THE ADAM PROJECT

HUGH A. FLOWERS

Cover Design – Niki Bradley-Fowler

Paperback-Press
an imprint of A & S Publishing
A & S Holmes, Inc.

ISBN 10: 1-945669-18-7
ISBN-13: 978-1-945669-18-7

ACKNOWLEDGMENTS

I'd like to give a special thank you to Niki Fowler for creating the perfect cover art for this book. You did a wonderful job.

My thanks also goes out to Norma Eaton for her editing help. Your time is appreciated.

Sharon Kizziah-Holmes, thank you for everything. You and Paperback-Press made publishing this novel possible. You are a professional in every way.

CHAPTER 1

Rafe Johnson was walking through the weight room on his way out of the health club when he was startled by a loud clang followed by a strangled cry for help. Following the sound he found a man trapped under a set of barbells pressing against his upper chest. His face was turning from red to purple as he struggled to breathe.

Rafe hurried over to the trapped man and, without thinking, lifted the barbells from his chest with his left hand while pulling him out from under with his right. Dropping the bells, he checked the man's condition.

Although the stranger was unconscious, he seemed to be breathing. Rafe looked around for a trainer and found one standing ten feet away staring at him in shock. current

"Hey, call 911! This guy is hurt!"

The EMT unit soon arrived and carted the injured man away. Rafe started to leave when the trainer pointed at the downed barbells. "Those bells were set at 200 pounds and you lifted them one handed! How did you do that?"

Rafe's mind raced as he faked a confused expression. "I don't know. I just reacted to the trapped man and did it. Maybe it was hysterical strength."

The trainer replied, "Weren't you using those weights earlier?"

"Yes, but that was over a half hour ago."

"But you were lifting that weight on your own. Maybe it wasn't hysterical strength after all."

Rafe shook his head ruefully. "I could never lift that weight one-handed, especially left handed."

"Left handed! You mean you're not left handed?"

"No. It must mean it was hysterical strength."

The trainer looked at him doubtfully. "Regardless, it was some feat."

"I hope you don't tell anyone what I did. I don't want the newspaper or TV getting word of this. It would make my life a living hell."

"Okay. The club doesn't want any publicity about an injury here either."

Rafe shuddered as he recalled pressing two hundred pounds with little difficulty after finishing twenty reps of 150 pounds. He must have forgotten to return the weights to the rack after finishing. He was a six-month member of the exercise club, gradually working his body into shape.

Earlier after completing his exercise for the day, Rafe showered and while drying himself he looked at his body in the mirror. He gave his reflection a smile of satisfaction. "Not bad for somebody on the wrong side of 70. In fact I look like I'm on the low side of 50," he said softly.

Rafe noticed a change in his body and general health about two years earlier. At first it was little things he noticed, like the liver spots on the back of his hands started getting fainter and then disappeared altogether. The bigger differences were the lack of leg pain, which had been bothering him for over a year and no joint and muscle pain when he stood up from a sitting position.

He soon joined an exercise club, which he used for about a year until he started getting comments about his improved physical appearance. He didn't want to draw any undue attention to himself, so he changed to this new club. He continued to become younger looking and stronger physically.

Something strange had happened to him that had never happened before. He didn't want to tell anyone because he feared the authorities would place him under study and he would never have a normal life again.

Rafe left the club in his red Mustang, a bucket list gift to himself just before the changes started. He was considering whether it was time to move to another exercise club, but this time he was considering using a fake name and address. Driving down Battlefield Road, hunger pains reminded him he hadn't eaten breakfast, so he headed the car toward a family restaurant that served an excellent breakfast and had a pretty, friendly waitress.

When Rafe was seated in his favorite booth, Sarah soon arrived to take his order and they began their usual friendly banter. Sarah, a recently married thirty-something woman was friendly and enjoyed talking with her customers. Rafe's wife died six years ago and although he enjoyed talking to a friendly woman, Rafe had no desire for a relationship. However, since his body had reawakened, his libido was starting to stretch its muscle and was telling him it was time to reconsider.

Rafe's children, Jerry and Peter, were both successful and had their own families out of state, each at least a thousand miles from Springfield. He corresponded by telephone and e-mail and occasionally visited them, the last time about a year ago. His greatest physical changes happened since that last visit and their only comment then was that he looked great.

He had few close friends and most of them lost interest in him after his wife died. Apparently, she was the one who attracted them. His remaining friends he now kept in touch by telephone.

He finished breakfast and decided to visit a nearby Barnes and Noble to see if he could find a new e-book to add to his order list. He was an avid reader and his most cherished new possession was an I-Pad he used as an e-book reader. Arriving at the bookstore he parked his red road burner as far from the other cars as he could manage to avoid door dings. While walking through the parking lot he was stopped by a man pointing a handgun at him. Without a word the man gestured toward a nearby open van door.

Without hesitation Rafe stepped into the van and the door slammed shut behind him. Before the door closed and shut off the light source, Rafe saw that the van had one bench seat and was fully enclosed in metal.

He also saw a woman sitting on the seat, who looked at him intently as she slid over to make room for him. He quickly eased down next to her and asked, "What's going on?"

The van started moving and they both grabbed an armrest for support. The woman replied. "You don't know?"

"All I know is that I was forced into this van at gunpoint!"

She replied. "Me too!"

"My name is Rafe Johnson, what's your name?"

"Vera Sparrow. I was putting groceries in my car when they grabbed me."

Rafe thought a moment before asking, "I'm trying to think of something common to both of us. Are you living alone?"

"Yes. My husband died last year."

"My wife died six years ago. What is your age?"

She hesitated a moment before answering. "A gentleman doesn't ask a lady her age. However, I'm 68."

Rafe chuckled. "A well preserved 68. You don't look older than your late 30's or early 40's. I'm 78, but look younger too. How long have you noticed you were getting younger?"

Vera gasped and grabbed Rafe's arm. "Do you think that's it? I've been wondering what was causing my physical change."

"It could be, but I have no idea why we have changed. However, I may have an idea who these people are. I've been keeping a low profile because of that uncertainty, but it appears we were being closely watched."

CHAPTER 2

Rafe and Vera lapsed into an uneasy silence as their journey continued. The van eventually reached its destination after about forty minutes and the door opened. The same gunman stood outside motioning them to get out. Rafe stepped out and then helped Vera out of the van which was parked next to an unmarked Gulfstream jet aircraft.

The gunman motioned them up the aircraft stairs where another man dressed in an obviously expensive tailored suit awaited them. He looked at them closely as they climbed the stairs before speaking. "Please follow me."

He stopped before a sofa and motioned for them to sit, while he took a seat opposite them. The gunman followed them onboard, securing the aircraft door before telling the aircrew to take off. No one spoke until they were flying at their cruising altitude.

The man in the expensive suit opened his briefcase and pulled out two files before speaking. "I'm Deputy Director James McPherson of the CIA."

Neither of the two new arrivals expressed any surprise at this disclosure, except for a lessening of body tension.

McPherson looked at Rafe as he opened the first file. "Johnson, you have had an interesting career before you retired. You were with the Green Berets during the Nam war reaching the rank of Captain before transferring to the CIA. You served as a field agent in various countries until retiring as Station Chief in Paris in 1993."

McPherson then opened the other file. "Sparrow, you were recruited out of Oklahoma University and spent fifteen years in the field before moving to Langley as an Analyst where you retired in 1999."

McPherson looked at the two former agents with a stern expression. "We don't know what's happened to you, but we want you safe while we figure it out. You are hereby reactivated and assigned to the Farm for retraining, while we investigate the cause of your condition and whether we determine this is an outside threat."

Rafe and Vera looked at each other a moment before Vera smiled. "I guess we have another common factor."

"Yes, we worked for the same business and somehow never met."

"I remember a Johnson as Station Chief for Paris when I was an Analyst. You were infamous as a hard-nosed bastard."

This comment caused Rafe to grin at her. "I worked hard to gain that reputation."

Rafe turned to McPherson. "That confrontation at the casino last Friday was your people?"

The gunman finally spoke. "Did you have to break their arms?"

"You were the observer? You should know that when three men come at you with foul intent, you can't take chances. You disarm and disable as quickly as possible."

Rafe shook his head at the gunman. "Shame on you for ganging up on an old man."

"Old man! You went through them like a knife through hot butter."

McPherson interrupted, "Meet Jason Peterson, your new training officer."

Peterson smiled slightly. "Those three were big, but we were going to cut them from the program because of their inept skills, and we wanted to see how rusty you were."

Vera interrupted, "Did you notice any other surveillance? I knew I was being followed, but wasn't sure who."

Rafe answered, "I had that feeling as well, but I could never catch anyone watching me."

Peterson interjected, "We don't think anyone but us was following you, but most of our surveillance was done by satellite."

McPherson spoke, "Have either of you any ideas how anything could have been introduced into your bodies?"

Vera frowned before answering. "I've been keeping a mental list on ways that could happen. Rafe and I need to list all doctor and/or hospital visits we've had in the past three years. Also, where we get our medications, restaurants we eat at, friends and other people we have invited into our home or visited elsewhere, home cleaning visits to our houses, and bars or other places where drinks are served. We need to compare these lists to see if there is a match where we both did the same thing. I personally can think of one match we need to check first. We both have mail-order meds since we are retired government employees."

McPherson grinned. "I hope it's as simple as that. I'll call ahead and have someone start on that right away. Meanwhile, Peterson give these people something to write on so they can start their lists."

After a short search, Peterson returned with paper and pens to begin their lists. Rafe was considering Vera's appearance. She dressed conservatively, like a woman her actual age, but her clothing did not hide the trim figure underneath. Without considering her last name, it was apparent she was of American Indian blood with her medium tan skin color and high cheekbones. To Rafe, Vera was a very attractive, exotic woman. The intelligence he could see in her eyes only added to her allure.

Vera caught him studying her. "What?"

He smiled slightly. "I was wondering what tribe you're from? I've got a little Quapaw blood in my family."

She nodded her head. "That's not unusual for this part of the country. I'm Choctaw of the Bird Clan. Our surname comes down from our Mother instead of our Father. My husband, Jack Hawk, was also of the Bird Clan. When he died I took back my Mother's name."

Rafe asked, "Do you have children?"

She wistfully shook her head. "No, I married late and Jack and I never had any. But now, maybe I'll have another chance."

"I've got two boys and seven grandchildren. Maybe we both will have a chance to attract a mate and have kids."

McPherson had been listening and interrupted, "Do you think your bodies' reproductive organs have regenerated?"

Rafe considered a moment. "I don't see why not. My body works like a forty-year-old and is getting better every day, but I haven't yet tried it out with a woman. What do you say Vera, do you want to take our new bodies out for a spin?"

Vera looked at him with wide eyes for a moment before realizing he was making a joke. "Don't joke about that, I might just take you up on it."

The other two men started laughing, especially when Rafe's face turned red in embarrassment. By the time they completed their lists, they were landing at Langley's private airfield. McPherson took their lists and Peterson led Rafe and Vera toward a waiting car, which was to take them to the Farm. In less than an hour they were going through security at the gate to the Farm.

Their first stop was processing at the Indoctrination Building. Two hours later after being photographed, fingerprinted, and given new clothing, they were told to billet in building 3B before heading to the mess hall. They changed into their training uniforms in their adjoining rooms.

Rafe knocked on Vera's door when he had finished his housekeeping chores. She opened her door wearing a form-fitting one-piece blue uniform, a duplicate of what he was wearing. He again noted that Vera had an attractive body shape that her clothing did not hide.

Most of the other classes had arrived and, as they entered the mess hall building all conversations stopped as they were observed as newcomers. Rafe and Vera knew they were different from the others who, except for instructors, were all in their twenties. The others knew they weren't instructors because of the color of their uniform. Rafe and Vera were something new and the others wanted to know if it was going to affect them.

Rafe smiled at Vera, who smiled back as they began walking toward the serving line. No one spoke as all eyes followed Rafe and Vera as they picked up their food and sat at a vacant table. Two instructors quickly joined them at their table, which ensured that other trainees would leave them alone. Conversation in the room soon resumed, but most of it was centered on the two new arrivals.

One of the instructors spoke, "I'm Jess Blake and she's Mattie Johnson. Your Training Officer will meet you here in the morning at six. Don't talk to the trainees about why you're here. We don't know and according to the scuttlebutt, we are better off not knowing."

"Do you want to know our names?" Rafe said.

"That's okay," Jess said.

Vera spoke up, "I'm Vera Sparrow and he's Rafe Johnson. Maybe a relative to you Mattie?"

Mattie looked at Rafe closely, and then shook her head. "Not that I'm aware of. When this is over maybe we can get together and compare notes."

Vera looked over at Rafe and winked. He nodded his head in acknowledgement of her point, and then smiled as Vera noticed Jess giving her a close inspection. They started eating while everyone else in the room was wondering whom they were and why they were there.

The next morning Rafe and Vera were back at the mess hall at the appointed time. Jason Peterson was waiting outside and followed them inside. He was wearing an instructor's uniform and when they had filled their food trays they all sat together. Apparently, the trainees knew Peterson as a senior training officer, which placed Rafe and Vera into a special category. Apparently satisfied that Rafe and Vera presented no threat to the trainees' own statuses they were ignored.

Peterson asked Vera, "Have you been exercising?"

"I'm a runner and I try to get in three miles a day."

Jason smiled. "How long have you been doing this?'

"I started running about eighteen months ago. I worked up to three miles a year ago."

Peterson looked at Rafe. "I know you've been exercising. How long have you been at it?"

"Almost two years. I joined an exercise club and I built up my muscles to a point where I can lift 200 pounds. I'd like to start running if I get the chance."

Peterson looked at the two considering what they might need in training. They were both fit, but might need retraining in hand-to-hand.

He asked, "When was the last time you two fired a handgun?"

Rafe replied, "Not since I retired."

"Me too. I qualified with a handgun, but I'm better with a rifle."

Peterson shrugged his shoulders. "Lets head over to the firing range to see how rusty you are."

CHAPTER 3

At the indoor range Rafe and Vera approached the range master's counter. He asked them their choice of weapon. Rafe answered, "I'll take a SIG Sauer P239."

Vera smiled at Rafe's choice. "I'll take the same."

They were given their weapons along with two loaded clips of 9mm ammunition. Peterson led the way to the range where they both selected a paper human figure target. Rafe motioned to Vera. "Ladies first."

After donning ear protectors, Vera set the target distance at thirty feet. She checked the pistol out before ramming a clip in and jacking a shell into the firing chamber before quickly firing three shots into the forehead of the target. She moved the target to fifty feet and quickly fired another three shots into the center of the target's chest area.

Rafe and Peterson murmured a soft, "Damn!"

Peterson said accusingly, "You said you qualified with a handgun! That's a little bit of an understatement don't you think? I don't even need to check how good you are with a rifle since you said you were better with them."

Rafe shook his head. "That's going to be hard to beat."

Rafe then went through the same procedure loading his weapon as Vera, adjusting his target distance to thirty feet before firing three rapid shots into the target's forehead. After adjusting the target to fifty feet, he fired another rapid three shots into the target's chest.

Peterson retrieved the two targets and compared the shot groupings. "Well shit! They're almost the same with Vera's grouping, just slightly tighter. We can forget about retraining on handguns because you both shot expert!"

Vera looked at the shot groupings. "I think Rafe shot faster than me, but not by much."

Peterson replied, "Maybe so, but I wouldn't want either of you two shooting at me!"

He asked Vera, "How good were you in hand-to-hand?"

"I qualified, but success was more due to their surprise because of my size. I'm more a thinker than a fighter."

Peterson nodded. "That's why your move to Langley as an Analyst. Was that at your request or Langley's?"

"Langley's. My Station Chief said I was wasted in the field."

Rafe interrupted, "Let's use that brain power. Do you have any thoughts why you and I were selected for this treatment or was it random?"

Vera considered. "First of all, why do you think it's only us? There could be others that we're not aware of."

Rafe shook his head and then thought for a moment. "Yes! You might be right. I think this organization wanted the government to become aware of this treatment, so they picked one or more of the investigating agencies' former agents to infect. The FBI may have had former agents infected as well."

Peterson's face reddened as Rafe expressed his theory. "Shit, shit, shit! I've got to call McPherson and let him know about this! You people go back to your rooms until I talk to him."

Vera looked at Rafe after Peterson hurriedly left the building. "I think he must have a fixation on shit. We have about two hours before lunch; do you want to run? I get antsy if I don't run."

"Sure, let's go back to our rooms and change into shorts and running shoes."

Heading back to their rooms the campus appeared mostly empty. He asked, "How long has it been since you were here last?"

She laughed. "Would you believe fifteen years ago this month. I did a three month tour as an instructor."

He grinned. "It's been at least twenty years for me and I was an instructor too."

They arrived at their rooms and changed into running clothes. Rafe went outside where he found Vera already well into her stretching exercises. He copied her exercises and when she stopped, he asked, "Where are we going to run?"

She grinned at him. "Follow me."

She started jogging down the street at a slow pace in an attempt to judge his ability. He followed her while admiring her form from the rear. After about a quarter mile she picked up the pace slightly, which he was able to match. Twice more Vera increased the pace until they were jogging at her normal speed. They were now at the halfway point in her normal three-mile run, and she was starting to feel the endorphins enter her blood stream giving her a slight rush.

Rafe's leg muscles burned. He wasn't used to this much exercise. Suddenly he too started to feel the endorphins enter his blood stream. He soon felt the rush and the muscle burn disappeared. His pace increased until he was running beside Vera. He gave her a big smile as he spoke. "I'm really starting to feel good and the muscle fatigue has disappeared."

"I know! Doesn't it feel great?"

Eventually, they ended up at their starting point. Vera continued to run in place for a minute or two before stopping. "Whew! I think we ran more than my normal three miles, but I feel great. How do you feel?"

"I feel great now, but are we going to have an adrenalin crash? I've never run that far before!"

She looked at her watch. "We did that run in thirty minutes and I'm guessing we traveled at least five miles. I've never had an adrenalin crash before, but I've never felt this high before either. Lets walk around the block and try to come down easy."

Completing the circuit they felt good, and they agreed to return to their rooms for a shower and then meet in Rafe's room to discuss what they experienced. Forty-five minutes later Vera was knocking on Rafe's door.

Rafe pointed to a little sitting area and said, "What surprises me more than the run we just did is the fact that I'm not even tired."

"You don't feel fatigued? How about leg or other muscle pain?"

Rafe shook his head. "No pain and I don't feel tired. Now that I think about it, I had the same reaction when I was exercising, but I thought I was just in good shape. How about you? Any fatigue or muscle pain?"

"No. I thought the same as you, but that run was not normal for me. I still feel high!"

Rafe thought a moment before replying. "Let's go to the Dispensary and have our blood drawn so that it can be checked while we still feel the buzz."

They were soon at the Dispensary where they had the nurse draw three vials of blood from each of them. They then carried the blood samples to the Farm's main office where they hoped to find Peterson. He was just hanging up the telephone when they walked through the door.

Peterson looked harried when he saw them. He motioned for them to come into the office. After shutting the door he asked them to take a seat.

"I just finished talking with DD McPherson and he thought your theory had merit. He's going to check with the other Agencies and see if they have noticed any of their current or retired agents suddenly getting younger. He also wanted you two to do a complete physical and blood workup."

Rafe chuckled. "Our minds seem to be working together. We brought blood samples for you to test. We just finished a five mile run and neither one of us were fatigued or had muscle pain and we still have a buzz going from something our body produced when we were pushing it."

Peterson looked intently at them for a moment. "Okay, things are starting to move now. I'm authorizing a copter to move you to our own private hospital so we can get this done ASAP."

CHAPTER 4

Rafe and Vera had been at the private hospital for three days running tests, and they had about all of this that they could stand. Peterson was meeting with them on a daily basis and so far they had found no other agents with their condition. The FBI had given the CIA the lead in their investigation, at least until it was determined the cause was from within the USA. Congress had given the CIA authority to operate only against foreign threats.

Rafe and Vera were meeting again with Peterson who told them, "We're done with these tests, at least until something new happens."

"Have you had any luck checking the source of our infection?"

"No, not yet. We don't know if it was a single infection or caused by a series of exposures, such as taking ninety days supply of blood pressure medication. If it came from the mail order supplier, medications may have been substituted in the mailroom. Other possible infection sources would be even harder to discover, but we're still working on it. The FBI is now involved with us."

"Wow! How did you arrange that?" Vera said with a surprised expression on her face.

"The Director asked the FBI Director for help in this matter considering its importance and the fact that they may have to take over the investigation. The doctors here agree with you on the need for further tests and DD McPherson wants you back at the Farm where we are going to put together a team to figure out what is going on."

They had been back at the Farm for two days and their team now consisted of ten new members, one-half of which were FBI, ensuring that both agencies had access to all the information gathered. Rafe and Vera's body scans appeared to show nothing unusual for individuals in their late thirties who were in top physical shape. However, their blood work showed something they had not been able to identify. In addition, their DNA had a slight difference in the area the doctor's thought might be what controlled aging.

Rafe and Vera had been appointed joint lead investigators by the heads of both agencies. They felt they had the experience and vested self-interest to get the job done. The other team members were selected by their agencies and all appeared to be experienced investigators. They were all quartered together in the same building, which included a large conference room where they were now gathered for their first meeting.

Rafe and Vera sat together at the head of the table looking at the new faces staring at them, some with anticipation and others in disbelief. Rafe and Vera both stood up which silenced all conversation.

Rafe spoke. "I'm Rafe Johnson and before I retired I was Station Chief in Paris. This is Vera Sparrow who was a field agent for many years before retiring as an Analyst at Langley. I'm 74 and she's 68, and we are getting younger every day. Our job is to determine: (1) why were we selected, (2) what is their purpose, and (3) does it present a threat to our nation or the world."

It was obvious some of the team members had some prior knowledge of whom Rafe and Vera were, but seeing them was still a shock. Vera spoke, "You can shut your mouths now because we really are who we say we are and we need to get started. Rafe and I agreed to set up three teams, each dealing with one of the three questions. We will meet at least daily with the full team to report our progress. The FBI members can select a member who can report back to their agency on a daily basis or if you prefer they can receive a copy of our daily briefings."

A senior member of the FBI group spoke. "I'm George Wendt and have been instructed to accept either briefings as offered. For now the FBI will prefer a copy of the daily reports."

Vera nodded her head in acceptance. "I see we have an equal number of men and women. I'd like at least one woman on each team. I don't want this to be a men against women contest, although we would probably beat you."

This brought smiles from the women and loud protests from the men. Before the teams were selected Rafe brought everyone up to date on their medical findings. Vera had written each of the ten members' names on slips of paper, which she placed in a large envelope. She then drew three names out for the team looking into the first question. By chance she drew two men and one woman. The second question team had four members evenly divided between men and women, and the third question team had three members two of which were women. All the teams had at least one member of each agency.

Vera had the three teams sit together and choose a leader. The teams immediately dispersed around the table and started talking among themselves until they had each selected a leader. Vera then spoke, "Great! There are three rooms down the hall that are marked for each team, one through three. Each room has a table, chairs, and writing material. You will use your own room's toilet when the need arises. Team leaders, I suggest you set hourly potty breaks so that your discussions are not unduly interrupted. For security purposes, monitor that no one takes anything from the room during the breaks and secure your paperwork in the room's safe during breaks and at the end of the day. During lunch breaks please sit together as a team. Your provided uniform is that of an instructor, so the trainees will not bother you. You may sit with any team member during breakfast and evening meals. Don't discuss what you are doing or who you are with anyone else. Rafe and I will monitor your progress and answer any questions you might have as we drop by from time to time. Now lets get to work!"

Rafe grinned at Vera. "Well that gets us started. Why don't you go to the first team and inform them of the lack of any other agencies' knowledge of other agents or people getting younger. You can join me at Team Two, and then later we'll go to Team Three. I'm curious to see what they come up with."

It became quickly clear that Team Three couldn't do anything but make wild guesses without a conclusion from Team Two, so the two teams were merged together before the first lunch break. Rafe and Vera agreed that this question was the most important. They needed to know the purpose behind infecting only two people.

The teams were late breaking for lunch so that most of the trainees were already seated when their group of twelve arrived dressed as instructors. The trainees knew something unusual was going on, as the rumor mill was strong at the Farm. The mess hall immediately became silent as they walked through the door. All eyes were on them as they selected their food and took tables slightly away from the others.

Rafe stood up and shouted. "EYES FRONT! You may carry on."

This seemed to work as the noise level returned to normal. However, the teams were still the subjects of most of the conversations. Vera gave Rafe a wink and a small smile before starting on her meal.

Two days later Team One's consensus of why Rafe and Vera were picked was pure chance coupled with the fact they were both living in the same city. That may have made it easier to infect both individuals.

Vera was reading the team's finding, then looked at Rafe. "Do you think it was that simple?"

"Maybe, but if they wanted our attention they got the results they wanted."

Vera nodded her head. "Now we need to determine what was their purpose. If we were their test subjects, they can monitor how we were doing and maybe even obtain our medical tests. Both of us were a little slow in acknowledging that we had a potential problem. I know I was too busy enjoying how my body was changing."

Rafe smiled. "I was too. Team Two has already agreed with us that we might be guinea pigs. We both have been infected about two years and we have shed about thirty or forty years. I wonder when this is going to stop?"

"I don't know! But I'm enjoying every minute. Well, maybe not all of it. I had my first period in about eighteen years this morning."

Rafe looked at her in surprise. "That probably means you can now have children. You should report this to the Medical Center, as they'll probably want to run some more tests. They already told me my sperm count was as high as a thirty year old."

Vera grimaced. "Okay, but I hope I don't have to go back there. I just hate hospitals."

Rafe gave her a hug. "Suck it up. It's not that bad."

While Vera was making her call, Rafe called everyone together in the main conference room. When they were all seated he spoke.

"Team One's consensus opinion is that it was probably chance, coupled with the fact we were living in the same city, for the reason Vera and I were selected for the youth bug. You now are all being tasked to determine the purpose behind this operation. So far all we have come up with is that we were picked as test subjects. This means we are being remotely monitored somehow. When we were examined they couldn't find any sensors on our bodies. Maybe they have some way of reading our medical files…maybe computer hacking? Let's think of ways they could do this and check if it's being done."

Rafe left the others as they started exchanging ideas while he went to check how Vera was doing. She was waiting for him when he entered her room. He could tell from her expression they wanted her to return to the Agencies Medical Center.

"When do you leave?"

"A chopper is on the way to pick me up. They said I should be able to return tomorrow."

Taking her in his arms, he said, "Don't worry. There's nothing we can do at this point to change anything, so why fight it. Let's just enjoy what we have and hope for the best."

He kissed her forehead and then looked into her eyes. "I think I'm falling in love with you Vera Sparrow."

She grabbed his head and pulled him down to her for a passionate kiss. "Me too, you big lug."

She then grabbed her overnight bag and left for the Heliport.

CHAPTER 5

When Vera returned the next day the first thing she did was find Rafe. He was still working with the others at the conference room. When their eyes met, the connection was immediate and they smiled broadly. He left the others and met her at the doorway where they kissed passionately. Taking Rafe's hand, Vera led him back to her room.

The others looked on in shocked silence until they left the room. George Wendt chuckled. "I guess its quitting time."

Several of the others laughed as they all helped clear the room of paperwork before leaving. Most of the women suspected the budding romance between Rafe and Vera, but the men were clueless.

Later, after their potent lovemaking they lay together on Vera's mattress, which somehow had fallen to the floor.

Rafe said, "Wow! We must have had a lot of pent-up emotion. I don't remember ever having an orgasm that powerful before."

Vera kissed him passionately before snuggling against him. "That was wonderful. Let's see if we can do one better."

Rafe groaned in anticipation, but found that his body was ready to meet the challenge. Afterward, Vera was able to coax one more session out of Rafe before he was completely spent. Later, they took a long shower together where they each discovered even more about their bodies.

There lovemaking left them ravenous, so they made their way to the mess hall. Normally, they had been getting their exercise by running before the evening meal. However, today they felt justified skipping the run.

Walking back toward their rooms, Rafe asked, "What did the Med Center say about your period?"

"I didn't have one today. The doctors said I was producing eggs again, which really blew their minds. They want to do a paper on me just for that, as if that would be allowed. They could find nothing wrong with me, so maybe I should be using protection now that I'm sexually active again."

Rafe stopped. "You may be too late! We don't know how are bodies are working now. Would you be unhappy if you got pregnant?"

"How about you? Do you want to be a father again? As for me, I'd like to have a child, but maybe not right now."

Rafe drew her to him, kissing her. "I wouldn't mind being a father again, but you're right, now might be a problem."

The team continued for the next two weeks with their search, but they came up with no new viable ideas. Peterson called Rafe and Vera to the main office for a meeting. When they arrived he had them take a seat before speaking.

"We have not been able to come up with anything at the mail-order pharmacy except for one former employee they can't now locate. He worked at the shipping department for only two weeks before quitting about two years ago. His paycheck was returned because of a false address. The FBI is still trying to get more information on this guy, but so far they are getting little from his co-workers."

Rafe smiled. "That looks promising. At least now we have evidence that someone intentionally infected us and not that we both picked up something on our own."

Vera shook her head at Rafe. "We never believed that. Neither one of us believes in coincidences."

Peterson said, "Nobody believed that. We think this is how you were infected. The dose you both received must have been in that ninety-day supply of medication. There is no way to tell which medication was altered, but I don't think it really makes any difference."

Rafe looked at Vera before speaking. "What about our team's purpose? It's like spitting into the wind until we know for sure why they picked us to infect. Until we know who these people are, how are we going to get any answers?"

Peterson nodded his head. "Both agencies think you were picked as guinea pigs by some person or agency and somehow are monitoring your progress. We are using several different methods in an attempt to trace the monitoring back to its source. You can stay here or you can return home, your choice."

Vera said, "I want to return home. What did you do with our cars?"

"I'm going home too. I hope you didn't skin up my mustang."

Peterson smiled. "Your cars are back in your garages and as far as I know there was no damage done to either of them. We will continue to watch over you and will provide both of you with an emergency locator device."

They were soon on their way back to the airfield where they had first arrived. Peterson informed them that the team was disbanded and had been reassigned. They were soon in the air in apparently the same Gulfstream jet they used before. A car was waiting for them when they arrived.

Smiling, Vera asked, "Is it okay if I ride home with you? I want to see how you live."

He grinned at her. "I don't know. It might be a little dusty. I hope you're not a compulsive housekeeper."

"I don't think so, although my late husband had a habit of dropping his clothes on the floor that got on my nerves."

"I hope that was not the reason he died."

"Fun-ney!" She said as she dug a finger into his ribs.

They pulled into his driveway thirty minutes later. Vera looked at the brick two-story home located in a well-established neighborhood. "Wow, you have a beautiful home and somebody has even mowed the grass. I wonder if they took care of my yard too?"

"Probably. They did that to keep the neighbors from thinking we had died," he said with a grin.

He led Vera into the house where he quickly turned off the alarm system and then started showing her around.

Vera said, "You must have a cleaning service for this house. It would almost be a full time job keeping it clean."

"I have someone come in once a week to take care of that. She has a key and I pay her once a month. I think I'm two weeks late getting her check out. I better call her and inform her it's in the mail. Since I've been gone there wasn't much for her to do except dust."

When they got to the master bedroom, Vera noted the king-sized bed before heading for the large walk-in closet. "What a closet! I could get lost in here."

"That's what I thought until Alice filled it up. My clothes don't fill a third of the space, especially since I got rid of the suits and other clothes that didn't fit anymore."

"Yes. I've got a lot of clothes that don't fit since I started running again. I've got to update my wardrobe now that I don't look 68 anymore. What about you?"

Vera started going through his suits checking the labels and sizes. "It looks like you already did a good job culling the old stuff."

Rafe hugged Vera and then with an ardent expression asked, "Do you want to move over here? As you can see I've got plenty of room and if we start having kids we've got the space."

Vera laid her arms over his shoulders, drawing her body up against his chest and looking intently into his eyes. "Is that a proposal, or is it just more convenient to be living together?"

He kissed her slowly, and then more ardently, building passion into the kiss as their lips pressed tightly together until she broke away to catch her breath. "I think I love you, but we both need to live together to really know each other. Can you do that or do you need a ring on your finger?"

She smiled at him. "Okay, but I'm not selling my house until we get married. Are you going to help me move what things I need over here?"

"How much are you moving? Do you need a pickup or a moving van?"

"No, I think we can get most of it in both of our cars."

"Okay. Before we start on that lets get something to eat. Where do you live?"

"I'll show you. There's a new place near where I live I've been wanting to try."

Vera told him where the restaurant was located before they left the driveway.

"I've driven past there, but haven't tried it yet," Rafe said.

After the meal Vera guided him to her home, which was located in the southern part of the city, only a few miles from Rafe's home. It was a small one-level brick house. Vera led him inside her home, saying, "It's not nearly as large as your home, but without kids we were comfortable."

The home had three bedrooms, one of which had been used as an office with a tabletop computer sitting on a desk. Rafe noted that Vera was not a pack rat as the rooms were attractively furnished with minimal appointments. Vera went to her closet and started putting the hanging clothes she wanted to take with her on her bed. Pulling a suitcase from under her bed, she started filling it with folded clothing.

Vera pointed at the hanging clothes. "Put those in my SUV if it's really in the garage."

They were back on the road toward Rafe's home an hour later. He couldn't believe how organized Vera was. The only things in his car were three boxes of odds and ends. Vera was driving her Honda SUV with everything else she wanted to bring with her, at least for now.

CHAPTER 6

Rafe and Vera marked their ten-month anniversary together and, except for the first month's adjustment period, they settled into their arrangement as if they had been living together for years. Their love life was typical for newlyweds, meaning they didn't seem to be able to function without the other and hated to be apart. Every moment was another opportunity to explore one another, mentally and physically.

The morning of their anniversary, Vera finished fixing their breakfast and when Rafe settled down ready to eat, she placed a pregnancy test devise down in front of him. "I'm pregnant!"

Rafe looked at the devise in surprise, then smiled at her. "Let's get married!"

Vera plopped down into his lap and kissed before responding. "Are you sure?"

He hugged her closer to his chest. "Yes. I've been trying to get up my nerve for months now. This just made it easier."

Vera held him close to her and whispered softly, "I'm scared. I've never been pregnant before and I'm sixty-nine years old!"

Rafe laughed. "Maybe, but you're body looks like you're only twenty-five. A gorgeous, well-stacked young woman, I might add."

She snickered into his ear. "I think you might be a little biased, but I appreciate the compliment. I want a wedding at my church as soon as possible. I want you to call your sons and tell them of our intention of getting married. I'm sure they both will want to get here quickly to try to talk you out of it, since you're a old man of almost seventy-nine."

Rafe said with concern, "They're going to have a heart attack when they see us."

Vera laughed. "I should meet them at the door when they arrive. They'll think for sure I'm a gold-digger after your money."

Rafe shook his head. "This is going to be hard. They can't tell anyone else about how young we look."

She replied after considering, "I'll try to get the wedding date scheduled for about a month from now, so they have time to plan their trip here."

"Yeah and we need to see about getting you the proper medical help."

As she promised, Vera consulted with her church and arranged for a Saturday wedding in six weeks. Then she went shopping for a wedding dress. They were going to have the reception in their home with family members only. Vera insisted that the day be an intimate family event.

Rafe called his oldest son Jerry first with the wedding news. Jerry's initial reaction was shock, and then he started asking questions. "How long have you known her? How old is she?"

Rafe interrupted. "We have known each other about a year and have been living together for ten months. Vera is sixty-nine and quite active for her age. She is of Choctaw American Indian heritage, and was married before. Why don't you and your family come a few days early and meet her. Call Peter and give him the news for me and ask him and his family meet you here early as well. I have other important news I need to tell you both when you arrive. I love you. See you soon."

Rafe then called his emergency number at the CIA. Eventually he got Peterson on the line and relayed the news of Vera's pregnancy and their impending marriage. He than asked him to arrange for medical help at a nearby location.

Peterson hesitated a moment before answering. "Well shit! You knocked her up. Okay, I'll ask the powers that be what we can do and get back to you."

Rafe didn't get a return call from Peterson until the next day. "We have an arrangement at the Kimble Medical Center on South National. Apparently, Dr. Jamie Kimble is one of the leading Gynecologists for your area. Vera has an appointment to see her tomorrow at 9:00 a.m., and she will have her full medical file to review, so tell her to speak freely. Now about your family arriving for the wedding, just tell them you don't know what's causing you to get younger and nothing about the CIA. Tell them to not tell anyone else because you don't want the attention and it might cause a panic. Any questions?"

"No. I was already going to use that explanation. Vera doesn't have any living relatives, so it's just going to be my family at the wedding.

Thanks for the help."

Vera came home soon after gushing about the dress she picked out and the fact it was on sale because some other customer cancelled her order. Rafe pulled her close, kissing her passionately before giving her the news about her doctor's appointment.

"I'm going with you, but I don't expect any problems. Peterson said the doctor will have your full medical file so we can speak freely."

Early the next morning they arrived at the medical center to fill out the required paperwork, but they were surprised to be shown into the doctor's office immediately. Dr. Kimble stood as they entered her office and she motioned for them to take a seat.

"Vera, I reviewed your file last night and I couldn't quite believe what I was reading until I met you. You really are sixty-nine and look like a woman in her twenties."

Kimble looked at Rafe. "I didn't get your file. You look like you're just a little older than her apparent age, but I bet you're much older."

"I'm actually almost seventy-five."

Dr. Kimble laughed. "What did you two do, drink from the fountain of youth? I'll run the standard tests for pregnancy and give you another full physical to compare with the previous tests. Mr. Johnson, my nurse will escort you to the waiting room until we are finished with Vera."

Rafe put his arm around Vera, drawing her close. "Honey I'll come back at noon and check on you. If you get done sooner than that give me a call."

He returned to the Medical Center at noon and was surprised to find Vera in the waiting room. She smiled when he arrived, which seemed to brighten the room. "I just got released, so we timed that perfectly."

Rafe kissed her. "Are you finished here?"

"Dr. Kimble told me it may be several days before all the test results come back and she will call us when she wants us to come back."

Rafe asked, "Are you hungry?

She shook her head. "Rafe, why don't we go home and change into our running clothes? I miss our daily run. Let's go to the nature center and do the long trail. I should be hungry when we get done."

Later, they had a late lunch at Vera's favorite restaurant, The Olive Garden. Rafe gazed at Vera, her face reflecting the glow from their run as they both still received a high from whatever was being released into their blood, but Rafe knew the glow wasn't entirely from the run. Vera's face glowed from his unborn child resting in her womb.

After ordering, Rafe placed a ring box on the table in front of Vera. "Vera, I want to officially ask for your hand in marriage."

Vera looked back and forth, from Rafe to the box, tears welling in her eyes. She had never been more beautiful to Rafe in that moment.

"Of course you big lug. I've been in love with you almost from the first time I saw you."

Vera opened the tiny velvet box carefully and looked inside. "Ooh it's so beautiful."

Rafe took the ring out of the box and slid it on her finger. Vera held her hand out and admired how the diamond sparkled under the light. She scooted over to get as close to Rafe as possible. Rafe bent to her eager upturned lips with such ardor it shook him.

Afterward, neither could remember what they ate. Vera spent most of the meal admiring her ring. Rafe was delighted to watch his bride-to-be being so happy. He was glad he took the time to purchase the ring while she was in the Medical Center.

Three days later they got a call from the Medical Center to come see Dr. Kimble the following day at 9:00 a.m. Vera was very concerned about the changes in her body, and worried about her first pregnancy, what was normal, what was not, what should she eat, what meds could she take, how long could she and Rafe enjoy their runs at the Nature Center? Was the baby normal, would she deliver okay? Would her body adjust to this new reality?

Dr. Kimble, being a very good doctor, tried to calm Vera, as she was obviously concerned. "Vera please settle down. I didn't find anything wrong when I checked your tests. However, it appears that you will be having twins and you are about sixty days into your pregnancy. I may be able to tell the sex of the babies at your next visit with me in thirty days. You still have that unknown factor in your blood and it appears to have gotten more prevalent since you became pregnant. However, it doesn't appear to have adversely affected your health. Do you have any questions?"

Rafe stared, not quite comprehending as Vera almost shouted, "Twins! Did you say twins? I can't be having twins the first time around!"

Somehow, it all seemed to be Rafe's fault. Rafe looked to Dr. Kimble for help, who quickly hid her smile. She then offered an explanation.

"I've seen studies that seem to suggest that when older women conceive for the first time, twins are more prevalent."

"But you said I had the body of a woman in her twenties! Don't give me that crap. There's got to be another reason."

"Honey it might be just the luck of the draw that we're going to be having twins."

Rafe recognized the squint in Vera's eyes, which meant she was really angry. Rafe wanted to head that off. He quickly took Vera into his arms and kissed her passionately until she stopped her struggles and settled into the embrace.

Once he released her, she smiled at him sweetly. "Rafe baby, you owe me big time and I intend to collect as soon as I can think of the proper payback."

Rafe took the next appointment time from the doctor and they departed for home. Vera didn't speak the entire trip despite his many attempts to engage her in conversation. However, once they entered the house she broke down and sobbed in his arms. He finally got her settled and she looked at him shamefaced. "Rafe I'm sorry I acted like that, especially in front of the doctor. What must she think? Ooh dear, how am I going to face her again?"

"Honey your hormones are all out of whack because of the babies. I'm sure she's seen that same thing many times before."

"Are you sure? I've never acted like that before. It was almost like someone else was saying those things."

Hugging her close, he kissed her until she needed to catch her breath. "Come on upstairs. You need to take a hot soak in the tub to relax, and I'll fix you a nice lunch."

"No, what I need is some of your lovin'. I can relax later in the afterglow," she said as she pulled him to the stairs.

Later, as she lay in his arms she said, "Now I'm hungry. What do we have to eat?"

Rafe chuckled. "I'll see what I can find."

CHAPTER 7

$\bigcirc\!\!\!\infty\!\!\!\bigcirc$

The day that Rafe's sons and their families were to arrive, both Rafe and Vera were anxious. About mid-day Vera sucked a big breath into her lungs when she saw Jerry and his family through the front picture window approaching the house. When Vera opened the door, Jerry looked at her in surprise and tentatively asked, "Is Rafe available?"

Smiling, Vera said, "He's in the bathroom. Come on in, we have been expecting you."

The family followed her into the living room area and they all sat down. Jerry's entire family was with him, including his wife, two teenage sons and a ten-year-old daughter.

Vera, although uncomfortable, started the conversation. "I'm Vera Sparrow, your father's bride-to-be and before you think he's robbing the cradle, let's wait until Rafe gets here. He wants to try and explain our predicament."

All eyes looked at her in amazement before Jerry blurted, "Dad said you were sixty-nine! You don't even look thirty."

Rafe walked into the room. "It looks like I saved Vera from having to explain our awkward situation."

Jerry interrupted. "My God Dad! What's going on here? You look like my younger brother rather than my father."

The other members of Jerry's family sat with their eyes and mouths open in surprise at Rafe and Vera's youthful appearance. Jerry's wife, Beverly, spoke, "Shut up Jerry, they're trying to tell you."

Jerry looked at his wife in surprise, and then grimaced. "I'm sorry, go ahead with your explanation."

Rafe smiled at his son. "I know its hard, but think about it from our prospective. About three years ago we both started getting younger. We don't know why, but we think an outside source infected us with something that is making us younger and stronger. The Agency has reactivated both of us and is helping us cope and try to find the source and purpose of this condition."

Jerry looked at Vera with new respect. "Reactivated both of you. Vera you were with the agency too?"

Vera nodded her head. "Yes, we both retired and were living here, but had never met until this happened. We fell in love with each other and have been living together for the last ten months. We decided to get married when we discovered I was pregnant with twins."

Beverly jumped out of her seat and hurried to Vera's side and hugged her. "Vera I'm so happy for you and Rafe. Have you had any children before?"

Upon Vera's soft "No," Beverly said. "You're having twins!"

She turned to Rafe. "What does the doctor say about her condition?"

Vera interrupted, "I've got the best baby doctor in town and she says I'm in perfect health for a twenty-five year old. I don't think my actual age has a bearing on it in this case."

Beverly looked at her husband. "Jerry, we have to give Vera some support, even if its only moral support. She doesn't have anyone but Rafe and she needs a woman to help her, especially just before and after she gives birth. When Peter and his family get here I'm going to discuss this with Jenny and we'll work something out."

Jerry's children were taking the whole conversation in with rapt attention. Alice, the ten-year-old daughter, said, " Mom, I want to help!"

Beverly looked over at her daughter and smiled. "Vera do you know your due date?"

"No, but it will be sometime in about seven months, that will make it in June or July of next year."

"Good. Alice will be on summer break and can help if needed. Rafe, how many people can you take care of in this house? Peter's family is six if he brings everyone."

Vera smiled. "We have it covered. We can put up either of your families here and I still have my own house which can handle one of the families."

There was a knock at the front door. Beverly told her husband to let Peter and his family in so that they could get the explanations over with. Vera looked at Rafe and raised her eyebrow. Rafe smiled and shook his head. It would all be over soon enough and his only hope was that it would end on an agreeable note.

Rafe's second son, Peter, walked in with his wife and four kids, two teenage girls, a boy of about eight years, and a girl who was about six. Rafe quickly repeated the same story he had told Jerry and his family only minutes before.

Beverly walked over and hugged her sister-in-law. "Jenny, Vera is pregnant with twins and this is her first birth. She is due in June or July and we need to put together some support for her when her due date approaches. Between us and our daughters we should be able to do something for her."

Jenny looked over at Vera. "Twins! Ooh my, you poor girl. Of course we'll help. She should be okay until the last month. We can start sending people down to help then and until a month or more after the births."

Vera came over and hugged both women. "I can't begin to thank you both for your offer of help, but is it really going to be that bad?"

The sisters-in-law looked at each other and shook their heads. Beverly put her arm around Vera. "Honey, I only had mine one at a time and it was almost more than I could handle. Two at once I can only imagine."

Vera wanted to talk more to her new daughters-in-law, but Rafe called for everyone's attention. "Nobody can repeat Vera's and my condition. Think of the problems we would have if the media got hold of this. You kids can't tell your friends either. No gossip, girls. No talk about this to anyone, ever, at anytime, to anyone."

They all agreed they would keep the secret among themselves even though it would make a terrific story.

Rafe and Vera's wedding day was sunny, but a little chilly. They arrived at the church in separate cars for the bride and the groom, to keep Rafe from seeing the gown. He did see a flash of white as his car arrived, but Vera was gone before his car stopped.

Rafe stood next to Jerry, who was his best man, with sweating palms and feeling strangely out of sorts as the wedding march started. He kept his eyes front until she was standing next to him. Their eyes met and Rafe thought she was the most beautiful woman he had ever seen when she smiled and a winked at him.

Later, after the wedding he couldn't remember anything of the ceremony. That was nothing, except for the kiss at the end. Rafe and Vera returned to the house for the reception and a little honeymoon he hoped to surprise Vera with.

The happy couple toasted each other and family before Rafe and Vera cut the wedding cake. Wedding pictures were taken together and with the family before they excused themselves and retired upstairs to change into their travel clothes.

After their suitcases were loaded into the mustang, Rafe and Vera were on their way.

Vera poked Rafe in the ribs and asked, "Okay you big lug where are we going on our honeymoon? It better not be to a beach because I hate sand."

Rafe faked a heart attack. "Oh no, don't tell me that. I spent a fortune for a hotel on the beach."

She laughed. "Yeah sure. I'm not biting on that. Come on and tell me. Pleaseee."

"Okay, I will if you are really good to me."

After being the recipient of a hostile glare, he relented. "We're going on a week's cruise in the Caribbean."

"Ooh good. I've never been on a cruise before."

CHAPTER 7

Vera's misgivings soon turned out to be prophecy fulfilled. About ten years later the decision was forced upon the Johnsons. Rafe and Vera were awakened from a sound sleep by a loud explosion downstairs at three a.m. The explosion was followed by the surveillance system alarm screaming through the house. Rafe and Vera grabbed their handguns from the gun safe and ran toward their children's rooms.

Heart pounding, Rafe lay on the floor facing the stairs while Vera quietly moved the children into a prepared safe room. When Rafe heard several minutes of automatic gunfire from downstairs, his training took over as he calmly covered the staircase. Several long minutes later Rafe heard the all-clear signal from their rescuers.

Rafe yelled, "We're okay up here. Do we need to move elsewhere?"

After a moment, he heard someone yell, "Stay there until we check the area. We don't know yet if it's safe."

Rafe mouthed a silent "think you" to the powers that be and then checked on his family. They were all well. Neither of his children seemed frightened, but rather interested in the developments. Twenty minutes later the lead agent, James Robb, from the protection detail came up the stairs to inform them no one else had been found in the area and the local police were canvassing the neighborhood to see if anyone was hurt by the gunfire.

Rafe rushed downstairs to check on damages and found that the front door was missing, having sustained severe damage from the blast. Four men dressed in black were lying on the floor dead.

He asked Robb, "Did you take any prisoners? Were any agents hurt?"

Robb shook his head. "No, and we were lucky. None of our people got even a nick. These guys acted like amateurs. I'm thinking this was just a feeler to see how prepared we were."

"Can we get to a safe house for tonight? We can't stay here unless you plan on moving these bodies soon."

"Why not move next door south until we can clean up this mess. There are two empty bedrooms there and the agents will keep you safe until we can get an idea on how to fix the damage here."

Moving next door the Johnsons tried to get some sleep in what remained of the night. The agents brought McDonald breakfasts for everyone in the morning. It was a hit for the kids, since Vera seldom allowed fast food. Agent Robb came by and told them, "It's going to take about a week to fix the damage and strengthen the entryway. I think it's safer to keep you here and move our agents into your house until its fixed."

Rafe asked Vera, "What do you think?"

She grimaced. "It's not home, but it's only a week."

"There's your answer. I want you to set us up with a training facility to teach the kids how to use a handgun. It looks like it's come down to that now."

Agent Robb seemed surprised, but nodded his head. "I'll get back with you on that."

The next day Agent Robb arrived with news about the training facility. "I'm sorry but the only thing I could find was the police department's indoor firing range, but we could use it every day. The only catch is that it has to be for one hour at six a.m."

Rafe and Vera conferred, and then gave Agent Robb the okay to finalize the agreement. Vera called the kids into the room after the agent left. "Kids, we've arranged a firing range for you to learn how to use a handgun. We think you can handle a small caliber pistol as it has little kick. We'll try that anyway and if it doesn't work we'll think of something else."

The Johnsons arrived at the range the next morning. The range master let them into the building, which was normally closed at that hour. Rafe brought two different caliber weapons to see which would work best. The first thing he taught the twins was gun safety. Once he was sure they understood the rules, he gave each of them an empty weapon. He watched as they checked the clip and the gun chamber to make sure it was indeed empty. He then took one of the weapons and showed them the proper grip and stance facing the target.

He demonstrated how each should hold their weapon and their stance, making some minor adjustments until he was satisfied. He had Adam take the .32 cal., load in a full clip and chamber a bullet. They all donned ear protectors before he asked Adam to take careful aim and fire at the target.

Adam's bull's-eye target was set at twenty feet and his first shot hit within the center ring. His second shot was closer to the center, and his third was dead center. Rafe had him stop shooting and instructed him to aim and fire as fast as he could. The boy looked at his father with a happy gleam in his eyes, then turned and emptied the gun at the target.

Rafe had Adam put the weapon down and retrieved the target. He marked the first two shots, but the others were in the center. Rafe looked at Vera, "Not bad for his first attempt."

Vera shook her head in wonder. "Well, Evelyn I guess you are up."

Evelyn went through the same procedure as her brother and used the same weapon. However, she had the advantage of watching and experiencing the firing through his eyes. She was physically a little smaller than her brother and the weapon felt big in her hand; however, she lined up on the target and fired her first shot, which hit on the rim of the inner circle. The second shot hit almost dead center, and the third made a bigger hole. Vera told her to fast fire the remainder of the shells. She smiled, then quickly emptied the weapon into the target.

Vera told her to put down the weapon and they retrieved the target. The first shot was easy to find, but the others were lost in a big hole in the center of the target. Rafe said, "Wow. Daughter is like her mother, a dead shot."

Vera pulled Adam to her and gave him a hug. "They both shot expert on their first try."

The kids then tried the .38 cal., and got similar results. Rafe and Vera decided to stick with the .32 caliber, as it was a smaller weapon. They could always use hollow point ammo for better stopping power.

Rafe and Vera then had to decide where to keep the weapons close by in case of need. After much discussion, the parents decided that to be of any use in a surprise kidnapping, the weapons had to be where they could be used within seconds of an alarm. They decided the bedside table drawer was the best of the options available. When traveling they designed a holster that fit in the small of their children's backs.

The twins thought being armed was neat and empowered them. It made them think they could control some part of their lives. They also felt they were somehow agents themselves.

Six months later, the new safety procedures were put to the test. The agency had given them a different vehicle to use when they traveled as a group to the Medical Center or other outings. The vehicle was armored and they traveled in a convoy of three cars with the Johnson car in the center. Their convoy was attacked while on the four-lane James River freeway to the Medical Center.

Rafe was driving and noted several big Hummers coming up fast from their rear. He hit the emergency alert button mounted on the steering wheel letting the others know to be alert. The first Hummer passed Rafe and sideswiped the lead car trying to push it off the highway, while the second and third Hummers tried to box Rafe's car in. The fourth Hummer concentrated on the rear car of the convoy trying to knock it off the road.

Rafe speeded up and rammed the rear of one of the Hummers in an attempt to spin it off the highway. After another try he succeeded as it slid into another of the Hummers causing both to leave the pavement and overturn as they crossed the median and bounced across the oncoming highway and finally slid to a stop against a rock embankment.

Rafe then tried the same strategy against the lead attacker, who was still trying to knock the lead convoy car off the road. Rafe's car hit the Hummer with such force it too skidded off the highway and overturned several times, leaving pieces of metal behind until it finally came to a rest. The two lead cars of the convoy then stopped to deal with the last attacker.

The last Hummer suddenly broke off contact and crossed the median fleeing in the opposite direction. Vera turned around to see if her children were hurt or frightened. They were both strapped in car seats, smiling back at her.

"Mom that was exciting. I didn't know Dad could drive like that," Adam said.

Evelyn laughed. "I bet Mom could drive like that too, couldn't you Mom?"

Vera breathed a sigh of relief seeing that her kids were fine. "I'm good, but your father is better."

The convoy got off the highway at the next exit and checked the damage to their people and vehicles. After determining they could proceed, the convoy continued toward the Medical Center.

They arrived without any further problems and the Johnsons entered the building leaving their security detail behind. When they got to the receptionist, she told them to go on to the doctor's office as they were expected. When the family entered the office, four strangers greeted them.

The two men and two women were pointing handguns at them. One of the men spoke with a slight accent and pointed his weapon at Rafe and Vera. "You two stand face first against the wall. You children stand over there by the window."

Once the children moved out the line of fire, the two women began to pat down Rafe and Vera searching for weapons. While the attention was focused away from Adam and Evelyn, the twins drew their weapons in concert and fired one shot at almost the exact same time. The two men fell to the floor dead from a shot to the head.

Startled, the two women turned from Rafe and Vera to find the children pointing weapons at them. The women didn't hesitate in raising their hands in surrender, as they knew from their dead partners' bodies that these children would fire at the least provocation.

Rafe and Vera disarmed the two women while their children covered them. Rafe pulled a little box out of his pocket and pushed a button. "We should get some help from our people now."

Soon, multitudes of people were running toward their office. Rafe called out, "We are okay in here but we need some help!"

Agent Robb took a quick look into the room before motioning the other agents to take up positions. Adam and Evelyn were still pointing their weapons at the two women who were now lying face down on the floor.

"The kids do that?" Robb asked, pointing at the dead men.

Vera nodded her head. "They saved us. I guess our decision to arm them paid off."

Agent Robb smiled. "You think. I didn't believe you when you said they shot expert. It must be in their blood."

Eventually, Dr. Kimble was discovered stuffed unconscious behind her desk. A doctor was brought in from another office in the Medical Center, and Dr. Kimble was moved to an examining room.

The agents removed the dead men and captured women to see if they could determine who was behind this abduction attempt.

The Johnson family was free to return home to await news. That evening Agent Robb brought news. "We think the attempts today were from two different factions and think the best defense is to move you to a different location. Do you have a preference?"

Rafe asked, "How far away do you recommend?

"We prefer a medium size city at least five hundred miles away, otherwise it doesn't make a difference."

"Okay. We'll have a family meeting and give you our top three choices in order of preference. How soon do you need it?"

"Soon. We need to get you out of here ASAP. We'll handle all the moving of your stuff. All you can take with you is an overnight bag for each of you."

Agent Robb left and the family got together with a map of the United

States on the dinner table. Adam took a compass from his school supplies and drew a 500-mile circle around their present location.

Rafe looked at Vera. "Do you really dislike sand?"

At her nod he said, "Well that eliminates Florida. How about the northern west coast?"

Vera asked her children, "How about you two. Do you have a preference?"

"We've seen pictures of Seattle and think that would be a good place to live," Adam said.

They finally settled on three locations: Seattle, Washington; Portland, Oregon; and Salem, Oregon. Each city was in the same general area, but three different sizes. Rafe called Agent Robb to tell him of their decision. He responded. "I'll get back with you, but be ready to leave by tomorrow night."

They were having lunch the follow day when Agent Robb joined them. "We picked Portland. Seattle was too large and too near the border from the security aspect. Portland was far enough south and just the right size city. We are leaving here at six p.m. and traveling in a convoy to the airport. Also, you will have a new team of combined FBI and CIA agents. It's been a real privilege to work with you, and that includes the kids."

They responded with their own accolades, while the two children ran over and hugged Agent Robb, with tears in their eyes. Later, when the family arrived at the airport and left the car, Adam and Evelyn stared at the waiting Gulfstream aircraft. They had never flown before and this was going to be a new experience for them.

CHAPTER 9

Rafe and Vera were surprised when Deputy Director McPherson met them at the Gulfstream's door. Rafe and Vera shook his hand and introduced their children to him. Evelyn asked, "Does this aircraft belong to you?"

"No, but I get to use it quite often. Why don't you all take a seat so that we can get airborne?"

Vera had the children take window seats so they could have a better flying experience, while she and Rafe took the sofa seat they used previously when they met with the DD. McPherson took the seat opposite them as before and waited until they were airborne so they could speak easily.

"The lead agent in Portland is Jane Patton with the FBI. She has been the Supervising Agent there for three years and has fifteen years' experience. She was faxed your family's packet today and has arranged a safe house until a permanent house can be arranged. Because of the repeated attempts to abduct you and your family, she's been ordered to double the previous security detail, which has required transfers from other offices. Most of those transfers were of CIA agents."

Rafe spoke up, "What have you learned about the people behind the abduction attempts?"

"We got nothing from those people who were in the Hummers. The one who drove away we never caught and the other vehicles' occupants were killed. The women you captured were hired mercenaries who never met their employer and were paid in cash. The place they were told to take you to was a dead end as well. In short, we know very little."

Adam interrupted. "The man in charge of the group spoke English with an French accent and his male partner was called George. The women were named Alice and Jane and were former U.S. military."

McPherson looked at Adam in surprise, but then smiled. "That's good to know. Maybe we can get further with that information. Did you hear them talking?"

Evelyn answered, "Yes, they were not very smart to give us that information."

The children then turned their attention back to the ground and clouds they had been looking at before. McPherson looked at them with a calculating eye before turning his attention back to their parents.

"Agent Robb informed us of the children's contribution at the Medical Center. Normally we wouldn't condone putting weapons into the hands of ten year olds, but in this instance it certainly paid off. He indicated they tested expert at the range. That was a little unbelievable until they each took out a man with one shot to the head."

Rafe looked at his children with pride. "You did know they both tested high genus. Just how high is a little early to tell. They are home schooled to grade eight. We will need help to properly educate them as they are rapidly approaching the extent of our abilities."

Vera interrupted, "They learn at a very rapid pace to the point I think a computer study program might suit them better. They can advance at their own pace that way. It would also eliminate the security issue a teacher would bring."

McPherson considered and said, "I'll tell Agent Patton to arrange two computers and the software they need. Any other comments or questions?"

Vera spoke, "What about Dr. Kindle? Is she okay and how did they know about our medical appointment?"

"Apparently, she just received a knock on the head and is back at work. The agencies are looking into the other question. If that's all lets have something to eat." He then motioned to the flight attendant to begin the food service.

The children watched with interest as the flight attendant prepared each passenger a hot meal and attached the food tray to the seat. Before starting on their meal they waited until everyone had been served. They watched the adults fold the cloth napkins on their laps and peel the plastic cover off the food package. Fascinated, the children watched steam rise from the food. Their mother never fixed a meal like this.

After everyone finished eating, the adults reclined their seats in an attempt to relax and get some rest before they landed in Portland.

However, Adam and Evelyn were busy mentally comparing notes with each other.

McPherson suspects we can read others thoughts you dummy. Dad told us not to reveal that to anyone and you almost blew it, Evelyn thought to Adam.

Thanks for the save. I think he bought it, but he's still suspicious, Adam responded. *We'll have to let Mom and Dad know about his suspicions when we are alone with them.*

They then settled back into their seat enjoying the luxurious surroundings of the aircraft. Eventually they were all alerted by the pilot's announcement they were preparing to land and everyone should buckle-up.

After landing, the plane proceeded to the General Aviation Terminal where they deplaned and were directed to an armored vehicle for transportation to the safe house. It took almost an hour to reach their destination, which at first looked like a business building. Their vehicle entered the building after an electronic signal raised a door for them, and closed behind their three-car convoy.

The parking area inside the building could hold fifty cars, but currently only ten cars, including the three recent arrivals, were parked inside. The Johnsons met other agents who directed them to a bank of elevators where they were taken to the fifth floor. They stepped into a small lobby area, much like a hotel, where they were told to take a seat for a few minutes until a meeting room was prepared.

Besides the Johnsons there were ten other people milling around, since the Johnson's had taken what chairs were available. Rafe looked at Vera and frowned as he whispered, "What a cluster fuck. We must have gotten here before they had time to prepare."

Vera frowned at Rafe and shook her head. "Be still! Let's see what develops."

Deputy Director McPherson and a striking angry looking woman entered the lobby. "Everyone shut up and pay attention!" She shouted.

"I'm Special Agent, Jane Patton with the FBI. This is a combined FBI and CIA operation and I'm in charge. This is Deputy Director James McPherson with the CIA. We have a combined total of forty agents working this operation to protect four people. Would the Johnson family please come over here and introduce yourself."

Rafe and Vera stood up and motioned for the children to follow them. Rafe faced the agents and started speaking.

"I'm Rafe Johnson and this is my wife, Vera, and our twin children, Adam and Evelyn. We have been reinstated as CIA Agents since our problems started. I don't think many of you are cleared to learn what those problems are; however, there have been three attempts to abduct us as a family. I really hope you all do your jobs and keep us safe."

Special Agent Jane Patton looked at the agents. "You should know that the Johnsons have all been rated expert with handguns and that includes Adam and Evelyn. In the last attempt against them, the children killed two men attackers with one shot each to the head. If another attempt is made against them I expect it will be of a larger scope than in the past. You will be given your individual assignments for this twenty-four/seven protection detail until we are relieved. All right, report to your supervisor."

Patton motioned for DD McPherson and the Johnsons to follow her back to the meeting room. She indicated that they should all sit and then told her deputy to close and guard the door.

Patton looked at McPherson and muttered, "James, this is a real can of worms you've given me."

"Jane it could be worse. These could have been civilians. At least they can defend themselves if need be, and they have performed well."

Patton looked at Rafe and Vera. "You two were retired when all this started. Just how old are you?"

Rafe smiled warily. "You already know that, but it is hard to believe isn't it? I'm ninety-one and Vera is eighty-one. We have the physical bodies of low twenties and lots of people want a piece of us. You're going to be kept busy. I would think you need another forty agents just to keep watch of the airports and the area around this building."

Patton studied Rafe. "You were Station Chief of Paris when you retired and Vera was an Analyst at Langley. That's a lot of brainpower to let go to waste. Why don't you two take a look at the blueprints of this building and the surrounding area and try to find some weaknesses? Your residence rooms are located on this floor in the center of the building. I imagine you want to get some rest and I'll see you early tomorrow."

An agent was waiting for them as they exited the meeting room. She said. "Follow me please."

The Johnsons followed her down a hallway that had several numbered doors along its length, much like an apartment building or a hotel. They eventually stopped at door number 528, which the agent opened and entered first. She then stopped and looked around the room.

"Stay here while I check the rooms out."

She soon returned and gave them a tour of the apartment. There were three bedrooms, living room, kitchen with an attached dinning area, and two full baths.

"My name is Anne Hawk. The fridge is stocked and your bags should be delivered soon. If you have any questions, now is the time."

Adam blurted, "Do you have cable?"

Anne grinned. "Typical kid question. Yes, you have cable and WiFi for Internet connections. However, you have only the one TV. If you need another let me know."

Vera smiled at the agent. "What tribe are you from?"

"Choctaw," she replied with a questioningly look.

"As am I. My maiden name is Sparrow, from the Bird Clan. My first husband was a Hawk."

Agent Hawk looked at her with sudden interest. "Was his first name Jack and did he die about twenty years ago?"

"Yes. Did you know him?"

"No, but he was my great uncle. I guess we are related by marriage. It's a small world. Wait a minute, that can't be right. If you were married to Jack you would have to be over eighty, and you're not nearly that old."

Rafe chuckled. "Now you know part of our problem and why we are under protection. Tell Jane Patton that you guessed our age and don't tell anyone else what you discovered. On another note, did we get approval for two computers and teaching software for the kids?"

Agent Hawk looked at Rafe and Vera, her dark eyes intent for a moment, "I really stepped in it didn't I? On the computers, I'll ask about that. Anything else?"

Vera placed her hand on Agent Hawk's arm. "Don't worry. If anything, it shows your supervisor how observant you are. I'll ask them to keep you on the detail if it goes badly."

After the agent left the apartment, Evelyn said, "Mom, Dad. Mr. McPherson suspects that Adam and I have the ability to read minds. He passed on that suspicion to Agent Patton as it was on her mind when she was talking to us. We're sorry we weren't more careful."

Their parents hugged both their children.

Vera said, "Honey, in the future when you have information like that, just wait until we are alone to tell us and we will make the decision how to reveal it. If it's life threatening you may have to take direct action like you both did against the bad men. Make sure its life threatening before you take that kind of action. Any questions?"

"No. We both really like Ms. Hawk. She seems to like us and her mind is sharp, not fuzzy like so many we've met," Adam said.

Rafe thoughtfully asked, "How do our minds compare to hers?"

The children looked at each other before coming to a consensus on how they wanted to answer the question. Evelyn spoke for both of them. "Your minds are unique from others. We can clearly read your surface thoughts, but you seem to have a block that prevents us from going deeper. We knew from your thoughts that those bad men had to be eliminated, so we didn't hesitate when we had the opportunity."

Vera breathed a sigh of relief. "Your father and I were worried we had ruined your moral compass when you killed those men. Killing is something that should be done only as a last resort. We both have killed before, but it was only to save our lives or others and we both suffered later trying to come to terms with it. Did you two have any misgivings about the killings?"

They both shook their heads. "We took no joy in their deaths. We knew we were threatened and there was no other way to resolve the situation. Besides we knew we had your approval before we did it," Adam said.

Vera smiled sadly. "Well, I guess that's as good as we can get. Why don't you two kids pick out your bedrooms, but leave the big one for us."

The parents then walked to the kitchen to see what they could put together for an evening meal. It wasn't long before Adam and Evelyn were brought to the kitchen by the smells of pizza cooking in the oven. Vera poured them glasses of milk, which they took to the dining table and watched TV while waiting for the pizza to finish baking.

After dinner, Rafe and Vera checked to see whether the beds held fresh sheets and needed any extra blankets while the kids watched TV. The exterior walls of the apartment were brick, so they then checked the exterior door. It was constructed of heavy steel and had a dead bolt lock. It even had a fox support bar that could be engaged when they retired for the night.

Rafe looked at the door, grinning. "Nobody is going to get through that without us hearing them in enough time for us to greet them."

CHAPTER 10

Rafe woke early the next morning and started the coffee pot when he realized the morning newspaper wasn't in the driveway as usual. Still wearing his pajamas, he disengaged the fox bar from the exterior door and opened it to investigate.

An agent was standing just outside. "Do you need anything Mr. Johnson?"

Rafe smiled at him. "Yes, can you have someone bring me a morning newspaper?"

"Yes sir." The request was passed on through his radio.

"Is there somewhere in the building where we can jog?"

"I'll pass that on, but I think you can use the garage on the ground floor. Agent Patton will be here at eight a.m. to go over some things with you, so you better put off the jog until then."

Rafe thanked him and shut the door, returning to the kitchen for his coffee. Vera, enticed by the smell of coffee, walked in to find Rafe reading the newspaper. She got a cup for herself and sat down across from him. Rafe wordlessly passed her the entertainment section.

Putting the paper down, he said, "Patton is going to be here at eight."

Vera looked at the time. "I've got over an hour. You can help me get the kids up and dressed. I want to enjoy my coffee and read this article before I do anything."

Rafe smiled at his wife and got up from the table. "I'll get them started," he said as he headed down the hall toward their bedrooms.

Banging on their doors, he passed on his way to take a shower. He could hear them moving around before he got to his own room. After he showered and dressed he stuck his head into Adam's room and found him holding up a shirt, staring at it doubtfully.

"What's the problem?"

"I wore this shirt yesterday and it's all wrinkled."

"Didn't your mother tell you that you wear a shirt only once before you change."

"Yeah, but I didn't bring but one extra."

"Go ahead and change and we'll worry about tomorrow later. How's the jeans look?"

"Okay, I guess."

"Hurry up, Agent Patton will be here at eight."

As he was leaving Adams's room Vera passed by saying, "Evelyn's doing okay. I'm heading for the shower."

Everyone was in the kitchen eating cereal when a knock sounded at the door. Rafe shouted, "Who's there?"

"Agent Patton. Let me in."

Rafe hurried over and let her and the two people with her inside. Patton pointed at the agent holding several boxes. "Those are the computers you asked for. Where do you want them?"

Vera pointed to the hallway. "Put them on the floor. We'll put them where they belong later."

The agent did as instructed and left the apartment. Patton looked at the family and smiled. "Last night you solved a problem for me when you discovered you and Agent Hawk were extended family. I've brought her into the inner circle of agents who know your history and she has been tasked with providing you with your every need."

Rafe and Vera gave Agent Hawk a sympatric smile. "We're so sorry you got stuck with that thankless job. We'll try not to be too much of a burden."

Vera looked at Patten. "You know of course that she is a very intelligent and perceptive agent."

"Of course she is or she wouldn't be here. Let's get to business. I've made arrangements to get you the blueprints of this building and they should be here sometime this morning. I've also arranged for you to jog in the garage. What time do you want?"

Vera said, "We prefer from 10 to 11 a.m."

Patton made a notation of the time in her blackberry. "Okay, Agent Hawk will stay with the children while you jog. You are welcome to eat in our cafeteria if you like. Actually, we prefer you do. It gives you an opportunity to see other people and it has a nice view of the Columbia River and the ship traffic. We also won't have to restock your apartment with food as often either. Agent Hawk will provide you the dining times. Your family is instructed not to reveal anything of your problem with anyone outside the inner circle. Any questions?"

Rafe asked, "Have you learned anything more about the attempts to abduct us?'

Patton shook her head. "Not much. We have some Intel that an al-Qaeda terrorist with a code name of Raptor may be behind that last attempt, but we are still looking for other leads. We have a firing range on the second floor. Let us know when you want to use it."

Patton left leaving Hawk behind to help the family. Rafe said, "Agent Hawk we all need extra clothing until our stuff arrives. Do you know when it's expected?"

"No, but I would think at least three more days. I'll check on that for you and in the meantime what sizes and what clothing do you need?"

Vera told her what they needed and their sizes for three changes of clothing. She added, if it takes longer we could always do laundry. Rafe asked Hawk, "How are you in setting up computers?"

"I'm not sure this is in my job description, but let's get to it."

They soon had the computers set up and the software loaded, before they moved them to the children's rooms. Vera handed them each a copy of the operating manual and instructions on using the software and told them to go at it and she would give the first one to get it running a prize.

Before Hawk left she said, "I'll be back before your ten o'clock run."

With the kids busy, Rafe and Vera were alone for a few minutes. He took her hand and led her to the couch, pulling her onto his lap where they kissed passionately for several minutes. He said, "Honey I really love you."

"You don't do that enough."

"What, kiss you or say I love you?"

"Both," she said with tears welling in her eyes. "I love you too you big lug," she whispered as she hugged him, laying her head on his chest.

Suddenly, Evelyn cried out, "Mom! I've got it working."

"Me too!"

"But I called first!"

Vera looked at Rafe and snickered. "Okay! We've got some bright kids."

"Yeah, and very competitive. They're a tough room."

Vera hurried to check on the kids and helped them establish a study schedule. She set a schedule for each, studying different subjects initially and then later the same subjects to see which was better. The initial subjects were at high school level and she had Evelyn start with algebra and Adam with biology. She would then switch subjects and compare the results. She would then have them study science at the same time and compare the results.

Rafe and Vera were ready when Hawk arrived to watch over the children while they went jogging. Another agent was outside to escort them to the garage. When they left the elevator they found the garage held fifteen cars that were parked so they had a clear path around the interior walls that looked like a tenth of a mile circuit.

Vera looked at the makeshift track and asked, "Twenty times around to start and then see how much time we have left?"

Rafe nodded and he followed her lead as they started on their jog. They didn't stop until thirty laps and would have continued except their time was almost up. Their escort was waiting at the elevator when they approached, along with five other agents waiting their turn to jog.

On the elevator ride, their escort thanked them for arranging the jogging track. "We have a lot of runners and this really helped. I don't think they are going to do thirty laps though. We measured it and ten laps is about a mile and an eighth, which means y'all ran almost three and a half miles."

Rafe and Vera made it back to their apartment and relieved Agent Hawk. The twins were engrossed in their studies, but it was lunchtime and Vera told them to save their work. Rafe and Vera shared a shower, which probably took longer than it should, changed and met the twins in the living room.

They followed their escort to the cafeteria and when they entered were surprised at the view overlooking the Columbia River, which looked to be almost two miles away. A ship was heading inland as they watched.

Adam and Evelyn quickly made their way over to the window and gazed in awe at the sight. Evelyn pointed at the ship. "Mom, what kind of ship is that with all the boxes stacked on top?"

"It's what is called a container ship." Vera then explained to the twins why merchants brought their business in that way. She then herded them into the cafeteria line where they picked out their food and took a table that offered the best view of the river.

Rafe was looking at the other buildings between there and the river and noted their building must be on a low hill as it was higher than any other he could see. He made a note to himself to ask Agent Hawk about other buildings nearby that he couldn't see. They stayed a little longer to let the twins observe the river traffic before heading back to their apartment.

Their days started to settle into a familiar routine of the children studying their lessons, while Rafe and Vera examined the building blueprints and other nearby buildings for possible security problems. They eventually received their shipment of personal items and clothing from their old home and everyone felt a little better about being displaced.

They were in Portland three weeks when Rafe and Vera decided to take Patton's offer of the use of their firing range. The twins seemed happy to take a break from their studies as they left the apartment for a chance to go shooting. Their escort took them to the second floor where two other agents were already firing. The Range Master gave them ammo for their weapons and paper targets and told them to use the far aisle.

Rafe decided to go first and after positioning the target at thirty feet told everyone to put their ear protectors on. After checking his SIG Sauer he slow-fired three shots into the target's head, then quickly fired four shots into the chest area. He repositioned a new target at fifty feet, and after reloading, quickly fired six shots into the chest area.

He retrieved the target, proudly showing everyone the results. He'd hit both targets within the kill zone; however, the first closer target had shots so close together they were almost one.

Vera shot next and used the same routine. Her results were almost exactly the same as Rafe's. The twins examined the targets in wonder. Adam asked, "Can we shoot the same routine as you just did?"

Rafe nodded. "The fifty-foot target is going to be harder with your .32 cal. weapons. You might want to take a test shot at that distance before fast-firing."

Evelyn wanted to shoot first and fired the same routine for both targets. She tore a large hole in the head and chest area of her first target. The second try had one hole slightly below the other shots into the chest area.

Vera pointed at the lower hole. "That was your test shot?"

Evelyn nodded. "I had to make a slight adjustment. Adam will do better."

Adam's results were the same as Evelyn's on the first target, but his second target showed all the hits in a tight group in the chest area.

Vera looked at her twins. "So, you do learn from each other's experiences. If only one of you study a lesson, does the other learn as well?'

Adam answered, "Yes, but not as well. When I studied a lesson that Evelyn had already done, I was able to complete it in half the time."

Vera nodded. "That's why I had you two study lessons separately and together. I think from now on the lessons will go faster if you learn your subjects separately."

The Range Master stopped them on the way out. "Do you mind if I post these targets? We need something to remind some of these yoyos what an expert shooter looks like."

Rafe laughed. "What does it tell them when our kids shoot as good or better than we do?"

The Range Master looked at the targets again. "Which ones are the kids?"

Rafe sorted through the pile and pulled Adam and Evelyn's out. "Are you sure you want to post them?"

The Range Master looked at them, astonished. "They shot these at the same distance you did using a .32 cal?"

At Rafe's nod the Range Master muttered, "Crap! I'm going to post them anyway. Most of these guys won't believe it."

That evening, the family entered the cafeteria as usual and after getting their food they started toward the tables, but were diverted to a large table usually reserved for Agent Patton, who signaled for them to join her. Agent Hawk was already sitting at the table and both stood as the family approached.

Patton motioned for them to take seats as she said, "Please eat with us. I've got some things I need to discuss with you."

Once all were seated Patton continued, "Posting those targets today raised a competitive spirit that I think will be useful. I'd like to have a shooting contest between the FBI and the CIA Agents. You two are already entered with that posting. The best ten scores from each agency will compete for honors and a plaque."

Rafe looked at Vera. "I really think the best shots are our kids. At a short range nobody can beat them with their .32's."

Patton looked at Adam and Evelyn, smiling. "I'm glad they're on our side and they have already proved their worth. However, what I want to do is show our agents from both agencies that each has the ability to get the job done. I'll let you know when the finals are set."

A week later the eliminations were completed. Rafe and Vera were part of the CIA team of ten agents and were to shoot against the FBI team that included Agent Hawk. The finals were to begin the next morning with five agents from the FBI shooting first, then alternating until everyone finished. They were to shoot one clip of nine at each of three targets; one at thirty feet, one at fifty feet, and one at sixty feet. Headshots would receive double points and shots outside the zone would not count.

Rafe and Vera were shooting at ten a.m. When Adam and Evelyn heard them discussing the contest they came and sat down near them. Evelyn said, "Mom, Dad how good are these other agents?"

Rafe smiled at their innocence. "Not many of the CIA agents are rated expert, but I don't know about the FBI. We are shooting as a team, not individually, so unless they have more expert shooters on their team it should be a close contest. Patton is trying to show that this detail is a team effort."

Adam frowned. "So if the strategy is more points then will you try for more head shots?"

"Only if I'm sure I can stay within the zone. Remember outside the zone gets no points. I'm sure I can get the head shots at thirty feet, but fifty feet and over is iffy."

Vera said, "I'll do head shots at thirty and fifty, at least until I miss more than one outside the zone. The double points makes it worth it to try for them."

Rafe nodded. "You've got a point and I'll do that too."

The next day after all contestants completed their round, the results were posted. The FBI and the CIA agents was within eight points of each other, with the CIA the winner. The individual scores told the story. Rafe and Vera were the high scorers of both teams by racking up eighteen headshots each. The closest to them was one FBI agent with nine headshots. No one else had tried a headshot over thirty feet. Aside from Rafe and Vera, the FBI outshot the CIA team.

A week later the family was eating lunch in the cafeteria when Evelyn said, "That's strange. I've seen that same boat pass by at least five times in the last two days."

Rafe looked out the window toward the river. "What boat?"

"That small white and blue boat with a cabin on top. See that man in back, he looks like he is looking this way."

Rafe rushed over to one of the agents relaying Evelyn's observation, pointing towards the river. The agent then talked over his radio, watching the boat. He nodded his head as if in agreement and the two returned to the family table.

Rafe introduced Agent Hodge to the rest of his family. Agent Hodge asked Evelyn, "When did you first notice that boat and the man looking this way?"

"I noticed it last Tuesday at lunch, but it may have been out there before that. What drew my attention was the man in back taking pictures. Maybe of us?"

Agent Hodge smiled at this revelation from such a youngster, but then his face hardened as he walked away talking on his radio again. The family noticed a helicopter suddenly flying over their building toward the river and then over the suspect. The helicopter hovered near the boat until a coast guard boat arrived a short time later and took possession of the boat and its passengers.

By this time everyone in the cafeteria was watching the action on the river. Agent Patton hurried into the room and joined the observers for a few minutes before coming over to the family and asking them to join her in the meeting room.

Agent Hawk joined them before they reached the meeting room. When everyone was seated, Agent Patton asked Evelyn to repeat everything she could remember about the boat and the men on it. When she was finished, Adam spoke.

"I started watching the boat when Evelyn took an interest in it. The camera the man used had a long lens, and another man on top of the boat had something he was holding to his eyes while looking this way. We both saw the boat twice before we left the cafeteria that day and we've seen it every day since."

Agent Hawk said, "They were using both telephoto lens and binoculars. I wonder how long we have been under surveillance?"

Agent Patton looked at Rafe and Vera. "Have you come up with any weaknesses here that we need to be aware of?"

Rafe said, "Vera and I think the building itself is quite strong. There is no way inside except through the garage doors. All other doors and windows on the first floor have been bricked over. The garage doors themselves should be strengthened to withstand a vehicle driving through it. The only other threat we could foresee is a gas attack to knock everyone out. A gas attack can come from a helicopter shooting canisters through the upper windows. We need gas masks and training on how to use them to protect ourselves from such an attack."

Agent Patton's face whitened at this information, but quickly settled into determination. "Okay! I wasn't really expecting you two to come up with anything this quick, but it's better to be prepared. Agent Hawk we need enough masks to stash throughout the building. In the meantime, every agent will be required to carry one on his or her person until we get a handle on this threat. Also, find someone who can strengthen the garage doors. It's going to be a hassle, but in the meantime we should park something big against the door to support it."

Agent Hawk excused herself and left the meeting to begin her new duties. Agent Patton looked at the two youngsters. "You two continue to surprise me. You of all the agents in that cafeteria were the ones to notice that spy boat and if you would have had a little more experience you could have warned us that first day."

Adam stared back at Agent Patton, eyes dark. "We are quick learners and the computer teachings programs have brought us both up to a college level. Are there any other courses available that might help us in this situation?"

"You are what, ten or eleven years old?" Agent Patton asked, looking over at Rafe and Vera.

"How do you keep ahead of these smart kids?"

Rafe smiled slightly. "We can't. All we can do is guide them and so far it's worked. Does the FBI have any computer courses they can take? Don't worry about their age. They can absorb anything we give them."

CHAPTER 11

The next day Agent Patton stopped by the Johnsons' apartment. Rafe could tell from her appearance she was exhausted and he asked, "Can I get you something?"

She responded with a weak smile.

"How about a shot of whisky."

Vera quickly brought her a shot glass, two shots of dark amber inside it.

"Wild Turkey alright?"

Agent Patton took a sip and sighed gratefully. "I haven't slept since I talked to you yesterday. We picked up three people in that spy boat and they cut a deal this morning. Apparently, they work for the same group that hit you at the Medical Center. They only had contact with one person and he was long gone by the time we knew who to go after. We're still checking, but we aren't hopeful. All we know for sure is they know where you are and they still want you."

Rafe frowned. "I wonder how they followed us here? I can think of only two sources, no make that three. There's a leak at our agencies or they followed our stuff that was shipped here."

Agent Patton took another sip of her drink. "Yeah! That has occurred to me too. I don't think it came from here, but who really knows."

Vera looked a little disgusted. "So, what's the plan now? They want us alive, so they won't try to blow up the building. I still think it's going to be a gas attack."

"I think you're right. We can't keep moving you around with that security leak, besides this place is like a fort and is easily defended. We stay here and take whatever measures we need to take. You should get your gas masks later today, so make sure they are adjusted properly. They are still working on the garage doors, but they should be fixed sometime tomorrow."

Agent Patton finished the rest of her drink and stood up. "Before I forget it, Agent Hawk is going to bring your kids some software they might enjoy."

* * *

Three weeks later the two agencies had taken every precaution imaginable and were now waiting for the proverbial shoe to drop. The kids promised computer software arrived also, mesmerizing Adam and Evelyn. The software contained various ways and methods used by terrorists to cause mayhem and methods the FBI used in detecting and using surveillance to apprehend terrorists.

The twins continued their other studies and were well on their way to earning BA's. They had yet to settle on a major field of study; however, Evelyn tended to have a feel for higher mathematics, while Adam liked general science.

The family was eating breakfast in the cafeteria when several helicopters approached the building. Rafe seeing them first yelled, "We're under attack! Everyone don your masks."

Rafe and Vera had been practicing with the children putting on their gas masks, so they were protected before the first gas canister burst through the window. The other agents had also donned their masks and were escorting the Johnson family into the hallway in an attempt to protect them if intruders should use the big windows as their entry point.

Adam and Evelyn were calmed by the single-minded thoughts of their parents. Rafe and Vera's thoughts were only on how best to protect their children without any fear for themselves.

They could hear gunfire from several different locations within the building as the agents moved them to a prepared safe room in a central location on that floor. Agent Hawk was the only agent with the Johnsons when the door was slammed shut and the other agents took defensive positions guarding the room.

The Johnsons and Agent Hawk quickly moved furniture to act as a shield in case someone breached the door. Standing behind their makeshift shield, they stood ready to defend themselves. Gunfire continued until suddenly it was right outside their door. They ducked lower behind their cover as a shot pierced their door.

The shooting continued for a short time, and then seemed to recede. Fifteen minutes later the shooting stopped and an agent outside yelled, "Are you alright in there?"

Agent Hawk responded, "We're all okay. We will stay in here until the building is secured."

"Understood. Hang tight for a few more minutes."

There was another short sprite of gunfire before silence returned. About thirty minutes later they heard a knock on their door. Agent Patton called out, "It's all clear and I'm coming in."

When Agent Patton entered she was no longer wearing her gas mask, so they all took theirs off too. "Follow me to the cafeteria. It's got better air."

The cafeteria's big windows were all open letting in fresh air to clear the remaining gas. It was a little cold, but the fresh air smelled wonderful after wearing gas masks.

Agent Patton had several agents pull several tables together before they sat down. "This attack group appears to be hired mercenaries like the last group. A quick count of the inside group is twenty, with three survivors. We are still tracking the four helicopters used in the attack. They also tried to ram the garage doors, but that attack failed thanks to our efforts in that area."

Agent Patton smiled at Rafe and Vera. "You two called it right on in this attack. I'll give myself a pat on the back for giving you that task."

Rafe nodded. "Thanks, but what were our losses?"

Agent Patton's face tightened. "We have two dead and six injured. The injured aren't too bad and are already on their way to the hospital."

Agent Patton looked at the open windows. "It's a little breezy in here now, but your apartment is not clear of gas yet. We're going to bring in exhaust fans and open all the windows until we get rid of the gas. Why not go back to your safe room where it's more comfortable until your apartment is clear."

Three hours later, they were back into their apartment. Rafe turned on the TV to see what the news was saying about the attack on their building. A talking head was reporting about the strange happenings at their building, but little in explanations were coming from the authorities. The station showed videos of ambulances leaving the building for the hospital, but that was all.

Rafe looked at Vera. "Honey, it looks bad. We may have to move again."

Vera nodded. "Maybe not. If Patton can keep a lid on it, this will soon die down."

That night they prepared their own supper because the cafeteria was still too cold. The twins didn't appear to be adversely affected by the excitement of another raid against them and were currently busy drawing. Rafe and Vera noticed the twins had shown an interest in drawing after finishing a lesson in Art. That evening they were admiring a pencil drawing of the Mona Lisa that Evelyn created.

"This was drawn from memory?" Rafe asked.

"Yes, it's quite good isn't it?"

"It's better than good. I think she has a real talent."

"If you think that's so good, look at what Adam did."

Rafe looked at the drawing in amazement. The drawing was also of Mona Lisa, but Adam added color, which almost made it look like the original.

Rafe watched the twins draw. "Adam, can you print me out this picture of Mona Lisa. I want to see if I can see any differences between the original and your drawing."

"Sure, it should take only a minute."

When Adam brought him a copy of the picture he placed it down next to Adam's drawing. Vera's eyes opened wide in surprise as she compared the two versions of the famous painting. Adam had used watercolor over his pencil drawing, which resulted in some variance in the color tint, otherwise the picture looked the same.

Rafe smiled. "You know, we might be able to use this in finding out who is behind these attacks."

"What do you mean?" Vera responded with an uncertain look.

"I was thinking if we could get those attacker survivors to give a description of the man who hired them to a sketch artist, we might be able to follow him to the group behind this."

Vera shook her head. "You know how poorly those usually turn out... Ooh, you want the twins to draw the picture. How are we going to work that without anyone knowing they were involved?"

Rafe smiled. "Let's put our heads together and see if we can come up with something."

Later, after they came up with a tentative plan, he asked Agent Hawk if she could arrange to have his family observe when the attacker survivors have their sketch artist sessions of the contact man. She soon came back with news.

"They have just started and Agent Patton approved you 'all to watch from an adjacent room through a one-way mirror."

Rafe had already informed the twins of their plan and their need to pull the image of the man in charge from these survivors' memories. The first man finished about thirty minutes after their arrival and they were all done two hours later. The artist told them after he finished a composite he would have them back to see how close the drawing was to the real men.

The family returned to their apartment and the twins immediately started on their drawings. After completing their individual drawings they compared the two and then started making adjustments based upon each other's comments. They then looked at each drawing before discarding Evelyn's. They concentrated on the remaining drawing while making several more adjustments before bringing it to their parents.

Adam held it out to them. "Should I add color? It would make it more lifelike."

Rafe looked at Vera and smiled. "No. Remember, this is supposed to come from the sketch artist and he works only in pencil. Now we have to substitute this drawing for the one from the artist."

Vera asked Agent Hawk to bring the final sketch from the artist to them so they could try to identify him from their contacts. They had already determined they didn't know him from their own drawing. The next day Agent Hawk brought the finished drawing to them. While Rafe and Vera were looking at it, Evelyn created a distraction by asking Hawk a question. When she turned back to them they had already made the switch.

"I'm going to take this to Agent Patton now before it's put through our picture I.D. program. I'll let you know if we have a hit."

Later that day they received visitors. When Rafe answered the door he was not altogether surprised to see Agents Patton and Hawk. He noted their solemn faces as he invited them inside. After they were all seated, Patton smiled ruefully.

"I laid a trap for you with that drawing. We suspected that some or all of you were telepaths and I thought if that was the case you might attempt this ruse. I went ahead and sent your drawing through the photo I.D. scan and we came up with a positive I.D. It's good you have a high security clearance because life has just become more complicated. The person ID is James Wright who's associated with several Islamic groups whose goal is to destroy the western world. He is English and is known to have his hooks into the security agencies of the U.S., England, and France."

"So what now? Are we safe here or do we have to move again?" Rafe asked.

"I've got a call into the Director with that very question. I still think you are safer here than anywhere else and we can make it even harder for anyone to get in when we fix the areas where they got in this time. What I want to know now is who are the telepaths?"

Rafe and Vera grimaced in unison. "We were dreading this moment, but I can see now we really need their talents. Both Adam and Evelyn are telepaths and can read most peoples' surface thoughts. They have other talents as well. Vera, show them the Mona Lisa drawings and the original picture."

Agents Patton and Hawk looked at the drawings and then at the twins. "You did this from memory and not directly from the original?" Agent Patton asked.

The twins grinned. "That's why Mom and Dad thought we could do a better likeness than the sketch artist," Evelyn responded.

"How deep can you probe other peoples' minds?"

"We really haven't done that. We read what they are thinking about. When those men were doing the sketch, they were thinking about the man they wanted to draw. It was just like a picture they were broadcasting to us," Adam said.

"Have you tried to probe deeper beyond their surface thoughts?"

"No! That would be wrong. I wouldn't try that unless they were really bad people and I needed the information to help our family."

Patton smiled. "Telepaths with a conscience. You two have raised some really good kids."

CHAPTER 12

Another week passed with no further sign of interest in the Johnsons from other parties. They thought at least two groups wanted to abduct the Johnsons from the past attacks in Springfield. Agent Patton wanted to make sure none of the local agents were compromised, so she arranged meetings where the Johnson family met every agent on the detail over a ten day period. Conversations always involved the recent attack and speculation on how they got inside information.

The twins only received one suspicious reaction, an individual who was brought back for another interview; only this time with Agents Patton and Hawk while the Johnson family watched from the next room through a one-way window. It was Agent James Shepley, an FBI transfer to Portland from Los Angeles to augment this detail.

Agent Patton started asking questions about his background in Los Angeles and where he had been assigned in the past, gradually moving toward the attack against this facility. Patton suddenly asked, "Agent Shepley why did you sell us out?"

Agent Shepley turned white and he acted before either of the other agents could fully react as he pulled a small glock from his ankle holster and fired at both female agents, hitting Agent Hawk first, then Agent Patton. Patton shot Shepley as she was falling to the floor, while Shepley staggered toward the door.

Rafe motioned to Vera to watch their children, while he drew his weapon and moved to intercept Agent Shepley. Shepley was leaving the interrogation room when Rafe entered the hallway and shot him in the leg. Shepley fell to the floor and dropped his weapon, which Rafe quickly kicked down the hall.

In seconds the hallway was filled with agents wanting to know what was going on. Rafe yelled, "Agents Patton and Hawk have been shot and need medical attention! Call for an ambulance! This piece of crap shot them, so be sure he stays alive to interrogate!"

Rafe checked on the two wounded agents. Patton was on the floor leaning against a wall with a shoulder wound, while Hawk was on the floor unconscious with a chest wound. The building had its own EMT who soon arrived to administer to the wounded agents.

Agent Patton's second in command, Agent Peter Stouts, arrived to take charge. Taking note of the carnage, he asked, "What the hell happened here?"

Rafe filled him in on their suspicions of Agent Shepley and how during the interrogation he suddenly pulled a weapon and started shooting. Rafe described shooting Shepley in the leg as he attempted to escape.

Agent Stouts looked at Shepley. "It looks like he's been shot twice; once in the shoulder and again in the leg."

"Yes. Patton got off one shot after she was shot. We need to make sure that bastard doesn't die before we get some information."

Agent Stouts nodded. "That's why he isn't already dead. You could have easily blown him away at this range."

The EMT was now trying to stop the blood flow from Shepley's wounds. Five minutes later more EMTs arrived to transport the wounded to the hospital. Three agents escorted Shepley to the ambulance and the hospital to make sure he didn't escape or prevent someone else from trying to kill him.

Later they received word that Agent Patton was doing great. The bullet had gone through her shoulder without hitting any bones and she would be released tomorrow. Agent Hawk was in ICU and was in much worse condition, with a bullet lodged near her heart.

The twins had formed a special attachment with Agent Hawk and wanted to go see her. Rafe and Vera wanted to see her as well, but it was too dangerous for them to leave the building. They were also told that due to the age of the children they would never be allowed in the ICU.

The next day Agent Patton returned to the building with her left arm in a sling. She came by the apartment to give them news of Agent Hawk's condition. Patton sat down on the couch looking completely worn out. Vera hurried to get her a cup of coffee, which she accepted gratefully and took a sip. She leaned back with a sigh.

"Agent Hawk is not doing well and is not expected to survive. That shit that shot us is doing much better."

She looked at Rafe. "Thanks for not killing him. We really need some more information to keep us ahead of the bad guys."

Adam and Evelyn stood up and approached Agent Patton. "We think we can help Agent Hawk. Our blood apparently has properties that heal our bodies from sickness and injuries. We have never been sick and cuts heal without scars. Give her some of our blood and we're sure she will get better," Evelyn pleaded, her eyes dark with concern.

Agent Patton looked at the two, tears welling in her eyes and then turned to their

Parents. "I'm willing to try if you approve?"

Rafe and Vera looked at each other questioningly before Vera replied.

"We will give our permission, but due to their age they individually can't safely give very much blood, maybe a half-pint each? We can give more blood ourselves. With our blood and theirs it might be enough."

Agent Patton called their EMT to come and draw blood from the family. As she was leaving the room with the donated blood, she said to herself, *I hope this is a universal blood type.*

The Johnsons were relieved that they tried to do something to help Agent Hawk. Vera made sure everyone was given orange juice and other fluids to replace the blood loss, along with a snack of peanut butter and crackers. Afterward the twins went back to their lessons while their parents worried about what was coming next.

The following evening Agent Patton returned. This time she had a big grin on her face as she entered the apartment.

"I've got great news. Agent Hawk has improved so much they intend to remove her from ICU tomorrow if she continues her progress. The doctors don't know I switched the blood transfusion bags. That's just between you and me. The doctors can't figure out why she suddenly started to improve."

Vera smiled at the news, but then had a sudden thought. "You had better seize her medical records when she leaves the hospital. The bad guys might even try to steal them before then."

"I'm way ahead of you. I've got four of our people watching over her and her records right now. My thought was they might try to grab her if they figure out she received some of your blood."

Rafe asked, "What about Shepley? How is he getting along?"

"He's about ready to be released to us and I want your kids to read him when we interrogate him again. Maybe this time we'll get something more than him trying to shoot us."

Adam interrupted, "When you accused him of being a traitor that same man in our drawing flashed in his mind. He must report to this man too."

"Ooh that would be nice if we could find James Wright. I'm sure we could go further up the chain of command if we caught him."

Two days later they wheeled former agent James Shepley into the interrogation room in a wheel chair. The Johnsons stood in the adjoining room again watching through the one-way mirror. Shepley looked at the mirror and curled his lip in contempt.

Adam said, "He knows someone is here watching. Your face is on his mind."

The interrogation went on for over an hour, when Adam spoke to his parents, "He's zoned out and is thinking of nothing but a calm lake. Let us try to get below his surface thoughts! Dad, let us try!"

Rafe thought about it and then motioned for Vera to step outside the room. When she followed him into the hallway and shut the door, she asked, "Do you think they should try this? We don't know what this will do to them. What if they get stuck inside his head?"

"You have a point. Let's ask them if they can take safeguards to prevent that."

Returning to the room, Rafe and Vera told the children of their concerns.

Adam and Evelyn looked at each other and communicated telepathically for a few minutes before Adam answered.

"Only one of us goes into his mind while the other monitors. If trouble happens then he or she pulls the other out. We don't think there will be a problem. We don't even know if we can do it."

"Okay, I'll let them know what you are going to do."

Next door, Rafe signaled for Agent Patton to come outside where he told her of the twins' plan. Patton called the other agents out of the room, but two guards were posted outside while Patton and Rafe entered the observation room.

Shepley appeared surprised he was left alone in the room and then he wheeled himself to the door to see if it was locked. Finding the door was indeed locked; he turned his attention to the one-way mirror, gesturing rudely.

Patton told the twins they could begin when they were ready. It was agreed between themselves that Evelyn would try first and Adam would monitor. She concentrated for a moment getting beneath his surface thoughts until she started to peel his memories back like an onion. Shepley's expression was surprise at first, and then upon realizing someone was in his head, he started screaming while holding his head in his hands.

After about fifteen minutes Evelyn finished her efforts. She turned to the others and smiled, while Shepley was sobbing in relief that she had left his head.

"We got mind pictures of several of his contacts and at least a portion of their names. The last known location of James Wright is at the local Sheraton Hotel in room 1028. He travels with six other people, three are bodyguards."

Agent Patton beamed at Evelyn as if she had just been given a pot of gold.

"I'll get back to you on the pictures and names, but right now I want to see if I can catch Wright," Patton said as she left the room.

After Agent Patton left they watched as a subdued James Shepley was wheeled out of the interrogation room.

Rafe asked Adam, "Was he in pain during the mind probe?"

"No. He was just frightened when he realized something was in his head. Although such fear could make him crazy if it continued much longer."

Rafe smiled slightly. "I'll bet he'll spill his guts at any future interrogation sessions to avoid that experience again."

The family returned to their apartment to await future developments. The twins started on separate drawings of the faces pulled from Shepley's mind. They wrote what names Shepley associated with the faces at the bottom of each drawing.

Four hours later Agent Patton returned to give them news, her face beaming as she entered the apartment and motioned for everyone to take a seat.

"We found James Wright in his hotel room and he surrendered without a fight. We also picked up two members of separate Islamic terrorist groups. The others were bodyguards and Wright's girlfriend. We are now trying to get as much information out of them as we can before we have to hand them over to Homeland Security."

Adam interrupted, "If you need help on James Wright, we are willing. You should look at the drawings we made. Dad said he might know one of them."

Agent Patton looked at Rafe with concern. "Is it one of ours?"

Rafe handed the drawings to her. "You tell me."

She looked at the first drawing and shook her head before looking at the second. Her eyes opened wide in shock before her face turned red in anger. "That bastard! No wonder we had a leak where you were kept. He's the Assistant Deputy Director of the FBI."

Rafe nodded. "To get rid of him we need credible evidence. I suggest Deputy Director McPherson directly contact your Deputy Director with what evidence we have against ADD Jackson. He needs to be taken out of the loop as far as this investigation is concerned or we are going to be burned."

"Sounds good. Maybe your kids can get more evidence out of Wright while I take care of this matter. I'll have Wright taken to the interrogation room where they can do their work from the adjoining room."

Later, Agent Patton returned to their apartment wearing a determined expression.

"Well, that wasn't fun. That was the first time I had to point my finger at one of my superiors. It's a good thing McPherson knows me or I would have had a harder time of it. I also told him to keep your kids' telepathic powers to himself and Deputy Director Samson. They needed to know how we got the information or it would never be believable."

Vera asked, "Will DD Samson believe that telepaths are possible?"

Agent Patton looked at her and smiled. "Maybe not at first, but I had McPherson tell Samson to look at the drawing the kids did of Wright and how that was from a mind probe. However, I think McPherson can persuade him to isolate Jackson until we get more evidence."

Rafe and Vera smiled at each other, which caused Agent Patton to say, "What!"

Rafe's smile became a grin as he replied, "Would an account number of a deposit account in the Cayman Islands in Jackson's name be enough?"

"How much money is in it."

"That's something you will have to determine, but according to Wright he made six deposits of $500,000 over the past two years."

Rafe handed her a page with the dates and amounts of the deposit, along with the name of the bank and the account number. He then handed over another page with the names of ten contacts of Wright, along with their addresses.

Agent Patton looked at the information with a big smile on her face.

"I'll contact DD Samson later and pass on this information, which should take care of our security problem with Jackson."

* * *

Three weeks later brought a number of disclosures including ADD Jackson's resignation from the FBI, his subsequent disappearance, and the sudden arrests of a number of high-level Islamic terrorist members. In addition, Agent Hawk had returned to the building to finish her recuperation from her gunshot wound. It made sense to do it there where she was under protection.

Agent Hawk was in the Johnsons' apartment visiting and trying to catch up on all that had happened since she was injured. The twins were eager to see her and hovered asking if they could get her something. Everyone suddenly stopped what he or she was doing when Anne Hawk answered one of the children's questions, a question not vocally spoken.

Anne looked around. "What did I say?"

Evelyn asked her another question telepathically.

Anne answered, "Yes I can hear you. Why do you ask?"

Look at my lips. I am speaking to you with thoughts instead of spoken words.

Anne was shocked, still not fully comprehending what had happened. She turned to Rafe and Vera. "Can you do that too?"

Vera shook her head. "No, only the children and now you."

"I don't understand. Why is this happening to me?"

Vera took Anne's hands in hers and squeezed them gently. "You were dying and we tried to save you by giving you blood from each of us. Apparently the half-pint you got from both Adam and Evelyn gave you the ability to be a telepath. As you get stronger you will probably start feeling other changes. I want you to come see me if it happens."

Anne looked at the family with a little fear and some eagerness.

"I'm turning into one of you by taking your blood. I'm going to get younger too, aren't I?"

"Probably. Adam and Evelyn got our blood. You got theirs and ours, so you may have different abilities. We'll just have to wait and see."

Rafe called for Agent Patton to stop by their apartment soon, as they had something important to discuss with her. Patton was there within ten minutes and when seeing Agent Hawk sitting still, seeming shocked, she asked, "You told her about the blood transfusion?"

"Not until she demonstrated that she was a telepath."

Patton looked at him in surprise. "It's your blood or the twins' blood that caused it. That's right isn't it?"

Vera nodded. "Yes, but she got blood from all of us. We don't know what effect that's going to be on her body."

Vera asked, "Anne, are you married or have a serious boyfriend?"

"I'm not married, but my boyfriend is assigned at Seattle. Why do you ask?"

Vera looked at Rafe and smiled. "We both got very randy when we were going through the change. You may have the same side effect we did. At the time we didn't have each other and we had to cope with our desires. I jogged and Rafe exercised until we got past that period."

Patton looked at them and shook her head. "We can't have Anne jumping my men when she can't control her emotions. What's your boyfriend's name and I'll see about getting him reassigned here?"

Anne finally spoke up. "You guys are so full of shit. I can handle my emotions better than that. If it gets too bad I'll take a cold shower."

Vera smiled at her. "That never worked for me."

Anne looked at the two women in frustration.

"Alright, I give up. His name is Peter Stephenson, but we had an argument and I'm still mad at him."

Agent Patton looked at Vera and winked. "That's great! There's nothing better than makeup sex to get the blood flowing."

Anne's face flushed crimson when she realized the twins had been following the conversation with avid interest.

"Hey guys! These kids have big ears and I think they know what we were talking about."

The adults all looked at the twins with speculation. The twins smiled innocently before leaving the room. Vera looked after her children with a worried expression while Patton informed Anne. "If you get other problems or abilities let me know and we'll try to help."

CHAPTER 13

A week later, Agents Anne Hawk and Peter Stephenson were sharing quarters. She was grateful she had a mate, as her current sexual urges reminded her of when she had turned thirteen, only now the urges were ten times worse. She jogged with Rafe and Vera and the high she got from that helped a little, but she was happy she had a potential life partner.

Now that Anne had an outlet for her sexual cravings, she could now concentrate on the other changes in her body. She was twenty-nine and was beginning to look younger. The wound and resulting surgery scar had disappeared. She could read the surface thoughts of others without effort, but had not tried going deeper. She had the same ingrained belief this should not be done without sufficient cause, and not just for idle curiosity.

The biggest new power was the ability to move objects by telekinesis. So far the largest object was only three pounds, but she could move it as far as she could see. The Johnson twins had not yet developed this power, but they were only eleven years old.

Four months passed since the last attack and the security of the building had been upgraded to fix those areas targeted before. The cafeteria windows were made bullet proof and all others were shuttered. The garage doors, while not breached, were redesigned to be even stronger. The threat of another gas attack was now deemed unlikely, and agents were no longer required to carry gas masks on their person. However, the masks were still available on every floor.

The FBI and CIA still had joint control of the Johnsons, and now included FBI Agent Hawks. The agencies decided the Portland building was their best bet to keep them safe.

Agent Hawk spent a large portion of her time at the Johnson apartment when Agent Stephenson was on duty, because of their shared condition and their close friendship. The children liked her too and were curious as she developed new abilities, because they thought they could eventually develop the same powers.

Adam and Evelyn continued to work on their computer courses, which now included advanced degree software. Vera had been looking into having them attend virtual classroom courses where they could ask questions of the instructor. The instructor would not know their real names or their actual age, but would require computer tests to be graded.

Evelyn wanted to attend an advanced physics class, while Adam preferred a class from MIT on advanced mechanical engineering. To enter these courses required minimum grades in other preliminary courses. Vera asked Agent Patton if she had some connections to get around these requirements.

The next day Agent Patton brought some paperwork by the apartment for them to fill out.

"My contact said there were two ways to get by the minimum requirements. The first is a minimum IQ of 120, or take a short test with a minimum score of 95. I think the short test is quicker, although the IQ marker may open other doors in the future. Why not do both?"

Vera sent in the paperwork that resulted in the twins each receiving an IQ of 200 and a score of 100 on the test. The children started their virtual classes the following week, which they both enjoyed. Their parents were very proud of them and what they had achieved at such a young age.

The Johnsons marked their first year in Portland by having a private celebration in their apartment. Adam and Evelyn appeared to welcome the change in routine and seemed to welcome a break from lessons. When Anne and Peter dropped by, the party started. Everyone considered Anne as part of the family, and Peter by extension.

Anne brought Peter into the secret after they were married, knowing he had already guessed she had changed into something similar to the Johnsons' condition. She was even considering giving him some of her blood so that they would age at the same rate.

Anne's telekinesis powers had grown much stronger to the point where she could use it as a weapon. She had been careful not to reveal the extent of her powers to anyone except her husband, the Johnsons, and Agent Patton. Patton had given her approval to bring Peter into the group if he wished.

After the cake and ice cream, Anne decided the time was right to let the Johnsons know of her and Peter's decision. "Everyone, I want to tell you that Peter has decided to join our little club, and God willing we will start another branch when we have children."

Rafe and Vera hugged Anne and Peter, but Vera sadly smiled at Anne.

"We knew through the children you were struggling with this decision, but short of Peter leaving you, this was the only logical conclusion. Rafe and I are the first model, our children are the second, and your family will be the third. Each version is stronger than the last. We have to stay protected until we become strong enough to protect ourselves."

Rafe said, "I think that was the reason Vera and I were selected to start this cycle. A normal lab study would never have survived outside interference. I should pass this information on to Agent Patton, if she hasn't already guessed."

Six months later, Anne and Peter gave them the good news they were expecting twins. Anne asked Vera, "Do you think having twins is going to be the norm for us?"

"It certainly has started that way, hasn't it?"

Vera and Anne looked enough alike to be twin sisters, with their Choctaw Indian heritage and apparent same age in the low twenties. Anne looked as though she had shed almost ten years since her change. Peter, while apparently older than Anne, was also starting to look younger.

The agent detail guarding them also noted the changes in Anne and Peter; with several rumors circulating that explained the cause. Eventually, Agent Patton was forced to give an edited version of the reason for the change.

Agent Patton said, "You are all aware that Anne and Peter are now part of the people being protected by the detail. Anne was changed by blood she received from the Johnsons when we thought she was dying from her gunshot wound. Peter's change was because he volunteered to receive blood from Anne. You need not fear they are contagious, because the change only comes from receiving blood."

After fielding several questions from the agents she warned, "You can imagine why another country or terrorist group would want to gain the powers these people have. Information on these people under our protection is Top Secret and any disclosure will bring down the full weight of the law. We already had one traitor in our agency exposed. Don't let anyone else betray us."

Later that day Agent Patton held a joint meeting with the Johnson and Stephenson families in the Johnson apartment. After everyone was seated Patton started speaking.

"We have been so concerned about protecting you that we have not been properly monitoring your individual health and progress of your abilities. Starting next week we are going to have a permanent medical and science staff to do that."

Rafe asked, "Who are these people? Since they have to be fully vetted for a Top Secret clearance, I want to be certain of their qualifications."

Patton shook her head. "I haven't seen a list of who is coming, but I was assured they would be qualified."

Vera sighed loudly. "If they aren't, my kids will make their lives miserable. They won't be able to fake it when they are dealing with a telepath."

Patton smiled. "I forgot about that. They can act as an additional security check as well."

The following week the medical and science staff started to arrive. Before they had a chance to talk to the Johnsons, Anne and Peter interviewed them. Anne's telepathy powers were now stronger than the Johnson twins and Peter's powers were almost as powerful.

They interviewed six people without any problems; however, the seventh person was a surprise. Joyce Graham was a member of the science staff and she was a weak telepath. When she first met with Anne and Peter, they could feel her try to read their surface thoughts. Anne and Peter slammed their mental doors and concentrated on her thoughts. She was a plant by another agency to find out what the FBI and CIA were hiding. They continued the interview with Ms. Graham none the wiser she had been identified.

Agent Patton was furious at first, but then thought maybe they could use her for their benefit. She called Deputy Director McPherson on their secure line.

"James, the Homeland Security Agency sent Agent Joyce Graham, who has telepathy powers, to us as part of the science staff. I assume they want to see just what we have here because for security reasons we have refused to update them. Should we send her back with her head in her hands or make use of her?"

"Ooh crap! You say she's a telepath?"

"Yes, but a weak one according to Anne."

"Well, we still have to worry about Homeland Security's poor internal security. We can't have her going back and reporting what we have here. It would be like putting an article in the newspaper. What do you recommend?"

"Let's box her in. We assign her to monitor Anne and Peter, who will feed her false information that will mislead Homeland Security into thinking we have only weak telepaths here. We have to let the other medical and science staff members know who she is and not spill the beans. Anne can monitor Graham's thoughts to be sure she hasn't learned the truth."

"That sounds like a plan. I'll inform your boss what's going on and if he has a different take on this he'll let you know."

Anne and Peter did find that one of the medical staff was a paid informer of the Al-Qaeda Islamic terrorist group. That man was taken into the interrogation room in an effort to extract additional information. After Anne and Peter finished with him, the FBI was able to apprehend five more members of the cell group before they scattered.

The medical staff gave both the Johnson and Stephenson families a full physical. This was to establish a base line for Anne and Peter, and to check for any changes since their last physical for the Johnsons. They also wanted to determine how Anne's pregnancy was progressing.

The science staff was interested in not only everyone's ability to rejuvenate their bodies from age and sickness, but also the other abilities they developed. Joyce Graham was kept in the dark about all their abilities except a possible telepathy power and was assigned the duty of trying to gage the strength of this ability in Anne and Peter.

The science staff was particularly interested in the IQ levels of Adam and Evelyn. They gave additional IQ tests in an effort to ascertain their true level, since the previous test they took only indicated they had exceeded the benchmark of 200. They took three more tests and the twins exceeded each test's benchmark. The only conclusion was that, at the present time, the twins' IQ could not be measured.

When the IQ tests were given to the adults, they were surprised to find they all tested high, none below 180. The agents were all tested when they were hired and none tested over 120 previously.

The twins did well on the virtual classes they had taken and were now moving on to other subjects of interest to them. They were getting a well-rounded education until they found an area they wished to concentrate on.

After reviewing the results of the physicals, the medical staff informed Rafe and Vera they were going to be having another child. Vera's face flushed with expectation as she asked, "Are we having twins again?"

Dr. Maxine Schmidt said, "We don't know yet because you're only a month into your pregnancy."

Rafe hugged Vera close, kissing her. "Honey, don't worry so much.

Your last birth of twins was not nearly as rough as you anticipated."

Vera jabbed her thumb into his side, "How do you know how much pain I had?"

She smiled at a thought. "Well, at least the twins will have older siblings to play with. That reminds me, I need to have a baby shower for Anne before she has her babies."

Rafe smiled at Dr. Schmidt and shook his head as they left the office. When they got back to their apartment, Vera called Agent Patton and they started making plans for Anne's baby shower.

* * *

A year later brought several changes for both the Johnson and Stephenson families. Anne's twins were both boys and Vera's were girls. They now had six children to raise and protect. Agent Patton made arrangements to move the Johnsons into a bigger apartment. Anne and Peter had already moved into a larger apartment after the birth of their twins.

Adam and Evelyn were now thirteen and confused and a little unsettled when their twin sisters arrived, but they soon got into the new routine. They helped their parents take care of them, except when it came to changing diapers. Their new identical sisters were named Mary and Jennifer, with each wearing a different colored name bracelet to tell them apart.

The Stephenson twins were not identical, but were so much alike they had ID bracelets as well. They were named Jack and Ralph and were four months older than the Johnson twins. Anne was a little overwhelmed with her duties as a new mother, even with the help of her stay-at-home husband.

Vera stopped by and offered her help before the birth of her own twins, which helped Anne establish a routine. However, it wasn't long before her twins let Anne know by telepathy what their needs were. Vera watched as Anne fed and changed her twins' diapers before they had a chance to get upset. She was even able to get them asleep by soothing them telepathically. After Anne had both boys asleep, Vera complained, "I wish I could do that with my children. Adam and Evelyn can read me, but I can't do the same with them."

Anne grinned at her. "Do you want some of my blood? It would solve your problem and probably give your kids stronger powers when they are born."

Vera thought a moment before answering. "I want to talk this over with Rafe, but I'm sure he'll ask for a pint for himself."

A month after the transfusion, Rafe and Vera were able to communicate with the others telepathically. They were initially weak, but as the blood worked its magic they quickly got stronger. Now, a week after Vera's twin girls were born, she could hear their minds speak.

Rafe and Vera were each holding one of the girls and speaking to them mind to mind. The girls each looked up at the parent holding them with wide intelligent eyes, basking in the love broadcast to them. The parents could feel Adam and Evelyn looking through their eyes at their sisters.

CHAPTER 14

Ten years passed by peacefully with no direct threat detected against the safe house and its occupants. The senior members of the Johnsons and Stephensons still appeared to be in their low twenties with no signs of aging. The Stephensons had another set of twins. The newest arrivals were named Mark and Sally and were seven years old.

Their brothers, Jack and Ralph, both strong telepaths, also had gained telekinesis and teleportation powers. Mark and Sally shared these gifts; however, their powers were not yet quite as strong.

The Johnson family shared the telekinetic and teleportation powers also which meant the two families together were a formidable group. Anne Stephenson's telepathic powers increased to a point she could detect someone thinking harmful thoughts about their group or the safe house from five miles away. She detected such thoughts twice in the past month, but in each case the thoughts were too far away to ascertain to whom they belonged nor what their plan might be. Agent Patton was informed of the possible threat and the agents were put on alert.

Agent Patton and Deputy Director McPherson were getting older, causing concern to the families. The two had been very protective toward them. If either were replaced because of retirement or otherwise, it could mean their present situation would drastically deteriorate.

They thought of making them part of their group, but doing so wouldn't change their mandated retirement ages and the Agents would be unable to explain their sudden change in appearance. Changing computer records would be a lesser challenge than reversing the age process. The families realized time was of the essence as they had less than ten years to think of a solution to this problem.

The two families held a group meeting setting forth their problems and assigning individuals to find solutions. Their children with computer and code breaking aptitudes were given the task of finding a way to change government personnel records without being detected. Others were tasked with how to hide or camouflage sudden age reversal. Those with the strongest telepathic powers were given the job of detecting any threat to them.

Adam and Evelyn were the oldest of the children at twenty-two years. They had accumulated eight degrees between them and were now working on a doctorate, and were old enough now that they could submit a visual virtual image of themselves when they presented their thesis for review by a committee. Evelyn's was in Mathematics from Yale, and Adam's was in Computer Science from MIT.

Their thesis reviews were scheduled for the following day and they were both nervous. Evelyn's thesis was a different take on Einstein's Theory of Relativity, while Adam's was a new type of computer operating system.

The next day they explained their theories as outlined in the thesis, and answered the committee's questions. Evelyn's dissertation went well; however, Adam was required to send them a working model for review. Thinking ahead, Adam had already constructed a model and shipped it to them.

Two weeks later both of them received confirmation of their doctorate degrees. In addition, Adam received a patent and an offer from Microsoft to further develop the operating system. When Adam received the offer he immediately went to his parents for advice.

Rafe and Vera read the offer with excitement and Rafe asked Adam, "It looks like you have two choices, a lump sum payment of $5Million, or $3Million now and $500,000 a year for ten years and one percent of the gross revenue for that period. The only stipulation for the second option is that you help on any glitches found in the introduction version. On the face of it the second option is the best deal, but we need to have in writing what is meant by help in correcting problems."

Rafe gave the proposal back to Adam. "Yeah, I had the same reservations. I want the second option because it is going to bring in over ten times the cash amount. I'm thinking we're going to need this money eventually. I'll query them and if it can be done remotely, I will pick the second option."

Rafe considered a moment, and then consulted with Vera. "I think we need to have this money deposited in a numbered account somewhere

where it will be difficult for others to gain information."

"Yes. However, with Adam's computer skills he can then move amounts to several different locations, which would make it even harder to trace."

Rafe spoke to Adam. "The amounts you receive from Microsoft will be taxed at the outset, but after that nobody but us is going to know what we do with it. We need to start looking for another location to move our group to. We are sitting ducks here."

Three days later, more thoughts started coming to them from people planning an attack against the safe house. The planners were close enough now that the entire group was receiving these thoughts, but none of the thoughts revealed a date for the attack.

Rafe called a meeting with Agent Patton to discuss the impending attack. The group met with Patton in the main meeting room and when everyone was settled, Rafe began.

"We have detected at least twelve different people planning an attack against us. They are too far away to do a mind probe to determine who they are or who is behind the attack, except the name Raptor was used more than once. We just have first names of people they are working with. They are no longer concerned about taking us alive. All they want this time is tissue samples. They are going to be coming in hard with high explosives and we don't know yet when the attack is scheduled."

Patton looked at the group members, her face ashen. "Well, we can't defend against that! We'll have to move you again. Get packed and we will move you tonight. I'll let you know where after I make a few calls."

Patton called another meeting six hours later. "We are going to convoy you three miles to a place where we can chopper you to an airport away from Portland. The National Guard will clear us a path to the choppers. Your destination is going to be Parris Island, the Marine training base. You have become too hot for a civilian location and the Marines should be able to better protect you. You will still have our protection too, but mostly from a distance."

Rafe asked, "You're not coming with us?"

"No. Remember, I did double duty here as Agent-in-Charge. I'm going to miss you, especially the kids. I want to wish you better luck at your new location."

The group members each thanked her and the children gave her a hug, while they all fought back tears. The convoy left the safe house at eleven p.m., following a route cleared by the National Guard to the helicopters. Four choppers lifted off to meet a plane waiting for them in Eugene, Oregon.

They arrived at the Beaufort Marine Corp Air Station, located just outside Parris Island, South Carolina early the following morning. The jet's passengers deplaned with the twelve members of the Group, and twenty mixed FBI and CIA agents. Boarding three camouflaged military trucks, they were taken to the Parris Island base. The trucks soon stopped at their new home, a series of small houses.

A marine major and four sergeants were waiting when they exited the trucks. After they were all assembled the major addressed them.

"I'm Major Lee Thomas and the Adjutant of this base. I've been apprised of your situation and want you to know that no unauthorized personnel will enter this base. I see you have brought your own protection detail. I will need to consult with the lead agent before assigning an outer perimeter of marines. My sergeants will show you which houses you are assigned and will take care of any problems you have. This is the housing area for married Officers and NCOs and they will be told not to disturb you."

The major nodded at his sergeants and left. The Johnson and Stephenson families were each assigned adjoining houses, with the surrounding houses taken by their protection detail. A sergeant followed the Johnson family into their assigned house and watched while they checked it out.

Adam asked the sergeant, "Can I get internet and WiFi?"

The sergeant wrote the question down and nodded at Adam. "I'll see to it."

Rafe looked at the Staff Sergeant. "Sergeant, this house only has two bedrooms and we have four children. Is there a house with more bedrooms available?"

"No Sir, I can see where this would be a problem. We have another house which the older children can be assigned."

Rafe looked at Vera and asked, "Is that going to work?"

Vera shook her head in frustration, and then looked at Adam and Evelyn. "How about it. Are you two ready to move away from us?"

Adam and Evelyn hesitated a few moments while they mentally consulted with each other before answering. "We're fine with it, but what about the Stephenson kids?"

Vera looked at the Staff Sergeant, sighing. "Make sure it is next door and the Stephensons are going to have the same problem, and their kids are much younger."

Adam interrupted, "Mom, we can take Mark and Sally to bunk with us if it's okay with Anne and Peter."

After Anne and Peter checked out the house their two youngest children were going to move into with Adam and Evelyn, they gave their approval. Mark and Sally loved the arrangement, as they were great admirers of their adopted Aunt and Uncle. Adam reminded the sergeant that it was he who wanted the Internet and WiFi connection.

Staff Sergeant Tim McGregor told them they would use the base mess hall after the recruits had finished, and gave them a schedule to go by. A bus would pick them up.

Two hours later they boarded the bus to go for breakfast. The younger children were fascinated with being on a military base and eating in a mess hall. No one had the heart to tell them the reason it got that name. However, when they exited the bus and got their first smell of powdered eggs and SOS, they understood. The families lucked out and ate at a different food line than the recruits did. They had scrambled eggs, ham, fruit, toast, and milk.

When they got back to their houses everyone pitched in and made beds. What clothing they carried with them they hung in the closets. They would be taken to the PX by bus to obtain anything else they needed until their goods arrived from Portland. Anne went with Mark and Sally to the house they would be staying at with Adam and Evelyn. The bedrooms each had twin beds, which Adam and Evelyn were trying to make. Everyone pitched in and they soon finished. Sally and Evelyn picked one bedroom, leaving the other for Mark and Adam.

Anne told her children she expected them to stay with her and only sleep here. They still looked at their rooms as a getaway from their family. Adam and Evelyn would generally have the house to themselves during the day.

They had been at the base for two weeks and were back into a routine. Nobody had detected any thoughts that were against the Group, or knew how long it would be before they would be tracked to this location. Adam received notice through the Internet that Microsoft made the first payment to their numbered account and were starting work on Adam's operating system.

Rafe called a Group meeting to tell them the news that they now had $3M toward independence. They were going to have to make a decision on where they should settle, urban or rural. After much discussion, they finally decided to settle in an urban area. They thought it would be easier to hide within a hive of people rather than an area with fewer people. Besides, they needed to hide their computer activity from outside scrutiny, which would stand out in a rural area.

Mary and Jennifer Johnson were identical twins, now approaching ten years of age. Their Psi powers had not reached their peak, yet when they worked in tandem and focused their concentration, they were the strongest members in the Group. They were taking virtual computer courses, much as their older siblings had and quickly found only one of them needed to take a course for both to become knowledgeable of the contents. They quickly surpassed the number of courses Adam and Evelyn completed.

The twin girls were alike in most ways, except their preference in boys. Each had a crush on different boy singers and constantly argued about which boy singer was coolest. Vera sighed as she shut the door to their room in an attempt to get some peace. It had been too many years since she went through this phase of growing up, and she didn't feel eager to repeat it.

The Stephenson twin boys, Jack and Ralph, while not identical, were much alike in appearance and personality. They were a few months older than the Johnson twins and had just started to notice girls. They still treated Mary and Jennifer as sisters because of their close association, but had acknowledged they were very attractive. They were also taking virtual computer courses, but did not have the mind blend the girls had experienced. Their Psi powers were still developing, but were not as strong as their parents.

Adam and Evelyn were working together on a project that would allow them to transfer funds through several banks until they made the trail disappear behind them. It would make the transfers untraceable and the last two test runs had been successful. Adam had installed a satellite link that had been a key element in the effort. They felt confident their efforts were successful.

They had also been working on another income generating project. They were ready to seek a patent on new computer hardware that would maximize the use of Adam's operating system. The hardware was the size of an iPad and was voice activated with a touch screen keyboard as backup, using a solar power source. They thought it should be in great demand if its retail price could be kept below five hundred dollars. The twins felt they had the world by the tail and they weren't about to let go.

CHAPTER 15

The Group had been at the Parris Island Marine Base for three years, busily making arrangements to move out on their own. They purchased a building in Savannah, Georgia, through a shell company, a building much like the safe house in Portland, Oregon, and they converted it to their needs without ever leaving their present location. The building had been financed from the proceeds of the inventions sold to Microsoft and IBM, which were still bringing in income.

Savannah was close enough to Parris Island that they could make the move in an hour's time, assuming everything worked as planned. The Group was waiting on a distraction to put the plan in motion. They knew of another attack being planned against them and that it was going to happen soon.

They learned through Staff Sergeant McGregor where the motor pool was located and what vehicles were being held there. The Sergeant was persuaded to give driving lessons to Adam and Evelyn and they learned where the keys were kept and how to get past security.

The following night the terrorist attack started with three recruits, who had been placed inside the base for this purpose, attacking the front gate guards. The noise alerted the perimeter marine guards and the agents positioned around the three houses of the Group. Luckily, the Group had already left and was approaching the south gate as the attack started. They had just passed through the gate when they could see the marine guards locking down the base by erecting barriers across the gate.

The Group was traveling in one of the buses of the same type they used to get to the mess hall. They arrived at their new building a little more than an hour after leaving the base. After punching in the code for the garage door they drove into the building and parked next to two late model SUVs. The building was finished and had been ready for them for almost a year. Six months ago they had instructed the attorney they had hired to form the shell company, to buy the two automobiles and park them in the building. The two families took the elevator to the third floor residence level to check out the apartments they had designed for themselves.

The plan was for each apartment to have five bedrooms in case they had a possible future need. They had also provided six extra apartments for growth in the Group. Their building was six stories with a helipad on the roof. The top three floors were empty. The only entrance was through the garage doors and they had parking room for twenty-five cars. The second floor was the work area and with hookups for the Internet and WiFi, as well as a satellite connection to a dish on the roof.

After giving the others in the families duties to perform, Rafe, Vera, and Anne left in one of the SUVs to grocery shop. Their building was located within a mile of a large grocery store. After loading the vehicle with groceries they returned to their new home within two hours. When they arrived they mentally called upstairs for help bringing the groceries inside.

The first meal in their new home was a joint affair as they sat down to a meal of bacon and eggs, while the younger children ate their favorite, cereal. After their meal, the six youngest children were sent off to bed, as it had been a long stressful day. Afterward, the adults, which now included Adam and Evelyn, sat down to plan their future.

The TV news programs made no mention of an attack on the Parris Island Base. Apparently the gunfire noise was noted as part of a training exercise. The families knew that the government was looking for them, but were certain that they had left no trail for anyone to follow. The terrorist group or groups who had been after them probably thought that the Group was still at the Marine Base. However, the government leaks would eventually start the terrorists looking for them again.

Anne smiled as she remembered something. "I overheard my kids calling themselves the SA Group. When I asked them what that meant they said its short for the Secret Agent Group."

The others smiled and then they all laughed at its meaning. "Kids have a thing with super heroes," Rafe said.

Adam rented a mailbox at a nearby shopping center so he could receive computer components and other items he purchased over the Internet. He had already obtained several different credit cards under different business names. After obtaining the cards, he hacked into the credit card files and deleted all the background information. He then hacked into the files of the company who maintained backup records for the credit card company and deleted all the files relating to his cards.

Adam worked for a month getting his workshop supplied and in operation. The building had infrared security cameras covering all its sides and the roof. He programmed his computer to analyze any movement and sound an alarm if it exceeded his parameters.

Adam had a security program that used a military satellite eye in the sky to watch the building and a mile radius around it. If anything suspicious moved on the streets, such as the same vehicle that would repeatedly come near the building, then an alert would appear on Adam's computer screen.

The children also used the workshop to study. Adam and Evelyn wired individual cubicles so that the children would have access to the Internet and WiFi. They were situated far enough away on the open floor space so they didn't disturb each other. The children used the fourth floor to play. They used roller blades to play soccer and other games, and their parents even gave them bicycles to ride around on in the open floor space.

Meanwhile, Rafe and Vera were getting worried about finding mates for Adam and Evelyn. They needed to be able to meet people of the opposite sex in their age group who might be compatible with them. Vera urged the two to get on the Internet and check out the Mensa Website.

Adam researched the site and sent the required background information on his IQ. He then read the available information and found that Savannah had a local chapter. Evelyn then entered the site and sent her IQ qualification information, so they now were both members. The next scheduled meeting was the following week at a local historic hotel. It was a dinner meeting, so they made reservations.

Rafe drove them to the meeting and parked close enough that he could read the nearby minds to determine if this might be a trap. Adam and Evelyn entered the hotel and found the Mensa Booth outside a meeting room. They presented to the woman at the booth their Mensa Membership cards. After receiving nametags they entered the meeting room and mingled with the others.

They quickly noted most of the members were middle aged or older, so they tried to make conversation with the few younger members. The twins approached an attractive young man and woman who were standing apart from the others. They introduced themselves and indicated they were new members who recently moved into the city.

The young man spoke. "I'm Charles and this is my twin sister Elizabeth Ellsworth. This is only our second meeting and we've been working at the local Metcalf University as professors teaching Literature and Biology. What do you do?"

Evelyn answered, "We're self-employed and have several patents in computer software and hardware. We each have Doctorates in related fields. Are you two in a relationship with anyone?"

They were shocked at her abruptness, but Elizabeth recovered and gave them a coy smile. "No, what do you have in mind?"

Adam answered. "You know what slim pickings we have and you both are attractive individuals. We want to see if you are compatible with us with marriage as the ultimate goal."

The Ellsworth twins looked at each other for a moment until they nodded. Elizabeth said, "Okay, let's pair off and get to know each other and see if we have common interests."

During the dinner they sat together and after the meeting they left the room to sit at separate tables in the hotel coffee shop. Adam and Evelyn had already concocted a cover story of their past life, so they were on safe ground when each told of their past experiences.

They found the Ellsworth twins grew up in the Midwest near Omaha and attended KU in Lawrence, Kansas. They were two years older than the Johnsons and were happy with the climate and atmosphere of Savannah. An important fact was that they were the only children of deceased parents.

They left the coffee shop two hours later after exchanging cell phone numbers. Adam and Evelyn stood outside the hotel waiting on their father to pick them up, each taking a turn at telling the other what they had learned from the Ellsworth twins. After getting into the car they told Rafe that they had a great time with the Ellsworths.

Rafe smiled at them. "I heard your mental conversations about the Ellsworths and they seemed perfect for you two. What did you learn from their surface thoughts?"

Adam and Evelyn looked at each other and blushed, and then Evelyn answered. "They both thought we were hot looking and wanted to get physical the next time we meet. They live in the same apartment, so they were interested in getting together. They both have had physical relationships while in college, but they could never make a deeper connection because of the difference in IQ's. They thought we would be different."

Rafe kept his thoughts locked behind a protective mental wall as they drove back to their building. When they got back to their apartment, Vera was waiting in the living room. Rafe and the twins took seats and waited for their mother's response.

"I heard what you told Rafe about the Ellsworth twins. How do you feel about them?"

The twins looked at each other and then smiled, nodding in agreement. Evelyn again took the lead. "We really like them, but they are more experienced than we are in relationships. We are a little afraid they won't like us when they find out just how inexperienced we are."

Rafe and Vera looked at each other and smiled before Vera answered, "Kids, that inexperience has its own attraction. However, you do need to know how to protect yourself against sexual disease and pregnancy. Evelyn you already know that the pill won't work against pregnancy for us, so be sure the man wears protection. You two can read from their surface thoughts what they desire, otherwise just do what comes naturally."

The next day Adam received a call from Charles Ellsworth. He and his sister invited the Johnson twins to come to their apartment for dinner that night. Adam looked at his sister and asked, "The Ellsworths want us to come for dinner tonight at seven o'clock, do you want to go?"

At her nod, Adam accepted the invitation and asked for their address. The remainder of the day passed in a fog for Adam and Evelyn, until they both sought advice from their parents on what to wear on their first date.

CHAPTER 16

Two months later the two sets of twins were seeing each other almost every night and apparently were in love. Adam and Evelyn thought it was time to drop the bomb about their Psi abilities. Charles and Elizabeth's reaction to this disclosure would determine whether they would tell them about their true past.

The Johnson twins met the Ellsworths at their apartment where they were going to leave to see a movie together. After the Johnsons arrived they asked the Ellsworths to sit down as they had something to tell them. The Ellsworth twins gave them an uncertain smile as they sat down.

Adam started speaking. "We have not told you everything you need to know about us. We both have Psi powers. We are telepaths and have other powers."

Elizabeth looked at Adam with astonishment. "You can read my mind! You're not pulling my leg are you?"

"No. Right now you're thinking I'm pulling a gag on you. Think of something else not related to us."

Elizabeth looked doubtfully at Adam, but then replied, "You are thinking of a dress you want to buy at Rothberrys."

Elizabeth's face turned red as she realized the truth of Adam's claim. "You really can read my mind. Both of you can read our minds!"

Charles asked, "How can you do that? I didn't have a clue you were doing it."

Evelyn answered. "We were only reading your surface thoughts. If we went deeper you would know that, but we normally would never

85

intrude on your memories. We can also move and teleport things. Before this relationship goes further you needed to know some of our secrets."

Shocked, Elizabeth looked at Adam. "You have more secrets! How much more is there?"

Adam looked at the two. "Discuss this and let us know if you can live with us knowing that we are telepaths. If you can't live with that then there's no point in going any further."

Elizabeth looked at them in confusion. "Wait here. Charles and I are going to my room to discuss this."

Adam and Evelyn waited for them to come to a decision, but they knew what they were saying to each other as if they all were in the same room. The twins looked at one another and thought, *they still don't understand telepathy!*

They heard Elizabeth crying for a few minutes, and then there was silence for a few minutes until there was the sound of water running in the bathroom. Charles and Elizabeth walked back and sat down, their faces grim but determined. Elizabeth spoke; her eyes still red from crying. "We can live with you being telepaths, it was the secrets we didn't like."

Adam nodded his head. "I think you will understand our reluctance to tell you before now when and if we tell you more. Do you still want to continue this relationship?"

They nodded their heads before Charles spoke. "Evelyn, I'm in love with you and I know, Adam, that my sister loves you. We can't abide not being able to see either of you again. Please don't put too much into our surprise about your powers. It was a shock to find out telepaths really exist when our minds were closed to that possibility."

Adam consulted mentally with Evelyn before replying. "We told our family before we came here that we were going to inform you of our Psi powers and depending on your reaction we were going to ask you to meet our parents. You will learn more of our secrets when we get there. Are you ready for this?"

The two nodded and with some anticipation Elizabeth answered, "Yes! We are ready to learn everything."

When they were settled in Adam's car, Evelyn handed them each a black cloth sack to put over their heads. "This is in case you change your minds after learning our secrets. It's not because we don't trust you, but there are other people who will be put at risk if you make any disclosures about what you learn. Do you still want to go?"

They nodded again and pulled the sacks over their heads. After Adam pulled into the garage and the door was shut, they had the Ellsworth twins remove the sacks. They walked to the elevator and went up to the residential floor and to their apartment. Vera met them at the door as they entered. Adam introduced her as Vera, their mother, and Rafe, their father.

It was uncomfortable, that first meeting with their lovers' parents, but this meeting was surreal. Elizabeth asked Vera, "You don't look old enough to be their mother, unless you were six when they were born."

Vera smiled at her. "That's one of our secrets. I'm 94 and their father is 104."

Charles looked at the two parents and smiled. "Not bad. You hold your age quite well. Will Adam and Evelyn have this same ability?"

Evelyn said, "We don't know, but all indications are that we will stop aging in a few more years. Everyone in our family has the same Psi powers. When our parents first stopped aging they were sixty-eight and seventy-eight and about two years later the CIA placed them into protective custody because they thought this might be a threat from outside the country. The CIA was the first to notice what was happening to them because they keep a loose surveillance on their retired agents."

Rafe broke in and resumed telling their history of attacks and changing safe houses over the years and the addition of other agents to their Group until they arrived in Savannah. He ended by asking, "Do you have any questions?"

Charles looked at him and exclaimed, "Wow! I had no idea. So you are on the run from both the government and terrorists. No wonder you have been careful in your outside contacts. If we marry your children, will we be given your blood so that we age the same as our mates?"

"That is the plan. You won't age and you will get our Psi powers. You will become one of us and will be sought after by both the government and the terrorists when they find out about you. Do you still want to pursue marriage with our children?"

Elizabeth said, "We love them very much and can't think of being apart. We would walk through fire for them, so this is just frosting on the cake as far as we're concerned."

Rafe looked at Vera, who nodded. "Okay, I want you to meet the rest of the Group, so follow me and expect to be surprised."

They took the elevator to the work shop floor where the others were waiting. The two adults and six children greeted the new arrivals with shouts of congratulations and welcome. After introductions were made and whose children belonged to whom, they settled down to getting to know each other.

Later, the couples returned to the Johnson apartment and started making plans for their marriage. Neither set of twins was affiliated with a church, so they decided to use a Justice of the Peace instead of a church wedding. Charles looked at the others and then smiled. "Why wait, we don't need a three day waiting period for the blood test. Let's just go down there and get it done now."

They all agreed, but Adam and Evelyn wanted their parents to witness the event so they were alerted to come up and get ready. The Justice of the Peace married them in a double ceremony and they soon returned to their building. When they returned to the residence floor, each couple was handed a key to their own apartment. The apartments had been made ready for them while they were gone and now each couple was truly entering a new married life.

The next morning the newlyweds were invited into the Johnson apartment for breakfast. Before eating, Adam and Evelyn each donated a pint of their blood to their new spouses. While the blood transfusion was in progress, the Johnson twins held the hand of their spouse in a gesture of their love and support.

After the transfusion was completed they all sat together at the dining room table. The Johnsons' younger twins, Mary and Jennifer, would normally have been considered too young for such a conversation. However, since they were telepaths they might as well get the information first hand.

Vera blushed a little before speaking. "Charles, you and Elizabeth will soon go through what we call the change. To put it bluntly, you both will become incredibly horny for about two months. Then you will start to exhibit your Psi powers. They will be weak at first, but eventually your powers will be equal to or stronger than your mates.

Elizabeth blushed and asked in a tight voice, "Just how horny will we get? I don't think I could get any more than I was last night."

Rafe laughed. "Trust me when I say you won't be able to keep your hands off your mate. Ask Anne and Peter how they dealt with it. I don't know if you considered this yet, but you need to take a leave of absence from your positions. There are two reasons for this: (1) you need to be close to each other during this period, and (2) for security. Until you have full Psi powers to protect yourself and watch for anyone interested in you or the Group, you shouldn't be anywhere without one of us.

They both looked disappointed, but they agreed with the logic. Charles chuckled. "It's a good thing we have a furnished apartment. We'll give notice for the apartment and ask for a leave of absence from the University. I think we can move everything from the apartment in two or three carloads."

CHAPTER 17

That night they completed all their tasks and moved into the Group's building. The next morning Adam and Evelyn brought their spouses down to the workshop and showed them what they were doing and explained their plans for the future. When Adam finished speaking, Elizabeth asked, "Honey, what is your IQ score? Mine is 125 and Charles is 127, but you must have a higher score."

Adam and Evelyn grimaced. "We both took all the tests and scored 200, which means there isn't any tests available to accurately measure our IQs."

Charles grinned slightly. "That just means you are off the charts. We have a good chance of having kids just as smart. What about the other kids in the Group, how smart are they?"

Evelyn said, "Our sisters have both scored 198 and the Stephenson twins all score in the high 190's. This is without a genus parenting them. We can be almost sure we will have smart kids, but they may be even smarter than us."

Elizabeth snorted and then laughed. "Your parents did a good job and they aren't as smart as we are."

Adam then asked Charles and Elizabeth what interests they had outside teaching to aid them. Both had varied interests and had settled on teaching as a way of making a living. Adam suggested that they help them in their current project, which was another potential moneymaker for the Group.

But first, Adam showed them how he was going to hack into the state of Georgia's database and change their marriage information so that if anyone searched for them they would be led down a blind alley. He also hacked into the Mensa database and deleted all the information related to both sets of twins.

Adam and Evelyn explained what they wanted their spouses to do. Charles and Elizabeth had good computer skills and they were taught how to be much better. A week later the two new families were ready. Before the attack at Parris Island they learned several bits of information from the minds of those in charge of the terrorist attack. They knew who was funding the operation and the information on one of the terrorist bank accounts.

Adam used that bank account information to trace it back to another account. That account led them to three other accounts located in different parts of the globe. They made four simultaneous transfers from these accounts to four separate accounts of the Group before moving the funds again to another account of theirs. As planned, the trail behind the transfers disappeared shortly after the transactions. They left the original terrorist account in place for evidence when the FBI investigated.

They then sent the FBI an e-mail detailing the information they learned about the attack and the original bank account. This e-mail was bounced around the world several times before its trail evaporated. Hopefully, the FBI could find this information useful even after the time delay.

The four accounts they raided brought the Group another $40 million. Not bad for a day's work, they congratulated themselves. They called a meeting of the adult members of the Group to explain what they had done. The eight adult members met in a boardroom they had constructed in a corner of the workshop. Adam explained what he and his crew had accomplished and the additional funds they had received.

Anne Stephenson made a motion. "We should give Adam and his crew a vote of thanks. What is the total of our funds now?"

Vera held up her hand as she made a notation on her iPad. "We now have a total of $80 million in four separate banks. I think we can use part of this money to obtain another safe house in case we have to move quickly. Does anyone have a preference on where it should be located?"

A lively discussion ensued, which eventually came down to three locations: Charleston, Jacksonville, and Macon. Macon won the vote. The board authorized Charles and Elizabeth to act on the Group's behalf to hire a Macon attorney to form a straw company to own the safe house they would purchase. Adam and Evelyn would accompany them as protection. They would also start soon searching for an appropriate building and would e-mail pictures of the choices.

A week later the Board looked at the choices before them. Three were older warehouse type buildings, much like what they were using now. One was a departure from what they would normally consider, a recently constructed ten-story condo apartment building with a basement garage. The building was in foreclosure and sitting empty, and a steal at $8 million. The other buildings ranged from $1 to $3 million, but would require another $1 to $3 million to refurbish.

The members asked Charles and Elizabeth the condition of the condo and why it was in foreclosure?

Charles answered, "It was constructed too far away from the metro area and couldn't get commitments from buyers. Part of the problem might have been its unusual design as a ten-story round column building. The developers eventually went belly up and filed for bankruptcy. The four rooms shown to prospective buyers are the only ones with furniture. The bottom three floors were originally intended for office space and are currently white space. Tenants would dictate their construction needs."

Rafe considered a moment before speaking. "So, we could camouflage our use of the building somewhat by leasing out the bottom three floors. That gives us the top seven floors for our own use."

Adam said. "We could even occupy part of the bottom floor as a computer security firm. We could call it the SA Group."

Everyone laughed except for Charles and Elizabeth, who looked at the others with a puzzled expression. Adam explained, "The kids called themselves the Secret Agent Group or SA Group for short."

Charles and Elizabeth let it sink in and then they laughed also. The board then authorized their Macon attorney to purchase the condo in the name of SA Group. Adam e-mailed the law firm information concerning the officers of SA Group, after filing false information with the Secretary of State, stipulating all future correspondence was to be by e-mail.

Peter and Anne's advice to Charles and Elizabeth was when they became overwhelmed by their sexual desire for their mates they should go jogging. Exertion would release endorphins into their blood stream, which would relieve the urges for a time. Sometimes both sets of twins jogged together in the garage, but more often it was Charles and Elizabeth alone. After almost two months their symptoms began to abate. The twins became strong joggers and were able to keep pace with their mates when they ran together.

The newlyweds were back working together and now starting to communicate with each other mentally, a pleasant surprise for the new telepaths eager to practice as they sensed the mind glow of their mates. They realized there are no secrets kept between telepaths and they became even closer to each other emotionally. They had yet to develop any other Psi powers, but it was still early. The phenomenon eluded the Stephenson's for six months before they became aware of their power to move objects, or telekinesis.

Until the novice telepaths could defend themselves, they still needed someone to look after them when they left the safety of their building. Adam and Evelyn wore disguises to alter their appearance as they and their mates returned to Macon to check on the progress of the Condo project.

Charles and Elizabeth took the lead when they met the attorney handling the condo purchase and renovation. After discussing what progress had been made they followed him to the site to interview the construction supervisor. Plans had already been approved for the ground floor office construction and the security lockout for the elevator advancing above the second floor without a keypad entry. A steel door would be installed in the stairwell to preclude anyone from going higher than the second floor, but would allow people to descend from the higher floors. The door would have fire department access capability, but Adam intended to add a stronger device for safety.

After inspecting the work in progress they were happy to find that the contractors were almost finished with the first floor work. They gave the contractor revised plans for construction on the third floor, which was going to be the SA Group's actual workspace and play area for the children.

Charles obtained the expected completion dates for the first and third floors, before they left for an appointment with an interior decorator. The decorator showed them her portfolio of pictures of office space, and based upon the first floor construction plans she provided drawings of what she thought they would like. After spending a couple of hours deciding what they liked, Charles gave her their approval on proceeding with the purchases of flooring, wall coverings, drapes, and furniture.

The decorator was told to leave the wall blank behind the receptionist's desk that faced the entry door. They intended to place a business logo of the SA Group there. After giving her an advance check to cover costs, Charles and Elizabeth checked in at the local Marriott Hotel. They had an appointment with a sign company the following morning.

The telepaths had detected no suspicious thoughts during this trip, so they decided to relax and have a nice dinner before retiring for the night. The next day they met with the sign company's sales staff on the design of the sign and logo of their new business. Eventually, they were satisfied and made arrangements to have the sign placed on the lawn in front of the condo building and the logo plaque hung on the office wall facing the entry. They left a deposit, with the remainder due after delivery.

The Group had decided to equip two floors with furnishings in place and ready for occupancy. To save time and money they picked the two adjacent floors having the most show apartments already furnished, floors nine and ten, which had four show apartments. This gave them seven apartments with four bedrooms on each floor. They called their interior decorator with instructions to furnish the remaining ten apartments the same as those already completed. Their job done, they left for home.

The next day Adam reported on their progress to the Board. The members expressed satisfaction and they started making plans for their expected move. Their two SUVs would carry twelve members, and a small rental van truck would carry the last two members plus all their possessions. They planned on leaving the Marine school bus in the garage out of sight.

A month later, Adam, Evelyn, and their spouses returned to Macon to find out whether they needed to make any final adjustments to their SA Group Building. The construction was finished and the residential apartments on the two top floors were now ready for occupancy. The fire department had given their approval on the final inspection. They made a final walk around the building checking the landscaping before inspecting the new double steel garage doors. Satisfied they had done all that they could do to at least delay a direct assault, they returned to Savannah.

A week later they had moved into their new operations building in Macon, Georgia. They shut down the Savannah building, but maintained a constant surveillance contact via a computer link. They wanted to keep the Savannah building as their fallback position.

Rafe and the older members of the Board wanted their last two members to be the public face of SA Group. Charles and Elizabeth were not known as associated with the old Group, and Adam had created new personas and background information that would hide their true identity.

They started advertising in trade magazines and the local newspaper that they were open for business. Their first client called for an appointment a week later. Jack Meadows was the CFO of Smart Co., a small niche market product manufacturing business.

* * *

Jack and his assistant, Lilly Chambers, arrived to meet with Charles and Elizabeth. After they were seated in SA Group's conference room,

Jack spoke. "We think we have a security problem we don't know how to fix. We manufacture items for wholesalers, usually with a limited demand, and we market the products on TV. Recently, two of these items appeared in a marketing campaign shortly after ours were introduced. Can you check to see if the leak is from our end, and if so, can you stop it?"

"I'm sure we can, but first I need some additional information from you. We guarantee our work and will not charge you if we don't succeed."

A fee was negotiated for SA Group to investigate a possible computer leak and another fee to correct the problem if a leak was discovered. If further surveillance was required, then an additional monthly fee was given.

Adam arrived at the business the next day at the appointed time and reviewed the computer system. He asked to get into the system where he installed a back door so he could get into it from off-site.

After Adam returned to his workstation he started reviewing the Smart Co. computer's activity. It wasn't long before he detected the possible source of the leak and started his trace. After documenting who the source was and that computer's activity log, he built a wall against any future invasions into his client's computer system.

The following day Jack Meadows and his assistant returned to the office of SA Group. Charles explained that the source of their computer leak had been discovered.

"You indeed had a leak and it was done from the computers of Able Mfg., Inc. Here in this packet is the computer documentation of what they did. We have already safeguarded your system from further attacks. If you want to sue them for damages, we will be happy to serve as a witness. Another option is that for a fee we can introduce a worm virus into their system which would destroy it."

Jack looked at them for a moment. "You can do that?"

Charles nodded. "There is some risk to us, so our fee will reflect that amount. What do you want to do?"

"What is the fee for the virus?"

"$50,000, and we will make sure the same thing will not happen to you."

Jack blanched at the fee. "I'll have to get prior approval from the President before I can agree with either option. I will get back to you on that. In the meantime I will send over the check for the agreed upon amount, or would you prefer a direct deposit for this and the monthly fees?"

Charles gave him the information about their local deposit account and they left. He then mentally called Adam. *They just left and I think they are going to opt for the virus. Why not start calling the other businesses that Able Mfg. raided? We need to get them all in line before we introduce the virus.*

Three days later all the other businesses were contacted about the raids on their computer systems. Two of the three businesses did not even know they had a problem until it was brought to their attention. They all opted to become clients of SA Group. One just wanted protection from future raids, while the other two wanted revenge and agreed to pay the fee to destroy Able Mfg., Inc. computer system.

Smart Co. also agreed to pay the $50,000 fee. When all the fees were collected, Adam shut down Able Mfg. by planting the worm virus into its computer system. A day later, Able Mfg., Inc. became another client. A month passed and they had twenty-five clients. The SA Group became one of the fastest growing companies in Macon.

CHAPTER 18

The SA Group now needed a receptionist to handle the business calls as none of the other adult Group members could expose themselves for the position, and the children were all too young. An ad was placed in the local newspaper resulted in a dozen responses. Charles and Elizabeth spent the first day interviewing and quickly found being a telepath came in handy. They ended up calling back two applicants for a more extensive interview, and finally hired a single mother who needed to return to the work force because her husband recently died.

Rose Marie Jacobs was well qualified and was soon running the office. Rose Marie believed Charles and Elizabeth were much too young to be running a business and made it her personal responsibility to look after them.

Charles told Rose Marie, "You are the only salaried employee of SA Group at this time. Do you have any experience setting up withholding taxes and other needed paperwork?"

She shook her head in disappointment. "I've had experience doing that in my previous job, but that was years ago. I'll check to see whether changes have been made since then and I'll set everything up for you. I'll expect to be paid more if I'm doing two jobs."

Charles agreed. "That sounds fair. How much do you think this extra job is worth?"

"Well, it's only me so far. Instead of $400 a week, another $50 should be enough. However, if you keep adding work then my salary will have to be adjusted."

Charles knew from reading her surface thoughts she thought she was worth more, but thought that since they were a new business this was all they could afford to pay her at that time. He made a mental note to give her a $200 raise after she had worked for sixty days.

Three months later the phones were ringing constantly and they had added another twenty clients to their business. New clients were now coming to them from outside Macon. Charles and Elizabeth's Psi powers were now powerful enough that the Board felt it was safe for them to travel without an escort. Adam had trained them sufficiently to install a back door into new client's computer systems so Adam or Evelyn could gain access from the SA Group location.

Charles and Elizabeth, while not yet as proficient as their spouses, were beginning to do more of the computer work. They handled most of the established clients and were taking some of the new ones under their spouses' supervision. Adam initially only wanted the business to serve as camouflage for the SA Group and provide operating money for them. He consulted with the other board members and made a decision to accept only five more new clients, capping the business at fifty clients. This gave Adam and Evelyn more time to expand their own interests and search for anyone with a direct interest in their Group.

Six months later brought news of a different kind. Elizabeth was two months pregnant, which caused the Group to start making plans for medical examinations for her and the baby or babies. Macon had several choices they could use, so they started investigating which would be best for her and their safety.

Initially, Charles went with Elizabeth to their first selection, Dr. Beverly Nunn, a Gynecologist with the Bowers Medical Center. Before they saw the doctor they asked for a tour of the Medical Center, making a note of the entries into the building, the floor Dr. Nunn's office was located on, and if there was any security in the building.

Dr. Nunn, a middle-aged woman, was a little surprised when she was told that Charles was the twin brother rather than the husband of Elizabeth, who explained that Adam was on a business trip and didn't want her to wait until he returned for her examination.

Dr. Nunn took Elizabeth's medical history and the prepared history of Adam. She asked in surprise, "Both you and your husband are twins? That's interesting. This could mean you are predisposed to have twins yourself. If you are carrying twins you should have no problems considering your age and physical condition."

Dr. Nunn examined Elizabeth and ordered tests that would be conducted elsewhere in the Center. She then made an appointment for her and Adam to return in thirty days, unless the tests required an earlier visit.

Rose Marie cooed over Elizabeth when she heard she was pregnant. She had always assumed that Elizabeth and Charles were married and not twins. She asked, "Where is this husband of yours and how come he has never come by the office?"

Elizabeth thought, *Oh bother, what now!*

"Adam travels a lot and is currently in New York. He's due back next week and I'll bring him by to meet you. Adam is a twin too and his sister, Evelyn, is married to Charles. We are one big happy family. Evelyn is going to take my place here when I'm further along with my pregnancy."

Rose Marie thought, *I'm going to have to check on her husband. He shouldn't leave her alone so much, especially now that she's pregnant.*

Elizabeth heard Rose Marie's thought. *I'm going to have to talk to Adam about him sweet-talking her with a story that's believable.*

* * *

The SA Group had been in business for four years. Adam and Elizabeth's twins were now three years old and were named Jacob and Linda. Charles and Evelyn's twins were six months old and were named Kaye and Sarah. The Stephenson twins were now nineteen and had married. Jack Stephenson was married to Jennifer and Ralph Stephenson was married to Mary. Both couples had been married almost a year.

Mark and Sally Stephenson at fourteen were the oldest of the six children of the Group. The SA Group's Board now consisted of twelve adults. They all had Psi powers of almost equal levels and were all geniuses. The Stephenson twins and their spouses had all developed an interest in computers and their applications in finding terrorist groups who had an interest in the Group. They specifically wanted to find their sources of funding, which they raided for their own use. In the two years they had been making use of this strategy they had added over $20 million to their own accounts.

Adam and Evelyn had guided their efforts and showed them how to avoid anyone backtracking their raids. Whenever they had evidence of a terrorist group's location in the U.S. or outside the country, they would notify either the FBI or the CIA in a manner that could not be traced back to their location. This had the effect of letting them know the Group was still operating and friendly to the U.S.

Rafe met Adam in the workroom. "Adam, would you check the personnel records of the FBI and CIA to determine if Agent Patton and Deputy Director McPherson are still active or retired. If retired, where they could be contacted."

"Do you think they would want to join us?"

"If they are retired I'm betting they are together now. If so, the odds are favorable they would jump at the chance to be able to start a family."

The next day Adam went to his parent's apartment. After hugging his mother and catching up on what she had been doing, he delivered his answer to his father.

"You were right, they have been retired for over a year and their retirement checks are delivered to the same address in Fredericksburg, Virginia. What now? "

"I assume you can get their cell phone numbers. I'm sure the agency will have a close watch on McPherson, but maybe not on Patton. We can send her an e-mail with an innocent notification of a bird watchers meeting in Richmond, Virginia, and have her e-mail RSVP to the sending e-mail address. You know how to do this so they can't trace it back to us, and we need an address for the meeting in Richmond."

CHAPTER 19

The next day Adam had everything arranged for a fake bird watchers meeting and the e-mail sent by a prepaid phone. The meeting would be held at a Marriott Hotel in Richmond, two weeks from today. The next day they received an RSVP plus one guest, from Patton.

Rafe and Vera arrived two hours early at the Marriott, and checked out the small meeting room reserved for the Virginia Bird Watchers Meeting. They were surprised to find several people outside the meeting room looking at the placard advertising the meeting. Rafe told them it was a closed meeting for electing officers. The onlookers left, disappointed. Vera looked inside to make sure no one else was there before they waited down the hallway for Patton and McPherson to arrive.

Twenty minutes before the time of the scheduled meeting, they could mentally hear Patton and McPherson talking to each other. Patton was saying, "I know it's them. Bird Watchers were code for Sparrow and Hawk. It's right down the hall to the right."

McPherson looked surprised, while Patton's face lit up as they caught sight of their old friends standing up to greet them. They met outside the meeting room and vigorously hugged and shook hands. Quickly, they went into the meeting room and sat down facing each other.

Rafe spoke, "We want to give you the opportunity to join us in our group with all the benefits we enjoy. You will have the ability to start your own family, and we will have the benefit of your experience and contacts. What do you say?"

Patton beamed with glee. "I knew it! I just knew it. I've been telling

Jim you might contact us, but he thought it would be too risky for you."

Vera said, "It was risky, but we took precautions and have the ability to read minds, so here we are. If you want to join us you will have to come with us now. If you drove a car it will have to stay here. We will take you to our safe house."

Patton looked at her husband, eyes pleading until he nodded. "Let's go before we're caught."

They retrieved their luggage from the parking garage. Rafe had them set the luggage on the pavement where he ran a scanner over it. He and Vera then carried the luggage to their rented SUV and loaded it up. They drove to another parking garage six blocks away where they exchanged the rental for their own SUV, which was a different color. Rafe figured if they were under satellite surveillance the change in the color of their vehicle would throw any surveillance off.

Patton and McPherson were anxious to hear of the Johnsons' exploits since they left Parris Island. Rafe and Vera told them of the changes within the Group, the marriages, and births that resulted in their numbers increasing to eighteen. They would be twenty now. Talking over each other at times, Rafe and Vera recounted how they tracked down various terrorist groups and raided their deposit accounts and informed the agencies of what they had discovered about each group.

McPherson interrupted, "That information you provided has resulted in at least three cells being destroyed, and your raiding of their deposit accounts has hurt them even more. They have started hand carrying funds now, which means the agency can follow some of these couriers to new cells which were destroyed before they could do any harm."

Rafe said, "Well, I'm glad we are still doing some good, even if we are no longer with the CIA."

McPherson gave a short laugh. "You both are still carried on the rolls, but are on the deep cover list. That has our highest security clearance."

They stopped at Wilmington, North Carolina for the night. Both Rafe and Vera were tired, and the McPhersons had already sacked out in the backseat. After a night's rest they got an early start. They timed their arrival in Macon during the middle of rush hour.

As Rafe approached the SA Group building he said, "This is our safe house. The SA Group business is ours and is used as camouflage for the condos above the third floor. It's been a good life. We're so much in demand we had to limit our client base to fifty."

They keyed in their special code for the double garage doors before proceeding into the garage. Rafe had mentally requested help with their luggage, so Anne and Peter Stephenson were waiting for them. The former FBI agents hugged Jane Patton, shedding a few tears. They then shook hands with James McPherson, congratulating him on his and Jane's marriage.

After collecting their luggage, they used the elevator to go to the third floor workroom where everyone else was assembled. The only other people the McPhersons knew were Adam and Evelyn, now older than they remembered. The other children they knew were now adults. The adults all looked to be about the same age, which was a little disconcerting.

Rafe introduced Jane and Jim to the adults first, along with the newcomer twins, Adam and Evelyn spouses. The children were introduced last by their parents. Jane was surprised by the changes within the Group and also happy the children found spouses when they grew to maturity.

The board members retired to the conference room with the McPhersons. Rafe explained to the new arrivals that all adults were members of the Board. Children were considered adults when they turned eighteen, or seventeen if married. Rafe brought the meeting to order and submitted the McPhersons' application for membership to the Group. The application was voted upon and approved with no dissension. The McPhersons' were then told they would each receive a blood transfusion shortly and reminded them of the side effect of extreme sexual urges and jogging as a way to cope with their longings.

Vera then used her and Rafe's experience and those of the younger members - Anne, Peter, Charles, and Elizabeth whose experiences were much stronger. She informed them of their attempts at finding relief.

Rafe closed the meeting and he and Vera escorted the McPhersons to their new home on the tenth floor. When they entered the condo apartment they were surprised at its opulence. They entered the living room slowly checking out the furnishings until they stood before the window looking out over the city. Jim and Jane held hands as they stood together enjoying the sight, before moving throughout the apartment checking out the bedrooms, large closets, bathrooms, and finally the kitchen and dining area.

Jim turned to their escorts. "You didn't skimp on the furnishings here. I can't think of anything I would change, and I see we have room for kids."

"That's right. If you need anything, call Anne and she will take care of it. I know you need food and we have set up apartment 1010 as our grocery warehouse. If you need anything not there and it's not urgent, just add it to the grocery list you will find on the bar. Once a week we make a trip to the grocery store. You two won't be able to leave until you get much younger in appearance because the agencies are going to be looking for you with a vengeance. We are going to send an e-mail to both agencies explaining that you have joined our Group, which might ease their minds."

Adam and Evelyn had been working on another invention that hopefully would be another source of income. It helped that the Group was comprised of geniuses. The members came by the workroom and barnstormed, giving them ideas that could lead to the next big breakthrough.

The current effort was a wireless miniature surveillance camera that looked like part of a building. It was solar powered with battery backup and had a range of one mile, but the distance could be extended by the use of repeater units. Adam was currently testing the cameras by having them installed on their building looking outward 360 degrees and with another ring of cameras around the surrounding buildings looking inward toward the SA Group Building.

The camera placement provided full coverage of the area around their building and should catch anyone approaching it. The camera's images were captured on digital recorders and reviewed in real time by Adam's computer, which was programmed to immediately alert him if set parameters were violated.

The cameras were in operation for over a month when the security program alerted Adam of a possible intrusion. Adam reviewed the recording and saw a man installing a device pointing in the direction of the SA Group Building. Other recordings showed several different men installing similar devices on other buildings, all pointing in the direction of the SA Group building.

Adam immediately called a meeting to report his findings. He and Evelyn were waiting in the conference room when the other members hurried in. Rafe called the meeting to order and then nodded to Adam.

"Our security cameras show several men installing cameras pointing in our direction. I've checked the Savannah building and so far there is no apparent activity at that location. We need to start making preparations to change locations if we deem this to be an immediate threat. I should know if we are in immediate danger by this time tomorrow."

Rafe spoke, "Okay, everyone knows what they need to do! Adam will let us know if we need to go to phase two."

Jane and Jim McPherson talked to Rafe after the others had left. Jim asked, "What about us, can we help?"

Rafe said, "Don't be too alarmed. We have gone through this three times since we moved here and have never gone to phase two. All you need to do is pack your suitcases in preparation for a move. If we go to phase two you will receive additional instructions."

Jane smiled slightly. "We have gone into the change and about all I can think about is getting Jim into bed."

Rafe laughed. "Yeah I can remember that time. At least you have Jim to help you through this patch. Vera and I wouldn't meet for another two years."

Adam and Evelyn started working on tracing the signals from the spy cameras back to their source. All four cameras' signals were being sent to a single location, which was about six miles away. Adam used the signal to gain access into their computer, which belonged to Strong Investigations. He started searching for their customer files which he downloaded into a file at his location. While searching through Strong's files he discovered correspondence relating to Strong's investigation of SA Group.

This client was one of their competitors, Patterson Security, out of Atlanta. Adam made sure there was no other mention of SA Group in Strong's files, before leaving their computer. He then used Patterson Security's Web Site to check who they were. He eventually got into the business computer through the personal computer of the Secretary to the President.

Adam hacked the secretary's files first and discovered the firm's president wanted to expand into Macon and found that SA Group had already locked that area up. He ordered SA Group investigated trying to find a wedge to shake loose some of the bigger clients.

Adam inserted a worm virus into the Patterson Security system causing it to crash. He then informed the Board members that the problem had been found and corrected. Adam then burned out the Strong Investigations cameras' transmitters. Stronger measures would be taken if the cameras were replaced or reactivated.

Adam was happy with the new camera's performance and filed a patent application in the name of SA Group. Two months later they received an inquiry from a purchasing agency of the U.S. Government. They wanted to purchase the patent rights for $20 million.

Adam called a meeting of the Board to consider the matter. Upon hearing the offer, Jim McPherson spoke, "We will have to sell to them eventually, because otherwise they will place a hold on the patent using for the good of the country as the reason. I recommend we make a counteroffer of $40 million and see what happens. If they come back with $30 million, take the offer."

The Board discussed the matter until finally instructing Adam to follow McPherson's recommendation. Two weeks later they received a direct deposit of $40 million into their local bank account. Adam transferred $36 million to one of their offshore accounts, where he did the dance of hiding it in multiple accounts throughout the world. He then had their accountant prepare the tax documents for a prepayment of $4 million to the IRS.

In the meantime, Jane and Jim McPherson were beginning to notice improvements in their physical condition. They both felt twenty years younger and their bodies were starting to change as well.

CHAPTER 20

Rafe and Vera were visiting the McPhersons in their apartment and commented on how good they looked. Jane took Vera into her bedroom and showed her the improvements she noted in her physical body.

Vera laughed. "Well, look at me. You are going to have a body like this in a few years. What you need to do is help it along by exercising or jogging. I preferred jogging and Rafe exercised before we met. Now we both try to jog every day. After about a mile your endorphins kick in and you get a nice high. That's what keeps you coming back."

Returning to the living room, Vera and Jane informed their spouses that tomorrow they were all going to jog together in the basement garage.

Rafe said, "Do you have jogging clothes?

"We've got running shoes and sweat clothes, but no true running clothes."

"Tell Anne what your sizes are and she will get them for you. Let her know if you need anything else."

The next day the McPhersons joined the Johnsons on their daily jog. The garage was round; similar to its upper floors and one circuit was about an eighth of a mile. After the first mile, the McPhersons started to pick up the pace as the endorphins started entering their blood stream. At the end of three miles Rafe and Vera stopped and asked them how they felt?

Jane looked at Jim, holding her legs. Jim said, "I'm good. I'm not even tired. How much longer do you guy's usually run?"

Rafe replied, "We usually jog three and half miles. How about another four times around?"

Jim started ahead of him. "Let's do it!"

* * *

Five years had gone by in Macon. The McPhersons' physical appearance was that of someone whose age was in the mid to high twenties, and they were parents of two-year old identical twin boys - Randy and Jackson.

Mark and Sally Stephenson were now nineteen, and like Adam and Evelyn sought mates through their Mensa membership. After a six-month search they found and married Jeri Reynolds and Grant Gleason and had been married about a year. The disclosure of the SA Group's history and their mates Psi powers was accepted almost exactly the same as Adam and Evelyn's courtship.

The children of the Group now consisted of three sets of twins ranging in age from two to eight, and there were now twenty-two adults. The Group's Psi powers were still their primary defense and they all practiced to improve their abilities. Whoever might attack them next would have an unpleasant surprise.

Every adult member of the Group was responsible for certain assigned duties. The adults added to the Group after the Parris Island move did most of the outside work; i.e.: shopping for clothing, food, and other necessities. Those with special abilities were tasked with that type of work. Adam's computer and special inventions detail now had ten members, and the children had one-on-one instruction coupled with computer lessons.

Generally, the special detail had several projects in process at the same time. The next item Adam's team concentrated on was finding the group or person responsible for funding the various terrorist organizations around the world. Jim McPherson gave Adam the names of five individuals the CIA suspected of providing funds to terrorists, but no proof was ever found.

They concentrated all their efforts on finding the deposit accounts of those five individuals. Three were oil rich Saudi princes, and the other two were billionaire arms dealers spreading chaos in order to sell more weapons. Two months later, they found the accounts of both arms dealers and one of the Saudi princes.

They first documented the deposit activity in the arms dealers' accounts, noting payments from known and suspected terrorist groups and their account numbers. They then found where these accounts were located and documented their activity. From that activity they were able to identify another Saudi's account and three more terrorist cells. When they had mined this activity for all useful information, they raided all the arms dealers' and terrorist's accounts of their funds. This brought the SA Group over $3 Billion.

They were now rich beyond anything they'd ever considered. They e-mailed the documentation they had accumulated to a special CIA address Jim McPherson provided them. They then turned their attention toward the accounts of the two Saudi princes. The activity in these accounts led to additional terrorist groups along with some they had already identified. The accounts of the newly identified terrorist organizations showed deposits from a third Saudi prince. After mining all these accounts of useful information they also raided their funds. This brought the SA Group an additional $25 Billion.

They then e-mailed the documentation from these accounts to the same CIA address. Adam decided they needed to call a Board meeting to address their accumulated funds. When the Group members arrived, Rafe called the meeting to order and gave Adam the floor.

"My team has been very successful in raiding the deposit accounts of terrorist groups and in some cases their sponsors. These funds and income from other sources have resulted in the accumulation of a sizable deposit balance of over $34 Billion."

There was silence after almost all the members, except the team members, gave a gasp of surprise. Then Rafe asked, "Did you just say $34 Billion? Not million?"

"$34 Billion! We need to formulate a plan to invest a large portion of this. Right now it's just sitting there."

Jim McPherson spoke, "I know someone who can help us, but we need to decide how the money will be invested. We can invest in stocks, bonds, or directly into a going business. We can start a political action committee to elect politicians that would listen to what we want to happen."

The Board started to work on several proposals on how to invest their funds. Rafe suggested. "Everyone, make a list; up to ten ways we can use the funds and from that let's come to a consensus."

The board members started making their lists and after they finished, Vera collected and started writing down the various ideas with a check mark to indicate a repeat. The top three proposals were: (1) invest most of the funds; (2) use some of the funds in a business that would benefit their Group; and (3) establish a Super Political Action Committee.

Rafe called for the Board to vote how much to allocate for each proposal and then they would decide how to use the funds. They eventually decided to invest eighty percent or $27.2 Billion, and another

$4 Billion into a business or businesses that would benefit themselves, and finally the remaining $2.8 Billion into a SPAC.

The Board authorized Jim McPherson to begin the process of investing the bulk of their funds, which they would review monthly. He then asked for volunteers to be on separate committees to handle the funds for the remaining two options. Rafe stated there should be at least five members on each of the two committees. The Board consisted of members with diverse interests and the two committees each filled with seven members.

A month later, Jim McPherson gave his report on the status of their investment portfolio. "Our financial advisor recommended we diversify, but not be too cautious. Our investment value had increased two percent, or $544,000 during the first month; however, don't expect this kind of return every month."

Vera Johnson chaired the committee centering on investment in a business that would benefit the Group. She gave the Board a list of businesses that would fall into this category, and stated they would continue the search until the Board agreed upon a choice.

Jane McPherson chaired the committee on SPAC. She said, "The best use of these funds are to pick a first time candidate for the House or Senate, someone who would support our views."

She gave the Board a list of five candidates she felt would qualify. The Group membership thanked the committees for their work and suggested they should study their proposals before making a decision.

* * *

A year has passed without any threats detected against the Group. During this period five sets of twins were born, and there are now sixteen children and twenty-two adults. At the annual Board Meeting it was reported that the Group's investments had done well, totaling $32.8 Billion. In addition, the group purchased controlling interest in two businesses, both located in the Silicon Valley - a computer chip company and a manufacturer of computers and peripheral equipment. Adam and his team channeled several of their inventions to them, which helped make them one of the leaders in their fields. The SPAC was sponsoring ten politicians of both parties, elected evenly between the House and the Senate.

Jim McPherson stated, "According to his informant, the raid on the deposit accounts of the three Saudi princes has caused the King to take a closer interest in the activities of his family, which has resulted in fewer funds reaching terrorist groups. The positive outcome was fewer terrorist attacks around the world; however, the negative result was a $10 Million bounty placed upon whomever was responsible for the raid."

Adam Johnson stated, "I don't think we have to worry about anyone tying us to that raid, unless there is a leak in the CIA, and even if that occurs no one knows where or what we are. Regardless, we are keeping a close watch on our neighborhood."

Rafe nodded his head in agreement and then brought up another subject. "I think we need someone on the ground in California to protect our interests. We can't have anyone with a surname the agencies know. Grant and Sally Gleason seem to fit our needs. Both have worked with Adam's team for years and can be our watchdogs. Our biggest potential problem there is industrial espionage, maybe with some terrorist or agency spying as well. Their ability to read minds should work well for us."

Rafe looked over at his two candidates. "Well, how about it? Do you want to go to the land of milk and honey?"

This was the first time any of their Group has been assigned an extended tour outside the safe house. They looked at each other with hope and a little fear until Sally nodded her head.

Grant and Sally stood and holding hands replied, "We agree, but want to know how long this assignment is for?"

"It's open-ended, but if for any reason you want to return we will make arrangements. I know with your twin babies being so young this assignment may be problematic, but we can get you the best nanny that's available."

CHAPTER 21

Grant and Sally Gleason had been in Sunnyvale, CA for a week and were just getting a handle on everything. Everything was new, the climate, the city, the house, and now the nanny. Their nanny, Janet Welford, a woman of about forty-five years whose own children had all grown up, married, and left the area was personable, widowed, and seemed eager to take care of their identical two-year old twin boys, Alex and James.

The house the Gleasons bought was an overpriced two-story older home that had recently been updated with modern appliances and new furnace and air-conditioning. It had four bedrooms and an office, which gave them plenty of room to grow in their family.

They were scheduled to be at the Albertson Electronics the next morning. Grant and Sally were not sure what kind of reception they would receive since they represented the majority ownership. They just wanted to be sure their children were going to be properly taken care of in their absence. Janet had handled the boys all day and she seemed to know what she was doing. They had no doctor here yet, but they weren't concerned because the Group's children had never gotten sick before.

The drive to the Albertson Electronics didn't take long and they were at the gate within twenty minutes. They were issued temporary passes and directed where to go for processing. After about an hour they had their first introduction to management.

They were shown into the office of President Sharron Blackman who shook their hands and motioned toward a separate informal seating area in her large office. From their mind scan they knew she was suspicious of their motives for being there. Grant decided to immediately get to the point of their visit.

"Albertson Electronics major shareholder has asked us to check your operation for potential problems. We have no desire to interfere with your daily operations, but would like an adequate office to interview some members of your staff to get a better idea on how we can be helpful. We don't know how long we will be here and we will also be visiting another nearby business that our employers also have a majority interest."

Sharron was listening intently. After he finished talking she thought, *these two are really young to be seeking management positions, so maybe they are troubleshooters.* "Can I ask what you are looking for?"

"We have heard rumors of industrial espionage and have been tasked with making sure you are clean. We don't want to create any waves, so we would appreciate if you would make a list of all your supervisors. From that list we will start our interviews. Can we count on your discretion to keep our mission a secret?"

Sharron nodded her head. "Yes, of course. Why don't you wait here while I make arrangements?"

Grant and Sally were in their new office thirty minutes later and making a schedule for interviewing the firm's supervisors. They allowed thirty minutes each for the initial list of twenty supervisors. The first was scheduled after lunch, so they hand delivered the schedule to President Blackman's secretary so that the interviews could be started on time.

Grant and Sally had an early lunch at the firm's cafeteria and watched the employees' reaction to their presence. The rumor mill was strong as they were the apparent subjects of almost every conversation among the lunch crowd. This was according to plan as it brought the employees' thoughts toward what Sally and Grant's purpose might be. Any with guilty consciences would have their transgressions first in their thoughts.

During their interviews they asked questions that brought thoughts of not only them possibly selling business secrets, but also other people they suspected of doing this. After the first day they had a short list of people the supervisors suspected, but so far the supervisors were all clean.

The Gleason's left early for home, as they were anxious about their twins. They had never been away from them so long before, but when they were about a mile from home they could sense their son's mind glow, which gave them immediate relief. They were mentally cooing to them before they pulled into their driveway.

They found Janet fussing with them as they entered the boy's room.

Janet turned to them. "I don't know what came over them. They were playing together in their playpen, when they suddenly got excited and started jumping up and down saying mommy and daddy, and then you showed up."

The reason for the boys' agitation dawned upon Janet. "They knew you were coming!" She accused.

Grant and Sally ignored Janet's comment as they each picked up one of the boys and made over them before trading who they were holding and each playing with the other. After quieting the boys they asked Janet how her day went.

"Well, it was no problem at all. The little guys like to play with each other and didn't cry a bit. When they wanted the bottle they pantomimed what they desired. I've never taken care of babies like them and they're only twenty months old."

"Yes, we noticed that they were pretty smart and they have already started walking. If you want you can stop using the pen and let them use the bedroom instead. Just make sure everything is placed out of their reach except for their toys. Put the door fence in place so you can check on them."

Janet nodded. "Okay, but if they're this smart I bet they can get through it."

Grant thought to Sally. *They would try to climb out of the playpen too, so to avoid a fall we better have them already on the floor.*

"I'll take a look at the door fence and see if it's strong enough," Grant replied.

They saw Janet out the door after making arrangements for the time she would return tomorrow. Grant and Sally generally took turns preparing the evening meal while the other took care of the twins. It was Grant's time to cook and he decided on spaghetti and frozen meatballs. The boys liked spaghetti and they tended to make a mess, but at their age they generally made a mess of whatever they ate.

Both Grant and Sally were beginning to enjoy being out on their own. Sally had never done this before and Grant hadn't been out very much since his marriage. It was up to Grant to ease her into the mainstream population ways. She had to watch herself and make sure she didn't answer a question vocally that was asked mentally when there were others present.

They returned to Albertson Electronics the following morning and continued the interviews during the week until they finished with the supervisors. They had no hits on the supervisors, but had five suspicious employees to check. The supervisors noted these employees had been living well above their income level. Sally made arrangements through their supervisors to have the suspects meet with them the following day.

Grant and Sally left after lunch and did some shopping before heading for home. They were beginning to enjoy setting their own working hours and being able to spend more time with the twins. This time they were careful not to put the twins on alert that they were approaching home.

After pulling into the garage they started unloading groceries and other purchases from their vehicle. Janet came down the stairs to meet them as they entered the kitchen. She started telling the parents all about the twins' accomplishments during their absence.

"They had started trying to get over the door fence, first by one standing on the back of the other. When that didn't work they tried piling objects in front of the fence in an attempt to climb over it. They were just climbing over it when I caught them in the act."

Grant looked over at Sally. "We can't have them doing that. I'll call and have a different type of door installed that they can't get through."

The next day Janet supervised the installation of a door with a steel mesh insert that was too fine for the twins' fingers to get through, allowing Janet to see and hear what they were doing inside the room and allow her easy entry when she needed to.

Meanwhile, Grant and Sally started their first interview with one of the employee suspects. They were not very long into the interview when they read from his surface thoughts that his wife's family was providing the extra funds they were spending. During their third interview they struck gold when interviewing Zack Barlow.

He had been with the firm about a year and had a gambling problem. To supplement his income he accepted Brightstar Electronics offer to steal certain data chips he was producing. The production line he stole from didn't have sufficient security, so it was easy for him. For the time being they left him in place and continued the interviews.

They finished the interviews without finding any other crooked employees. They notified Barlow's supervisor of his actions and the need to strengthen their security procedures. Grant suggested they add an electronic marker to all chips that would trip an alarm if anyone tried to carry one outside the production room.

They also asked for a meeting with President Blackman to report their findings. When they were shown into her office, Grant and Sally were not surprised to find all the supervisors present as well. They knew from their thoughts that they were in the room before they entered. Blackman asked the new arrivals to make themselves comfortable. Extra chairs had been brought in to seat everyone; however, the large office was a little crowded.

Blackman started the meeting by asking how they had found the thief in such a short period of time. Grant replied, "Actually, your supervisors gave us the names of the suspects when we interviewed them. We were interested in people who seemed to be spending much more money than their salary would support. Using this as a starting point we dug deeper until we had a suspect that we concentrated on. During our interview with him he inadvertently gave himself away. We checked his financials and found where he received large cash deposits three times over a period of six months. We then checked the financials of your firm's closest competitors and found matching disbursements from Brightstar Electronics. Since the data we collected was not obtained legally I don't think we can go after them with a lawsuit."

Blackman's face reddened with anger as Grant's explanation continued. When Grant finished she angrily blurted, "I want payback! I want them to feel pain for what they have done."

Sally smiled at her. "Let's have these other people get back to their jobs before we do anything else."

After all the other people left the room, Sally asked President Blackman, "Why don't we sit down together and discuss our revenge."

Sharron looked at her sharply as she motioned them to the informal seating area. "Why don't I have my secretary bring us in some refreshments before we start?"

After they were all settled with coffee in hand, Sally looked intently into Sharron's eyes. "We have a way of getting back at them that is not legal and if caught could bring severe penalties for us. Are you still interested?"

The two telepaths closely followed her thought process as she came to a decision.

"How risky is it?"

Grant answered. "We will probably be suspected, but there won't be any evidence to use against us. We plan on using a computer virus to shut them down and destroy their backup files. They may not be able to reconstruct enough files to continue doing business."

Sharron's face reflected her glee as she said, "Let's do it!"

CHAPTER 22

⊂⊗⊗⊃

Two weeks later the Brightstar Electronics firm suffered a complete computer failure that included the deletion of their backup files. Experts were called in to get them working again, but they could do nothing except try to reconstruct some files from stand-alone computers. Albertson Electronics increased their production to handle the business formerly held by Brightstar Electronics.

Grant and Sally made arrangements to meet the management of their second majority held firm, Ingram, Inc. They spent two days at home following the debacle at Brightstar and enjoyed being with their children. The Group's children generally didn't develop Psi powers until they turned ten to twelve years of age. Janet worked every weekday whether the parents were at home or not. It ensured that she wouldn't leave for a better paying job and gave them a little more freedom to do other things.

Returning home after a shopping spree, they found Janet waiting for them at the garage door. Her face was strained as she motioned for them to follow her upstairs. Grant and Sally realized Janet was almost in shock because of something she refused to even think about. Just before reaching the boys' room she held a finger up to her mouth indicating they be quiet.

They were startled to see two teddy bears chasing one another in a game of tag in the air above the boys' heads. Sally thought to Grant. *Oh poop! How are we going to explain this?*

Grant motioned for Janet to follow them downstairs. They sat her down at the kitchen table. Sally hurried to fetch a glass of water. They let her take a drink before giving her an explanation she might accept.

Janet seemed to settle down and collect herself before asking, "What is that all about?"

Sally took Janet's hands in her own and looked into her eyes. "It's a big secret. We are part of a government experiment to develop extra sensory perception, or ESP. This wasn't supposed to happen until they were older, but apparently they have stronger powers than any of the others. We want to keep you on as their Nanny, but you can't reveal anything that you see. We will even double your salary if you decide to stay."

Janet intently looked at them for a moment before asking, "How about you, do you have powers too?"

Sally mentally moved a vase of flowers from a nearby table to a spot directly in front of Janet. "Yes, a nice parlor trick isn't it?"

Janet grinned at her. "Oh pooh! I just thought I was losing my marbles. Now that I know what's going on I don't have a problem. But that salary increase is nice too."

Sally mentally returned the flower vase to its proper place and then patted Janet on the shoulder. "Why don't you go check on the boys while Grant and I bring the rest of our things inside?"

Janet smiled and then headed upstairs to continue her nanny duties. Grant thought to Sally. *That was quick thinking on your part. It had just enough truth to be believable and the government-sponsored part keeps her quiet about what she sees.*

The next day they drove to Ingram, Inc. to introduce themselves to management. An hour later they were sitting in President Ralph Ingram's office explaining why they were there, using the same reason as they had at Albertson Electronics. Ralph Ingram was the son of the founder and has been its CEO for over six years. He was in his early forties and unlike his father had a head for finance as well as being a computer hardware innovator.

After making arrangements for an office to conduct interviews and a list of supervisors, Grant and Sally left President Ingram's office. They were following Ingram's young, curvaceous private secretary toward their assigned office when Sally hip-bumped Grant and mentally said *that's enough of that! Keep your eyes off those hips.*

Grant smiled, *I was just comparing hers with yours and thought yours were much better.*

You better. I bet I could swing my hips like that if I was wearing a skin-tight skirt like hers.

You would certainly make her jealous if you did, but then I would have to fight off the men you would attract.

The secretary stopped at the door to their office and told them she would return soon with the list of supervisors. After they received the list and made a schedule of appointments, they returned to the secretary so she could notify each supervisor of their time to appear. The first was not until one p.m., so they went to the firm's cafeteria for an early lunch break and to let the employees see them.

The first day was a bust as far as getting any suspects, and they were anxious to get home and see if the twins had exhibited any more Psi talents. They entered their home without finding Janet waiting for them, which was a good sign, as they continued their way upstairs to the boy's room.

They found her and the twins playing a game where they competed by mentally stacking blocks higher than the other. They watched from the doorway as she asked them to spell their names using the letter blocks. The blocks started moving in the air arranging themselves until one spelled Alex and the other James.

The impressed parents started clapping their hands and voicing kudos at how well the boys had done. When the boys heard their parents' voices, the blocks fell to the floor and they hurried toward them in glee. Grant and Sally picked up their children and hugged them, congratulating them on their feat.

Later, before Janet left, she told them, "They take instruction so easily. They are so smart, I just can't imagine children this young being able to do what they can. I showed them what their names looked like by putting the letter blocks together just once, and then they did it on their own by using their minds to move the blocks. They really like using their minds to move things. It's fascinating to watch them play. I'll look forward to coming back tomorrow to see what they do next."

After Janet left Sally and Grant looked at each other, relieved. "It's a good thing we have her on our side with the children now starting to show their talents. We have to let her know of the other things they may start doing."

Grant replied, "If Janet is not able to handle their talents, one of us will need to stay home."

"I hope that doesn't happen, but you're right that we need to watch the situation. So far she has done pretty well."

The next day they returned to Ingram's to continue their interviews. During their third interview Grant and Sally thought they might have a lead with a new hire the supervisor had been having a problem with. His work performance was not as good as his references would indicate. They flagged his name and continued with the interviews. When they finished with all the interviews, they had three individuals the supervisors had misgivings about. They arranged meetings with these suspects through their supervisors.

The first suspect was Gene Compton, who was a recent hire and didn't live up to his references. When he entered their office he appeared a little surprised to find Grant and Sally. He expected someone older to be over his supervisor. By reading his surface thoughts, Gene was expecting to be called to task because of his poor work performance. When asked about his references his thoughts went to the person he had paid to create them for $1,500. He thought he could bluff his way through the job for a couple of months until he was fired.

After Gene left the room, they notified his supervisor of the false references. The next suspect was Jane Rush who appeared to be overqualified for the job she applied for. She had been with the firm six months and according to her references she could be working at a much higher level. Her supervisor noted she appeared bored when on the job and took frequent breaks, but still out-performed her co-workers.

When Jane entered the office she noted Grant and Sally waiting for her, but before anyone had a chance to speak they felt her try to read their thoughts. Sally responded with a strong mind probe of her own, causing Jane to stumble back against the wall. Grant and Sally helped her into a chair and watched her closely as she recovered.

Sally sent another mind query. *What are you doing working here when you could earn more at a higher-level job?*

Who are you people? I have never met another telepath before and you're really strong.

Answer the question! What are you doing here?

I had to leave my last job because people were beginning to suspect I could read their minds. This was the only job I could find on short notice.

Your application states you're twenty-seven, single, and apparently over qualified for your job. I'm going to arrange for you be transferred. What do you prefer?

You can do that?

We represent the majority owner. If you don't like it here, maybe we can arrange a change.

Jane looked at them in wonder a moment before relying, *I like it here, but it gets lonely because I can't share being a telepath for fear they will think I'm crazy, or they become frightened of me. With you here I've got someone to talk to and maybe be friends with.*

I'll recommend you be transferred to the same type job you held before until we learn more about you. I think you are going to be happy with the change, but remain silent about your gift.

Gift! I've always considered it to be a curse. Okay, I'll wait to hear from you.

Jane smiled at them as she left the office. Grant and Sally waited until they no longer could feel her mind glow before speaking. Sally spoke after considering several options.

"We need Adam to thoroughly check her background all the way to her birth to make sure she is not a plant. She may be just who she says she is, but we need to be certain."

Sally sent an encoded e-mail to Adam with Jane's references and job application and described her ability and their concerns. They then called the President's secretary and arranged to have a meeting with him that afternoon. They then held their last interview of the supervisor's suspects.

It seemed there was no one employed by Ingram, Inc. they needed to be concerned about, except for Jane Rush. They met with President Ingram and informed him of their negative findings. They strongly recommended the firm transfer Jane to the more responsible position she was qualified for as it was in the company's best interests.

Grant stated they would return soon to make a further analysis of the firm, and then they left to return home. No new surprises awaited them when they entered their house, so they went upstairs to check on their children. Janet had devised new games to tweak the twins' interest in strengthening their talent.

When the parents arrived at the boys' room they were mentally moving an inflated ball through an obstacle course with the intent of not touching objects along the way. They were so focused on the game they didn't notice their parents watching them. When they finished, Grant and Sally gave them loud applause and rushed over to pick the boys up and kiss them.

Janet smiled at the boys and gushed over their accomplishments. "They are getting much better in their ability to control objects they want to move. They even lifted and moved that playpen when it got in the way of their games."

Grant immediately went over and started taking the pen apart and moved it out of the room. Sally spoke, "We don't need that anymore. Honey, let me help you take that out to the garage. We can store it in the attic later."

Three days later they got a reply to their e-mail. Adam had personally done the background check and Jane Rush appeared to be who she said she was. The Board had approved her acceptance into the Group contingent upon their own final interview. Sally looked at her husband and frowned.

"I was hoping we didn't have to do the final interview."

Grant nodded his head. "You know that you have to do it because you have the training and are one of the strongest telepaths in the Group."

"I know, but I still don't like doing it."

CHAPTER 23

The next day they returned to Ingram, Inc. to make contact with Jane Rush. After their arrival at the firm they summoned her appearance before them. She tentatively entered their office and took a seat. Sally started to mentally speak to her.

I did a background check on you to make sure you aren't a plant. We have many enemies both foreign and domestic. We would like for you to join our organization, which would entitle you to many valuable benefits, but first you must submit to a memory scan. If you don't agree, there will be no repercussions and you may retain your position here. I'll give you five minutes to make a decision.

Will it hurt?

If you relax and let me have free rein, it should be painless.

Okay, I agree. When do you want to do it?

Right now. Please lie on the floor and relax.

After Jane found a clear area, she lay down on her back and tried to relax as instructed. She listened to Sally's voice in her mind asking her to clear all thoughts as if preparing herself for sleep. Sally's mind voice was soothing and Jane didn't feel Sally enter her memories, going deeper until she was satisfied nothing was amiss.

Sally awakened Jane slowly with her voice until Jane was fully awake. "How do you feel?"

"I feel fine. Are you finished?"

"Yes. Did you feel any pain or discomfort?"

"No, nothing at all."

How about now? Do you feel any pain now that I'm talking to you mentally?

No. I feel great! Did you do anything while you were in my memories?

No, except that I told you that being telepathic was a gift and not a curse and that you should feel proud of it and not guilty. Now before you agree to join us you should be aware that both the government and terrorist organizations are trying to locate us. The government wants to protect us, but they haven't done a very good job in the past. The terrorist groups want to kill us and have placed a bounty on us.

That's the stick, what's the carrot?

Our organization is still small, but is growing. We need professional people in our ranks and have been recruiting by members marrying both inside and out of the organization and having children, which have always been twins with genius mentalities. We currently don't have any males in our organization old enough for you to marry. We would like for you to pick a professional man, a lawyer or doctor is high on our list if you can find one that is compatible with you. They have to be deeply in love with you for them to want to follow you into the organization. The carrot is a long life in a body of a twenty-two year old with full Psi powers.

You've got to be kidding me!

No, our leaders were in their late sixties and early seventies when they started getting younger. They now have the bodies of people in their low twenties.

How about their Psi powers?

Every person in our group has these powers; some are stronger in some areas than others.

How about you two?

I married Grant, who was outside the organization. He has the same powers I do, but I'm one of the strongest telepaths in the organization. Once we give you the treatment you may be a much stronger telepath than you are now.

Wow! This is so unbelievable. An organization of genus people who have full Psi powers and as a bonus keep a youthful body. Where do I sign up?

Listen; there is a downside on taking the treatment. We prefer that new applicants be married because during the change they become so horny they can hardly keep their hands off each other, especially the younger people.

Are you serious?

It doesn't affect those who are born into the organization, like me, but

Grant was after me pretty hard for the first two months.

Two months of constantly making love, how did you handle that?

Well, after a while Grant did all the work.

Okay, if I find an older man to marry, the young body carrot balances everything out. Getting a doctor may not be as hard to do as I thought.

Don't find one too much older than you. Remember, the younger people are affected more than the older ones. You don't want to kill him with sex if he can't keep up with you.

Yes Mother. It is a good thought though. I'll start looking tonight. How do I get in touch with you?

Sally handed her a card with her cell phone number and e-mail address. "Let me know if you have questions or need advice."

Jane left the office with a big smile on her face. Grant and Sally discussed what they should do next. They decided to return to Albertson Electronics and called to let them know they were returning and to make sure their office was available. They then left after giving President Ingram's secretary their contact number.

Grant and Sally checked in with President Blackman's secretary after arriving at Albertson's, who informed them the President wished to see them when they arrived. They waited a few minutes until Blackman finished a telephone call, before the secretary showed them into her office.

Sharron got up from her desk and met them, shaking their hands and then motioning toward the informal seating area. After everyone was seated, she hesitated a moment marshalling her thoughts.

"Yesterday, I was visited by an FBI Special Agent. He was checking firms in the Silicon Valley for anyone with knowledge of the whereabouts of people he had on a list. He just said it was a case of National Emergency they be reached and he left a card in case I heard anything."

Sally asked, "May I see the list?"

Sharron handed over a copy of the list of names. "Somehow I know he suspected I would know who to contact."

Grant and Sally quickly looked at the list and verified that the names were mostly those of the original members of the Group. Sally looked up at Sharron and asked, "May I have a copy of the agent's card? I think I know who to contact to get the information he wants."

Sharron handed over the card with a smile. "Keep it. I don't think I'm going to be needing it."

Grant asked, "Is there anything else we can help you with?"

"No, you two have done quite well since you've been here. Since Brightstar Electronics failed, our company's profits have substantially increased, due in large part to your efforts. I'm very glad you showed up here when you did and if you need my help don't hesitate to ask."

Grant and Sally returned to their office and sent an encoded e-mail to the Group, with the list as an attachment and the FBI Special Agent information. After finishing sending the e-mail they looked at each other, concerned, before going to the cafeteria to mentally eavesdrop on the employees.

CHAPTER 24

Rafe called a Board meeting immediately after receiving the e-mail from Grant and Sally. After everyone was seated he passed around copies of the correspondence and had them read it.

"Jane, do you know this Special Agent McAdams?"

"Yes, as I remember he was second in the SF office. This National Emergency worries me. I think we need to contact him soon."

Rafe looked at her with concern as he turned to Adam. "Adam, is there a way we can safely call from here?"

"Yes, no problem. I'll go get one of the prepaid cell phones and be right back."

Adam brought the cell phone back and Rafe pointed to Jane. "You call as he knows you and you're on the list he had."

Referring to the information on the card, Jane initiated the call. "McAdams here."

"Jock, this is Jane Patton McPherson. What can I do for you?'

"Jane! It's good you got right back to me. We have a problem that your organization can help us with. When can we meet?"

"McAdams, this is Rafe Johnson. You know we have a security problem and your agency has been known to have leaks. How much help do you need?"

"We have information that an attempt will be made to bomb the SF Mint in the near future. We need telepaths to give us an early warning."

"Are you sure that the Mint is the actual target and not just a decoy?"

"My people think its ninety percent certain. Can you help us?"

"I'll call you right back after I discuss this with my people."

Rafe looked at the Board. "Okay, what are your thoughts?"

Jane spoke. "We do have members already there; however, they aren't trained for this type of work. They will need to be accompanied by agents who will watch over them."

"Any reason we should not help? Okay, all those who want to say Nay hold up your hand."

"Motion carried with no negative votes."

Rafe then called McAdams back. "McAdams here."

"Rafe here. We have people in your area. Where is a good place to meet and when. They will need to be accompanied as they are not trained, but they do have powers for self-protection. These are our children so please take care of them."

McAdams gave Rafe the information he asked for and pledged his protection of their people. Rafe then had Adam e-mail Grant and Sally with the information they needed to meet with the FBI.

When Grant and Sally received the e-mail from Rafe they just looked at each other in astonishment. Sally then called Ralph Ingram and cleared Jane Rush's absence for the remainder of the day. She then mentally told Jane to meet them at Ingram's front security gate in twenty minutes. Later, when they picked up Jane, she asked, "What's happening?"

Sally grimaced. "We've been asked to save the world! Well, almost. The FBI wants our help to stop a bombing of the SF Mint by using our telepathic skills. How far away can you read peoples thoughts?"

"If there are not many other people, I can read thoughts a block away."

"Oh Poop! Well, you can still help. Three locations are still better than two. We need to leave now to meet our contact with the FBI."

Before they had left the parking lot at Albertson's, Grant exchanged his car's license tags with ones he had borrowed for just this type of reason. While they were driving toward their contact point, Jane looked at Sally and asked, "Oh Poop! Where were you raised?"

Sally blushed. "I was home schooled, alright? I get enough of this from Grant without hearing from you too."

Grant laughed. "I keep telling her not to use that term around our twin boys or they're going to be kidded unmercifully when they get older."

"You have twin boys? I'm jealous! I don't have a real life yet. I'm twenty-seven and still single."

"Oh poop! I need to call Janet and tell her we might be late getting home."

"Who's Janet?"

Grant replied, "Our Nanny. We can't function without her help. The boys are starting to mentally move things."

"How old are they."

"Almost two and they should be at least ten before they do that."

"Wow! I thought I had problems. I'm going to have to go through this too."

Grant drove into the parking lot of a Marriott Hotel just off I-880 and pulled into the lobby drop-off lane. Grant got out of the car and held up a paper sign that read PTO. A man hurried over and told him where to park and then they would get into another vehicle.

They were soon on the road again in the typical black Chevrolet Suburban the government uses in all the movies. They were on the road another twenty minutes before they reached their destination. When they exited their vehicle, Agent McAdams met them.

He looked at the three telepaths and asked, "Who's in charge?"

Sally answered, "That would be me. I'm the strongest telepath. Jane here is not yet a full-fledged member and has a range of only about a block. Where do you want to place us?"

"I'm going to put two agents with each of you and you just follow their lead."

McAdams wanted them to be their early warning alert so they would have time to stop them before they reached the Mint. They were looking to intercept a vehicle, as a single person couldn't carry enough explosives to do much harm. Those streets not covered by the telepaths were blocked using street repairs as the reason.

They had been in place for three hours when an armored truck approached Sally's location. She immediately knew from the thoughts of the driver this had to be it. She told the nearby agent, who passed the information on. Suddenly, a dump truck pulled out from a side street blocking the armored truck, which immediately tried to back up when another truck blocked its movement.

The armored truck remained motionless for a few minutes until it suddenly blew up with a loud explosion, scattering debris everywhere. Sally had taken shelter behind the vehicle she had been using as her surveillance point when the truck blew. She immediately dropped to the ground and put her purse over her head, while using her Psi powers to repulse objects from falling on her. When things stopped falling from the sky she got up and looked to where the armored truck had been, but it was gone with the two blocking trucks now only burning wrecks.

Sally could tell there was no way anyone could have survived inside those two trucks. They had to wait for transportation because their vehicle was too damaged to drive. After about fifteen minutes another Suburban arrived with Grant and Jane inside, which took them to where

McAdams was waiting.

He thanked them for their help and then talked to Sally aside from the others. "Tell Rafe we really thank him for sending you to help us. I don't think we could have stopped them without your help. You saved a lot of lives today."

"I wish I could have saved those two in the trucks."

"I know. But it couldn't be helped. I'll have one of my agent's take you back to your car. Thanks again for your help."

"Wait, before the truck exploded, the driver was thinking about someone named the Raptor. I hope that helps you."

"It might! Thanks again."

They were taken back to their car and then the agent departed with a wave. Sally took a device out of her purse and turned it on as she walked around their car. It beeped when she got to the left rear of the car. Grant stooped down and looked under the car, then reached under and removed an electronic tracking device. Sally made another turn around the car before she was satisfied there were no others. Grant looked around the parking area to make sure there was no one near, before putting the correct license tags back on his car. He then attached the tracking device to another similar colored car.

Grant thought to the others. *That should confuse the satellite trackers.* They then returned to Ingram Electronics so that Jane could retrieve her car. Grant and Sally thanked Jane again for her help and wished her well in her hunt for a husband before heading for home.

They pulled into their driveway at six-forty p.m., much later than they ever had before. They entered the house to find Janet cleaning up the kitchen after feeding the twins, who were watching cartoons on TV. Upon seeing their parents, they ran to greet them. After awhile they settled down and returned to watching TV, while Grant and Sally talked to Janet.

Sally apologized to her for being so late, but explained that something had come up at work that needed their attention. Janet smiled at them and winked. "That wouldn't have anything to do with that big explosion near the Mint today, would it?"

Surprised, Sally said, "Don't ask and we won't tell any lies."

Sally looked at the twins as she asked, "How were they today?"

"Oh, the boys are great and really well-mannered for their age. My own kids were never as good as these two. They've started something new today. Instead of moving objects they have graduated to moving themselves. I blame the cartoons they watch where the characters fly around."

Sally put her hand over her mouth as she muttered, "Oh my gosh!"

"Yeah, only I used stronger words."

"Honey, what can we do?"

Grant considered a moment before answering. "For them it's just another learning experience, like walking was for us. You fall and get up and try again. For them a fall is going to hurt more. Maybe if we put helmets on them we can protect their heads."

Sally shook her head at him. "I'm going to try reasoning with them."

She went into the living room were the twins were watching TV. She turned it off and taking their hands she sat on the floor and pulled them into her lap. Using her mental voice she started speaking to them.

Boys, your father and I don't want you moving yourself or other people around in the air like you were flying. You may hurt yourself or other people if you continue doing this. Do you understand me?

Alex and James looked at her intently and then nodded their heads before mentally replying. *Yes Mommy, we won't do it again.* She hugged them and gave each a kiss before saying. *That's my boy's. You can go watch TV if you want to.*

The twins got up from her lap and turned the TV back on, while Sally watched them for a few moments before joining the others. Grant hugged his wife. "How did you know they would understand your mental voice?"

"Oh Grant. We have been mentally talking at them since they were born. We just never asked them a question before."

"Did you really expect them to mentally answer you?"

"No, but I wasn't that surprised either. After all, they are progressing faster than any of the other children."

Janet interrupted. "Wow! You are all telepaths too. This is the most interesting thing I've ever experienced."

Sally smiled at her. "Well, to us it's an everyday experience. It's not new if you live it. I guess we have everything under control now, so you can take off if there's nothing else?"

Janet nodded her head and waved goodbye as she left the house. After Janet left, Grant and Sally hugged each other and kissed. Grant was still holding her as he buried his face in her hair and said softly, "I didn't know if I'd ever see you again when I heard that explosion. It was a tremendous relief when you let me know you were alright."

"I was scared too when that truck blew up. I thought at first that I was going to die."

They held each other tightly for a few more minutes, gaining strength from each other. They were not hungry, but fixed a snack and watched the boys in the other room until it was their bedtime.

Before Grant and Sally turned in for the night, Sally e-mailed Rafe reporting what had occurred at the Mint and the tracking device they discovered. The next morning they returned to Albertson Electronics to continue their observations.

CHAPTER 25

∞

Rafe read Sally's e-mail to the Board who sat without comment until he finished. "I think we can safely say our children performed quite well considering their lack of training."

He looked at Peter and Anne Stephenson. "You must be very proud of your daughter."

Anne wiped her eyes, visibly composing herself. "Sally was always a little bit of an introvert, but she certainly took charge when it counted. We did give them some training as evidenced by their looking for and finding that tracking device. The FBI may be grateful for our help, but that didn't stop them from trying to find us. We need to give all our adult non-agency background members training in how to avoid surveillance. We have six former agency members to take care of that task."

Rafe took an affirmative count of hands and the motion carried. Vera volunteered to make a list of classes after they decided on the techniques to be taught. Rafe then brought up another matter.

"Our new member Jane Rush volunteered for this mission with only her natural telepathic skills. According to Sally, Jane will make a valuable addition to the Group, especially if she achieves her goal to marry a medical doctor."

Laughter from the Board burst out at that comment. For years the Group wanted to attract a doctor and a lawyer to their Group. Rafe held up his hand for quiet as he continued. "Sally also reports that Albertson Electronics has received substantial new orders because of the computer failure at their competitor, Brightstar Electronics."

That brought smiles to faces of the Board who knew who caused that computer failure. Rafe asked for any other comments or matters relating to Board action before adjourning the meeting. Rafe and Vera met with Peter and Anne to discuss what they should teach about anti-surveillance procedures, when Jim and Jane McPherson joined them.

"That little device that Adam cooked up to detect electronic trackers and bugs has already come in handy. We need to check with him to see if he has anything else we can use," Jim said.

"Did I hear my name said in vain?"

Rafe laughed. "We were just wondering what other gadgets you have that might come in handy."

"Well, I have a software App that can be installed to computers and iPhones that automatically routes e-mails through enough destinations it would be impossible to trace. I also have a device that when turned on scrambles any bugging device in the room where it is used."

Jane spoke up, "Adam, I think Sally could use both of those items. Better safe than sorry."

Grant and Sally had been alternating weeks at the two firms the SA Group had a majority interest in for the past six months, when they received an e-mail from Jane Rush saying she wanted to talk to them. They arranged to meet at a restaurant that evening after she confided she was bringing her fiancé with her.

They arrived at the restaurant and were waiting a few minutes before Jane and her companion arrived. He was a distinguished looking man who appeared to be about twenty years older than Jane. Jane introduced everyone. After they were seated, Jane explained that Dr. William Sheldon was an M.D. practicing internal medicine, whose wife died three years ago in a car accident. He had no children because his former wife was infertile and they didn't want to adopt.

Jane placed her hand over Bill's and said, "We're madly in love with each other and want to spend the rest of our lives together. I've told Bill I'm a telepath and he says he doesn't have a problem with it, but I don't think he really understands the full meaning of a telepath."

Sally smiled at Bill and touched his hand. "Bill, let's wait until after dinner and then we'll go somewhere private to discuss something you need to know."

She could tell Bill was confused about what the big deal was, but would go along with the flow. After dinner, they decided to continue their conversation at Bill's house. Bill was a personable individual and a good conversationalist during their dinner. They were about to see how much he loved Jane.

Bill showed them into his den, asking if anyone wanted a cocktail.

Bill took orders and prepared drinks quickly. Sally then began the conversation.

"Bill, we belong to an organization of people who are long lived and have extraordinary Psi powers. Since you have expressed your love for Jane and wish to marry her, we offer you membership. You will become younger, eventually becoming the apparent age of Grant and myself after several years. You will also gain other powers, such as telepathy, telekinesis, and teleportation. Jane is a natural telepath, but has not yet been granted full membership because we currently require couples, and all our children are too young for marriage. Now is the time for questions."

"You say I'll get younger, as young as you are now! That's pretty hard to believe. Jane and I could start a family and I would live to see them graduate from college."

Bill then looked at Sally skeptically and asked, "Would you mind showing me a little telekinesis?"

Bill suddenly found himself floating in the air above the others, and then he started moving around the room until Sally put him back into his chair. "How's that? Are you convinced now?"

"Yes, but what kind of treatment is required?"

Jane got up and sat in Bill's lap and with her arms around his neck, she passionately kissed him.

"That's not the treatment is it?" He said with a laugh after getting his breath back.

Sally smiled as she shook her head. "No, but it's as simple as getting a blood transfusion. The reason we require couples is that there is a side effect of the change. About ten to fourteen days after the treatment, the change starts which lasts about two months. The people getting the treatment suffer an extreme sexual urge that limits their ability to function normally. If you desire to join our organization you should first turn your practice over to another doctor, or at the very least take a leave of absence. Jane would need to resign her position as well. Our organization has plans for both of you."

"What do you mean extreme sexual urges?"

Jane laughed. "She means we can't keep our hands off each other, me more than you because I'm younger."

Bill hugged her closer. "That doesn't sound so bad."

Grant grimaced. "After a week it's almost maddening that you can't control your urges. Sally was born into the organization and didn't need to take the treatment, so she had to put up with my urges."

Bill looked at Jane with new understanding. "Wow! I didn't realize. I guess the saying, too much of a good thing can hurt you."

Two weeks later the two couples and twin boys flew to Atlanta where they rented a car for the trip to Macon. Bill and Jane would receive their treatment and acclimation into the Organization. Grant drove into the SA Group garage after entering the code and watching the massive double steel garage doors open. Jane Rush Sheldon murmured an awed, "Wow!"

All of the adults were waiting for them in the third-floor boardroom. Rafe introduced himself and the other members. Sally's mother, Anne Hawk Stephenson, hugged her daughter tightly and kissed her cheek, welcoming her back home. She then picked up her grandchildren and mentally welcomed them home too.

The two new Group members were a little overwhelmed by their reception, but they quickly adjusted and started to find out who these people were. Rafe called for attention and told the new arrivals a brunch had been laid out in the boardroom. Everyone started around the table picking out what they liked and moving on into the work area finding a place to sit and eat, while still talking to the new arrivals.

After everyone had finished eating, Rafe and Vera took Bill and Jane upstairs to their apartment. After looking at the opulent surroundings, they were suitably impressed and expressed their delight. Rafe then gave his and Vera's history and the start of the Group. Bill was looking at the founding couple in awe and asked, "Rafe, just how old are you?"

Rafe smiled at him. "I'm 109, but feel much younger."

Jane snorted as she replied, "You look younger than me. It's almost unbelievable. Everyone here looks to be in their low twenties."

Vera nodded. "Yes, everyone who takes the treatment gets younger and so far they are free of disease. The kids have never had any sickness. We really need a doctor we can trust to do research on our new branch of humans. Follow me and I'll show you our make shift health clinic where we do our treatment."

When they got to the clinic, Dr. Sheldon found it was a cubicle on the third floor Work/Board Room/Play area. Vera explained, "We only use this area for the blood transfusion treatment and would construct whatever lab area you needed. We have already drawn donated blood and you can use it now for your treatment."

After Bill and Jane completed their transfusions, they retired to their new lodgings for rest and contemplation of their new life. Bill immediately started thinking about what he would need in equipment for the new lab. Anne Hawk Stephenson came by their apartment and informed Jane about the food storeroom and how to request items they needed that might not be currently stocked. Also, since Bill was not known to the agencies he would be included on the list of people who would shop for needed items.

"Jane, I know you were seen and probably photographed by the FBI; however, they didn't know who you were. I think we only need to put a wig on that beautiful red hair of yours to change your appearance enough that you won't be recognized. You probably have a little over a week before the change happens, so prepare now as it's not likely you will be able to do much once it starts. We found that exercise helps fight the sexual urges, but jogging in the garage is the most popular. We will try to help you during the change, such as getting you food. Any questions?"

"Can we get back to you on that, this is a little overwhelming right now."

Anne nodded her head and left them to their thoughts.

A year later brought several changes to the Group. Dr. Sheldon had established a lab in one of the vacant apartments on the fourth floor and was busy trying to discover how the blood changed the human body. Jane Sheldon was already one of the most powerful telepaths in the Group and was still not yet at her full strength. Her other Psi powers were gaining in strength as well, but appeared to be only average to others.

CHAPTER 26

Grant and Sally Gleason returned to Sunnyvale, California, with Ralph and Mary Johnson Stephenson joining them later. The Group had acquired a majority interest in Brightstar Electronics on the cheap after its problems, and now wanted to replace some of the key management positions under the supervision of the Stephensons. Later they sent Jack and Jennifer Johnson Stephenson to watch over Ingram, Inc.

Grant and Sally would now watch over only Albertson Electronics, but consult on the other two firms as needed. Rafe wanted to start expanding their reach and spreading their risk in case of an attack, giving the three families a chance to socialize and be themselves without fear of exposure. The Stephenson families had two year-old twins they needed to find day care for. Mary and Jennifer were the twin daughters of Rafe and Vera Johnson, while Jack and Ralph were twin sons of Peter and Anne Hawk Stephenson, and they asked Sally for her help in finding them a nanny.

Sally asked Janet Welford. "We have two new families who are also in the government project moving here. Do you know of anyone else who would fit as nannies for them?"

Janet considered for a moment before replying, "I could do them all until we found someone. Are they as well behaved as the boys?"

Sally smiled. "All our kids are angels. You know how parents are. These twins are both one of each sex, so you will have some girls to take care of. I don't know if that is good or not, but when we get them all together the parents can mentally tell them what is expected of them. If you keep them busy with your games, it might work out okay. My boys are about a year older than the others, so I'll ask them to instruct the new twins."

Janet nodded her head. "That may work. The play room may get crowded with six children, but we'll see."

The next morning the other families brought their children to the Gleason home. When all the children were together, each of the parents mentally told them what behavior they expected of them. *No moving people or themselves in the air, no fighting among themselves, and to obey Janet when she vocally asks you to do something. She can't hear your mental voice, so use your speaking voice to let her know your needs. Alex and James can help you if you have any questions.*

When all the parents left the house for work Janet observed the children as they interacted. At first the new arrivals stared at the Gleason twins as if they were talking mentally with each other. Then they all turned and looked expectantly at her. She thought, *now it's my turn.* Janet then started the first game, one she had played before with the boys so they could help the others get started.

When the parents returned that afternoon they were a little anxious, as this was the first day the Stephenson family's children had been under the care of a nanny, and the Gleasons were uncertain whether Janet could handle six children. When Jack and Jennifer arrived, Sally met them at the door with a smile.

"The kids are just fine and they are all taking a nap. I thought we would wait until Ralph and Mary arrived before waking them all up."

Jennifer replied, "Well, this sounds encouraging. I hope they weren't too much for Janet."

It wasn't long before Ralph and Mary arrived to find everyone else already there. Sally led the other parents upstairs where they found Janet sitting in a chair reading a book. She smiled at the others and pointed to the sleeping children lying on the floor. Before waking them she asked, "Are you ready to pick them up?"

At Sally's nod, she softly hit a small gong, which immediately awakened the children. They sat up rubbing their eyes and, on seeing their parents, the children ran to them hugging their legs. Then realizing they were getting ready to leave, the children ran back to Janet, surrounding and hugging her legs. They then left her and returned to their parents.

Janet had tears in her eyes as she said, "Goodbye, see you tomorrow."

After seeing the others out of the house, Sally turned to Janet and asked, "How was your day? I'm curious how you handled six kids."

"It helped that Alex and James were there to answer the others mental questions, but really it was not that much different than looking after just the two. They all liked to play games and I guess I wore them out, because they needed a nap in the morning and the afternoon."

"So, you're okay taking care of all six?"

"Oh yes. I'm really looking forward to three times the income too. You know, the little girls are different than the boys. The boys just start doing things by trial and error, while the girls watch the boys and learn from their mistakes. I think these girls are smarter than the boys, at least in that regard."

The Gleasons started hosting weekly covered dish dinners with the other two Group families so they could keep in close contact with each other, especially the twin brothers and sisters. They found that Janet might have been correct in her guess that the two girl children were smarter than the boys. Vera and Clara seemed to mentally communicate between each other more than the boys did.

They were at their third weekly dinner when they decided to mentally listen in on their children's thoughts while they were upstairs playing. The boys were mostly thinking about what they wanted to do, while the girls were planning their moves together. It was obvious that working together they could outdo the boys. Neither of the two younger twins could vocally speak as well, as their physical bodies were still developing.

The parents were all happy with the way Janet kept changing the games to challenge their children. Sally had suggested to Janet that she document what she was doing so her methods could be used elsewhere. When extra money was offered, Janet immediately started writing down what she was doing and the results of her efforts.

On a Saturday, the three wives and their children were shopping together while their husbands played golf. The children could walk, but the mothers had elected to use double baby strollers so they had better control of them. While at the mall, this caused more attention than they wanted when other women caught sight of three sets of twins together.

It wasn't long before they had a group of women surrounding them asking questions. Sally's sense of humor almost got them in trouble when she responded to a question with, "We are members of a twin club. You have to have twins to join."

That answer got more questions about the club's name, how can one sign up for it, and was there a website? Jennifer quickly told them. "It's a new club and only has the three members, but we may open it to other members later."

It was another thirty minutes before they could break away to continue they're shopping. Later, they had lunch together and were returning to their vehicles in the parking lot, when a van pulled up beside them and three men got out with the intention of kidnapping them. The women, using their mental powers, immediately knocked the men out. When the driver checked on the delay he was disabled as well.

The women consulted mentally on what they should do next. Sally took charge. *We load these men into the van and Mary and Jennifer will drive them to my house where we can interrogate them. I'll follow with the kids, but I need some help with the car seats.*

While the other two women removed car seats from their vehicles, Sally mentally called Grant and told him of their problems and where to meet them. They soon returned to Sally's house and pulled into the garage, shutting the door behind them. Jennifer stood watch over the would-be kidnappers while they waited on their husbands to arrive.

They kept the men inside the van for convenience, as they would probably have to move them later. The husbands soon arrived and Sally explained, "We can't make any plans until we find out who these people are and what their plans are. Okay, we women are the strongest telepaths here and we will each take one and peel through his memories. You guys watch the fourth man until we get to him."

It was soon evident this was no grand conspiracy. They were just targets of opportunity, three women with their children. They thought they were easy targets and easy money. They had made no plans beyond the snatch and grab attempt. Now, the Group had a quandary of what to do with them. They couldn't turn them over to the police, not after how they had disabled and questioned them.

Sally pulled out the card FBI Special Agent McAdams had given her and considered her options for a few minutes. She then called Rafe Johnson on the special number he had given her. When he answered she gave him the details of the problem they faced. He told her he would consult with Jane McPherson and get back to her.

Thirty minutes later, Jane called. "I've talked to Agent McAdams and you can drop the van with the four men at the same Marriott Hotel parking lot you used before. Rent a gray car using one of your fake identities and use it to pick up your people in the van, and then exchange it for another rented black or white car parked in a covered parking garage. This is to confuse satellite surveillance. Your meet time is at five p.m. today, so get cracking and good luck."

Sally told the others what the plan was and Grant and Jack knew of a parking garage they could use. Sally would drive the van to the meet at the Marriott Hotel with Jennifer along wearing a red wig, hoping to mislead observers into thinking she was Jane Rush. Grant would drive the gray car to pick them up at the hotel, reinforcing the idea they were still the original three the FBI knew about. Mary and Ralph Stephenson would remain behind to take care of the children.

Grant was to use gloves when driving the gray rental car to avoid fingerprints. Sally and Jennifer would use gloves as well and while on the trip to the hotel would try to remove any prints they might have left while in the van. They made the trip to the hotel and the pickup without any problem. When they got to the garage they parked and did a final wipe down before transferring into Jack's rental car. They then waited until another gray car left before they followed it out of the garage. Once they left the garage, they returned to the mall to abandon their rental and pick up the other two cars left behind at the kidnapping site.

When they returned to the Gleason house they all breathed a sigh of relief. Sally called Rafe and told him they had returned home and as far as they knew it went according to plan.

CHAPTER 27

Rafe called a meeting of those members with agency backgrounds. He informed them of the apparent successful mission in Silicon Valley.

"Our people, under Sally's leadership, foiled the kidnapping attempt and quickly left the scene before anyone raised the alarm. They then pulled information from their minds that confirmed it was a criminal kidnapping and not a terrorist attack. She then notified me of the attack with her conclusions and a possible remedy. She respected the chain of command and waited for us to make a decision on its conclusion. We need to use this operation in our classroom so the others in our group can learn by this example. None of our people there had agency training, yet they prevailed. The next time Sally is here we should give her special recognition."

Anne agreed with the accolades Rafe gave her daughter. "I'm very proud of Sally the way she stepped up and took charge. Maybe being raised with three brothers had something to do with it, or having parents who were former FBI Agents. In any case she has done us proud."

Adam's team continued to look for terrorist activity, but since the money pipeline had been shut down to a trickle, they spent the majority of their time on developing gadgets they could use to hide their own activity or discover if anyone was watching them. Every month they would report to the Board anything new they had developed, and a sample was placed on a table outside the Boardroom. This table was starting to get full and all members were encouraged to ask questions about their use.

* * *

Six months later at a regular meeting of the Board, Rafe suggested they consider another location for some of their members. "I think we need to further spread our risk of loss if we are attacked here. Two locations come to mind, Columbus and Augusta, Georgia. Augusta is closer to our fallback position in Savannah, and Columbus is next to Ft. Benning. We could even establish a presence in both locations. We already have six members in the Bay Area. If we relocate two couples in both Augusta and Columbus, our presence here would drop to six members, or thirty percent of our members. I don't think we want to risk any more than that in any one location. Let's talk about this some more and come up with a plan."

The Board soon gave their approval to add two new locations for their Group and authorized teams to travel to Augusta and Columbus to find suitable quarters. Mark and Jeri Stephenson went to Augusta and Dr. William and Jane Sheldon traveled to Columbus. Their instructions were to find a location that could support up to six couples and their children and was isolated from nearby neighbors. It should also be sturdy enough to withstand a light to medium attack.

Both teams were gone for almost two weeks when the team from Columbus returned. They found three locations that would fill the requirements, but one was their top pick. That location was near the main gate of Ft. Benning and was currently a small refurbished apartment building with twelve units. It was vacant because the owners had priced the units out of reach for military families. List price was $600,000, but would probably sell for $450,000.

Three days later the team from Augusta arrived. They had also brought three locations for them to consider. Their top choice was located south of the main part of the city, just off the I520 loop. This was also a small apartment building with fifteen units and was currently empty. The building had been remodeled two years before and converted to condos. The investors had gone into bankruptcy and the building was listed at $800,000, but probably could be purchased for $600,000.

Rafe called a Board meeting to discuss the possible purchase of a building in each of the two cities. The Board agreed with the top picks for each city and started asking questions about their concerns. Both buildings had basement parking and were of steel and concrete construction. The bottom floors of both buildings each had four outside doors that would have to be strengthened, and all windows covered. The garage entrance for both buildings were open and would need double steel doors added with security code access.

The Board approved the purchases with the stipulation they get the best price available. They soon had purchase contracts for both buildings, $480,000 for the Columbus building and $610,000 for the Augusta building. They hired the building contractors who had done the last refurbishing to put steel doors on all ground level exterior exits and cover all ground floor windows with steel covers. Installing double steel doors on the garage entry way was the most expensive change.

Two months later four couples, with their children, left Macon for Augusta and Columbus. The McPhersons, and Peter and Anne Hawk Stephenson moved to Columbus, while Charles and Evelyn Johnson Ellsworth and Mark and Jeri Stephenson moved to Augusta. This left Rafe and Vera Johnson, Adam and Elizabeth Johnson, and Dr. William and Jane Sheldon at the Macon address.

The families at each of the new locations soon got into a routine about where to shop and otherwise know their new location. Before they moved into the new buildings, Adam had connected them into a video network where they could teleconference from all locations, including Sally's house in Silicon Valley. Everyone felt better knowing they could still see and talk to each other.

Dr. William Sheldon was making some progress in understanding how the blood of a Group member changes the body of the recipient. He took a blood sample from both himself and his wife before their transfusion to compare how their blood changed afterwards. He noted their blood changed in several different ways over a two-year period before it stabilized. The white blood cells became more numerous and vehement, attacking any infection by outside contaminations, which explained why they didn't get sick. In addition, their DNA changed slightly in the area researchers thought might control aging. He compared his DNA with Rafe and Vera's and couldn't find any deterioration. It was anyone's guess on what his or her new life span was going to be.

Jane Sheldon was taught how to help her husband in the lab and also manned the SA Group office on a rotating basis with Elizabeth Johnson. Rose Marie was still employed as their receptionist and did most of the work. She missed Charles and Evelyn, but quickly became friends with Jane, especially when Jane told her she was expecting twins in six months.

Back in the Bay area, Sally hadn't noted anything that would indicate they were under observation. She and the other Group members used their telepathic skills at maximum every few hours each day to determine if they could read any thoughts pertaining to them, but so far their efforts were negative.

The three firms they were monitoring hadn't had any problems, except in one instance Jennifer's mental eavesdropping discovered an employee who had thoughts of doing harm to her supervisor. The employee was contemplating how to do away with her supervisor because of his continuous sexual harassment.

Jennifer sat down at the table where Joanne Bigalow was drinking coffee. Joanne looked at her in surprise and trepidation, as she knew Jennifer was a troubleshooter for the firm.

"I understand you have been having a problem with Mr. Jackson?"

"How do you know that? I haven't told anyone yet."

Jennifer smiled at Joanne. "I've got my sources. Do you want revenge or just want him to stop harassing you?"

Joanne looked into her eyes trying to judge how serious she was. Eventually, she made a decision. "I want both! However, I'll settle for stopping his harassment."

Jennifer nodded her head. "Both it is then. I'll clear you for taking the rest of the day off while I take care of him."

"I would really like to watch you take care of him, but be aware he is a big bully and wouldn't hesitate to hurt you."

"Sorry, I don't want any witnesses to what I plan. Just be grateful you won't have to deal with him again."

Jennifer talked to the human resources department and told them the problem with Jerry Jackson and asked how much trouble it was going to be to fire him? Mary Gibson snorted. "It would be easier if you can get him to quit, otherwise we have to go through a warning period, then deal with the Union."

"Okay, if he quits do we have to give him a severance package?"

"No, nada. That's the best for us."

"Okay, have him report to me in my office ASAP."

Jerry Jackson soon arrived at her office and Jennifer told him to take a seat. She sat and watched him without speaking for several minutes while she read his memories. He was starting to get nervous, as he had no idea what she wanted. His mind went back to several things he had done that she might want to accuse him of doing, including harassing Joanne and three other women.

Jennifer smiled cruelly, which immediately gave him cold shivers.

"Mr. Jackson I've been checking up on you and you have been a very bad boy. You've stolen from the firm in at least three instances, with a laptop computer being the most recent. What I dislike the most is your sexual harassment of three women you supervise. I intend to have you fired and have these charges placed in your personnel file, or you can quit and nobody will know what you did. Your choice, which do you prefer?"

"How about I beat the crap out of you or you drop the charges."

"My, you are aggressive aren't you? No, you disgust me. I think I'll just fire you for threatening me."

Jackson's face turned red with anger and he stood and was about to lunge at her when he was thrown backward against the wall. Stunned, he slowly slid to the floor. He quickly got back onto his feet, but suddenly he was thrown even harder against the wall. Jennifer then mentally picked Jackson's body up and started spinning it faster and faster, while Jackson started screaming. She then dropped him to the floor, where he lay sobbing.

He eventually got to his feet, shaking in fear.

"Are you going to quit, or do you need additional convincing?"

When he didn't respond, she caused his body to shake. Eyes wide with terror, Jackson yelled, "I quit!" Before running out of the room.

CHAPTER 28

Adam's computer program that watched for key words sent over the Internet paid off. The program sent him a message that an alarm had been tripped. He reviewed the chatter that tripped the alarm and then did a further search going back a month. The messages taken individually appeared innocent; however, when combined with other messages, it was clear a plot involving the Group was in progress and again involved the code name Raptor. So far all the messages were between addresses outside the U.S., but that didn't make Adam feel safe.

Adam mentally called for his parents to meet him in the workroom on a matter of importance. Rafe and Vera soon joined him and he showed them the messages. Rafe asked, "Did you run these through the decoding software?"

"Yes. If there's a code, they must be using a common book as the vehicle. All I can glean is they are actively looking for us, but there is no indication they know where we are."

"Okay, tonight we will teleconference everyone. E-mail them that the conference is set for eight p.m., and see if you can find the servers the messages are going through."

Rafe started the teleconference that evening by acknowledging each of the locations on a split screen and asking, "Have any of you noticed any unusual activity at your location? The reason I'm asking is that today Adam has discovered chatter outside the U.S. involving us. It appears to be in some kind of code we haven't yet cracked, but we think someone is actively searching for us. Any questions?"

Sally asked, "We have taken the usual precautions. Is there anything else you would recommend?"

Jane McPherson spoke, "I think you should start taking different routes to work or shopping and become aware of the vehicles that keep showing up in your travels. However, if there are people following you that close, you would have heard their mental voices."

James McPherson spoke, "I would recommend you periodically check your house and vehicles for bugs. Be proactive in your activities and if you're not already doing it in the Bay Area firms, check all new hires personally."

Rafe asked everyone if they had anything else to discuss before he closed the teleconference. Later, Rafe looked at the others in the Board Room. "Is there anything we can do differently to better protect ourselves here?"

Adam looked at Jane while saying, "Our main exposure is the SA Group office area. We can close the office and transfer the telephone service to another location. Rose Marie can even operate out of her home until we get a better handle on this threat. Do you think this will work?"

Jane nodded. "It should work. We can post a sign that the office is being closed for remodeling and show a telephone number where we can be reached. The hard part is going to be what we tell Rose Marie."

Adam nodded his head. "You and Elizabeth have had the closest contact with her. I've only talked to her a few times and don't have the close relationship you two have with her. I would suggest you tell her the office has had a threat made against it and we are taking these steps to ensure everyone's safety until things are resolved."

Elizabeth stuck her tongue out at her husband. "Coward! You make the women do the dirty work. Okay, we'll do it, but you owe us one."

Adam smiled. "Okay. As soon as I can get an extra line installed in Rose Marie's house we'll close the office down."

Rafe looked at the others. "Any other thoughts or comments?"

Vera cleared her throat. "Just remember when you get the alert to take shelter, that everyone drops what they are doing and immediately head toward the basement bunker."

A week later the office was closed, and Rose Marie was handling the business from her home. Jane, the strongest telepath, hadn't picked up any thoughts of a threat against them.

It was a month later that Jane got her first hit of someone thinking about them. The person was in Macon, but not anywhere close to their location. Every adult was now concentrating on trying to get any other thoughts from this source. Two hours later they all picked up someone thinking of them and the thoughts were closer. The person was apparently talking to a realtor who was driving them around the city. When they were approaching the SA Group Building, the person asked about its history as they stopped outside. Apparently satisfied with the answer the person mentally crossed this location off his list and continued on his way with the realtor.

That night Rafe teleconferenced all locations and informed them of the drive-by of someone looking for them. They didn't know anything about the individual, aside from the possibility he could be with a government agency or terrorist organization. They were reminded to keep alert and report any contacts.

They continued getting sporadic readings of someone thinking of them, but so far nothing threatening. Jane volunteered to hide her red hair under a blond wig and follow this individual until they could identify him. Although Rafe was concerned for Jane's safety, he knew she was trying to do the right thing.

"How strong are your telekinesis powers?"

"According to Adam I'm stronger than he is, but it's all relative isn't it. I just need to be strong enough to defend myself. It's up to me to not put myself in harm's way. Besides I have other powers I can use."

"Bill, how do you feel about your wife acting as our go to girl?"

Bill hugged his wife lovingly and looked into her eyes. "If she thinks she can do it I'm not going to stand in her way. But, I'll kick her ass if she gets hurt."

"Okay, go ahead and start your surveillance when you're ready."

* * *

Jane changed into her shopping clothing, donned a blond wig, and drove in the direction of the telepathic thoughts. She eventually pulled into a restaurant parking lot where she sat in her vehicle for a few minutes trying to zero in on the individual until she was sure he was in the building.

Before Jane got out of her car, she used her powers to ascertain if anyone else was nearby that might have an interest in her. She did attract the usual attention a young attractive woman would get as she entered the restaurant, but nothing more. She was shown a small table near the center of the room where she was soon able to identify her target.

Jane concentrated on two people sitting together in a booth about twenty feet from her table. At the moment they were both concentrating on their meal, which made it easy for Jane to slip into the woman's memories. The man in the booth was the woman's co-worker and they were both agents of NSA and wanted to find the Group to ask for their help on a job.

Jane quickly let Rafe know mentally of her findings and asked how she should proceed. He gave her approval to make contact and then they would play it by ear.

Jane got up from her table and approached the couple. They immediately were put on guard as she stopped at their table. Jane held her hand out to the woman and spoke.

"Hi Mary Anne. It's great to see you again. Is this Jack, the man you've been telling me about? May I sit?"

Mary Anne looked at her as if she was a cougar, but made room for her to sit. Jane smiled at the now wary couple. "Okay, what is it that you want from the Group?"

Mary Anne looked at her in dawning realization that the one she was looking for was right beside her. "We can't talk here. Where can we go without being overheard?"

Jane smiled sweetly at her as she responded, "I don't think that's possible with your NSA network, but let's go to the bar located in your Hotel."

Entering the Hotel Bar, they selected a booth away from everyone else. After drinks were ordered and they were alone, Mary Anne spoke.

"We know about your arrangement with the FBI and CIA where you share info you have gained in your quest to raid Terrorist funds. That source has pretty much dried up as they have started using other methods to fund their operations. We offer you another way to continue, maybe even as profitable."

Jane told them to wait a moment while she passed on this information. She then mentally informed the others of NSA's request. Rafe told her to inform Mary Anne that another member who was knowledgeable of the topic under discussion would soon join them, and fifteen minutes later Adam joined them at their booth.

Jane was soon lost in the complexity of their discussion, but basically the NSA had discovered that certain countries' governments, friendly to the goals of the terrorists, had indirectly been funneling funds to them. The NSA would provide bank account numbers from origination to final disbursement to the terrorists. Since the transactions involved so-called friendly governments, their hands were tied.

Adam said. "Our hands have no such restrictions, do they?"

Mary Anne handed over a memory stick. "This is the information you need and we wish you good luck. Is there some way we can reach you in the future?"

Adam handed her a card with a website address. "If you need to talk leave a number where you can be reached."

Mary Anne handed him a card with a number on it. "If I need you to call, the message will say - Andy call home."

Later, after they had returned to the SA Group Building, they recapped everything that had occurred since Jane had left to seek the person looking for them. Adam ditched the card Mary Anne had given him after writing down the number, because he feared it might have had a tracer attached to it. Adam and Jane had driven to another Hotel and each parked their vehicles in its underground parking garage to avoid satellite tracking them to their home base.

Instead, they shared a taxi ride home. They decided to abandon both vehicles the following day rather than risk satellite tracking. Someone in the Group would pick them up later from the tow truck lot and trade them for different vehicles.

Adam consulted with the in-house Group members on whether they should take on this project given them by the NSA. Rafe suggested this was no different than what they had done when they discovered this same type of information on their own. He told them they should verify that the funds did indeed go to terrorist organizations and flow through the accounts as described. Everyone agreed to proceed if the information checked out.

A week later, the Group deposited another $2.2 Billion in its accounts. This loss from the treasury of the three countries caused such uproar within their governments that changes were made, including resignations and several suspicious suicides. Rafe suggested they make large contributions to any charitable relief organizations planning on coming to the aid of these countries. Their own goal was achieved when they deprived the terrorist organizations of their funds and brought the corrupt government leaders to the attention of the world. They planned on returning all the funds they raided back to the people of those countries. Everyone returned to his or her watch status until the terrorist situation became clear.

CHAPTER 29

$$\infty\!\!\infty\!\!\infty$$

After two months the SA Group office was reopened because no further chatter was heard from anywhere in the world indicating that someone was still interested in finding them. Rose Marie arrived back at their office with a fresh bouquet of flowers and as far as she was concerned, everything was right with the world.

The Stephensons and McPhersons had gotten used to their new housing in Columbus and made sure that the apartment building's façade didn't look like a fortress. Frescoes were painted on the steel shutters covering the ground floor windows and flowerbeds were scattered around the building and sidewalk borders.

Jane Patton McPherson enjoyed taking her children out for walks in the late morning to show them the multitude of different kinds and colors of flowers. She was usually joined by Anne Stephenson to help her control the two sets of twins. The apartment building had a much larger lot and was located on a quiet side street with little traffic once everyone had left for work. They even had a small pond where different waterfowl lived.

Jane and Anne were sitting on a bench watching the children explore nearby. Jane sighed with satisfaction. "This is so much better than in Macon. Here we can actually get out of the building and enjoy the scenery and nice weather. I wonder how the others are doing in Augusta?"

Anne said, "Their building is much like ours and according to Rafe they took our lead in painting over the steel shutters on the ground floor windows. They have three sets of twins to take care of and Jeri, my daughter, says she is ready for more. They are going to have their hands full."

They both looked up as a black panel van pulled into the circular drive. Both women mentally contacted their husbands informing them of the arrival of the van. The women watched as two men got out of the van and looked around the grounds until the children's voices caught their attention.

One of the men went to the rear of the van and opened its doors. Two more men got out and started talking to each other. While they were doing this, Jane started calling her children to her and Anne was mentally informing James and Peter that they could be in danger.

Anne was trying to use her telepathic powers to find out what the men's intentions were. At this point, all four men started walking toward them. They all wore similar gray coveralls and ball caps and as they got closer they started to spread out. Jane and Anne were standing in front of the children and Anne shouted at them when they got about twenty feet away.

"Stop right there! What do you want?"

The men hardly hesitated their forward movement at Anne's call to stop. Both women used their mental powers to push them backwards about ten feet, where they landed on their backs. They quickly got back on their feet and were about to charge them again when the women knocked them out with telepathic attacks against their minds.

Their husbands, who quickly took in the situation and decided that Peter should fetch the van so they could move the bodies into the building's garage, soon joined the two women. While the men moved the attackers into the building, Jane and Anne moved the children back into their apartment. Anne then went to the garage to help the men with their captives. The van had nothing in it they could use, and only the driver had any identification - a driver's license that was possibly fraudulent.

Anne started to mentally review the driver's memories. He and the others had been assigned to find the Group and they were following a lead to Columbus. This was their first stop, having arrived today, of a possible three locations. The three possible locations were the choices they were using in the final selection. The real estate agency they used may be the source of the leak, but if that was the case, Anne wondered, why use old information.

Anne dug deeper into the driver's memory and came up with the leak coming from inside the CIA. Her target was a lower tier employee who discovered the information in a trashcan after someone inadvertently discarded it. The question now was how the CIA obtained the information.

Anne sent Rafe a coded e-mail explaining their problem. Rafe immediately replied, be prepared to move. Bill McPherson was told to e-mail the special number at the CIA and ask them to pick up the van near Ft. Benning. They soon received an e-mail from the CIA to leave the van at the main gate of Ft. Benning at four p.m. Rafe sent a message to everyone in Columbus, ordering them to return to Macon that night.

They pulled into the parking garage of the Macon Marriott Hotel at midnight, where they transferred into other vehicles for the trip to the SA Group Building. After settling the children into their old rooms, with Jacob and Linda Johnson watching over them, all the adults met in the boardroom where Rafe called the meeting to order. "The Columbus location is burned for us. The CIA and the terrorists knew of its location and we can never return."

Bill McPherson was so angry one could almost see smoke rising from the top his head. "I want to arrange a teleconference between us and senior CIA officers. It might not do any good, but I need to vent my frustrations on their apparent unprofessional behavior."

Adam spoke. "I'm pretty sure I can arrange it without them knowing where our signal is coming from."

Rafe seemed a little peeved as well as he responded. "Okay, use the special e-mail address and get the proper codes to make this happen. We don't make any further moves until we talk to them."

Rafe adjourned the meeting and left it up to Adam to take care of things, while everyone else got some sleep. After breakfast the next morning, the adults met again in the boardroom for an update from Adam.

"The teleconference is set for two p.m. Apparently heads have rolled since our message yesterday about the van full of terrorists. They say they have gleaned a little more information from them that they will share with us during the meeting. Have you all cooled down some since last night?"

Rafe looked at Bill. "Bill and I have agreed we need to establish some ground rules for our future relations with the CIA. As the former Deputy Director of the CIA, I'm going to let Bill take the lead on this. In fact, most of our members talking to them are former agents of the CIA or the FBI. This should be an interesting meeting."

Everyone was in place in the boardroom when the teleconference started. Six people were present from the CIA, and eight from the Group. Rafe held up his hand to get their attention. "I'm Rafe Johnson and to my right is Vera Sparrow-Johnson, my wife. We are both former CIA agents. To my left is James McPherson, the former Deputy Director of the CIA, and his wife Jane Patton McPherson, a former FBI agent. To their left are Peter and Anne Hawk Stephenson, both former FBI agents. To the right of my wife are our son, Adam, and his wife, Elizabeth Johnson. Who is present from your side?"

An older man held his hand up. "I'm Deputy Director Sam Patterson, to my right is Assistant D.D Clara Simpson, and Assistant D.D. Peter Cushing. To my left are Assistant D.D. James Campbell, Assistant D.D. Janie Morris, and Assistant D.D. Alice Peterson. I hardly recognize you Bill. You look like a young whippersnapper now; in fact you all look much younger than your files indicate. Rafe, for a man of your advanced age of 110, you look as young as your son."

He then grimaced. "I understand you have a bone to pick with us, so let's get to it."

Bill McPherson smiled at Patterson. "Right to the point. I always liked that in you Sam. What I don't understand is the lax security that prevails in the agency since I left. Paper left in a trashcan. How in hell could that happen? Don't you all use shredders now? Besides the lax security, why have you continued to look for us? You know we left the agency's protection because of your poor security. We felt we could operate better on our own without having to worry about leaks. Just look at our record on how well we have performed against the terrorist organizations. We struck their money supply until they had to shift to a different method. Terrorist attacks have declined substantially because of our efforts, so why do you continue to look for us and put us at risk again?"

Patterson looked at his assistants grimly. "The operation that failed so miserably was not authorized by me, but was an effort initiated by someone in Homeland Security with the help of one of my former assistants. The person in Homeland Security has also been reportedly relieved of his duties. The security failure was unfortunate and has been corrected. Do you have any questions?"

"This person in Homeland Security, how sure are you he is no longer a problem?"

"Not sure at all. That place is a mess, right hand not knowing what the left is doing. We know his name and are watching for it to turn up."

"Let us have it and we'll watch too."

"His name is J. Graham."

"Is that Joyce Graham?"

"Could be. All we had was an initial. You've had past history with her?"

"Yes, she was a weak telepath Homeland sent to us in Portland. We'll make sure she doesn't bother us again. What about the terrorists we gave to you in Columbus?"

"Based upon the information you gave us, we were able to trace their movements since they arrived in the U.S. at Jacksonville. Their mission was in two parts, determine your location and plant a bomb at Ft. Benning. We found where their explosive package was stored and took possession of it. Apparently this plot was planned by a al-Qaeda terrorist, code named Raptor."

Bill McPherson smiled at Sam. "Now comes the good part. Since your actions caused us to lose an expensive piece of real estate, we want reimbursement. I think $1 million should cover our expenses."

"Where do you want me to send it?"

"Not even an accounting? Okay, here's the bank and account number. We plan on continuing our relationship as before. We share information and you don't look for us. We continue to be patriots, but don't have a desire to be scapegoats for anyone. If you desire to contact us, you may leave a message on our website, secretagent.com."

They ended the teleconference and sat looking at one another for a few moments in silence. Rafe finally smiled. "I think that went well, don't you?"

CHAPTER 30

Rafe met with the Stephensons and McPhersons. "Do either or both of you want to stay here or move to Augusta?"

Anne asked, "We can stay here or move? Let us discuss this for the remainder of the day and we'll let you know tomorrow."

Jane nodded her head. "Yeah, I think that's a good idea. We will let you know tomorrow."

Rafe turned to Adam. "See if you can find Joyce Graham and let's see if we can make her life interesting, and see what you can learn about this Raptor terrorist."

The following day the McPherson family, former residents of Columbus, decided to move to Augusta. They had fallen in love with the smaller city lifestyle of Columbus, which Augusta promised to replicate. Peter and Anne Stephenson decided to stay in Macon, at least until they were needed elsewhere.

James and Jane McPherson, and their two sets of twins, returned to the hotel garage to pick up their car. They then drove to a used car lot where they traded for a different vehicle, before continuing on to Augusta. When they arrived at their new larger apartment building, they were pleasantly surprised it was so attractive. They mentally received the garage code and were met there by the other residents.

Jane let her children out of the car, who immediately rushed toward the two families they were going to be living with. The children they were approaching were a little older, but that didn't stop the children from having fun. The McPhersons greeted the Ellsworth and Stephenson families, who helped carry their luggage to the elevator and gather all the children for the ride up to their apartment. All three families were staying on the third floor and the apartments were similar in size and furnishings as they had in Macon.

Evelyn Johnson Ellsworth pulled Jane McPherson aside, while the others were helping Bill get settled into the apartment with the children. "What happened in Columbus that caused you all to move?"

"Terrorists showed up at the apartment building while Anne and I and the kids were enjoying a beautiful day outside. Since our location there was blown, we were told to hand over the terrorists to the CIA and return to Macon. Your father and Bill had a teleconference with the hot shots at Langley where they reamed the CIA for their lax security procedures. Bill's replacement at Langley had already cleaned house and vowed nothing like this would happen again."

"Gosh, that must have been scary when they showed up."

"I didn't get scared until afterward and then only because of the kids. You know, when we told them to get behind us they followed orders just like little troopers. Anne and I just mowed those guys down, first with a mind pushback, then when that didn't stop them we gave them a mental knockout."

"Would you go over that again with the others in case we ever have a similar problem?"

"I'm anxious to see how you all landscaped the grounds around the apartment building. The kids and I really enjoyed going outside at Columbus and I hope we can here too."

Evelyn gave her a big smile. "Oh, I think you're going to like the way we've got it fixed up. We have about two hours before the rush hour starts. Why don't we hurry outside with the kids and enjoy the fresh air."

When they got outside Jane was pleased to find a small lake similar to what they had in Columbus, and a playground set of swings and a climbing mound. Her children took one look at the swings and made a dash toward them. The adults even had park benches to sit on while watching their children. Jane sat with the others watching the children play and felt her tension melt away.

* * *

Adam found that Joyce Graham was still with Homeland Security and had even been promoted to one of the assistants to an assistant director. Adam hacked into her personnel file and retrieved the last two performance evaluations, which he changed to reflect an unsatisfactory job performance, with the last evaluation recommending termination within thirty days.

Adam then hacked into the personnel file of Joyce Graham's supervisor and changed his last two performance evaluation forms to reflect his declining and currently unsatisfactory job performance along with an observation of his continuing sexual affair with Joyce Graham, whom he supervised.

Adam thought this might take care of two bad birds with one shot. He made a note to check the Homeland Security personnel records at a later date to see if the goal had been achieved. Adam then mentally informed Rafe of the steps he had taken regarding Joyce Graham.

His computer searches for the terrorist Raptor brought little additional information. It appeared that the mysterious Raptor took pains to keep his name off the Internet, which made him harder to track.

* * *

Fifteen years later brought several changes within the Group. Numerous children had reached the age where they desired marriage with a suitable mate. Seven marriages had occurred in the last two years, all but one were within the Group. Sarah Ellsworth married Phillip Seymour, an attorney she met in Augusta. His situation was similar to that of Dr. William Sheldon, in that he was a forty-two year old widower without any children and had experience in his field.

Phillip Seymour met Sarah at a Mensa meeting and they quickly fell in love. Phillip was fascinated that Sarah was a telepath and when he met her parents, Charles and Evelyn Ellsworth, and found that they looked the same age as their daughter, he was hooked even before he learned of the rest of her abilities. He had been the Group's attorney for over a year and was happy in his work of handling the affairs of such a large organization.

The Group purchased another small apartment building in Athens to replace the one in Columbus. All locations now housed four couples and their children except for Macon, which housed five couples. The Seymours moved from Augusta to the headquarters building at Macon, so that Phillip could better handle his duties as the Group's attorney.

Rafe was satisfied with the almost even split of the Group's membership between the various locations, with the largest concentration at less than thirty percent. Rafe also decided that any additional locations would have to be outside Georgia, perhaps establishing one in NYC.

Dr. Sheldon's lab work had not brought them any further revelations, other than their oldest members had yet to exhibit any aging of their minds or bodies. Rafe as one of the two founding members was now almost 135, while Vera was over 125 years old and was pregnant. Dr. Sheldon stated that he was sure this was a new record for anyone becoming pregnant, but since she had the body of a woman in her low twenties and had already given birth to two sets of twins, he didn't expect any problems.

The Group purchased a controlling interest in another Silicon Valley electronics firm, which Randy and Linda Johnson McPherson were assigned as supervisors after their move from Augusta. Sally and Grant Gleason helped them find a house near the other Group members and gave them pointers on how they should conduct their supervision of Frazier Electronics. This firm was under a new government contract to produce bomb sniffer equipment. Randy and Linda were to check all current employees and new hires to make certain no terrorist ties or industrial spies existed.

President Sharron Blackman left a message for Grant and Sally Gleason to contact her when they arrived for work at the firm. Sally and Sharron had become close friends and due to the length of time they had known each other and their apparent relationship with the FBI, Sharron suspected they were more than they appeared. Sally and Grant appeared at the President's office and were immediately shown in.

Sharron was an attractive woman in her late forties and was now inspecting the two twenty-something looking individuals. She winked at Sally and asked, "What is your secret formula for staying so young?"

"Good genes and clean living. You look pretty good yourself for being thirty-nine."

"I wish! I've got a message for you from the FBI. They want you to contact a Special Agent Margaret Fisher at this number," she said as she passed the note to Sally.

Sally and Grant's brows furrowed and then they turned back to Sharron. "Anything else? These messages from the FBI usually mean they want our help with something and we may be gone for a few days. If you have a problem while we are gone you can contact me at this number."

Sally wrote down the information, and gave it to Sharron before they left the room. Back in their own office they called the FBI number.

"Fisher here."

"This is Sally. What can we do for you?"

"McAdams used you before on an important job and you came through big time. We have another use for your talents and want to meet so we can make arrangements. How about that hotel we met before at one p.m.?"

"Okay. We'll see you then."

Sally then called her brother, Jack Stephenson, and informed him of her call from the FBI. She asked him to call the others and put them on notice they might be needed on an FBI job. They left the firm and rented a different colored car to take to the FBI meeting. On the way to the meeting they parked their car in an enclosed garage, while continuing on in the rental.

Sally and Grant arrived two hours early and parked in the hotel parking lot. Killing some time they treated themselves to lunch at the hotel. They were seated in a booth where they could watch people arriving and departing the hotel. At noon, three black Suburban SUVs pulled up to the hotel entrance, where twelve men and women in plain clothes jumped out.

All but two immediately spread out around the hotel. These two entered the hotel and soon were at the dining room door looking around at the patrons. Sally looked their way and held up her hand to get their attention. The two quickly headed their way and sat down with them.

Sally looked at the woman. "Special Agent Margaret Fisher, I presume."

"I was looking for an older couple. You two haven't aged a bit since the last operation about twenty years ago. So that information is still correct. We need you and several more of your organization to help us catch and stop a terrorist organization from setting off a series of bombs throughout the bay area. Our Intel is sketchy. We don't know what the targets are or when they plan on doing it, except that it's soon. Do you have any ideas on how best to spread your people throughout the bay area?"

Sally thought a few moments before speaking. "Unless they are already in position, we could have people in helicopters travel over the main highways until we find someone thinking of bombs. I can get six more telepaths to use if you have the birds?"

Fisher looked at her in astonishment for a moment. "How soon can they get here?"

"I can have them gather at a place where helicopters can pick them up, just give me an hour."

An hour later eight helicopters were in the air over the main highways of the bay area. Three hours later while flying over I-280, the first hit came from somebody thinking of bombs. The FBI immediately shut down all the bay's main highways. This caused a major gridlock and three more locations of bomb thoughts. The telepaths soon had four bombers pinpointed on the highway, with highway patrol cars heading their way, and a helicopter oversight.

Suddenly, another bomb thought was detected traveling on a

secondary road toward Silicon Valley. Two helicopters soon located the vehicle carrying another bomber. When the bomber started to ram his vehicle into a highway patrol roadblock, the two Group members in helicopters caused the vehicle to leave the road and crash into a ravine, where it blew up.

Group members mentally disabled the terrorists at the other four locations before they could detonate their bombs. Another four hours went by before the highways were moving again, which were newsworthy even for the bay area.

Helicopters returned the other six Group members to where they were picked up, while Mark and Sally were returned to the hotel. Sally climbed out of her chopper and was met by Agent Fisher, who shook her hand. "You people did a great job and saved a lot of lives. You need anything, just let me know and I'll do my best to take care of it."

Sally said, "I'll hold you to it. Who knows, next time we may need your help."

Mark landed in his helicopter and after checking for bugs on their rental, they left the hotel for the garage where their car was parked. They were soon home where they called the other three couples to make sure they were okay. Satisfied, Sally e-mailed Rafe with a coded message explaining how they had helped the FBI again.

CHAPTER 31

∞

After receiving the message from Sally Gleason, Rafe wanted to call a special meeting of the Board. He asked Adam to set up a teleconference with the other locations so all members could participate. An hour later they started the meeting with all members represented.

Rafe called the meeting to order and read the e-mail message from Sally about her team's actions in helping the FBI stop the bombing attacks in the bay area.

"Due to her team's efforts only one bomb exploded, which killed only the bomber. The FBI lead agent gave her credit for saving many lives. Sally, I want you and your team members to stand while we give you the applause you all deserve."

After the applause finished, the Silicon Valley Group sat back down with red faces of embarrassment and gratitude for the approval of their families and friends. "Sally, I need you and your team to put together a written record of your actions so they can be studied by others in our organization, especially the children. We are going to issue you and your team memorial plaques for your last two actions with the FBI. These and other plaques are going to be placed on the board room wall to remind members of your heroic actions."

Rafe turned the meeting over to family members so they could talk to each other before the conference ended. Rafe asked Adam, "Have you detected anything suspicious at our safe house in Savannah?"

"No. Why do you ask?"

"I think we need to reassess the building's livability since it hasn't been used in years. I'm thinking of sending Peter and Anne Stephenson to Savannah to see what needs to be done."

The next day Peter and Anne traveled to the safe house. After arriving in Savannah, they drove around town trying to get a feel for the changes that had taken place since they had left. Savannah was still a beautiful city, but it had gotten larger and the area around their safe house was undergoing rejuvenation with warehouses being converted into residential apartments and condos.

Once they arrived, they started their inspection of all the floors. Two hours later they looked at the list of things that needed to be done. The roof had developed a leak and water damage had occurred on the top two floors. All the apartments needed to be updated with new furniture and kitchen appliances. In addition, the electrical wiring needed to be checked for problems because rats were present in abundance.

Peter and Anne contacted a roofing company to take care of the roof and then hired a local contractor to fix the water damage and to remodel the kitchens and bathrooms. They would take care of the furnishings after the construction was finished. They then had an electrician check the building's wiring for problems and hired a pest control man to take care of the rat problem.

Two days later everything was in process. The rats had gotten into the wiring and the electrician wasn't sure how big a problem it was going to be. Peter and Anne determined he was speaking the truth when they used their telepathy powers on him. The roofing company had to redo the entire roof of the building and they noted some problems with the brickwork that needed to be fixed.

Two months later they were ready for an interior decorator to start work on the interior walls and furnishings for three floors. The price tag for the repairs and renovations cost the Group almost $400,000.

At the next teleconferenced board meeting Rafe brought the matter of maintaining the Savannah building as a safe house up for a vote. Rafe wanted to use the building as a future new location. Upon discussion the Board sided with Rafe's recommendation as a future new home. The way the Group was growing it was not going to stay vacant for very long.

Alex and James Gleason married twins they had met at a Mensa meeting in the Bay area. The fact that Alex and James were also identical twins seemed to have tipped the scales in their favor. The Gleason twins were one of the first within the Group to gain their Psi powers early and were now very powerful.

* * *

After three months of dating, both twins were deeply in love with the Blake twins, Vanessa and Vicky. They had no problem telling each other apart. What endeared Vanessa and Vicky to the boys was that they always knew whom they were with, even when they tried to confuse them.

When the Gleasons were sure about the girls, they proposed to them together, but told them to wait a moment with their answer until they told them about a secret they had. Vanessa and Vicky were eager to marry the Gleasons and were inpatient to hear their little secret. They wanted to get on with their life together.

Alex and James could hear their mental confusion and together they said, "We're telepaths!"

The Blake twins looked at them in surprise, before Vicky blurted, "You mean you can read our minds?"

Alex answered, "Do you want a demonstration?"

Vanessa suddenly frowned. "That's how you always knew who we were! You sneak!"

"Now, now. How is it that you think that's worse than you trying to trick us?" Alex said.

Vicky looked at James and asked, "What am I thinking now?"

James and Alex grinned at each other before James whispered into Vicky's ear.

Vicky face turned beet red as she turned away from them in embarrassment. "Vanessa don't think anything personal because they really can read minds."

The two women walked away and started discussing this revelation and how it was going to affect them. After a few minutes they returned to confront James and Alex. Vanessa said, "That's really unfair! You know what we're going to say before it leaves our mouths and we won't have any secrets at all."

Alex said, "We really love you and we can fix it where you would have the same powers as we do. When that happens you would naturally block another telepath's attempt to read your mind."

The Blake twins were visibly relieved. Vicky said, "How are you going to do that?"

James replied, "Before we get into that we've got to know if our being telepath's makes you not willing to marry us?"

The Blake twins nodded at each other and Vicky said, "Of course we want to marry you. We love you very much and want to have your children."

Alex replied, "We need to take you to meet our parents, who will explain further. Are you willing to go now?"

They agreed and quickly drove to the Gleason home. Sally was expecting them and answered the door, ushering everyone inside and had them take seats in the living room. Alex introduced his mother and father and his identical twin sisters to their betrothed.

Vanessa looked at Grant and Sally in shock. "Why, you look as young as we do! How can that be?"

Sally smiled at the two young women. "I'm not bad looking for a woman in her forties, am I? If you marry our sons, that's another perk you'll receive. You know we are all telepaths, but we also have other powers. We can also levitate and move objects, and have a long life span. My twin daughters also have these powers and they are only sixteen. Do you have questions?"

Vanessa and Vicky sat on the couch, astonished with their mouths open for a few moments, before Vanessa spoke. "Wow! I thought this was possible only in sci-fi, but seeing is believing. How do we sign up?"

Sally said, "After you get married you'll travel to Macon, Georgia where you girls will receive a treatment."

She explained the change to the Blake twins and what their bodies would endure because of it.

"You didn't go through the change?"

"No, I was born into the Group and married Grant, like my boys are marrying you two."

The Blake women looked at their love mates, brows furrowed with concern. Vicky asked, "You're willing to put up with us during this period?"

James answered, "It's the only way we can be together. You would get older as we stay young if you don't get the treatment. Many others have done it and survived, we can too."

The twins got married, took the treatment in Macon, and later after they suffered through the change, they were assigned to the new station in Athens. The newly married twins experienced the old adage of too much of a good thing can be bad. They were slowly getting back into what they considered a normal sexual relationship.

The Blake twins were also starting to miss their family back in the Bay area and now had a full understanding the restrictions they had to live under. They used a prepaid cell phone to call home every week and their family could reach them in an emergency by calling a special number, so they stayed in touch.

CHAPTER 32

Twenty more years elapsed and the Group's membership increased to 239, plus 142 children. Phillip and Sarah Seymour opened a SA Group office in Manhattan to be closer to the financial markets. Phillip continued as the lead attorney for the Group, and now two more Group member attorneys assisted him.

Dr. William and Jane Sheldon moved the lab out of the Macon Headquarters building into one they acquired majority ownership of in Atlanta. Three M.D.'s and six technicians who are also Group members joined Dr. Sheldon in their research of the Group member's condition. Apparently, Group members would not live forever. Rafe and Vera Johnson started showing signs of aging, but at a much slower rate than normal humans. At the current rate of aging, Dr. Sheldon estimates they could live another 200 years.

Dr. Sheldon was quick to point out that the current mutated version could have a different lifespan. He wanted to give Rafe and Vera blood from a recent version to see if it would rejuvenate their bodies, but not before he did further research. Dr. Sheldon's' research was being conducted in a closed laboratory so that no contamination from an outside source would occur. In addition, periodic mind scans were done of other non-Group employees to make sure no one was trying to steal any samples.

The terrorist threat seemed to have abated, but the Group remained concerned. Federal agencies requested the Group's help four more times, all with successful outcomes. However, the Group refused to leave the country on one assignment, which caused some senior bureaucrats to have harsh words with Rafe Johnson, who informed them the Group would help with their personnel only within the continental United States and would not physically leave the U.S. on any mission. Only trained agents should do that type of duty.

The Group's Super PAC financed the successful elections of over thirty politicians in both houses of congress. Many of those men and women were in control of the committees approving funding for critical branches of government. Should a bill be introduced counterproductive to the Group's beliefs, it died quite often in committee. However, should a bill arrive in the Group's interest, it got a fast track toward a positive vote.

This behind the scenes manipulation is standard practice among politicians, but the Group's record of success garnered the attention of other special interests that traced the Super PAC's funding. Phillip Seymour, the SA Group's lead attorney, received a request for an appointment from Charles Gilbert to discuss the current political climate. Gilbert was the head of another Super PAC whose political leanings sometimes were at odds with the SA Group's.

The two met the following day in the SA Group's Manhattan office. Seymour selected his office location with care. It took over the entire fifteenth floor of a high-rise in the center of the financial district. Many of its employees were non-members of the Group, but they had been selected with care for their expertise and loyalty. They were also periodically mind-scanned to determine if any had been approached to act as spies.

Seymour stood as Gilbert was shown into his office and they shook hands in greeting. Neither had met before, so they discussed possible mutual friends and acquaintances they might have in common. Finally, Seymour asked, "How may I help you Charles?"

"There's going to be a bill coming up before the finance committee soon that I'd like to see get fast tracked. It will benefit mutual friends of ours and put a crimp in the tail of the Fowler Coalition. The purpose of the bill is to finance construction of a fast rail system along the eastern seaboard. It's planned to give service from Boston south to Charleston, and then later south to Miami."

"That's an ambitious plan. What's the price tag?"

"Boston to Charleston is estimated to cost $60 Billion, but is to be funded in $10 Billion increments."

"How are the contracts going to be awarded? You know if any kickbacks come to light, there's going to be hell to pay."

"The GSA is responsible for awarding the contracts, but kickbacks generally occur between who gets the contract and the subcontractors, and that's going to be difficult to monitor."

Seymour nodded. "I agree, but let's put some language in the bill that places severe penalties on the contractor if they are caught receiving bribes. If this passes I'm going to put my own watch dogs on them."

"So you agree to push for a fast track?"

"Yes, if you put the penalty clause in it."

"What penalty do you want?"

"How about the amount of the bribe plus one million dollars for each infraction?"

Gilbert smiled as he replied, "Done! I think we can get this bill through."

They shook hands before Gilbert left, and Phillip returned to his desk and sent a coded e-mail to Rafe, explaining the agreement made with Charles Gilbert and his Super PAC. Based upon Phillip's mind scan of Gilbert, Rafe was sure that Gilbert was honest in his representations of the bill.

Rafe e-mailed him back and asked if it was possible to add a clause to the penalty that would offer a ten percent reward to any person who paid a kickback if they would offer proof of the transaction. It would be a powerful incentive for any contractor not to accept a bribe. Seymour passed this information on to Gilbert, who responded positively.

Denver was another new station for the Group, which gave them a Midwest location. Denver had become an important exporter of space technology, of which the Group had become a large investor. Corporate money was driving space technology and exploration when the government could no longer politically justify the cost.

SA Group had majority ownership in two such businesses, Star Bright Venture and Star Explorations. Star Bright constructed vehicles that catapulted man into space, and Star Explorations designed and constructed space vehicles to leave Earth orbit to explore the Solar System.

Star Bright now had two reusable test vehicles that could fly from the ground to Earth orbit carrying a payload to construct a Space Explorations station that would eventually build space vehicles. In order to meet their desired time frame, they needed at least ten more vehicles to carry materials to space. Star bright was also making vehicles for commercial use and had an initial order to build twenty such vehicles to shuttle tourists and others around the world in a short amount of time.

The factory to construct these orbital vehicles was located in Wichita, Kansas where aircraft manufacturing had been done almost since flight developed. In addition, the flat land was excellent for long runways for takeoffs and landings, which made it perfect for a staging area to fly materials to Earth Orbit. Wichita became a boomtown again and people were flocking to where the jobs were.

Space Explorations moved their headquarters to the area to be closer to the action and Rafe also opened a new station for the Group with three couples and their children. He needed Group people there in various capacities to ensure there were no terrorist threats or industrial spying. Rafe envisioned that Group members would eventually leave Earth and follow mankind when it left to seek other planets to colonize.

CHAPTER 33

Rafe Johnson decided to take Vera on a vacation, away from the stress of supervising the operation of the SA Group. Rafe thought back to when the two of them first met in Springfield, Missouri more than fifty-five years ago. Who would have thought they would be the catalyst for a movement the Group has become. The SA Group now had over 380 members with assets exceeding $205 Billion.

The Group's influence was felt in both business and politics, and the general public had no idea of its existence. The U. S. Government had a good working knowledge of what the SA Group was, but most of the other world governments had only rumors and spotty intelligence of the Group. For their safety Rafe made certain that none of their members ever left the continental United States.

The SA Group members also had to keep moving around to avoid their contacts noticing they never aged. Now that their numbers had increased, it was easier to move members around about every ten years. Most of the people Rafe and Vera knew at the beginning of this odyssey were now retired or dead. Rafe's first family decedents thought he had died, but all six of his and Vera's children and twenty grandchildren were Group members.

The Johnsons now lay on a Florida beach enjoying the winter sun on their youthful bodies. They felt a duty to keep their bodies strong and jogged every day to stay in shape. Vera had agreed to the Florida vacation, despite her dislike of sand, because she felt Rafe needed this break. They were so much in love that neither one of them noticed the admiring stares from members of the opposite sex.

Rafe and Vera were staying at a nice beach hotel in Miami and on their third night decided to explore the nightlife. Walking along a crowded sidewalk, trying to decide on which restaurant to use, they detected they were being followed. It didn't feel like they were in imminent danger so they picked a restaurant that appealed to both of them and ignored the mental images.

After being seated they noted that a young couple soon entered and were seated near them. From their mind scan it was apparent they were the ones who were following them. Rafe soon knew what the attraction was for the two. The young woman was sure she recognized Rafe from a family photo and was trying to work up the nerve to ask if she and Rafe were related.

Feeling sorry for the girl, Rafe approached their table. He looked down at the woman and asked, "I'm sorry, do we know each other?"

The woman blushed and then pulled a picture out of her purse and showed it to him. "My name is Alice Roberts and this my husband, John. You look just like this picture of my great grandfather when he was my age. His name was Rafe Johnson and our family lost contact with him many years ago, but heard that he died."

"Why not join me and my wife, Vera, for dinner and we'll discuss this picture?"

The couple looked at each other a moment before agreeing and then moved to Rafe's table. Rafe looked at the picture a moment before asking, "Who is your grandfather?"

"Peter Johnson."

"Alice, are Peter and Jerry still alive?"

Alice's stuttered, "How did you know about Jerry?"

Rafe smiled reassuring and pulled out his driver's license. "Because I'm Rafe Johnson, the great-grandson of the man in the picture."

"Oh! This is really something. We're related. Both Peter and Jerry are still alive, but are not well and are in a nursing home. The only reason I had the picture was because I was tracing my family tree. Can I get some family history from you to complete this branch of the family?"

Rafe agreed and gave her false names and dates that supported the time Rafe disappeared. They ordered dinner and Rafe caught up on his family through Alice. After dinner, Rafe and Vera returned to their hotel, Vera chiding him for telling such whoppers to the earnest young couple.

"Well, it made her happy and it explained the photo of me. I even got to hear news of my family, so everyone is a winner. I'm thinking of paying my sons a visit before it's too late."

Alice visited her grandfather and great uncle in the nursing home a few days later and presented them with a new branch of the family tree with their father, Rafe Johnson. Reading it they looked at each other in surprise, before Jerry asked, "You say this man who looks like our father is married to a woman named Vera?"

Alice nodded her head. "Yes. She looked like she was an American Indian and was really pretty."

The brothers smiled at each other, as they were sure that was their father who Alice met. After Alice left they discussed their father's appearance. Jerry suddenly blurted out, "When we attended Rafe and Vera's wedding it was obvious something physically was happening to them that they couldn't explain, and they are even younger now. That meeting with Alice was pure Rafe. You know how his mind works. He didn't want Alice involved, so he came up with that plausible story she accepted, hook, line, and sinker."

Their train of thought was interrupted when Rafe appeared out of nowhere. "Alice is a smart girl, but she hasn't been exposed to the world like we have. How are you two?"

Jerry and Peter looked at Rafe and Vera in surprise as they entered the room. Jerry smiled and greeted them. "Well, if it isn't our long lost father and Vera. You both look to be about twenty-two and in excellent health for people over 100 years old."

Rafe smiled at them and pulled Vera to his side. "You should know that you have four half-sisters and two half-brothers since we last met. These new bodies have allowed me to raise a new family. I was wondering if you might want to join us in being young again?"

Surprised, the brothers sat up straight. Peter said, "You're serious, you can do that?"

"Yes, but it has a downside. You will have to cut yourself loose from your family and have no contact after you start changing."

"We were going to die soon anyway, so we'll leave word we're taking a bucket list trip before dying. Let's do this before it's too late."

Two hours later they all were flying from Miami to Macon on a chartered jet. Adam met them at the General Aviation Terminal in a rented Suburban, driving them to the SA Group Building. Once inside the clinic, they were immediately given the treatment and shown their new apartment.

The brothers were still in their wheelchairs as they looked outside at the Macon skyline. Jerry lightly punched Peter's shoulder. "Well, this is quite a turn of events. Yesterday I was wondering how many days I had left and now I'm considering how many years I have before me. Rafe, just how long can I expect to live?"

"Assuming the treatment works for you, and it hasn't failed yet, you will live anywhere from two to four hundred more years. Everyone is a little different, but the doctors are working to try to get a more definite time line."

"You two are a little older than Vera and I were when we got our start, and you were given a more advanced mutated blood treatment, so we all are going to watch how it's going to affect your bodies."

"Peter, it's been too long for either of us to fit back into our old jobs. We old dogs are going to have to learn new tricks to fit our new bodies."

Rafe chuckled. "We'll bring you up to speed on what the SA Group is and what our goals are. The reason we need to keep a low profile is that we have powerful enemies and friends that want to be too friendly. After you go through the change in about two weeks, we will help you learn to use your new Psi powers safely."

Peter blurted out, "Psi powers! You mean like reading minds?"

"Yes, but each person develops their powers at a different rate and strength. You should develop telepathy, telekinesis, and teleportation powers, but each will probably be at a different level of strength. Adam is a strong telepath, but his other powers are weaker. It's rare to have strong abilities in all three powers. Another benefit of the treatment is that you become smarter. All Group members have genus IQs."

Rafe could tell the brothers were intrigued. Adam started telling his half-brothers about their other siblings and where they were located. He also explained how the apartment housekeeping worked and where everything in the building was located. He explained that one of the members would be with them until they began to feel better.

Both brothers were able to walk again and felt much better within a week of the treatment. They were left alone now except for check-ins every four to six hours. They ate all their meals with Rafe and Vera, exchanging family information and gossip. Ten days after the treatment they both started the change.

Rafe and Vera took them to the garage and introduced them to jogging. Physically, they were still in bad shape, so they slowly jogged two circuits, walked one, and then jogged two more. They used this routine until they were able to complete ten complete jogging circuits before gradually increasing the circuits until they could do twenty, and finally were able to stay with Rafe and Vera for three miles.

After finishing their first three-mile run, the brothers looked at each other with satisfaction. They were now in better shape than when they were in there fifties, and they were even starting to look younger.

CHAPTER 34

One year later, Jerry and Peter Johnson were still living together in the SA Group Building. Their apparent age was in the mid-fifties and they were now the public face representing the computer security business of SA Group. Adam was only a thought away in case a customer's question needed his expertise. The brothers were also taking computer courses relating to finance and computer security. They very much wanted to contribute to the Group in a positive way for their new lease of life.

The brothers continued their close relationship with their father, and during an evening meal with Rafe and Vera, Jerry brought up something that had been in their thoughts.

"Dad, we're lonely and want to meet someone we can share this new life with. How would you recommend we proceed?"

Rafe and Vera smiled in understanding. "You want a wife, not just a girlfriend?"

"Yes. We're too old for the single women here in the building. We want to meet women of our own apparent age, and if they are willing, join us in the Group."

"Others have met their future mate at Mensa meetings. You need to be tested and then join the local chapter of Mensa."

Vera retrieved some papers from a desk drawer and passed it across the table, saying, "These are instructions on how to get tested and the address of the local Mensa office. Don't worry about the test, as you should test high. You were smart even before the change."

Two months later Jerry and Peter were members of Mensa and were on their way to their first dinner meeting. They entered the meeting room forty minutes prior to dinner and started mingling with the other members. They approached a group of four women who appeared to be about their apparent age and introduced themselves as new members.

The brothers' telepathy powers were helpful in selecting two women who immediately showed interest in them, each selected one they preferred, easing the woman away from the others so they could speak privately. After dinner, the two couples continued talking at the hotel coffee shop.

The courtship continued for two months with Jerry dating June Carter and Peter dating Patty Walker. The women were close friends from their college days and were divorced without any children. They were double-dating the night Jerry and Peter thought the time was right to pop the question. They had finished eating a late dinner after attending a movie and the two couples were sitting in a booth without anyone else nearby.

Placing a ring box in front of their respective girlfriend, they asked together, "Will you marry me?"

To say June and Patty were surprised would be an understatement. Each looked at the ring before them and then at the man who had just proposed. They were in love with their boyfriends, but didn't fully realize the feeling was reciprocated.

June said, "I love you Jerry, but we have only known each other for a few months. Are you sure you know me well enough for marriage?"

Patty held Peter's hand and asked the same question. The brothers mentally came to a decision they needed to tell them one of their secrets. Jerry nervously cleared his throat before speaking.

"We are both telepaths and know you better than if we lived together for years."

The women looked at them in silence for a moment. June then nodded her head. "So that's how you knew what kind of flowers I liked and didn't want you giving me candy, and most of all how I wanted to be made love to."

Patty was still holding Peter's hand, when she suddenly squeezed it hard. "That's not fair! You knew every thought we had about you, every fantasy we dreamed up. It's just not fair."

Peter gave her hand a gentle squeeze. "All's fair in love and war. It's because I know you so well is why I want to marry you."

"That goes for me too. We wanted to come clean about this before you gave us your answer about marrying us. Please don't be too mad, because we do love you."

The women looked at each other and smiled before picking up the rings and trying them on for size. June looked at Patty wistfully. "We had to fall in love with brothers."

Jerry said, "Before you give us your final answer we need you to meet our father and stepmother tonight. It shouldn't take long and it really is interesting."

The women agreed and they were soon on their way to the SA Group Building. The brothers mentally prepared Rafe and Vera that they were on their way with their prospective wives. June and Patty had driven past the SA Group Building many times, but had never given it much thought until that moment as they drove into the garage. When they reached Rafe's door, the brothers took a deep breath before knocking.

Vera invited them inside where Rafe soon joined them. After introductions were made they all sat down together. June and Patty were in a state of shock meeting their boyfriend's parents who appeared to be younger than themselves.

Rafe chuckled. "I see the boys haven't told you everything yet by your expressions. We are long lived and are much older than we appear. Jerry and Peter are my sons from a previous marriage. I met Vera later after my first wife died. I was 74 and she was 68 when we married, but we appeared to be in our thirties. We eventually stabilized at our now apparent age. Jerry and Peter are also older than they appear and are still getting younger. If you decide to marry my boys you will also receive the treatment and age the same together."

Rafe then described the good and bad aspects of becoming a member of the Group including the body's reaction to taking the treatment. "In addition, government agencies desire control of the Group and make use of its abilities. We have helped them in the past, but on our terms and we keep our locations a secret from everyone. Any questions?"

June asked, "What if we decide not to marry these guys?"

Rafe said, "I know you don't mean that, so what is your real problem?"

"Damn. I can't hide anything from a telepath can I?"

"When you go through the change and receive your powers, you can keep others from reading your memories. The Group generally does not read other members' thoughts as we consider that a breach of personal privacy. We do communicate with each other over distances using telepathy."

June and Patty nodded their acceptance. June held up her hands and said, "Uncle, where do we sign up?"

Rafe smiled. "Welcome aboard. When you get married do you have anyone in your family or friends you want to invite? Remember after the treatment you are going to have to sever all ties because of the changes in your bodies' appearance."

"Can we gradually sever the ties? Just how fast are these changes?" Patty asked.

"After the treatment your change will start within two weeks and lasts about two months. If you sever the ties within six months of the change no one should notice; however, everyone is a little different."

The women wanted a church wedding and, as soon as it could be arranged, they had a double wedding followed by their treatment that evening. The women had already moved their clothing and a few personal items into their respective apartments, which they loved. Everything else they placed in storage and listed their houses on the market.

Two weeks later, the two married couples were jogging together in the garage. June and Patty were no strangers to jogging, but were hard pressed to keep up with their husbands. When they complained about the pace, Jerry and Peter slowed down and apologized to their wives.

Later, after returning to their apartments the women told their husbands that the run did help their sexual cravings, but not enough to keep them from wanting the real thing. Eventually, the cravings subsided and they were able to function normally again after almost two months. June and Patty wanted to contribute to the Group as well and offered their services wherever they were needed.

CHAPTER 35

Rafe and Vera received a coded e-mail from Dr. Sheldon to come to their Lab in Atlanta at their earliest convenience as he had something of importance to discuss with them. The next day they met and from the expression of glee on Dr. Sheldon face, they assumed he had good news.

"The most recent version of mutated genes from the blood of one of our children shows a greater reaction in the aging sector. I believe if you take another treatment with this blood, you have an eighty percent chance of at least delaying the aging process."

Rafe and Vera mentally asked each other if they wanted to risk the procedure. Rafe asked Dr. Sheldon, "What do the tests indicate about the odds of a bad reaction?"

"Less than one percent chance you would be worse off."

"Alright, but I want to be the test subject. Vera can wait until we see how it affects me."

"Bull crappy! If something happens to you I don't want to go on without you."

Seeing how distressed Vera was, Rafe took her into his arms, holding her tightly. "Alright, we do it together. When do you want to do this Bill?"

"How about now? Everything is ready and you won't need to take very much blood. Tests indicate you need only a quarter pint each."

After the treatment, Dr. Sheldon and his wife, Jane, watched over Rafe and Vera, monitoring their vitals. Ten minutes after the treatment Rafe and Vera's heart rates and respiration increased moderately before returning to normal levels a half hour later. Both subjects suddenly experienced a hot flash followed by extreme thirst as their core temperature started to rise, but stabilized at 101 degrees for two hours before returning to normal.

Rafe asked Bill, "Is this normal? Has anyone else had these reactions?"

"No! This is all new for me too. Both of you are experiencing changes to your body that no one else has ever reported. I'm excited about what else is happening we can't see yet."

Rafe and Vera's reactions seemed to stabilize and they napped for two hours where they dreamed of flying high above a city they recognized as Washington, D.C. Jane woke them up with a surprised shout, and they fell back onto their bed.

Jane was still looking at them with a surprised expression when Dr. Sheldon hurried into the room. He asked, "Jane, what happened?"

"They were both floating above their beds sound asleep, when I came to check on them because of the strange brain patterns they were producing."

Dr. Sheldon asked Rafe and Vera, "Do you remember anything about the experience?"

Confused, Rafe said, "Vera and I were flying above D.C. when we were awakened."

Vera excitedly said, "I remember that too."

Dr. Sheldon tried to calm them down as he asked, "What do you mean flying, like a bird or in an aircraft?"

Rafe and Vera chimed in together, "Like a bird."

"Prognostication! I think you both were experiencing something that is going to happen in the future. You already had the ability to fly, but maybe not to that extent. Do you remember anything else?"

They shook their heads, and then Rafe said, "I got the impression we were on a mission, but what eludes me."

Dr. Sheldon asked, "How do you both feel?"

They both stated they felt fine, but Vera said she needed to go pee. Jane unhooked her and escorted her to and from the toilet.

Bill said, "I want you to stay here overnight so I can monitor you and if everything looks okay in the morning I'll release you."

Vera asked, "Whose blood did we use?"

"Two of your Grandson James' kids. Jessie and Katie were ten when I took my first test sample and twelve when I took a half pint each for my use here. It looks like I need to place them on a special watch as they may already be having prognostication episodes."

"I'll talk to James myself when we get back to Macon. He and

Melissa need to be looking for this and any other special powers they may have."

The following morning Dr. Sheldon released them because nothing else of interest occurred during the night. Their grandson James and his family were living in Macon, so Rafe and Vera dropped by their apartment soon after they returned to the SA Group Building.

Melissa answered the door and invited them inside. When asked about James, she replied, "Oh, he's out grocery shopping with three others while I look after the kids. What's up?"

Rafe asked, "Are Jessie and Katie at home?"

"No, they are studying with the others on the fourth floor."

"When do you expect James back?"

"Anytime, but now you have peaked my interest. What's going on that includes Jessie and Katie?"

Vera touched Melissa's shoulder, "We just planned on telling you together and not with the kids present. We just got back from the Atlanta Lab where we received another treatment using your kids' blood. We both got unusual reactions shortly after the treatment, which included what we think was a prognostication episode. Have they mentioned any unusual dreams to you?"

James interrupted their discussion as he entered the apartment carrying a box of groceries. When seeing his grandparents, he set down the box and came over and greeted them. He then noticed that Melissa had a strange expression on her face and asked, "What's the problem?"

Melissa answered, "Rafe and Vera just told me they just came back from Atlanta after taking a treatment using Jessie and Katie's blood and they think our kids may have the ability to see the future."

"What! Let's go through this again and let me catch up."

Vera repeated what she told Melissa, and then again asked, "Have they told you of any unusual dreams?"

Melissa blushed. "Oh my gosh. They both have had this recurring dream about being in Washington, D.C. and seeing a Presidential motorcade when you two suddenly appear out of the sky and stopped a bomb from killing everyone. I just thought it was their imagination, but now I realize with them both having the same dream that reoccurs at least once every two or three nights, that I should take notice."

"Did they have any clue as to when this was supposed to happen?" Rafe asked.

"You will have to ask them. I can mentally call them home?"

Rafe nodded, "Do it."

Jessie and Katie soon arrived in the apartment asking what the problem was, when they realized that Rafe and Vera were present.

Rafe said, "I want you to pay close attention to what I'm going to say. Vera and I have had a similar dream that you've been having. We believe it's a new ability to be able to see into the future. Do you have any clues as to when this is going to occur?"

The two girls looked at their great grandparents in awe and said, "Wow!"

Katie then muttered, "Let us think a minute. We saw this happen almost ten times. I remember seeing cherry blossoms and the president's car was closed, not open."

Jessie excitedly said, "And it was sunny, hardly a cloud in the sky when you two dropped down in front of the cars, causing them to stop. Then grandfather did something to a police car causing it to move away from everyone else where it seemed to implode. I didn't know you could do that grandfather."

Rafe hugged her. "Me either, but I must be able to since you saw me do it. Vera and I saw ourselves flying above Washington, but we woke up before we saw anything else."

"Wow, you can see things too!"

"Not until we took another treatment using your blood. You girls have some powerful genes and we're going to pay close attention to your dreams in the future. Who knows, we might see each other in our future dreams."

The girls hugged Rafe and Vera tightly. "We're glad we can help," they said in unison.

Before they left the apartment, Rafe told James and Melissa there would be a board meeting that evening. He then mentally told Adam to schedule a teleconference for all members at 7:00 p.m. Rafe and Vera tried to determine the time this event was to occur based upon the clues they had. Rafe wanted it clear in his own mind before the meeting.

By the time the meeting started everyone in the building knew of Jessie and Katie's dreams of the future. Rafe started the teleconference with the revelation, "Vera and I took another treatment using Jessie and Katie Johnson's blood and discovered later the girls appeared to have the ability to foresee the future. The four of us all shared the same dream where Vera and I stopped a bomb attack against the nation's President."

Rafe then related the clues they had of the date of the attack. Since it appeared to happen in early spring, they had at least ten months to prepare. He wanted everyone to think about the clues and then advise him immediately if they have a theory of the date and their reasons.

After the meeting Rafe told Adam he thought the date was next year because of the frequency of the dreams. He asked Adam to arrange a teleconference between himself and Vera, with the heads of the FBI and the CIA. He didn't know anyone with the Secret Service and doubted they would take him seriously unless he had the backing of the other two agencies.

It took a while to arrange the meeting, but finally everyone got together at six p.m. the next day. When the meeting started, Rafe apologized, "What I'm going to tell you is without any proof. It is only my word that it is true. Two of our young members have developed the ability to dream of events in the future. They are twin sisters who related these dreams to their mother who thought they were just dreams. Vera and I recently underwent a treatment that involved DNA from these sisters. Shortly after, we both had the same dream the girls experienced. The dreams involved a bomb attack on a presidential motorcade in Washington, D.C. during the time the cherry trees were in bloom. It happened on a clear day with few clouds and Vera and I flew down and stopped the bomber from killing anyone. It does sound a little crazy, but I thought you needed to know."

There was silence from the two agencies, until FBI Deputy Director Ferguson spoke. "This is a new ability your Group has achieved?"

"Yes, and we don't have a handle on how accurate it's going to be. But, based on the frequency of the girls' dreams and the fact it agrees with our dream, we felt you should be aware of the possibility this might happen. In the dream, we were flying down, stopping the cars, and then moving a police car away from the others before it seemed to implode as if it was smothered. I should tell you that unless I develop these powers in the future, I couldn't do that."

FBI DD Ferguson nodded his head. "Okay, thanks for the head's up and we'll pass this on to the Secret Service, but I don't think they'll do anything unless you can give us more information."

After the conference Rafe looked at Vera and said, "At least they didn't laugh at me."

"You did your duty and you really didn't expect more did you?"

"No. Maybe we'll get more information in our future dreams."

CHAPTER 36

⬤⬤⬤

During the next two weeks Rafe and Vera didn't experience any additional Psi abilities, nor did they have any prognostication dreams. They began to think it was going to take more time for their bodies to adapt to the changes taking place. Rafe and Vera had just gotten out of bed on the eighteenth morning of their treatment, when they heard Evelyn thinking of them.

They immediately attempted to mentally speak to her and she replied, *Mom, Dad are you here in Augusta?*

Vera replied, *No, we heard you from Macon. Nobody has ever used telepathy this far before, why you're over 100 miles away!*

Your mental voice is strong too. It must be the treatment you took, have you noticed any improvements in your other abilities?

No, but we haven't really checked before. We'll talk to you later, bye.

Rafe then telepathically checked with other member locations within Georgia who could mentally converse with him. He then tried New York, Denver, and Wichita without any problem. Rafe asked, "Do I dare try calling Sally in California?"

Rafe is that you? I didn't know you were out here.

Sally, I'm still in Macon and apparently Vera and I can reach anyone inside the United States. I've already contacted all our other locations and was just thinking of trying to reach you when you replied. It must be the new treatment we took.

Well, I want the treatment too. Just think of the advantages of being able to reach our members wherever they are.

I agree, but there might be some bad side effects we don't know about yet. I guess Vera and I are the test subjects until we know what we have here. Talk to you later.

Vera hugged Rafe. "Well, that certainly was a surprise. I wonder if we have any limitations on our range now?"

"We won't know until we have members in other countries or in outer space. Let's try our other powers and see if we have other surprises."

After breakfast, they mentally called Adam and asked if he was free that morning? When he heard what they wanted to do he agreed to meet them in the garage. Adam drove them out into the country away from any major roads or houses. When he thought they were isolated enough they left the car and he prepared to test Rafe and Vera's abilities.

Rafe had been able to levitate himself before, but now he tried to fly. He slowly rose above the ground and then started moving in a circle around them, going faster and wider around them as he gained confidence. Finally he shot away from them going faster and higher until he was out sight, then suddenly he was right before them again as he landed on his feet.

"Wow, that was fun!" Rafe was exhilarated. "I first used telekinesis to fly and then teleportation to return. Your turn Vera."

Vera began to slowly levitate and then copied Rafe's flight and sudden return. "That was fun! Adam when you get this treatment you have to do that."

Rafe spoke, "Jessie and Katie said they saw us drop out of the sky and stop the motorcade. How did we stop the cars?"

Vera considered. "We must have used a strong push back, but not too strong or it would harm the cars and their occupants. What can we practice on?"

"Maybe if we picture a bubble around each car and quickly slow their movement until they have stopped?"

Adam said, "I'll drive toward you and you can practice on stopping me."

After several practice runs with Rafe and Vera both stopping the car, they thought they had the right idea. They thought they would have to start the maneuver while they were above the motorcade in order to reach all the vehicles at once. Now, what could they use to smother the explosion in the police car?

Adam suggested, "Why not use the bubble idea, only bring it down tightly around the vehicle as you are moving it away from the motorcade."

Vera hugged her son. "I knew you were a genus, now you just proved it." She kissed his cheek.

Rafe considered a moment before speaking. "What's going to keep the Secret Service from shooting us when we release them from the bubble?"

Vera chuckled. "Rafe! Think about it, we just teleport back home. They may not even know we were there."

"That's wishful thinking isn't it? Even if they don't see us, they know about our warning about the bomb attempt. But you're right it does take us out of the line of fire."

After they returned to Macon, Rafe asked Adam to monitor anything regarding Raptor, bomb, or presidential motorcade. Maybe they would get lucky. Vera checked in with James and Melissa and asked if the girls were still having the same dreams? Melissa indicated they were still getting the same dreams and nothing new had been observed.

* * *

Ten months later, Washington's cherry trees were in full bloom. Adam hadn't been able to detect any terrorist activity regarding a bomb attack. Jessie and Katie's dreams still occurred, but no new information was noted. However, the news services reported that the next day the President was going to escort the Israeli Prime Minister from Reagan National Airport to the White House, where he would sign a new treaty with the Palestines over a joint homeland with Israel.

When Rafe saw the news report he said, "Bingo! I bet this is it."

Vera agreed, "We don't know the time or the exact place of the attack. We can't just hang around in the air hoping we get there in time."

Rising from his easy chair, Rafe said, "Let's go see Jessie and Katie."

Melissa let them inside and said the girls were eating breakfast. Rafe and Vera took a chair and sat down at the table with the kids. Rafe asked what they were having?

By now Jessie and Katie were used to seeing their great grandparents, but their two younger siblings were almost in shock when Rafe and Vera sat down with them. Rafe and Vera were the group's founders and had almost godlike fascination for the youngsters because of their relationship.

Katie grinned at Rafe. "We're having toaster waffles grandpa, and they're good too."

Melissa hurried to fix the new arrivals a serving, while the younger siblings watched them with their mouths open, fascinated.

Rafe asked Katie, "Can you tell me what is near the motorcade before we arrive out of the sky?"

Jessie and Katie mentally compared their memories. "They had just went over a bridge and passed a big white square building. I think it was the Lincoln Memorial, and that's when you showed up with the sun behind you."

"How high was the sun?"

The girls conferred a moment before Katie replied, "It was almost half way up."

Rafe said, "That's great. Do you remember anything else or has the dream changed any?"

They conferred again and shook their heads. "No, nothing new."

Melissa placed a plate of waffles in front of Rafe and Vera, whereupon Rafe said, "Let's eat, I'm hungry."

Melissa introduced her two youngest children to Rafe and Vera, who didn't react until Rafe spoke to them mentally, *You have really smart sisters and I bet you grow up to be just as smart.*

The two young twins grinned at him and then returned to their food. Rafe winked at the older siblings and they smiled back at him. Rafe and Vera stayed an hour with them before leaving and returning to their own apartment where they planned their movements for the next day.

Rafe mentally called for Adam to join them for a planning session. He and Vera brought Adam up to speed on what they had learned that morning from Jessie and Katie. They were sure the attack against the President would take place tomorrow morning around ten o'clock between the Lincoln Memorial and the White House, probably not far from the Memorial. They needed to decide where they could teleport in that area so they could watch for the motorcade without causing attention to themselves.

Adam brought with him a map of the District of Columbia and spread it on the table. Tomorrow was a weekday with the rush hour over by ten. They needed somewhere high so they could see the approaching motorcade. The problem was they needed somewhere they had been before to be able to teleport there. They could teleport to the Iwo Jima Monument and walk to an overview of the highway, or teleport to the Kennedy Center.

They knew they needed to be at one of the two choices early enough to avoid tourists. All the other options were too busy, with people moving around. Adam suggested that during the morning rush hour there would be fewer tourists to worry about, so they decided on seven o'clock at the Kennedy Center.

The next morning, Rafe and Vera woke up early, ate breakfast, donned warm clothing for their wait at the Kennedy Center, and at seven they teleported to their destination. It was a beautiful sunny day in Washington, just as the girls dreamed. The cherry trees were in full bloom, and they walked beside the Center until they found a bench that overlooked the north bridge across the Potomac River.

At nine o'clock they noticed an increase in military helicopter flyovers and started to pay closer attention to the bridge traffic. Fifteen minutes later they spotted a motorcade starting to cross the bridge heading toward them. Looking around, they didn't see many people on that side of the building, so they flew over the building and started looking for their bomber ahead of them.

Maintaining a height of about a thousand feet above the street, they hoped no one was looking up at them as they continued their search. When the bomber saw the motorcade approaching, his mental thoughts were recognized instantly, indicating which car he was in. Rafe and Vera dropped from the sky toward the motorcade and stopped it before it reached the parked police car with the bomb. Rafe then turned his attention to the bomb car, moving it further away as he encased it in a bubble, compressing it until it imploded into a ball of twisted metal.

Rafe and Vera then released all vehicles from their bubbles and teleported back to Macon. When they arrived back into their apartment they turned on the TV news and watched for a report. Fifteen minutes later the network broke in with a news flash. Apparently, the Presidential motorcade had been attacked, but no injuries were reported.

CHAPTER 37

That afternoon they received a message on their website to call home. Rafe, Vera, and Adam were present when Rafe called the CIA special number. The Deputy Director himself answered. "Rafe was that you and Vera this morning saving the bacon for the Secret Service? When I heard that the President was going to be in a motorcade this morning I called the Director of the Secret Service reminding him of your warning and he blew me off. He blew me off! I even called the FBI and when he tried to warn the SS, he was blown off too. He's either dumber than a Christmas turkey or he was bought off."

"I would have called you about the powers Vera and I developed, but our ability to see future events was still unproven. So, we just followed the forecast and took the bomber out. Do you want me to check this SS joker out or can you and the FBI handle it?"

"The President was pissed when he heard we were warned and still operated as if nothing was wrong. This joker is toast whether he's dirty or not. Good work, by the way. If you hadn't warned us, I don't think anyone would have known you and Vera did it. Talk to you later."

Looking around, Rafe shrugged his shoulders. "I guess it turned out alright for everyone but the Secret Service."

Adam said, "I wonder which group is behind this attempt. It was a perfect target for terrorist groups, a two for one with both the President and Prime Minister of Israel."

Rafe nodded, "Keep looking, you might get lucky."

The next day Rafe got a mental call to visit James and Melissa. He and Vera returned to their grandson's apartment with some apprehension, as they expected to hear about another prognostication from Jessie and Katie. After entering the apartment they found the whole family waiting for them.

Before anyone could speak, Rafe went over to Jessie and Katie and hugged each one.

"You two were responsible for us being able to save the President of the United States and the Prime Minister of Israel from being killed. I'm going to recommend to the Board that you each receive a plaque for your efforts."

Melissa and James looked at their daughters, tears of pride welling in their eyes. Melissa then said, "They both have received another dream! They see themselves and you two with the President receiving some kind of an award. Does this mean they're going to Washington?"

Rafe grimaced and looked at Vera, "It appears so. I was hoping to keep this as low profile as possible. Maybe I can request that it be a private ceremony with no news coverage. I didn't want the whole world to know of our existence, at least not yet."

Vera asked the parents, "What about you? How do you feel about your girls going to Washington with us?"

James and Melissa looked glum. "We're afraid this is going to change their lives forever. So far they are the only people who have this talent, aren't they?"

"Not entirely. We may start getting more dreams ourselves and their siblings will probably have this talent when they get older. But right now you're right."

Vera said, "It's a valuable talent, but currently all the visions involve themselves or the Group. If they start seeing random disasters then it becomes valuable to the world. But, let's not ask for problems we currently don't have. Now back to the question, do you want them to go to Washington?"

James nodded, "Since you're going with them we don't have a problem."

Rafe smiled at the parents. "We'll keep them safe."

He then asked Jessie and Katie. "What other talents do you have and how strong are they?"

Jessie said, "We have strong telepathy and telekinesis powers, but haven't yet tried teleportation."

"How about defensive moves in case of an attack on your person?"

"Mother said we didn't need to know that yet."

Rafe looked at Melissa. "They need it now, even if they are with us."

Melissa looked stricken. "Yes, you're right. My girls are going to be out in the world and they need to know how to protect themselves. Could you and Vera do that?"

Rafe smiled at her. "We'll be happy to. Girls, let's go down to the garage and practice some moves."

Jessie and Katie quickly got up from their seats and hurried after their great grandparents. When they reached the garage level they looked around for something they could use as a training tool. The elevator shaft was located in the center of the garage and along the shafts outside walls were storage units for the apartments. Inside one of the units were several pieces of luggage, which Rafe and Vera moved and stacked near an outside wall.

Rafe had the girls picture in their minds invisible hands pushing against the luggage. Suddenly the luggage jumped back against the wall.

"That's what we call the push back move. Now use your minds to stack the luggage again and then only Jessie uses the move."

The luggage restacked itself and then with a crash it flew back against the wall. "Now, restack it and Katie does the move."

The result was the same for Katie. "Remember, unless you want to hurt someone, don't use as much force against them. Now, let's try teleportation. Jessie, mentally pick up one of those suitcases and visualize that it should be as far away as you can see in the garage."

Jessie could only see about thirty feet because of the circular floor and elevator shaft in the center of the garage. She mentally picked up a suitcase that momentarily floated in the air before disappearing with a pop, and a bang when it fell to the floor thirty feet away.

"Okay that was perfect. Now you do it Katie."

The result was the same. Vera had everyone go to the teleported suitcases and examine them. She had them open them up and inspect them for damage before teleporting them back to the other suitcases. The girls looked at the stack of suitcases with satisfaction, pleased with their progress.

Rafe then had Jessie, using the same method, teleport herself to the right of the stack. At first she was doubtful, but she visualized where she wanted to go and then willed herself there. She disappeared with a louder pop and reappeared to the right of the stack. Katie, encouraged by Jessie's success, followed her example and arrived to the left of the stack.

"Great, you're doing everything perfect. Are you sure you haven't done this before? I want you both to teleport to your room and then back here, okay?"

They nodded their heads and suddenly disappeared with two pops. Moments later they were back, grinning from ear to ear.

Rafe and Vera smiled with satisfaction. "Where have you been recently away from Macon?" Rafe asked.

Katie spoke. "We went to the Augusta house three weeks ago to visit Uncle Peter."

"Can you clearly visualize his apartment? Mentally compare your memory with Jessie and if it's clear, teleport there and then back here. You don't need to worry about hitting anything as two objects can't occupy the same area of space."

When the girls were ready they disappeared with pops of air filling a void. Rafe and Vera started to worry after three minutes, when the twins suddenly reappeared with ice cream bars in their hands.

Jessie held up her ice cream. "We were delayed by Uncle Peter, who wouldn't let us leave without a treat."

Rafe and Vera smiled at their success. "We don't know yet what our limits are, but since Vera and I teleported to Washington, it's likely you can too. You two have never been in our apartment. I want you to visualize our memory of our apartment and teleport there and then back here."

The girls knew accomplishing this feat would require strong concentration. Furrowing their brows, they did as instructed, visualizing what they saw in Rafe and Vera's minds. When they were ready they disappeared with two pops and then soon reappeared.

They both grinned as Katie said, "That's fun, what else can we do?"

Rafe laughed. "That's it for now except you need to put those suitcases back where they belong."

After they mentally moved the cases back into their spot, Rafe told them to teleport back into their apartment and tell their parents what they had accomplished. The girls disappeared with pops, and Rafe and Vera took the elevator to the work area to talk to Adam. After telling Adam about Jessie and Katie's latest vision of the future, Adam asked, "Have you received an invitation to the White House yet?"

Rafe said, "No, but if it happens it should be soon. I have a feeling the Israeli Prime Minister may want to be present as we saved his neck too."

Rafe and Vera were eating lunch when Adam mentally told them that a message was left on their website to call home. Smiling at Vera, Rafe said, "Want to take a bet on what they want to say?"

After they finished eating, Rafe placed the call to the special CIA number. When the Director got on the line he said, "The President wants to present you and Vera with a special award for your action in preventing the terrorist attack against him and the Prime Minister. Can you be here tomorrow evening at six?"

Rafe responded, "We would feel uncomfortable if you didn't include our great grandchildren, Jessie and Katie, in the presentation, because it was their prognostication that allowed us to be there."

"How old are these children?"

"They just turned twelve."

"I'm sure that will be satisfactory. Anything else?"

"Yes, will you please tell the President we would appreciate it if the presentation be kept private and not reported to the news media. We can teleport to the main white house gate at six if you can have someone meet us there."

"The presentation is private and I'll arrange for someone to meet you."

"We'll see you tomorrow then. Bye."

Vera then mentally contacted Melissa. *The meeting with the President was on for tomorrow evening at six and did the kids have suitable clothes to wear?*

No! Would you come with us and help pick out clothes for them?

Okay, let's meet in the garage in thirty minutes.

Vera looked at Rafe as she started getting ready. "Have you got a tux that's in style?"

"I don't know, come with me and we'll check. What are you going to wear?"

Later, when Melissa and the girls reached the garage they found that Rafe and Vera needed to shop for clothing as well. Six hours later they had purchased what they needed for their trip to Washington, including a recent color picture of the White House main gate.

The following evening they were all gathered in James and Melissa's apartment checking to be sure they were dressed properly, the parents checking their children, Rafe and Vera checking each other. All this attention to detail was starting to make the girls nervous.

Vera stooped down to eye level with the twins and said, "Take a deep breath. Now let it out slowly. Now do it again. Is that better?"

The girls' smiles were weak, but they nodded their heads. Katie said, "I've never met the President before."

Vera winked at her. "Me neither. Buck up. He puts his shoes on just like you."

That got the girls laughing and then they had to go to the bathroom. When they returned, then Vera had to go. When they were all together again Rafe had everyone concentrate on the main gate picture while they held hands. Once everyone had a mental picture of the destination firmly in place, they teleported.

CHAPTER 38

$\infty\!\!\infty\!\!\infty$

They arrived at the gate a few minutes before six, but their escort was there and she took charge leading the way through the security checkpoints into the White House. Eventually they arrived in the Oval Office where several people had gathered, including the President and the First Lady.

Director Bishop of the CIA made introductions to President Charles Stevens and First Lady Grace, followed by Prime Minister Goldstein, and the new head of the Secret Service and the other agency heads. The First Lady, who was tall for a woman, stooped down and talked to the girls.

"I understand you two were partially responsible for saving my husband. You must be identical twins, yet you don't try to dress alike. I was a twin too, but my brother was a pain to be around."

Jessie said, "Everyone can tell us apart because we're all telepaths, but we understand about brothers since we have two younger ones. Do you have any children?"

"Yes, but they have all grown up and have their own families now."

"Your grandparents look young for their age. Does everyone stay young?"

"We don't know. No one ever gets any older looking than our great grandparents so far."

The President cleared his throat and everyone looked his way. "We are here to present the Freedom Award to Rafe and Vera Johnson for their fateful action in saving the lives of myself and the Prime Minister.

In addition, I understand these two young people helped by foretelling the event so that action could be taken. There isn't anything I can officially give them except our heartfelt thanks."

The President shook Katie's and Jessie's hands. When he touched Jessie, she stiffened and fell to the floor in a faint. Vera quickly knelt beside her, checking her pulse, and then asked for a wet cloth. Jessie soon came around and then whispered into Vera's ear. Vera mentally told Rafe what Jessie told her, as she helped Jessie off the floor and onto a chair.

Jessie mentally repeated the message to Rafe and urged him to take action. Rafe cleared his throat. "Mister President, Jessie had a vision when you touched her. She saw you in a helicopter that explodes. She thinks it will happen soon, so I recommend you stay away from all helicopters until this is resolved."

The President looked at his Chief of Staff. "Bill, have my helicopter thoroughly checked out and I'm not flying again until Jessie clears me."

Rafe said, "Mr. President let me consult with Jessie and find out just what she saw. We might be able to pin this down where the cause is easier to find. Jessie, tell me everything you saw."

"When the President touched me it was like a electric shock, then I saw him get into his helicopter. He flew toward the Washington Monument, but then veered toward the river. I then saw something streak toward it and then there was a big explosion."

"Can you tell what time of day it was? Was the sun high or in the east or west?"

"Which way is west?"

"Toward the river."

"Okay, it was late afternoon because the Sun was below the top of the trees."

Rafe turned to the President. "We just learned it wasn't a bomb on your helicopter, but more likely a rocket. If you have anything scheduled soon that includes a helicopter flight in the late afternoon, I would recommend sending up a decoy and see if you can find the rocket launcher. Our target has to be between the Lincoln and the Washington Monument near the Mall."

The President said, "All you agency heads take note of what he said and use the decoy method. I was planning on leaving tomorrow just like Jessie said. Let's get this done."

The President then shook Rafe's hand and he and the First Lady left the room. The Prime Minister came over and shook Rafe and Vera's hands as well. "I would like to talk to you later about a matter of importance. Where might I reach you?"

Rafe wrote their web address on a piece of paper and handed it to the PM, which caused him to laugh when he read it. "I see you have a sense of humor."

Rafe asked, "Is the treaty signed?"

"Yes, but making it work is going to be the hard part. That is what I need to talk to you about."

"How long are you going to be in the U.S.?"

"A few days and then I must return before something happens back home."

"On your way home in three days why not stop in Paris for a few hours. Unless there has been a change in your Embassy there, the Rose Garden was beautiful about three in the afternoon. It might clear your mind for the task ahead."

The Prime Minister gave him a slight smile. "Yes, the garden remains beautiful. I think I'll take your advice and clear my head."

They shook hands again and Rafe looked around to discover that all the Agency heads had departed. He mentally asked Vera. *Is Jessie clear headed enough to teleport back home?*

Jessie answered. *I'm fine now. Are we ready to go home?*

Not quite yet. I need to check something.

Rafe opened the case presented to him by the President earlier and then used the device Adam invented to burn out any tracking feature it might contain. He then mentally told Vera and the girls to teleport back to James and Melissa's apartment. They all arrived at about the same time surprising the family watching TV. Vera told them about Jessie's vision after the President attempted to shake her hand and the excitement that had created.

Melissa looked at the girls with a hand over her mouth as she said, "Oh my! Were you frightened?"

The girls hugged their mother, "No, Mother. Rafe and Vera were there and we knew nothing bad was going to happen. It was fun meeting the President and the First Lady. She was lonely and missed her grown children," Katie said.

Before they departed, Rafe told the parents to let him know if they had more dreams or visions. Both parents hugged their girls and agreed. Rafe then mentally asked Adam to meet them in the workroom.

Rafe handed Adam the Freedom Award the President had given them and asked him to test it and the case for any kind of tracking device. Adam placed it in a lead-lined case and said he would look at it tomorrow. Vera happily described the excitement created by Jessie's vision when the President touched her. When Vera finished the story, Adam asked how the children were?

"Oh, they took it all in stride. Not bad for twelve-year-olds. Rafe met and talked some with the Prime Minister of Israel."

"Oh, what was that about Dad?"

"I set up a meeting at the Israeli Paris Embassy in three days. Do you and Vera want to come? No, I forgot you can't teleport that far."

"What are you going to talk about?"

"He said it was a matter of importance, but I'm sure it's about the new treaty he just signed sharing Israel's homeland with Palestine. He needs a way that both parties can be sure no one is lying to them. If both sides had a telepath it would eliminate this fear."

Adam scratched his chin, thinking. "You know if the Palestinians get a telepath, then eventually it's almost certain a terrorist group will have this power."

"What do you recommend?"

"Tomorrow let's go to Atlanta and talk to Dr. Sheldon. Maybe he has a solution to our problem."

Rafe and Vera supplemented Adam's teleportation ability by including him in their mental visualization when they teleported to Dr. Sheldon's office in Atlanta. He was expecting them and had his wife, Jane, with him. Rafe explained what he was contemplating with Israel and Palestine and asked, "Is there a way of limiting the transfer to only the telepathy ability?"

Dr. Sheldon raised an eyebrow and smiled at Jane. "That's fortuitous isn't it?"

He then shook his head and laughed. "We just isolated the gene that gives us telepathy and it can be transferred without a transfusion. I can put it into a gel capsule that doesn't require any special handling."

Rafe asked, "Do you know if it will have any side effects or will the ability be transferred to offspring?"

"Who knows? I just got this much done. The people who take it will have to take the risk."

Rafe mentally consulted with Vera and Adam about whether to pass this ability on without testing. Eventually, they all agreed this risk was better than letting the Palestines have access to their abilities.

Rafe said, "I think you may have saved me from making a big mess. Can you quickly prepare four capsules because I will need them in two days?"

"If you wait I can work them up within two hours."

"Great, maybe Jane can show us around the Lab while you get to it."

"No, I'll do that. Jane can do this far faster than I can."

While Jane was working on the capsules, Dr. Sheldon proudly showed them his current project. The lab was a busy place with at least twenty people working at various tasks. Rafe asked Dr. Sheldon, "Are all these people members of the Group?"

"Yes, we are running three shifts, which total about fifty members. We have been fortunate that we have recruited so many talented people. Best of all we have no turnover."

Jane brought the capsules to Rafe in two small containers. "Try to keep these out of the sun. They really should be kept in a cool place."

"Okay, I'll pass that information on. Thanks for your help, Jane. Did you ever think you would be doing this when you first joined our Group?"

"This is the happiest I've ever been in my life. I'm really glad Sally found me when she did."

The three teleported back to Macon where Rafe and Vera started to get ready for their trip to Paris while she was thinking this is a great opportunity to shop.

CHAPTER 39

Rafe and Vera found the Prime Minister smelling the roses when they arrived in Paris. He must have heard something because he turned and saw them walking toward him. "Mr. and Mrs. Johnson, it's so good to see you again so soon."

Rafe and Vera shook his hand without any prognostication episode, which was a good start.

Rafe asked, "What can we do for you?"

Prime Minister Goldstein pointed to a nearby bench in the shade. "Why not make ourselves comfortable and enjoy the garden for a moment." They sat for a few minutes without talking; however, both Rafe and Vera were scanning for any thoughts pertaining to them.

PM Goldstein gave himself a little start as his mind came back into focus. "I am sure you're aware of the problems we face in maintaining a peaceful co-existence in Israel with Palestine. We need a way to ensure we continue to trust what we say to each other."

"What you need is telepaths talking to one another. You can't lie to a telepath."

"Exactly!"

"We won't give you the secret to our treatment, but we have recently isolated the gene that gives us telepathy and are willing to give you that power."

"Just like that. No demands or asking of favors?"

"It's in our own best interests that this attempt at co-existence succeed, so we are willing to take the small risk of others with telepathy.

Besides, it's never a bad idea to have you owing us a favor."

Rafe handed over the two bottles of capsules. "There are two capsules in each bottle. I recommend combining the two bottles in the presence of the Palestinians, shake them up and then place two in the empty bottle and ask them to choose which bottle they prefer. I recommend that you each have a man and woman on your teams. We don't know if there are any bad reactions to these capsules, but with the full treatment our people were subjected to extreme sexual urges about two weeks later, which lasted for two months. I don't expect that with this treatment, but who knows since it hasn't been tested. It might take up to three months for results to begin, so be patient."

PM Goldstein looked at the bottles. "I hope this works. Do you have any other thoughts?"

"Nothing, other than maybe the four candidates should stay together so they can get to know each other and watch how the others react to the treatment."

"If this works, your people will have a friend for life in Israel."

Gratified, Rafe and Vera said their goodbyes and teleported to a nice mid-range hotel Rafe was familiar with. Rafe had not been in Paris for over eighty years, but the city's charm continued to enchant him. They had already checked in with their luggage and now all they wanted was to bathe and change into fancy clothes for an evening in Paris.

They returned to Macon the following day where Adam told Rafe their web site had a message for him to call the CIA. Rafe mentally asked Vera, *Do you think they know we were in Paris talking to the PM?*

Maybe being in Paris, but how could they know about the PM?

Rafe said, "I guess I better call and find out."

The Deputy Director answered. "The SS and the FBI jointly caught that guy with the rocket. They staked out three vans along the suspected route and when the decoy chopper took off he was caught before he could arm the rocket."

"If you want help getting info out of him we'd be happy to volunteer."

The line went silent for a few moments. "I'll pass the offer on and they'd be crazy not to take you up on it. I'll get back to you."

Rafe turned to Vera, "I'm glad they got the guy. It would be helpful if they eliminated the whole terrorist cell, otherwise they are going to try again."

Vera took his hand. "Come along, I've got something for you in the apartment."

"What did you get for me? I thought I was with you the whole time. Oh, I get you," Rafe said, patting Vera's rear end.

The next day a message on their website asked them to call home.

The Deputy Director answered Rafe's call. "We have him at Langley and both the FBI and the SS have approved your use of telepathy on him. They'll worry about the legal aspects of how it was obtained later."

"I can come now if that's what you want? I can teleport into the Wall of Stars room in thirty minutes."

"That's perfect. We will have time to get an escort there for you."

Rafe asked Vera, "Do you want to come too? It will be like old home week for you."

Vera grinned at him as she remembered the years she had worked there, and then agreed. "I'd like that, but there won't be anyone left that I knew."

"Vera is coming too. See you later."

Later they arrived together holding hands before the Wall of Stars, each star representing an agent killed in the line of duty. They stood before the wall in reverence for a few moments before turning to look for their escort. A woman was standing in the center of the room, turning slowly until she realized they were looking at her.

Hurrying to them, she handed them a visitor's badge. "I'm Assistant Deputy Director Alice Reynolds and I'm happy to meet you both. Among the higher circles of the agency you both have achieved star status. What you and your group have done fighting terrorism is almost unbelievable."

"Alice, Vera used to work here as an Analyst many years ago. I was wondering if we could do a quick walk through on our way to where you want us?"

Alice did a double take and stared at Vera. "I'm sorry, I can't quite wrap my mind around how old you two are. Sure that won't be a problem, just don't tell anyone who you are or that you used to work here."

Alice took them into the Analyst Division section and stopped at the Division Heads office. The walls of the room were filled with pictures of the past Division Heads, and Rafe quickly found a picture of Vera, looking about thirty years older. The current Head was also a woman who looked up in surprise as they arrived. The department generally didn't get people with a visitor's badge. ADD Reynolds introduced Rafe and Vera as children of a former analyst to DH Eloise Black. Black immediately fixed her eyes on Vera, who could see her mind trying to determine where she had seen Vera before.

DH Black went over to the wall and pointed at Vera's picture. "This is either you or your grandmother." She then looked at Rafe and then quickly back at Vera. "It's you! So the rumor is correct after all."

ADD Reynolds said, "Shit! Black, keep your voice down. Tell me about this rumor mill! Wait a minute!" She hurried over and shut the door.

"That two of our former agents have had a super security lock placed on their files. Remember what we do here, we analyze. For instance we knew you two had married when you both were about seventy and your pensions were placed on hold. Not stopped as if each of you died. Also, that you were under protective custody at the time the hold was placed on your pensions. This was before the security lock, yet even after that we heard stories of terrorist attacks against two of our people."

ADD Reynolds then asked, "How did you put it all together so quickly when we came in here?"

Vera spoke up, "Because she's good at her job. Maybe almost as good as I was."

"Your face stuck in my mind when I first looked up at you. When I placed it as one on the wall, a young woman with a young man who I remember seeing a picture of when he was the Paris Station Chief, it all clicked into place."

Rafe looked at ADD Reynolds. "She's wasted here. She should be in an ADD position supervising this Division. If you don't, I may try to steal her from you."

DH Black looked at him with speculation. "Obviously, you are no longer in protective custody and have at least an equal relationship with the agency."

"See! I told you. You better get cracking or I'm going to be making my move."

ADD Reynolds looked at DH Black with appreciation. "You know that nothing you heard here can be repeated. Okay, I think he's right, you are wasted here. I'll get back with you soon."

Vera shook Black's hand, and then followed the others out of the room to their next destination. They went through two security checkpoints before they reached the room where the terrorist was being held. They watched through a one-way window while the interrogation went on.

Rafe asked, "How long has he been interrogated today?"

"Six hours and this is the second interrogator."

"I think I can get the information you want in twenty minutes."

The agent in charge of the interrogation snorted and said, "He hasn't told us anything and you tell us you can make him talk in twenty minutes. This I want to see."

Rafe replaced the other interrogator and sat down, staring at the terrorist for about three minutes while he gauged the man's mental condition. The prisoner was so exhausted that Rafe easily started searching through his memories, and had all he needed in fifteen minutes; however, he concentrated on two faces, which he sent to Adam so that he could draw them and send them back to the CIA.

Rafe left the room to where the others were waiting. "You helped by breaking him down and making it easier for me to get into his memories."

Rafe revealed the terrorist's name, and the names and location of the other two members. He also gave them the names of the team's planners before they left a Saudi desert camp.

"I asked my son Adam, to draw pictures of the two planners which he will send here when he's finished."

The lead interrogator looked at him, mouth open in surprise. "So, it's true. You are a telepath. But, how did you let your son know what to draw. You can mentally talk to someone that far away?"

"Some of us can and eventually all of our Group will be able to. Adam said it will take about two hours to finish the drawings, but that's because he's such a perfectionist. I'm thinking the name of the planners, Raptor, is a code name of their organization. We've heard the name used for the past forty years, so they are not a new group."

ADD Reynolds took Rafe and Vera to a break room while they waited on Adam's drawings. The agency was busy assembling a strike team to go after the other members of the terrorist cell.

CHAPTER 40

It was almost three hours later before they brought the drawings to where they waited in the break room. Rafe compared them to his memory and deemed them almost perfect. He asked for a pencil and made some minor changes before handing them back to ADD Reynolds.

"These drawings are really excellent. Your son is an artist. It looks almost like a photograph."

Vera answered, "Yes, both he and his sister have this talent which we discovered when they were about eleven and did a drawing of the Mona Lisa from memory."

ADD Reynolds said, "I'll be right back. I want to start comparing these against known terrorists."

They were kept waiting in the break room for about thirty minutes. Several agents used the room while they were waiting, but no one talked to them. A surface reading of their minds indicated they had been instructed not to interact with the couple with visitor's badges.

ADD Reynolds returned, smiling. "I checked with DH Black first with the idea that with her memory she might know who they were. She had some recent Intel on them and pulled their files for me. One of their close associates was our rocket man. Now we have the top brass looking at the files to determine their next moves."

Rafe said, "I told you she was wasted there."

"I know, but we need someone good to take her spot."

Vera said, "I bet if you asked her, she'd know whom to recommend for her old position."

Reynolds smiled. "I'll bet you're right. I'm going to start the ball rolling."

Rafe nodded, "I think our work here is done for now. Unless you want something else, we'll head home."

"Wait a moment while I check with my boss," Reynolds said as she picked up a telephone and punched in a number and asked if the Johnsons were needed for anything before they left. She nodded and turned to them.

"The Deputy Director wants to ask a favor of you before you leave. He said it wouldn't take long."

Rafe nodded his head. "Okay, let's go."

Fifteen minutes later they were in DD Gregory Wilson's office. He was alone and pointed to his seating area. "Take a load off and catch your breath. You have been busy since you've arrived and I appreciate your help, even finding talent within the agency we were not fully aware of."

He hesitated a moment before adding. "I was wondering if you would share those capsules you gave Israel?"

"I would be happy to share, but why not let them test them first. We just isolated the telepathy gene when Israel's need arose. We don't know if there are any adverse side effects or if they work. When Israel finishes with its field tests, how many do you want?"

"Assuming the capsules work, we need enough for our interrogation and field agents. I assume the other agencies want a supply as well."

"Okay, but we want to control the supply. We'll charge you our cost, which is a thousand dollars a capsule. Also a million dollars from each agency that wants it, to cover our research costs. In the meantime we will start production so that we will have a supply when you want it."

"I didn't realize you had the ability to produce the capsules in that volume, but the cost appears reasonable. How long do you think it's going to take before we know if the treatment works?"

"Another three to six months on the side effects and how well it works. It might take less time, but it's all new for us."

"Okay, go ahead and start production and if it doesn't work we will reimburse you for the extra expense."

They said their goodbyes and teleported to Atlanta. When they entered Dr. Sheldon's office he looked up in surprise. "Hi guys. What can I do for you?"

"Those telepathy capsules you gave me have stirred up a lot of interest. What needs to be done to produce two thousand of them?"

Dr. Sheldon said, "Well, we can't do it here. I need to ask Jane what she thinks."

He hurried out of his office and returned with his wife. "They want to know what we need to do to produce two thousand of those telepathy capsules?"

"Just the one batch of two thousand?"

"That depends on whether a booster treatment will be needed and how many agents they want with the ability. Maybe, another two thousand at a later date."

"It will be easier to contract this small batch out rather than buy a drug company, but it will require an FDA certification. Maybe Adam can fudge that for us as a cold medication. We can provide the ingredient and the drug company does the manufacture of the capsules. How many for each bottle?"

"We want to try to control these treatments; how about ten per bottle. We need to ask each agency to maintain internal controls of inventory and disbursements that will be subject to our review. We want them to think we have at least an illusion of control over who uses the treatment."

Dr. Sheldon asked Jane, "Who do you think we should approach?"

"I don't know yet, but it's going to be expensive for such a small batch."

Rafe said, "I told them a thousand dollars per capsule and a million per agency. Is a thousand per capsule too low?"

"No, that should cover it and if it's a little low the million per agency will take up the slack. When do you want it?"

"I told them three to six months to test the original Israeli capsules, but try to have them ready within two months. Go ahead and do four thousand capsules if it bring down the individual cost."

"Dr. Sheldon, when can you start giving other members the new treatment? Since the newest members are already the strongest, why not start giving it to the oldest members first."

"Since we have to wait awhile to draw blood again from Jessie and Katie, Adam and Evelyn will have to wait. It'll be three years before we can obtain blood from Jessie and Katie's younger siblings. So far no one else has exhibited these same gene factors. You and Vera can give blood every three months, and that will provide treatment for at least eight members."

Rafe looked at Vera for confirmation. She nodded her head, "Let's do it now and each of us can carry the treatments to where they should go."

Later, Vera teleported to Augusta carrying a treatment for Evelyn, while Rafe took three treatments to Macon for Peter and Anne Stephenson, and Adam. The other two treatments would go to the Stephensons first born, Jack and Ralph, who were in Silicon Valley. Vera would teleport those treatments to Sally's home where the brothers would take the treatment.

The plan was that after one or more members of a location received a treatment, they would later provide the blood for other members at that location. They would then teleport blood to wherever it was needed. Dr. Sheldon estimated it would only take between three and four months for every member to receive the treatment.

This was Vera's first trip to California and was surprised when everyone showed up to welcome her. Sally introduced the other members Vera hadn't met and her older brothers who were to receive the new treatment. Jack and Ralph Stephenson had been born when the Group was in Portland, but Vera hadn't seen them since their marriages.

After visiting with the other Group members and bringing everyone up to date on what had been happening to them, Vera explained what powers the new treatment would give them. She also told of the strange reactions their bodies had shortly after the treatment and the interrupted prognostication episode Rafe and she experienced. Vera also told of the episodes Jessie and Katie Johnson experienced concerning the President and warned them that an episode can be initiated by a touch with another person.

"Within days of this treatment your other powers will be greatly strengthened. You will be able to contact any member by telepathy or teleport anywhere inside the United States, or maybe further as Rafe and I teleported to Paris from Macon and back. The same rules apply that you must be able to picture your destination in your mind. We used a recent color photograph of the White House's main gate and teleported without a problem."

Vera also told of Rafe and her use of a protective bubble to protect the Presidential motorcade and another bubble to cover the terrorist's car, while using a pushback power to move it further away. She revealed how Rafe constricted the bubble around the bomb car until it imploded, either by the terrorist or the pressure.

The members discussed among themselves the various ways they could use the new stronger powers. Vera took Sally aside and explained that Jack and Ralph should each draw blood in fifteen days, which would provide eight more treatments. When everyone received a treatment, she should let Macon know and they would decide where to teleport future blood treatments.

"When can Jack and Ralph give blood again?"

"Not for three months and we may not need any by that time."

"Wow, that's going to be quick work."

Vera asked, "How's everything out here? Anymore requests for help from the FBI?"

"It's been real quiet. Our people keep busy, but I miss the excitement those FBI assignments gave me."

"Be careful what you wish for. Rafe and I have been real busy recently and I'm starting to wish for some quiet time. My youngest twins, Joseph and Elizabeth, are almost twenty-one and are seeking mates, so it won't be long before I'll be a grandma again."

After supervising treatments for Jack and Ralph, Vera told everyone bye and teleported back to Macon.

CHAPTER 41

$\infty$$\infty$

The CIA related that they captured one and killed two others at the raid on the terrorist location in Alexander. The cell was located in a house that was in a congested neighborhood and when they started moving the neighbors out, they were fired upon with automatic weapons resulting in several civilians being wounded. The strike team then assaulted the house. The surviving terrorist was not talking, but they would keep him in isolation until a telepath could be located.

Sixty-four days later all the Group's members had received the new treatment. No one reported having any prognostication visions or dreams, including Jessie and Katie. Rafe was beginning to wonder what triggered these episodes. The CIA reported the Israelis were happy with the results of the telepathy treatment and wanted a first shipment of one hundred doses. Rafe e-mailed them back with their bank information and instructions to pick up the shipment in the Star Room at six p.m. the next day.

Rafe mentally called Dr. Sheldon and informed him of the arrangement for the first delivery of the telepathy treatment drug. He gave Dr. Sheldon a clear mental picture of the Star Room where the shipment would be delivered. Two weeks later, they received another order from the CIA for eight hundred doses, followed by five hundred for the FBI, and a total of two thousand doses from five other agencies. They still had a reserve supply of 1,100 doses.

The drug cost for the Group was $3.2 million and so far they had received $9.9 million. Six months later their reserve was down to 500 doses, but the demand seemed to have been satisfied. Rafe called DD Wilson of the CIA.

"Greg, I'm curious how effective your telepaths are? How strong are they and what distance is their limit?"

"Wait a moment and I'll let you talk to one."

About two minutes later a new voice answered, "ADD Reynolds here."

"Hi, this is Rafe Johnson. I was wondering how strong the new telepaths are?"

"Maybe you can tell me. I have no problem mentally talking with other telepaths until they get about a mile away. Our interrogators have no problem getting information out of the terrorists' memories, but there seems to be a block against another telepath."

"You are what we call a stage one telepath. My first twins were born as stage two telepaths before they got upgrades. As a comparison, we now consider ourselves stage tens. We don't normally try to read other telepath's memories unless our safety is at risk, and we don't scan surface thoughts just for curiosity. I'll give you an example of our strength. Right now you are thinking, what's he doing giving me moral lessons."

"My God, you can reach this far!"

"With great power you must set moral limits. We are giving you small steps to see how you react. You have no idea of what we can do. We must police ourselves so our members don't exceed our own moral guidelines. How's Black doing?"

"She's an ADD in charge of her old Analysis Division, and her handpicked replacement is working out well."

"It's always better if you promote from within. I'm curious how Homeland Security is using their telepaths. Based upon their past performance, they're probably using them as enforcement tools rather than for investigation. I'll have to check on that. Thanks for the update and I'll get back with you later."

Rafe tried to mentally feel his way hoping for a familiar mind glow. He was surprised to find the mind glow similar to Joyce Graham, who was with Homeland Security and had a senior position as Deputy Director. Rafe quickly determined she was the daughter of Joyce Graham and had inherited her mother's telepathy powers. Maybe she could help him in his quest to find how their telepaths are being used within the agency.

DD Stout was a weak telepath and apparently not any stronger than the ones she supervised, which caused her some anguish. Rafe was correct in his suspicions about how the telepaths were being used, and he started taking notes of the people who were responsible. Apparently, the

Director was clueless about what his Deputy was doing, which to Rafe was almost as bad.

Rafe considered his next move before he consulted with Vera, Adam, and mentally with the McPhersons. He explained what he learned about Homeland Security's use of their telepaths and asked for their input on how it could be stopped. Both James and Jane were disgusted that the DD would take such action, but based upon their own past history with her mother it seemed to follow a pattern. The consensus was only the President had the authority to take action.

James McPherson asked, *Do you think you have enough pull with the President that he'd listen to you?"*

Maybe, but I would have to get close to him to ask. However, if he's a telepath maybe our problem is solved.

Rafe followed the President's mind glow until he found him reading a newspaper article. *Mr. President this is Rafe Johnson and I need to speak to you on a matter of importance.*

Rafe! I'm on Air Force 1 over the Atlantic. How could you reach me this far away?

I've recently received an upgrade. The matter of importance is the Senior Management of Homeland Security. Deputy Director Freda Stout is the daughter of a weak telepath, which she inherited before I gave the agencies the ability to make their own telepaths. Stout used her ability to blackmail her way up to her present position. Currently, she is using her agency's telepaths to consolidate her power base. You have a rotten apple at Homeland Security, poisoning the entire agency. The Director does not appear to be involved, but he is not smart enough to clean house. I recommend you ask the CIA loan you Assistant Deputy Director Eloise Black. She just started as an ADD, but is a firecracker and sharp as a tack, plus she has no ties to Homeland Security.

My God, my people have been telling me about problems there, but this is a bomb waiting to go off. I'll have my Chief of Staff get right on it. Thanks, Rafe.

Rafe mentally told his advisors. *I talked to the President and he said he would take care of it. Now let's watch the fur fly.*

Two hours later Rafe got a message to call the CIA. Deputy Director Wilson answered at Rafe's call. "Crap, Rafe you've raised a shit storm here. The President wants ADD Black on loan to clean house over at Homeland Security. I don't know if it's even legal."

"Will Black do it?"

"I have her here with me now and she wants to talk to you."

"Rafe Johnson here, I told the President you were the person to do this. If you haven't had the telepathy treatment, take it now because you will need it. Don't go over there alone; take agents from other agencies that have telepathy powers to help you. It's going to be like walking into a hornet's nest. The Queen is DD Stout and she is a bad one. Please take this on, it should be a challenge."

"Thanks for the vote of confidence. I just hope I don't get my tits in a wringer."

"Don't worry; I'll give you a position here if the government kicks you out."

"From what I hear that's not a bad gig. Talk to you later."

The following week Homeland Security was in the news reporting several early retirements in the higher positions including the Deputy Director. Not reported were several transfers out of Washington to less favorable duties in Alaska. A month later the Director of Homeland Security resigned to pursue other interests. His replacement was a former Director of the FBI, Mark Richards.

Two days later Rafe received a message on their website to call home. DD Wilson answered the call. "Mark Richards, the new Director of Homeland Security wants you to call him at this secure number. He wants some input on what happened there."

"Is Eloise Black still at Homeland?"

"Yes, and I don't know if I'm going to get her back. Damn Rafe, I know you brought her to my attention, but we could really use her here too."

"Sounds like she has job security no matter where she decides to settle. You sure you want her there. She probably likes being a Deputy Director. Talk to you later."

Rafe smiled to himself as he called the Homeland Security number. "Mark Richards here."

"Hi, this is Rafe Johnson answering your call."

"Rafe! Thanks for giving me a call. Acting DD Black says you were instrumental in letting the President know of the problems here and recommending her to clean it up. I've never met anyone quite like her before. She's already got this agency back on track and given me a list of things that need improvement."

"Yes, she impressed me too. About two months ago I met her when she was the Head of the Analysis Section of the CIA, before she was promoted to ADD of the Analysis Division. Are you going to keep her there?"

"I'm not stupid. I've already been talking to the Chief of Staff trying to make her move permanent."

"You better ask her if she wants to stay. Women like to be consulted about their future."

"Good point! I'll see if I can make it worth her while."

"If you haven't already taken corrective steps, Homeland has had a history of poor security. Other agencies have left them out of the loop because of it."

"Yeah, it was that way when I was with the FBI. Black has already taken steps to correct that situation. Thanks for giving us the telepathy ability. It has made this whole cleanup effort so much easier. Feel free to use this number if you have the need."

"I will. Until later, bye."

CHAPTER 42

$\bigcirc\!\!\!\infty\!\!\!\bigcirc$

Five years later Rafe, and Vera teleported to Atlanta to complete their annual physical workup. Dr. Sheldon wanted to check their DNA to compare with their previous medical history. He also asked about their prognostication abilities. Neither Rafe nor Vera had any visions since they received the treatment the first time.

Apparently, such episodes would only occur when they or someone close to them was involved, or if touched by someone affected by them. Dr. Sheldon informed them that all the Group members now have these same abilities and no limitations were found.

Rafe and Vera decided to visit all their locations for a firsthand look to determine if any changes needed to be made. Rafe contacted the senior member at Savannah to get a clear picture of the garage area, since it had been so long since they had been there. When they teleported there, the first thing he saw was the marine bus they first arrived in. Rafe smiled at Vera and said, "Do you think we should give this bus back?"

"I remember that house in Parris Island were we lived vividly. Let's teleport it there, right in front of the house."

Rafe and Vera mentally compared images, but stopped when they realized they needed to check the bus for anything left in it. Satisfied, the bus disappeared with a loud pop. Without the bus the garage looked larger.

Mary Jo Stephenson Wilson gave them a tour of the Savannah building which appeared much more lived-in with forty-two families in residence. Rafe and Vera met with the adults in their work area and Rafe spoke, "This house is the Group's first safe house under our own control. I notice that someone has placed a plaque to that effect in the boardroom, but are you aware that we arrived here during a terrorist attack at our previous location? During those early years we suffered through several such attacks until we became strong enough to take care of ourselves. We have expanded our numbers and locations across the United States and in the future maybe even to other planets as humankind expands. Vera and I would like to visit with all of you and answer any questions you might have before we leave tomorrow."

Rafe and Vera were surprised at some of the changes the residents made to the building's interior in their absence. They left the next morning, satisfied with their people's confidence in themselves. Their next stops were Augusta and the other Georgia houses before heading toward the east and west coasts, and returning to Macon through Denver and Wichita. Their intent was to show everyone their founders' faces and give them an idea of what the future would be under the Group's influence.

Arriving in Macon, they mentally informed everyone that they had returned. Adam answered that they just received a message for Rafe to call the FBI number. Deputy Director Ferguson answered their call.

"Rafe thanks for getting right back to me. Our agents with telepathy have discovered there is going to be another bombing attempt here, but instead of targeting the President; it appears they are going after the monuments. No specifics yet, but we expect the attacks to be soon. Is there anything you can do to help us?"

"Any guesses which monuments are to be targeted?"

"All the major ones. The Washington, Lincoln, and Jefferson Memorials, and maybe the war memorials on the Mall and in Rosslyn, in other words multiple targets."

"Okay, I'm going to send at least one Group member to each of those memorials named. They will be wearing yellow armbands so don't get trigger-happy. If you get additional information let us know and we'll do the same. Give us thirty minutes to get into place. Anything else?"

"No. I'll pass the word."

Rafe mentally called all the Macon members for a meeting in the Board Room immediately. Five minutes later, Rafe explained the problem and was assigning pairs to individual memorials, recommending they use constricting bubbles to secure any bombers should they appear. Rafe and Vera took the Washington Memorial because of its elevated position on the Mall. All the members were wearing yellow armbands when they teleported to their assigned positions twenty minutes later.

Rafe and the other assigned Group members immediately heard

several bombers' thoughts, upon arrival. Rafe mentally told a nearby FBI telepath that the attack was in process. Rafe and Vera zeroed in on three men approaching their position wearing large backpacks. Rather than wait any longer, they formed constricting bubbles around the three and when they were certain these three were bombers, they tightened the bubbles until they imploded.

Rafe and Vera monitored their other members as they handled their own attacks. Later they found that four monuments were attacked, including the Washington Monument. None of the attacks were successful and no one was hurt other than the bombers. After the attack, all the Group members, except Rafe and Vera, teleported back to Macon. Rafe and Vera waited at the Washington Monument for the FBI to arrive. The Deputy Director arrived thirty minutes later to find them sitting on one of the benches surrounding the monument.

He walked up to them and took a seat. "Thanks guys. That was a close one. If you had been ten minutes later, this would have been a disaster."

Rafe smiled at him. "I guess having agents with telepathic powers was a good idea."

"No shit! Too bad we didn't get anybody to ask questions of, but with bombers you can't take risks."

"If you get anything from their vehicles, let us know so we can update our own files. I'm guessing this is another Raptor operation. I wonder where they are getting their funding?"

The DD shook their hands and thanked them again for their help before Rafe and Vera teleported back to Macon. The others reported back to the boardroom upon their arrival for a recap of the day's activity. When they finished, Rafe congratulated everybody on a successful operation and told Adam to have a plaque made to remind everyone of their bravery.

* * *

Five more years brought many changes to the SA Group. The Group's membership had increased to over 500 and now had new residences in Los Angeles, Seattle, and Houston. Rafe opened new residences when the others reached eighty percent of their capacity. Dr. Sheldon's research found Rafe and Vera's DNA had stabilized again and was no longer deteriorating. He estimated they had only aged two years before receiving the last treatment, and now had no idea what their lifespan was going to be.

Several members had received prognostication episodes, which alerted them to dangers they were able to avoid. So far all such episodes involved the member or someone close to them.

Rafe and Vera's youngest twins, Joseph and Elizabeth, were now married and living in Houston, having married within the Group and had produced grandchildren. Now, with the Group's increased teleportation powers they were able to visit each other almost daily. Jerry and Peter from Rafe's first marriage, and their wives had also produced children making the Johnson family one of the largest in the Group.

Phillip Seymour, the Group's Attorney, requested Rafe and he meet to discuss future political strategy. The following day Phillip and his wife, Sarah Ellsworth Seymour, teleported to Macon to meet with the founders. Phillip brought Rafe current on their burgeoning influence in Congress. He suggested, "We would be even more effective if we had several Group members elected to Congress. "

"I agree, but remember even if they were elected at a young age, when it became apparent they didn't age, the cat would be out of the bag."

Phillip replied, "I talked to Dr. Sheldon and he said they recently isolated the DNA aging gene and he believes he can stop the appearance of getting younger and yet greatly slow future aging. The other benefits would remain, giving them full Psi powers."

"That sounds promising. We just need to find someone in there forties we would trust with these powers. Do you have anyone in mind?"

"Two in fact, one in the Senate and another in the House. Just think of the advantages they would have in committees they chair."

"Who are they and are they married?"

"Senator Margaret Chase and Representative Ben Grimes, and they are both single. Both are in their mid-forties and each belongs to different political parties. They will be able to help each other when combined with our other people. Both have spotless backgrounds. I have met them both and based upon my mind scans I recommend them."

"This sounds better all the time. Get them to your office soon so Vera and I can give our approval. Do you think they will be receptive to our offer?"

"Yes, if we are honest in our motives for wanting them on our side. These people have a desire to help the country and not to make themselves rich. I'll let you know when we arrange a meeting time. Let's now go see how Sarah and the others are getting along."

The following week Phillip mentally let him know the meeting with the two candidates was scheduled for the following afternoon. The next day Rafe and Vera teleported to Phillip's office fifteen minutes early. They had never met the politicians before, but had seen their pictures in the news.

At the appointed time Phillip's secretary showed Chase and Grimes into his office. They appeared to be surprised when they saw Rafe and Vera, who they didn't know or expect. Phillip introduced everyone and stated that Rafe and Vera were the head of the SPAC that had been financing their political careers.

Senator Chase looked at Phillip and stated, "I thought you were the head of the SPAC."

"Yes, you're right as far as the public is concerned. However, we are members of a Group they head and wish to make both of you a proposition. Please don't interrupt until they are finished, then they will answer your questions."

Rafe smiled at the two politicians, who looked back at him with confused emotions.

"The Group we belong to is small, but is growing larger every year. It is now about eighty-five years old and began with Vera and me when we were about seventy. As you can see, membership has its benefits. We eventually got into politics in a small way to try and influence government policies toward benevolent actions for those it governs. We now have financed the political careers of over thirty in both houses of congress. We didn't favor either political party, but instead hoped to appeal to their natural desire to better the lives of the people who voted them into office. You may ask questions now."

Chase and Grimes processed the information for a few moments before Senator Chase spoke. "You say you both are 150 years old? How is that even possible?"

Vera answered, "Actually I'm 147 and Rafe is 157. We are both retired CIA Agents who were infected at the same time by an unknown person or group. We think they wanted to use us as a test vehicle to see how the human body adapted to the infection. It made us younger to a base line of about twenty-three and protected us against all other infections. No one in our Group has ever gotten sick. When Rafe and I married and had children, the infection mutated and gave our children Psi powers. Every time children of our group intermarried, it mutated again giving them stronger and other types of Psi powers until now we can read minds and teleport to anyplace on the globe."

Representative Ben Grimes asked, "What do you want of us?"

Rafe answered, "We want to ask you to join our group. Normally, this wouldn't work for us because your appearance would give you away. However, our medical team isolated the DNA gene for aging and altered it so it no longer makes you younger, but retains its ability for a long life. If you agree to join us you can expect a life span of at least two or three hundred years and full Psi powers."

Senator Chase asked, "In exchange for this what do you expect in return?"

Rafe said, "Nothing more than what you have done before, but you will be much more effective with your new powers, especially your telepathy powers. There are no secrets when you deal with a telepath."

Grimes and Chase looked at him with their mouths open as it suddenly dawned on them what they were being offered. Representative Grimes brought his mind back into focus as he asked, "What's the downside of this offer?"

Rafe answered, "Initially, we had the protection of the FBI and CIA because of terrorist attacks trying to kidnap us. Later, as our numbers and abilities increased we escaped and have been living in secret places avoiding direct contact with Federal Agencies. Since our teleportation powers increased we have worked closely with several agencies against al-Qaeda terrorist cells, but they still don't know exactly where we reside. There is still a $10 million bounty on us by al-Qaeda. We don't know what, if any, side effect this treatment will have on you because it hasn't been tested. The regular adverse reaction begins about two weeks after the treatment and lasts about two months. The symptom is extreme sexual cravings. Normally we require married couples when one of the pair takes a treatment because of this side effect."

Senator Chase frowned. "Just how bad is this craving?"

Vera answered, "It depends on your age when you get the treatment. The younger you are the worse it gets and the older people are less affected. Both Rafe and I were single and had not yet met when we went through the change. It was still very hard for us, but was partially relieved by exercise. Since you won't get younger, maybe you won't have this side effect."

Chase said, "If we do this, we had better exchange phone numbers in case it gets bad."

Grimes asked, "When do you want to give us the treatment?"

Rafe smiled, "If you both agree, we can do it now. We can teleport both of you to our treatment center."

The two agreed and were teleported to Atlanta for their treatment and then returned to NYC. Before they left Seymour's office, contact numbers were exchanged and Rafe and Vera then teleported to Macon.

CHAPTER 43

Three weeks later Rafe received a e-mail from Senator Chase advising she and Grimes had not yet suffered any side effects from the treatment other than they both felt great. Rafe passed this information on to Dr. Sheldon so he could update their medical files.

Rafe and Vera kept themselves busy by mentally checking in with the member in charge at each Group residence location. They were able to ascertain what problems had developed and how they planned to solve them. Usually, everything was running fine except when they contacted Randy McPherson in Los Angeles, he brought forward a problem they hadn't encountered before.

Today, our members mentally heard several sources thinking about using a ground-to-air shoulder mounted missile against several aircraft flying into LAX. We're not sure, but one of these may be Air Force One. I was about to give you a heads up when you called me.

Randy, good catch. I'll call Homeland Security and get back to you soon.

Rafe called Mark Richards. "Richards here."

"Mark, you have a big problem in LA with terrorists thinking of taking down aircraft with shoulder fired rockets flying into LAX. Air Force One may be one of the targets. You better get the warning out to all the agencies involved and let me know if we can help."

"Hang on! I'll get Eloise on the line and you repeat that."

"No need. I've already mentally informed her and she's on it. Give me a call if you need me."

Thirty minutes later, Rafe got the call he was expecting from Eloise. "Rafe we need your people to ring LAX and stop those rockets. Air Force One has been diverted to San Diego."

"If they fire from a boat we may have a problem. I'll get back with you as soon as we get more information."

Randy, Homeland Security wants our help in stopping those rockets. Air Force One was diverted to San Diego. They want us to ring LAX with our people, but if they fire from a boat we can only stop them if some of our people are in the air. Do we have a time line on the attack yet?

No! We only have ten adults here and need at least fifteen more.

I'll send them to you. Where should they land?

Manhattan Beach at this location. Randy then gave Rafe a mental picture where he wanted them.

Okay. Meet them in twenty minutes.

Rafe then mentally sent for five members each from Silicon Valley, Augusta, and Athens to meet at the designated place, then Rafe and Vera teleported there as well. They were the second group to arrive behind Sally Gleason from Silicon Valley. Minutes later the remaining members arrived. Randy quickly outlined his plan of defense and dispersed the members to their positions.

Randy looked at Rafe and Vera. "The attack can happen at any time and I need you two out over the water."

Rafe and Vera nodded and started west, flying low over the water below the flight path of the aircraft. Two miles from shore they encountered two sixty-foot boats with occupants who were thinking of rockets and aircraft. As they got closer they were able to determine everyone on board the boats were terrorists and they enclosed them in bubbles just as a rocket was fired from one of them. The rocket exploded causing the boat to explode as well. The occupants of the remaining boat gazed in fear at the two people floating in the air 100 yards away.

One of the terrorists started firing at them with an automatic rifle; bullets ricocheted back into the boat hitting several terrorists, including the shooter.

Soon, they could see a Coast Guard Cutter approaching, so they moved to the far side of the terrorist boat to avoid discovery. When the terrorists were under the guns of the Coast Guard, Rafe and Vera released the bubble and teleported back to Macon.

Rafe mentally called Randy McPherson and told him about the two boats they took out and asked about the others' status.

You got most of the action. Sally's people took care of one other group before they could fire and they were turned over to the FBI. Everyone teleported back home and I don't think the public was even aware of what was going on.

Randy, you and your people did a good job and you will get a plaque to remind everyone of your actions. Both of your parents are very proud of you and will speak to you later. I need to talk to Homeland Security and see what the situation is there.

After mentally speaking with the heads of the other three locations that participated in foiling the terrorist attacks, Rafe called Eloise at Homeland Security. *Eloise, have you got it all tied together yet?*

Yes. I want to thank you for giving us some prisoners to interrogate. Maybe we can get a handle on who was behind this attack.

What was the Coast Guard's response to what they found on the shot up boat?

They couldn't figure why they started shooting at each other and they never saw you. We'll try to keep your people out of the records.

It looks like interagency cooperation worked well this time. Can you see any improvement?

It really helped that you contacted us first so that we got the ball rolling to the agencies involved. It worked like it was supposed to for once. I really like this job you helped me get and it feels good when it all comes together.

Give me a call if you need help or advice. Bye.

Rafe and Vera continued their mental checks with the heads of the remaining Group houses. After finishing this task they decided to visit one of their children and grandchildren in Savannah.

* * *

A year later Rafe and Vera were mentally called to NYC to meet with Senator Chase and Congressman Grimes in Phillip Seymour's office. When Rafe and Vera arrived they found they were the last to appear and immediately greeted the others.

Rafe asked, "Have either of you had any ill effects from the treatment?"

Margaret Chase answered, "No. We both feel fine. Really we feel better than fine. I may look the same age, but I feel over ten years younger. We never had the side effect you warned us about, but we both have discovered we aren't finished with our sexual nature. We have tried to keep it a secret, but Ben and I have become engaged."

Vera was ecstatic. "Well, you two won't be the first to become a couple with mixed political backgrounds. I want to congratulate you both."

"Do you think I can conceive? I still get my period, but normally my age would risk the baby having problems."

"Why don't you make an appointment with Dr. Sheldon. I'm sure he can check you out and answer your questions."

Rafe asked, "Phillip said you two have a proposal you want to run by us?"

Margaret said, "Yes, I got sidetracked. We have a good chance to push through the Chase Bill. As you know I drafted this bill to provide education funds for at risk children in poor school districts. We think we have the needed votes to pass both houses, but aren't confident the President will sign it. Do you think you can influence him to not veto it if it lands on his desk?"

Rafe thought a moment before answering, "It might be possible, but I'm not holding much hope for my chances. This might be a budget buster for him. Can you think of a way he can get the funds from another source?"

The two politicians mentally compared possible solutions before agreeing. Grimes spoke, "There is a military aircraft boondoggle that needs to have its funds pulled. It is enough to pay for this education bill twice over."

Rafe nodded. "I think it's worth a try. Why not wait while I give him a mental call.

Mr. President. This is Rafe Johnson; do you have time to speak to me?

Not right now, try me again in twenty minutes.

Rafe turned to the others. "He said to call back in twenty minutes. Margaret why don't you try to contact Dr. Sheldon about your question while we wait."

Margaret made her mental call to Dr. Sheldon and shortly turned to the others. Ben, he wants us to teleport to his office later today at three p.m. for tests before he can give us an answer.

After twenty minutes had elapsed, Rafe tried to mentally call the President again.

Mr. President, its Rafe Johnson again. Can you talk?

Yes, what can I do for you?

I'm interested in your signing of the Chase Bill if it gets to your desk. I understand you are concerned about the cost when you have a tight budget, however, I have a possible solution. You can kill the Military's failed Star Fighter Project, which will provide more than enough funds. Of course the Military will want to use the funds for other projects, but the children need it more.

Let me look into it and get back to you. I can still use that number you gave me?

Yes. Thank you for your consideration, Mr. President.

Rafe smiled at the others in the room. "Well, he didn't turn me down. He said he would look into it and get back to me."

A month later the Chase Education Bill passed and was on the President's desk for his signature. The Military Lobby had gotten wind of funds being diverted from the Star Fighter Project and were putting up a media fight to keep the Bill from being signed. However, after a week of controversy the President signed the Bill into law.

CHAPTER 44

Senator Chase and Congressman Grimes were married and expecting a child. The couple was happy and living together in a Georgetown townhouse after selling both their former homes.

Rafe and Vera were in Macon supervising the various Group houses and its numerous financial interests when one night they shared the same dream. Awakening, they found themselves floating above their bed, much like their first shared prognostication of future events. Rafe grabbed Vera's hand and slowly they settled back onto their bed.

Vera pulled herself against Rafe's chest, hugging him tightly as she shuddered in anger and fear. "Honey, what are we going to do?"

"First let's recap and see if we remember the same things. The first thing I remember is us flying over a long big lake with trees everywhere. The lake had ocean-going ships on it heading in both directions, and there was suddenly a huge explosion from one of the ships followed by a mushroom shaped cloud. What do you remember?"

"The same as you flying over a lake with ships on it. The ship that exploded was a grain hauler from White Star Lines heading southwest. Based on the size and shape of the lake, it had to be either Lake Ontario or Lake Erie. The trees were in color, so this will happen in the fall."

"Wow! You do have a memory for details. If it's going to happen this fall we have three or four months to prepare. I'm going to let Homeland Security know what we foresee and then let's fly over the lakes and see if we can pinpoint which lake it is."

Rafe called Deputy Director Eloise Black of Homeland Security.

Eloise, this is Rafe Johnson, can you talk?

Yes. What's up?

Vera and I had a vision where a grain hauler had a nuclear explosion on what we think is either Lake Ontario or Lake Erie in the fall of the year. We think it's going to happen this fall and Vera and I are going to do a fly over to try and locate the spot we visualized. Depending on the wind, the fall out would cover most of the northeastern seaboard. Canada would probably be affected as well.

Crappola! I'll start the ball rolling here while you try to find the location. Talk to you later.

Rafe and Vera teleported to Erie, Pennsylvania and then started flying northeast along the U.S. shoreline until they reached about the mid-point of Lake Ontario. When they were sure they found the location, they took a GPS reading and teleported back to Macon. Rafe and Vera found Adam in the workshop and told him of their problem.

Vera then spoke, "Adam, concentrate on the grain hauler in my memory and draw a picture we can fax to Homeland Security."

Adam concentrated on his mother's memory of the ship. "I think I got it," he said before starting on the drawing.

Two hours later he gave his parents his first draft. Vera made a few adjustments with a pencil.

"Adam I think it might help if you added color to this drawing. The ship's hull is white with rust streaks here and there along the water line. The bridge is red with a big white star on its side and the name of the ship begins with the letters A-D."

Two hours later Adam finished his revised color drawing. Vera considered it carefully, looking for any detail she could add. She handed the drawing to Rafe. "What do you think?"

Rafe looked at it in amazement. "Babe. I knew you had a good memory, but this is like looking at a photograph."

"It is good, isn't it? However, that's because of Adam, not me. Adam, this is as good as I can remember. Add the latitude and longitude and fax it to the number Homeland gave us. Wait a minute; add the tree color to the drawing. Maybe they can get the time frame to within a couple of weeks."

When Adam finished and got Vera's approval on the drawing, he faxed it to Homeland Security. Two hours later, Rafe called Eloise.

Eloise this is Rafe. Can you talk?

Yes, but you got a shit storm started after we got that picture you faxed. At least we know now where to start looking.

Vera thought it was a White Star Line ship and you might get a better idea of the time frame from the tree color at that location. If you need anything call us.

Two months later Eloise called Rafe. *We've determined the ship in the drawing is the ADILE with the White Star Line. She is now heading toward the St. Lawrence Seaway from her last port of Bandar-e Abbas, Iran. She was there for three months, reportedly doing a refit. She'll be in Canada's territorial waters within twenty hours, but Canada refuses to take any action based upon the information you gave us. Our only recourse is to sink it now before it reaches Canada's waters, but that will surely bring serious backlash from the Middle East. Do you have a solution?*

How soon do you need to know?

Two hours at the latest.

Okay. I'll get back to you.

Rafe immediately called a mental Board Meeting where he informed the members of the approaching terrorist attack and what the political problems were. Rafe asked,

Does anyone have any ideas other than our own direct intervention?

Sally was the only member to answer. *We are the only ones with the ability to do this. Can we make it look like an accident? Maybe causing the devise to explode prematurely?*

That's not the problem. If it goes off it's going to take a bunch of ships with it and that's not even considering the fallout, Rafe said.

Sally replied, *What if we teleported it into space toward the Sun?*

That might work. I wonder how many of us it will take to do that?

Vera answered, *Let's get twenty of us together with another twenty in reserve and try it. We need a platform to work from; I bet we have some surface ships near there.*

Rafe said, *I'll have Eloise arrange a ride for us and every other member can follow our thoughts and join in the effort.*

Eloise this is Rafe, can you talk?

Yes. What have you come up with?

Arrange for twenty of us to come aboard one of our ships near the ADILE and we will teleport it into the Sun. We will need a picture of the ship and if there's a telepath aboard that would help.

Check back with me in thirty minutes.

Rafe mentally picked the twenty Group members during the wait and told them to be ready to teleport when they received a destination. Thirty minutes later he mentally called Eloise.

Eloise, this is Rafe. What do you have for me?

I'm looking at a picture of the USS Gregory, a Helicopter Attack Carrier that is ten miles away from the ADILE. There's no telepath aboard. Can you use my eyes to key on this ship?

Yes, I think so. You volunteers key on my memory of the ship and teleport on the count of three. One, two, three.

Twenty Group members suddenly appeared on the flight deck of the USS Gregory. Lt. Commander George Meadows hurried over and asked to speak to the leader. Rafe said, "That would be me. Is there somewhere we can all get out of the wind and still see the ADILE when we get within two miles of her?"

"I'll check with the Captain, but you will all fit on the Bridge."

"I thank you. I didn't take into account the difference in temperature from where we came from and here."

Captain Jack Walker welcomed the Group members onto his Bridge and Lt. Commander Meadows introduced Rafe to him. After shaking hands, the Captain ruefully said, "When I was told to expect twenty people to suddenly appear on my ship I thought somebody upstairs had lost their marbles. Now what can I do for you?"

"Captain, head for the ADILE and when we are close enough we are going to try to teleport it into the Sun."

"Why do you want to do that?"

"The ship is full of terrorists with a nuclear device they intend to explode while they are on Lake Ontario."

"Shit! You crew members who heard that and are about to see other things, be aware it is top secret and not to be repeated unless you have been given clearance to do so."

Captain Walker shook his head and muttered, "Nobody tells me anything and when they do I can't ever repeat it. Helmsman, head toward the ADILE at twenty knots."

The USS Gregory approached the ADILE at a twenty-five degree angle from the rear. When the Gregory was five miles astern of the ADILE, Rafe told the Captain to hold his position.

Rafe mentally informed other members of his plan, which was to place a bubble around the ADILE and then teleport the ship into the Sun. The entire membership using Rafe's mental image placed a large bubble around the ADILE, visualizing it vanishing into the Sun.

The ADILE suddenly disappeared, leaving a large hole in the ocean, leaving nothing of the ship behind. Captain Walker stared at the spot where the ADILE disappeared.

"Mr. Johnson, should I make any kind of response to what happened here?"

"I would recommend you make no log entries, but write a confidential letter to your Fleet Superiors detailing what happened here. I'll tell Homeland Security to grease the skids so it gets to the right people. I want to thank you and the crew of the USS Gregory for your help in this matter. I wouldn't be surprised if your ship received a Presidential citation for this job."

Captain Walker shook Rafe's hand and wished him well before the Group all teleported back to their original places. Rafe and Vera arrived at their apartment, relieved that another terrorist attack had failed. They decided to clean up and go out for dinner to celebrate.

CHAPTER 45

Ten years later the United States was in the process of electing a new President. Senator Margaret Chase was running as a Democrat against Republican Pat Tucker, the former Governor of California. The previous President had resigned in disgrace due to allegations of illegal drug use.

The SPAC of the Group was providing substantial campaign funds to support Senator Chase. Chase's husband of twelve years, Republican Congressman Ben Grimes, was openly supporting her to the dismay of Tucker. The Republican Party was even threatening to kick him out of the Party, but Grimes retaliated saying if he ran again he would run under another party's banner. Three months before the election the polls showed Chase ahead by almost twenty points.

Former Governor Tucker couldn't seem to open his mouth without offending some group or organization and the poll numbers continued to widen until Election Day. Senator Chase won by a landslide, with Governor Tucker only carrying four southern conservative States and didn't carry his own state of California.

Rafe and Vera mentally congratulated the now President-Elect Margaret Chase and wished her well in the coming years. The Democrat Party also elected a majority in both houses of Congress, which ensured the end of gridlock that had plagued the government in the previous four years.

Rafe and Vera received an invitation to attend the Presidential Inauguration and a private meeting following in the White House. Rafe mentally informed the Group members of the invitation and asked any who were interested to mentally follow the proceedings though his viewpoint.

The day of the Inauguration Rafe and Vera teleported to the office of Congressman Ben Grimes, where his Chief of Staff escorted them to their assigned seats near the President-Elect.

Rafe spoke to Vera. *It's a fine clear day for the swearing in isn't it? I'm really glad you insisted on bringing our heavy coats because it's got to be below freezing.*

After that trip we made to the USS Gregory you'd think you would remember the temperature difference between Macon and Washington, especially in the winter. Burr, it's really cold. Do you think anyone would notice if I turned on the heat?

Funny! I thought you were going to wear your long johns and thermal socks?

They were then distracted by the arrival of the President-Elect and her family, who all sat down in front of them. Ben Grimes winked at them before helping his daughter Vera, into the seat next to her mother. After taking her seat, Vera turned and smiled at the people she considered her Uncle and the Aunt she was named after.

The ceremony seemed to go quickly with President Chase gaving a stirring address before an appreciative audience. Later, Grimes' Chief of Staff collected them and took them to a waiting black Suburban driven by a Secret Service Agent. The agent was a telepath, but made no attempt to read their minds.

Curious, Rafe asked, *Agent Remoras how long have you been a telepath?*

Five years sir. I have been briefed on your past history and was told not to initiate any kind of communication, but could answer your questions.

I'm curious about the term past history. How many years would that cover?

The file I read started with the two of you saving the life of President Charles Stevens.

Has being a telepath helped you doing your job?

Yes, in so many ways. Personally, I wish I could turn it off when I'm off duty.

No one has taught you how to block thoughts of others?

No, I didn't think it was possible.

After we get to our destination, I'll give you a lesson on how I do it. It should work for you as well.

The car pulled up to the back gate to the White House and went through security. When they stopped at the White House, Rafe mentally showed the agent how he blocked outside thoughts. After trying it the agent's face glowed with satisfaction.

Rafe chuckled. "Don't forget to turn it back on."

Thanks, I already did.

Rafe helped Vera out of the vehicle and were met by two more Secret Service Agents who escorted them into the White House after first giving them a quick metal scan.

Rafe looked at Vera and shook his head in disgust. *Old habits are hard to stop. If we wanted to do harm we could teleport into their presence.*

The older agent smiled at him. *Tell me about it. We still have to follow guidelines we know are meaningless when we encounter you. Since there isn't that many of you, we need to continue the practice. Please follow me and I'll take you to the elevator to the President's living quarters.*

Rafe and Vera stepped off the elevator where they were met by Vera Grimes who immediately gave each of them a hug before taking her Aunt Vera's hand and started walking down the hallway, *they're waiting just down the hall to the left.*

Aunt Vera said, "You've grown since I last visited you. You must be almost ten now."

"Almost eleven and you already knew that Aunt Vera. You already teleported my birthday present last week. By the way, thanks for the dress. I'm going to wear it tonight when we go ball hopping."

Still holding Aunt Vera's hand, Vera led them into the sitting room where the President and First Gentleman were waiting. They were still wearing their formal wear, but were relaxing with a drink in hand. Ben Grimes held up his glass. "Care for a refreshment?"

Rafe smiled and answered, "We'll take what you're having."

"Jack and Soda?"

Vera shuddered, then answered, "That sounds too strong for me, what are you drinking Maggie?"

"Ben, get her a Vodka Collins. Vera get yourself a soft drink and sit with us."

After they were all seated with refreshments in hand, President Chase looked at her benefactors with a small smile on her face. "When you brought us into the Group, did you have any inkling that this would come to pass?"

Rafe smiled at her. "Well, I knew one of you had a good chance if circumstances fell into place, but realistically I only gave you a twenty percent chance of making it. You even beat the odds by being the first female President."

"Actually, being a female helped me in this election. I want your help in picking my staff. I want a large portion to be from the Group. My Chief of Staff, James Seymour, is a member and can show the others we bring in how to do their jobs. Having telepaths on my staff will greatly enhance my abilities."

"How many do you want? You will need to bring the Secret Service and FBI into the loop of who they are to get by the background checks for security clearances."

"Darn! I forgot about that. I guess I'll have to use my Presidential muscle to get that done. Anything else?"

"What are you going to do about selecting your cabinet, especially the Heads of the Homeland Security, FBI, CIA, Secretary of State, NSA, and DOD? These should be people with that type of background and not just payback for political favors. I personally like those currently heading Homeland and the FBI, but don't know about the others. We need professionals heading the CIA, NSA, and the DOD. I would recommend using the best of their DD's for those positions."

President Chase nodded. "You have a point with the Heads of Homeland and the FBI and if they don't want to work with me I'll check out their Deputy Directors. I'm thinking of leaving James Gilmore as the Secretary of State. He has done a great job for the past four years under trying conditions and is as nonpolitical as anybody in his position can be."

"Do you think he would be interested in staying on?"

"I have a meeting with him scheduled for next week, but he is a man who really likes his work. He will be even better if he has telepathic abilities. My predecessor, among his other faults, was not smart in how he doled out the telepath pills."

"Your daughter, Vera, is very excited about attending some of the balls with you. Is she going to have an escort she can dance with?"

"Aunt Vera! Can you get someone my age who can actually dance?"

"Oh, I'm pretty sure I can find someone. Do you want someone shy or one that has a take charge attitude?"

Vera considered a moment. "A take charge attitude and maybe two years older."

Aunt Vera looked at the President, who appeared to be having a stroke. "Maggie, what do you think?"

The President visibly calmed herself before answering, "Honey, are you sure you want to do this. You don't even know him yet. What if he's two inches shorter than you and stumbles around the dance floor?"

"Aunt Vera will pick one just right. Won't you?" She said, looking at her Aunt with imploring eyes.

Vera looked at Rafe and asked, "Robbie Gleason? His mother was a dance instructor and he is quite handsome for his age. I'll have him teleport here now and you can decide if he is acceptable."

Vera mentally contacted Millie Gleason and asked her if they could borrow Robbie as an escort for the President's daughter. Ten minutes later Robbie was standing before them. He looked a little peeved as this was not his idea, but when he saw Rafe and Vera his frown became a smile as he greeted them.

Rafe introduced him to the President and her husband and then to Vera. It was obvious Vera liked the looks of this young man before she asked, "Aunt Vera says your mother taught you how to dance. Can you demonstrate a waltz with me?"

Robbie looked at her and smiled. "It would be easier with music."

Ben Grimes went to an old fashioned turntable and motioned him over to select a waltz from the LPs available. Robbie picked out one and gave it to Ben who started it playing while Robbie and Vera took their position in the center of the room. When the music started, Robbie led Vera around the room in a graceful waltz while she gazed at him in happy fascination.

When the music ended, they both bowed to the President as if they had rehearsed it. Vera turned to Robbie and blurted, "You're a great dancer! Will you be my escort tonight?"

Robbie smiled at his dance partner. "I would be happy to, but I don't have a tux."

President Chase said, "No problem. I've been told there is a selection of tuxes available here. I'll just get one altered to fit you. In the meantime, let's have a late lunch and we can get to know each other better."

Robbie was at his best behavior, his mother taught him well in the social graces. He and Vera Grimes were seated next to each other and found they shared common interests, as they were only eighteen months apart in age. Vera's parents seemed to relax after watching the two interact with each other. After the meal concluded, a tailor was waiting with several tuxes to select from and fit to his size.

While the tailor was working on the tux, Vera wanted to practice several waltzes that would be played at the balls. Rafe and Vera stayed with them while the President and her husband tended to other matters.

Later, everyone gathered for a photo session before they departed the White House for the balls. Robbie and Vera were a perfect couple in miniature, Robbie only two inches taller than her. There were group pictures of the First Family, one with Robbie added, one with Rafe and Vera included, and one of only Robbie and little Vera.

After the photo session, Rafe and Vera teleported back to Macon. The others started their ball hopping. The President's party attended four Balls, staying only long enough for one dance at each and back into the White House three hours later.

Robbie said his goodbyes to the First Family, but before leaving he kissed Vera on both cheeks and said he had a great time. He then teleported back to his home in Houston, while Vera looked at the spot where he had stood with a wistful expression of regret that their time together had ended.

CHAPTER 46

The next day Rafe and Vera were watching the media coverage of the Presidential Balls. The networks were all ecstatic about the dancing performance of the President's daughter and her escort, comparing them to Fred Astaire and Ginger Rogers.

Someone had recorded one of their dances, which had become viral on the Internet. This seemed to fuel the interest in the young couple and dancing began to be popular again. The media frenzy continued for a week cumulating in all three major TV networks showing the dancing couple and speculating on how they had met.

Rafe contacted Robbie Gleason and asked, *how are you holding up under the media attention?*

At first I hated it, especially when my friends in the Houston house started teasing me. But after watching the dance replayed, I'm kind of proud of our performance. I wonder how Vera is taking it?

Why don't you contact her and find out. She might need a friendly person to confide in.

Thanks. I'll try and contact her. Bye.

Vera Grimes, this is Robbie, can you hear me?

Yes! Oh Robbie have you seen us on the news?

I thought we looked really good. My friends in the Houston house teased me pretty badly for a few days. They finally admitted we looked "Fine". How about you?

The same. My friends at school wanted to know who that handsome boy was I was dancing with, but I told them I was sworn to secrecy and you were my Secret Service protection.

Are your parents okay with it?

No problem with them. They were worried about me. I guess the next time we dance it will have to be in private.

Yeah. Is that an invitation?

Yes! I'll ask and get back to you.

Okay. I'm home schooled here. What grade level are you studying at?

I'm at second-year college level and it's really boring. What about you?

I've finished my BA and I'm now working on a Masters in Computer Science using computer courses. I can study at my own speed that way. Why don't you try it, I promise you it won't be boring. I've got access to some cool courses.

Can you send me a list before I hit my parents up for this?

I'll teleport a copy to that table in the sitting room where we first met. Is that okay?

Okay, but contact me first so I can get to it before the house staff finds it.

I'll talk to you later. Bye.

Bye.

Vera couldn't stop smiling, thinking of Robbie contacting her. When the family gathered for their evening meal, she showed her parents the variety of computer courses available and told them how fast Robbie had advanced in his own studies.

When Margaret heard that Vera had been in contact with Robbie, she asked, "How is Robbie coping seeing his face on TV so much?"

"Apparently, he's living in a closed environment and he got teased a little by his friends, but he said we looked really good dancing together."

"How about you Vera. How do you feel with all the attention focused on you?"

Vera shrugged. "Much better now that I've talked to Robbie. It helps to have someone who shared the experience give his support. I've invited him back here so we can dance in private together. When you can find the time, he said he would be happy to pop in."

Margaret looked at her daughter for a moment. "Your friends at school don't meet your social needs, do they?"

"No. I'm too much younger than those who are at my grade level, and any my age think I'm either too smart or stuck up. Robbie likes me because of who I am, nothing else. I feel like I'm falling behind in my potential by taking classes. I want to try different fields of study."

"Vera, first you can tell Robbie he can pop in here anytime one of us is here to supervise. As far as the computer courses go, make a list of what you are interested in and we will go from there. Finish the courses you have already started at school before we pull you out. Anything else?"

Vera smiled at her Mother. "No Mother. Thanks for listening to me. I promise Robbie and I won't cause any problems, at least not until I'm eighteen."

Margaret looked up in alarm at that last comment, but then smiled as she detected from her daughter's thoughts the little dig she gave back to her parents for the requirement of parental supervision when Robbie was present.

* * *

Sally and Grant Gleason were working in their office at Albertson Electronics. The new President of AE, Peter Whitestone, was only a figurehead and the Gleason's made all major decisions. Former President Sharron Blackman had retired six years ago. Under the Gleasons' direct control the business had shown steady growth, helped somewhat by the occasional new invention from Adam Johnson.

Sally's cell phone pinged. It indicated the FBI was calling. She looked over at Grant muttering, "Oh poop! It's the FBI."

"This is Sally, what can I do for the FBI?"

"Special Agent James Walker here. We have a developing situation here in the Bay area we need to consult with you on. Can you meet me in my office ASAP?"

"Are you a telepath? If so, picture your office in your mind."

"How's that?"

"I can read you now and I'm on my way."

Sally and Grant teleported to SA Walker's office, who surprised, hung up his telephone. "Okay, I'm here. What's the problem?"

"I'll call my team together and we'll meet them in our conference room."

Once in the meeting room SA Walker asked if they wanted any beverage while they waited on the others to arrive. Five minutes later six more agents arrived and took their seats while staring at the apparently young Group members.

SA Walker cleared his throat, bringing the attention of the others back to him. "Fellow agents, I want to introduce Sally and her husband…"

"Mark."

"Who you are aware has helped the Agency several times over the past thirty plus years. Those of you who are telepaths should be aware that their powers far exceed yours. Sally, can you tell me what your telepathy limits are?"

"Unknown. We've talked to other members throughout the United States."

"Jesus!" Said one male agent, and two others faces went pale in shock.

"Yes. Like I said, they are powerful telepaths. For example they teleported into my office by reading my mind picture of it. This is why we need them on this project."

SA Walker then proceeded to tell them of their problem. When he finished, he asked, "Can you help us?"

Sally and Grant mentally conversed. After a few minutes Sally turned back to SA Walker and answered, "I'll need to get approval from Rafe and Vera for this situation. Why don't you 'all take a fifteen minute break while we consult."

Sally and Grant initiated a mental call to Rafe and Vera.

Rafe-Vera, this is Sally and Grant Gleason. The Bay Area FBI needs our help with a special situation developing here. Their own telepaths have learned of a probable attempt to destroy both bay bridges coupled with another attempt to use a bio bomb. They want our help to locate and stop the terrorist attempts. I estimate we will need at least thirty members; more would be better.

How many adults do you have in the Bay Area?

Twenty-six and I think eighteen in LA.

I don't want to take more than half from you or LA. I'll get the rest from the other houses. Will fifty be enough?

Yes, I think so. If we need more I'll let you know. Send them to this location.

Let us know if you need any help.

I will. Bye.

Bye.

Sally then mentally called Jessica McPherson Blake in LA and arranged for eight members to teleport to her location. When the other agents returned from their fifteen-minute break Sally informed them the operation was approved and fifty members would be arriving soon. They were planning on where to place the members as they started to arrive.

To make room for other arrivals, they were told to wait outside the room in the hallway until called back inside. Thirty minutes later all had arrived, including Rafe and Vera. Rafe told Sally she was the leader of this operation, he and Vera were there to observe and offer help as needed.

Two member teams were placed at the Bay bridges and single members placed throughout the city monitoring mental thoughts of bio weapons or bombs. Sally and Mark were responsible for receiving any alerts from her people or the FBI telepaths. After three hours, they started relieving people on a rotating basis until they got their first hit. The second day both bridge teams received thoughts of people driving trucks with bombs aboard.

Sally instructed the teams to place bubbles around the trucks and teleport them into the Bay. Surprise and concern erupted when two large explosions burst in the Bay near Alcatraz Island. The explosions brought a sprite of thoughts about a bio weapon from three locations. Sally's people quickly determined the locations and informed the FBI. Two locations were in apartments three miles apart in heavily populated areas. The third was in the downtown business district.

Sally consulted with SA Walker on the best action to take. The terrorists were not moving from inside the buildings and based upon past history, they would detonate the weapon if attacked. Sally suggested her Group members mentally disable the terrorists. They could move or disable the weapons afterward.

SA Walker agreed to Sally's plan and after placing her teams nearby, but out of sight of the terrorists, Sally ordered her team to mentally knock them out. The FBI then quickly entered the buildings and apprehended the terrorists and retrieved their bio weapons. They found one of the weapons was activated with a timer. Sally ordered her people to place a bubble around it and teleport it into the Sun.

The other two weapons were placed in bio containers and transported to a safe location. The six captured terrorists were searched and placed in restraints before being transported to the FBI office for interrogation. All Group members except for Rafe, Vera, Mark, and Sally, teleported back to their home locations. The others returned with SA Walker to the FBI office.

When they were all back into the conference room, SA Walker breathed a sigh of relief.

"I want to think you all for your help again. We couldn't have done this job without your help. I especially liked how you disposed of that active bio weapon. I didn't even think that would be possible."

Rafe said, "We are happy to help and don't hesitate to call on us again if needed. However; please don't mention us or our actions to the media. We perform better out of the public's eyes, plus what the terrorists don't know won't hurt us. If there is nothing else, we will take our leave."

SA Walker replied, "No, that's all. I'll give you a call if I need you."

CHAPTER 47

Sally and Mark teleported back to their home, with Rafe and Vera following them. Seated at the dining room table with Rafe and Vera they completed an after action report. Rafe began.

"You did well, probably as well as Vera or I could have done. You asked for help in a timely manner, analyzed your manpower requirements and dispersed them in a logical way. You quickly made adjustments in your manpower after realizing the time factor, and brought the problem to a satisfactory solution. Vera, tell her of anything she could have done better."

Vera's fist hit his shoulder playfully. "Well, you could have told us to buzz off, but that wouldn't have gone over very well."

That brought an unexpected laugh from Sally. "Vera, you shouldn't put such thoughts in my head," she said, controlling her laughter.

"I do appreciate your feedback and I'm happy you think I did a good job. What is going on with my grandson Robbie?"

Vera replied, "Oh, Rafe drafted him to act as escort to Maggie's daughter for the Inauguration Balls. He is a great dancer and he and little Vera danced beautifully together."

"I know, I saw them on TV. How is he handling the media attention?"

Rafe said, "I talked to him and he seems okay with it. Apparently little Vera got it much worse, being the President's daughter. Robbie talked to her and she seems okay now. Robbie says he's been back to the White House twice now to dance with her."

Sally snorted. "That little scamp. Why he's barely thirteen. Maggie better keep a watch on those two."

Vera replied, "Don't worry about that, at least for another four or five years. Little Vera has a crush on Robbie, but they are both smart enough to want to finish their education before getting too involved with each other."

Vera reflected for a moment. "Maybe I should visit little Vera and get a read on just how much of a crush she has on Robbie."

Sally said, "May I come with you? If she's going to be a possible future mate of my grandson, I'd like to meet her."

Vera smiled at her. "I sometimes wished I had interviewed my grandchildren's love interests before they committed to marriage, but I'm afraid we don't have much say in who they fall in love with, but I'll try to get a date from Maggie when we can visit."

After contacting the President they were invited for dinner that evening at seven. Sally looked over at her husband. "Mark, now that I'm going I'm having second thoughts about grilling the President's daughter."

Vera smothered a laugh with her hand. "What! Sally Gleason afraid of offending the President of the United States. Besides, you aren't going to be grilling anyone. You are there to get to know her and establish a bridge between the two families. Besides, it's just going to be us women talking among ourselves. This could be fun."

Later that evening Vera and Sally arrived in the Sitting Room of the residence inside the White House. Margaret Chase and her daughter were waiting for them. Vera introduced Sally to the mother and daughter as Robbie's grandmother.

Margaret's face reflected her knowledge of Sally's many exploits against terrorists on the West Coast, and now her family tie to Robbie brought another factor into play. Little Vera's face reflected her understanding of Sally's interest in herself.

Vera started the conversation. "Maggie, Sally wanted to meet Vera since she saw Robbie and her dancing on TV. She thought a closer relationship between the two families should be encouraged as long as the two continue as close friends."

Margaret clapped her hands. "Wonderful! Why don't we proceed to the dining room and continue this conversation over dinner."

After everyone was seated and served by the wait staff, they began to eat while slowly getting background information on each other. After dinner, they declined desert and began talking to each other in earnest.

Little Vera was very interested in Sally, as she had heard some of the stories relating to her past exploits, so she asked, "Sally, you are legend among the Group children I've met. Robbie says you are his hero and hopes your genes influence his future."

"Robbie is still young and has not yet had many opportunities to make his mark. However, you both have made world news with your dancing. I know you both didn't intend to create such media frenzy, but with you being part of the First Family almost anything you do is news. Unfortunately, you have made yourself a bigger target for terrorists."

Margaret interrupted, "Have you heard anything specific from that plot you and your people broke up today?"

"No. The FBI had just started their interrogation when we left. I would suggest the First Family's security detail be increased and Vera's outside activity be curtailed for her own protection. You may get prognostication dreams if your family is threatened, but I wouldn't rely on that. Just be careful in what you do and be alert, you may have to defend yourself. Vera, how strong are your powers?"

"Not as strong as yours, but I am telepathic and can teleport myself a short distance, as well as move small objects."

"Good! You need to practice if you want to use your powers for defense. Later, you can learn offensive moves. The next time you see Robbie, ask him to help you with defensive moves."

Vera asked, "Maggie, what training have you and Ben had with defensive moves?"

"None. We didn't think we needed to until now."

Sally exclaimed, "Poop! We need to show you some basic moves, which you can pass on to Ben. Where is your exercise room?"

The President led them to the exercise room where Vera and Sally looked around at what was available. They used their mental telekinesis powers to move the weight and running machines off to one side, then moved the punching bag out into the center of the room.

Vera said, "The push away move is the most versatile. Watch the bag as I mentally push against it."

The big bag jumped away as if hit by someone.

"Maggie, you try it"

The bag moved slightly. "Use more power!"

The bag jumped back further than when Vera moved it. "Okay. Vera, now you do it using your full effort."

The bag jumped back almost to its limit. "Good work Vera. You need to practice on what effort you need to make to achieve your goal."

"A knockout move is where you concentrate your effort on the attacker's brain. This is a move you can't practice as it always disables and sometimes kills the attacker. Use it only if you are directly attacked. Another defensive move is mentally placing and maintaining a bubble around yourself or a close few. This bubble can't be entered by anyone or by bullets, but shouldn't be maintained too long as no air can get in. Watch what happens as I visualize a bubble around the bag."

A nearly transparent bubble appeared around the bag, but then disappeared as Sally released it. "Maggie, you try it."

A similar bubble appeared around the bag and then disappeared when Maggie was told to release it. "Okay, that was great. Vera it's your turn."

A bubble appeared and disappeared on command. "Okay, you both have been doing great. Let's try telekinesis. See that big ball over in the corner. I'm going to use it as a weapon."

The ball left the floor and swiftly struck the bag. "Use a smaller and harder object when you select a weapon. Your turn Maggie."

Both Maggie and Little Vera successfully used telekinesis as a weapon. "You can also use teleportation as a defensive move. Just move yourself far enough away to avoid the attackers. Just don't panic. You have the means to take care of yourself and those around you if you stay calm and plan your moves."

Little Vera beamed. "No wonder you kicked terrorist butt. I had no idea how my powers could be used in a fight."

Maggie frowned at her daughter. "Watch your language! But you're right, no wonder the FBI uses her as the go-to person when they have a problem."

Vera said, "She comes by it naturally. Did you know her three times Grandmother is Anne Hawk Stephenson? Rafe and I were the original pair of the Group and were retired CIA Agents. Anne and Peter Stephenson was the second branch and were active FBI Agents. Both Anne and I are full-blooded Choctaw American Indians from the Bird Clan. She is a Hawk and I'm a Sparrow, and we are related by marriage through my first marriage to a Hawk. In fact all the other Group members now share our blood lines."

Little Vera exclaimed, "You mean I'm related to Robbie?"

"Remotely, like a cousin three or four times removed."

The President grimaced. "Vera, you would pick out that one piece of information to zero in on."

Sally said, "Well, it makes sense she's concerned if Robbie's an eligible man to consider for a future mate."

Little Vera reddened in embarrassment. "Why, I'm too young to even consider that."

Vera answered, "Apparently you are or you wouldn't have asked the question."

"Aunt Vera you tricked me! I like Robbie, but we haven't even kissed except a peck on my cheek. I don't even know whether or not he likes me that way."

Maggie said, "Oh, he likes you. He is young and may not yet know what his feelings are, but he would never have braved coming to the White House to meet you if he didn't."

"Maybe I'm just a good dancer and no one at his house is better."

"You do look good together when you dance, but I don't think that's the attraction for him. What do you talk about when you're together?"

"About each other's background and family. We talk about our studies and what we want to do when we are adults, what our parents want us to do or expect from us. Just getting to know each other."

Maggie smiled sadly at her daughter. "Oh my! Have you had your first argument yet?"

"Not really. We have disagreed on some minor things, but we didn't argue. Why do you ask?"

"How did you feel when he didn't agree with you on something?"

"A little hurt, as if my thinking was flawed somehow. But we both have strong personalities and we talked it though until we resolved it."

Maggie looked at the other two women and sadly shook her head. "Well, I'm glad you two came calling. At least now we know what we have developing here. If it continues I foresee an eventual joining of our two families. Whatever they do in the future, I predict a substantial impact will be felt."

Little Vera looked at her mother and then the others. "Was this an intervention or just an attempt to find out how serious Robbie and I are?"

Maggie hugged her daughter. "Honey you're not even twelve yet and we wanted to find out just how emotionally you feel toward Robbie. We discovered you both have edged past simple friendship but had not yet reached full love for each other. I want you both to continue your studies and discover what you want to do with your life, either separately or together. Your families will support you in whatever you decide."

CHAPTER 48

When Vera returned to Macon, she informed Rafe of what she, Sally, and Maggie learned about Little Vera and Robbie's relationship and how they had left it.

"What's been happening here while I've been gone?"

"Not much. I wonder if we should take a more proactive approach toward the terrorists instead of just reacting to what they initiate."

Vera nodded. "We know Iran was directly involved in that attempted nuclear attack against the U.S., and I bet they were involved in the recent Bay Area attack. What can we do that will cripple or kill their nuclear program?"

"I bet I can ask someone who has a vested interest in that goal."

"Israel?"

"Former Prime Minister Goldstein said Israel would be our friend for life. I think I'll try to cash in on that, and he should know who we need to talk to."

Rafe mentally tried to contact Goldstein, hoping he had taken a telepathy pill. By chance Goldstein had and Rafe found his mind glow.

Prime Minister Goldstein this is Rafe Johnson, can you talk?

Yes. Is this really you?

I wasn't sure you had taken a telepathy pill, but luck is on our side. I want to have a face-to-face meeting with someone who has good knowledge of where to strike Iran's nuclear capability where it will do the most harm. Can you arrange that?

Does your government sanction this?

No. I want to do it in such a way that it appears to have been an accident. That way, they can't point a finger at anyone. Will you do it?

Please contact me this time tomorrow and I will have an answer for you.

Sounds good. I'll talk to you then.

Rafe turned to Vera and grinned. "They are going to consider it and I'm to get back with him tomorrow. I want you to come with me if we teleport there. You have a good mind for strategy."

The following day Rafe contacted Goldstein.

This is Rafe Johnson. What can you do for me?

We need to discuss what you want to do and why. Will you meet us here in Israel?

When and where? If you picture a mental image of the meet place I can immediately be there.

Wait a moment while we decide.

All right, we have decided. You can come now at this place. Whereupon he projected a mental image of a conference room he was standing in.

Okay, I have the image and I am bringing my wife.

Rafe and Vera teleported to the conference room that contained Goldstein and four other individuals. "We bring gifts," Rafe said as he and Vera set two medium size boxes on the table.

Goldstein eyed the boxes in anticipation as he asked, "What might this be?"

"I thought you might have need of some more telepathy pills for your security services."

"How many doses did you bring?"

"Five hundred. If everyone is here, let's begin our discussion."

Goldstein introduced the others in the room to Rafe and Vera and then asked, "How are you going to be able to enter and do damage to Iran without anyone knowing you were there?"

"You saw how Vera and I teleported ourselves here from the United States. If we have a firm target destination in Iran, we can repeat the process. The damage we can do depends on the location. Why not show us what would be the best targets and we will come up with solutions."

Aviva Donati looked at the two Americans doubtfully, but Goldstein vouched for their abilities, and she witnessed their arrival seemingly out of thin air. She pointed to the conference table.

"We have put together what we believe are the strongest targets. Any one, if destroyed, would cripple Iran's nuclear production. If they were all destroyed it would stop production for many years. However, they are widely separated and one accident cannot explain more than one being destroyed."

"How many targets do you have and where are they located on the map?" Asked Vera.

"Six, and as you can see more than thirty kilometers separate the two closest targets."

"What is the purpose of each target?"

After receiving this information, Vera considered the various factors before asking another question. "This location here is used to separate uranium from ore and at this location forty kilometers away is where they enrich it to make it more useful. These two locations, if destroyed, would keep them from making any more bombs until they were replaced. Where do they keep the processed nuclear material?"

"Right here, thirty-five kilometers north of the other two locations."

"What is the prevailing winds this time of the year?"

"South! If we can explode the nuclear material the fallout will make the other two locations useless."

Vera looked at Rafe. "Honey, what can we do to make nuclear material explode?"

"Heat, pressure or a combination of the two. Or we can place a small nuclear device at its center." Rafe turned to Goldstein. "You know of any place we can get one of those?"

"I might. It just so happens we recovered such a device when al-Qaeda agents tried to smuggle it into Israel. We believe it was made in Iran, and I think it's appropriate we return it. I'll ask for the necessary approval. It might take several days, how can I reach you?"

Rafe gave him one of their prepaid cell numbers and they teleported back to Macon. Three days later the anticipated call arrived. "Approval has been given. When can you return?"

"We shall be there in thirty minutes."

Rafe turned to Vera. "Looks like your plan has been approved. Do you need to do anything before we leave?"

"Let's tell Adam and put the houses on standby alert before we leave. We don't know what Iran's reaction will be."

Thirty minutes later they were back in the conference room. Goldstein pointed to the backpack sitting on the table. "It was controlled by a trigger button, but we added a fifteen minute timer. Do you need more time?"

"No, but we do need a picture of the nuclear storage site. I assume it's underground, but we need as clear a picture of the site that you have."

"We have high resolution satellite pictures. Here are pictures beginning at one kilometer, 1,000 meters, and finally 100 meters. Is this sufficient?"

Rafe and Vera looked at each picture and finally selected the 1,000-meter picture as the best one for their purpose. When they were sure they had the location firmly in their memory, Rafe turned to Goldstein and said, "Activate the timer!"

"Done! You're ready to go."

The backpack disappeared from the table. "We placed it. Now we find out if it works and what the reaction is going to be."

Twenty minutes later the conference room telephone rang and Goldstein answered. His grave expression didn't change as he hung up the receiver. "Our instruments just picked up a large explosion in the Iran region. Now we wait for Iran's reaction."

Rafe and Vera said their goodbyes and teleported back to Macon. The international news from Iran was sketchy as little was emerging except that one of their nuclear sites apparently had an accident, causing a large explosion. Details were not available.

Two days later Rafe mentally contacted Goldstein. *This is Rafe Johnson. What have you learned about the effectiveness of our project?*

The prevailing winds carried the fallout all the way to the Persian Gulf, which has temporarily shut down all shipping. The surrounding nations have condemned Iran for this nuclear accident and have called upon them to cease all future nuclear activities. Apparently, the two other sites are receiving large doses of radiation, which will make them useless for many years. I think we achieved the goal we were looking for and I want to thank you again for the help you have provided Israel.

We were happy to provide help to our friends; however, what we did also helped reduce the nuclear threat to us from this terrorist source. If you need us again don't hesitate to ask for our help and we will do the same.

Rafe smiled at Vera. "It looks like your plan worked perfectly except the price of oil will probably go up in the short term while the Persian Gulf shipping is shut down. Israel doesn't think Iran has any idea the explosion wasn't an accident. Let's not tell anyone else we had anything to do with it. We were just innocent bystanders."

"I think you're right, but I know some government agencies are going to suspect we had our hands up to our elbows in it."

"Better they suspect than know. Their internal security is better than it was, but what they don't know won't hurt us."

CHAPTER 49

$$\infty\!\!\otimes\!\!\otimes$$

Five years later brought several changes within the Group. Two female Group members married foreign nationals who were brought into the Group and now lived in their country of origin. Bruce Wilson married April Stephenson and returned to his home in London. Cabot Gachet married Eva Johnson and returned to Paris.

Bruce met April in Atlanta at the Group's lab where she worked as a doctor. Bruce had business with the lab, which he extended after meeting April. It was love at first sight for both of them and they dated every day for two weeks until his return to England. The forced absence from one another resulted in extreme emotional distress until Bruce returned a month later.

Bruce was soon introduced to April's family and to the secrets of the Group. He was so much in love with April that nothing they told him deterred him from wanting to marry her. Three days later they were married and spent their honeymoon and the next three months in the Group's Atlanta house. After he recovered from the change, they flew to London where he introduced his new bride to his family, who owned a well-known pharmaceutical firm.

Cabot met Eva in New York where she worked as an attorney in Philip Seymour's law firm. Cabot was a banker with a business relationship with the law firm. The pair dated several times for three months while Cabot was in NY. They came to realize after each parting how much they missed each other. At Cabot's next business visit he stayed over an extra week. Eva took vacation time and they spent the week together. When it came time for Cabot to return to Paris, he couldn't leave Eva and took another week off, proposing to her.

Eva took him home to visit her parents where he received disclosures he did not at first believe, but after demonstrations of the Group's powers he realized that they were real. Eva and Cabot were married three days later, and he talked his bank into giving him a three-month leave of absence. The newlyweds spent most of this time in the NY house suffering through the change and recovery before Cabot brought Eva to Paris to meet his family. Cabot's family was a majority owner of the investment-banking firm where he was currently employed.

The newly married wives were soon employed by each family's business. Eva already had a working knowledge of French and with her husband's tutoring was soon fluent. The Group's first members were now established outside the United States. The women's husbands had not yet reached their full powers, but they made use of their weak telepathy powers in their business.

Eva Johnson Gachet was settling into her new job as an investment banker by reviewing existing client records and learning the documentation requirements under French law. While doing this she discovered an unusual set of transactions involving several of the bank's clients.

Eva noted there were transactions between other accounts to cover withdrawals from two large accounts. The activity was an attempt to cover a large embezzlement from the two large accounts. The account manager over these accounts was one of the firm's senior executives. Eva's further investigation indicated weekly transfers from the two accounts to the account manager's personal account.

Eva gathered all the documentation of the embezzlement and showed it to her husband. Cabot looked at the documentation Eva had brought him and after reviewing it asked, "How much has he stolen?"

"This documentation is only for three months and amounts to 40,000 Euros. A full audit needs to be done to discover how much is missing."

Cabot's glum face turned into a smile. "His accounts were audited less than nine months ago, so our firm's liability should be limited to activities since then. Let's give this information to father and go from there."

Cabot and Eva entered Jacob Gachet's opulent office, informing his secretary they needed to see him on a matter of importance. Jacob stood up and came around his large desk to greet them.

"Cabot, Eva, how nice to see you. Eva, how are you doing in your new job?"

"Father, Eva discovered an embezzlement from the accounts managed by Walter Gephardt. I want you to look at what she has documented here," Cabot said as he gave the file to his father.

Jacob took the file as if it was a snake instead of paper. "Cabot, you and Eva take a seat while I review this."

Fifteen minutes later he looked up at Eva and asked, "How much has he taken?"

"40,000 Euros for that three month period. Cabot told me he was audited about nine months ago, so we probably have more liability. Are we insured?"

"Our 100 Million Euro blanket policy has a 500,000 Euro self-insurance clause; however, each account manager has a 100,000 Euro Bond policy. Hopefully, this embezzlement is less than that. I'll need to notify our Board of a special meeting to discuss this and also notify the police of Gephardt's actions. Cabot, inform security to remove Gephardt from this building. Freeze his accounts and change all his computer codes. Eva, please stay here while Cabot does these tasks, I want to talk to you."

Cabot gave his wife an encouraging smile as he left his father's office. *Don't worry, Father's bark is worse than his bite,*

Jacob continued sitting at his desk for a few minutes thinking before he looked up at Eva and said, "Eva, you have done us a tremendous service by uncovering this embezzlement in a timely manner. Did you do this type of work at your last position?"

"No, not specifically. My attorney duties dealt with investment contracts with firms such as here. I was learning French document requirements when I came across these transactions. It was pure chance that I picked these accounts to review."

"Chance or not, I'm not going to overlook an opportunity like this. I want you to continue your education in our documentation requirements and also look for irregular transactions of any kind. As you gain experience I foresee a possibility of you heading an audit department for the bank. Do you think you would be interested in this type of position?"

"Thank you Jacob. Would the bank pay for accounting courses to make this happen sooner?"

Jacob smiled at his daughter-in-law's request. "Yes, and I'll even give you time off to attend day classes. I like your attitude. Cabot better watch himself or you will soon be making more salary than him."

* * *

April Stephenson Wilson was used to living in a large city, so her main adjustment to London was learning her way around the city and public transportation between her flat and the lab. Bruce took off work an additional week showing her how the public transportation worked and special points of interest until she felt confident moving around alone. He also introduced her to his family who were happy he brought another doctor into the family.

Eventually the time came for Bruce to show April the family business, Wilson Pharmaceutical, Ltd. A car picked them up and delivered them to the company's main business office near the manufacturing building. Bruce led the way inside and showed her his office, which according to its size and window placement indicated his high importance to the firm. He then got on the intercom and made an appointment to see his father, who was the firm's President.

Bruce turned to his new bride and said, "We have a few minutes before he can see us. Take a seat and I'll arrange for us to have a spot of tea."

Bruce's secretary soon brought in a tea service. Bruce waited on his wife and discussed decorating the flat while sipping their tea until it was time to meet his father. They entered the President's much more spacious office, where he told them to make themselves comfortable.

President Rudolph Wilson, a man in his late sixties, prided himself in keeping fit and looked the part of the man in charge. He smiled at April as he said, "Bruce tells me he met you in Atlanta where you worked in the Falstaff Laboratories. What kind of work did you do for them?"

"I was senior in development of new strains of antibodies relating to cancer cures. I can't reveal any details because of the propriety agreement I signed when I joined the firm."

"So your field is research. If you are interested in that type of work, I'm sure we can find a position for you. Dr. Cheryl Fieldhouse is the head of our research department, and if you agree I'll make an appointment for you to meet her."

"Yes, that would be the field I'm interested in."

President Wilson buzzed his secretary to get Dr. Fieldhouse on the line for him. Shortly his phone rang and he started talking to the Doctor, arranging the appointment. After hanging up he turned to April.

"Dr. Fieldhouse will see you at one this afternoon. Bruce, when you get April settled, I want a word with you this afternoon."

Bruce led the way out of his father's office and took April to Personnel so the paperwork could be started for her employment with the firm. April met Bruce back in his office later and they took a long lunch before April returned for her appointment with Dr. Fieldhouse.

Dr. Fieldhouse was a woman in her early fifties and appeared on the surface to be friendly, but her thoughts were how she was going to put up with this young American woman who had snagged the President's son. Her thoughts turned to surprise when she learned of April's research background and she asked, "How can you have done all this being so young?"

"I look younger than my age, and I finished school when I was eighteen and interned at John Hopkins. I started at Falstaff Labs two years later. I'm sure I will excel at any task you give me, but if you continue to think of me as a gold-digger you are going to lose me to one of your competitors."

Dr. Fieldhouse looked at her in surprise. "You can read minds too?"

"I didn't need to. Your face and posture said it all."

Fieldhouse searched April's face before speaking. "Very well. I need a smart researcher on a project we are just starting. We will see just how good you are. If this works out we'll both benefit."

CHAPTER 50

President Margaret Chase was on hand to cut the ribbon officially opening the Boston to Washington, D.C. leg of the nation's first high speed rail system, designed for speeds exceeding 120 mph. Eventually, the east coast system would reach Miami before they would start on tracks to the west coast. The project's cost was under budget at 15 Billion Dollars; however, the cost from Washington to Miami was estimated at two-thirds of the previous leg.

After the ribbon cutting, President Chase met with Phillip Seymour and Charles Gilbert who were largely responsible for obtaining Washington's approval to build the system.

"I want to commend you gentlemen on your foresight in putting controls on the contractors and subcontractors who bid on this project. When this project first started, there was much moaning and groaning about how unrealistic the controls were, but a year later it proved itself when everything started to come together under budget."

Seymour chuckled as he said, "That's not to say several didn't try to get around the controls in order to stuff their pockets. After two contractors and three subcontractors were caught and fined a total of three million dollars, that made a believer out of the others who might have had similar ideas."

"Gentlemen, I want your help in getting the military back into space. The civilians can handle the science and spacecraft design and manufacture, but we need the military to police disputes and possible encounters from outside the system. We also need them when we start exploring outside this system. I want a defense force able to handle any problems we might encounter. Do you think we can get this started?"

Seymour and Gilbert looked at each other for a moment before Seymour answered. "Madam President this won't be as expensive for the government as you might think. Initially, all we need is two or three ships configured with long-range weapons. They can be used as training platforms for future additions to an Earth Fleet. I think we can get this passed by both houses if we go at it as helping the overall economy. We might get several other countries interested in providing manpower and capital to the project. What do you say Gilbert?"

"I agree. I've already heard several members of congress wondering why we don't have a military presence in space. Your idea of other countries providing manpower and money is brilliant. We want an Earth Fleet, not a U.S. Fleet. We don't want different countries competing with each other over control of another planet. Now is the time to set this in motion."

President Chase smiled at the two men. "That's what I am going to include in the Bill I will submit to Congress. I want you two to get everyone behind this so I can sign it during this session."

The two heads of the largest SPACs pledged their support and then departed to plan their strategy. Later, Phillip Seymour mentally called Rafe Johnson and informed him of the President's pending bill and asked if he had any thoughts.

Phillip, I put this idea in Maggie's head about six months ago and am happy she has followed through. We need to get some of our people positioned to be part of this Fleet at its inception. We need at least one member on each ship for its protection and instant communication. Hopefully at some future time we will have a ship with all Group members.

Rafe mentally contacted every house head and asked them to check with their members for anyone interested in becoming part of the crew of a military spacecraft. All volunteers would be transferred to Houston to begin training for space and operation of a spacecraft.

A week later, Rafe had just finished a mental conversation with Prime Minister Shaul Allon who sought his help in sponsoring an entry from Israel in the next Earth Fleet School. The prestige of having someone from Israel on one of the Fleet's space ships would do wonders for morale.

He had promised he would try his best to fulfill his request. Rafe then mentally contacted President Chase and related the Prime Minister's request. *Wow! Do you know what the entry fee now is to enter that school?*

No, but I'm sure that's the reason for PM Allon's end run through me. How much is it?

$50 million! Those ships are not cheap and each new one is going to be an upgrade over the last.

Are you going to pay his way into the school? The SA Group can chip in half if that helps.

Why don't you pay the entire fee and I'll reimburse you for our half. I don't want anyone tracing our payment for Israel's share, as it would set a bad precedent.

Understood. How goes the romance between Vera and Robbie?

They are both attending graduate school at MIT and taking the same classes. So far she has kept her word about finishing school before getting married, but they are now living together and from her mind glow, I see she is completely in love with Robbie and he with her.

Well, we all knew that this would probably happen after their first date. Can you imagine the children those two will have?

I know. That's been my solace. I think of the problems they will cause her when their children get to be three through their teen years. She'll ask for my help and then I'll be right back into it again. Darn!

Sic their Aunt Vera on them and they won't know what hit them.

Between all of us we should be able to handle them. Yeah, that worked pretty well with Vera and Robbie. Maybe we will be okay.

Rafe turned to his wife. "Vera, did you get all that conversation with Maggie?"

"Yes, but I don't see the big problem with little Vera and Robbie. Living together should relieve the stress of graduate school and since they're taking the same classes, that should speed up the process."

"With Maggie, I think her problem is that Vera is an only child and she feels abandoned with her out of the house."

Vera snorted, "She needs to have another child as soon as she gets out of the White House. I'll talk to her soon."

Rafe hugged his wife. "How about you, are you ready for more children?"

Vera immediately dug Rafe in the ribs with a stiff finger. "I've already had three sets of twins, thank you very much. I'm not ready to go through that experience again, at least not in the near future. I'd rather dote on my many grandkids and spoil them rotten."

Rafe smiled at her while rubbing his sore ribs. "Yeah, with them we can always go home when they get too active and noisy. I haven't heard from Evelyn in over a month. What are she and Charles up to?"

"Still getting the Seattle House ready for occupancy. Do you want to ask if they need our help?"

"No. I'd like to see her again, but it might look like we don't trust them in getting it started. Maybe a month after they move in. We could mentally call her for an update if you like?"

"I just talked to her two days ago. We could visit Joseph or Elizabeth, they both live in Wichita and it's been ages since I've seen their kids."

"Six months, if I remember correctly. They will have changed a lot since then. Let's see if we can visit them without causing a big ruckus."

Vera mentally called her two youngest children and asked if it would be convenient for her and Rafe to come for a visit. Both children were thrilled to have them come for a visit tomorrow, but suggested they come to Joseph's house because it was larger and Elizabeth and her family would join them.

Vera relayed the plan and shook her head. "Elizabeth was never a housekeeper and with her twins to take care of, I bet her house is a mess she doesn't want us to see."

"Maybe she's going to help Brenda clean up the bigger house."

"Maybe, but Brenda would hire help if she needed it."

Rafe and Vera teleported to Joseph's house the next day and knocked on the front door. They could hear mentally and vocally the twins' glee that their grandparents had arrived. Brenda answered the door looking like she had run a marathon, while the twin girls peeked around her legs with huge smiles on their faces.

Brenda urged them to come in, while shooing the twins away from the door. Once inside, the grandparents surveyed the two-year-old twins who stood before them with matching smiles and dresses.

Vera pointed at one of the twins. "You must be June because of that dimple, and that means your sister is Rachael."

The twins both shouted, "No fair! You peeked into our minds."

They then climbed into Rafe and Vera's laps, giving them both a wet kiss. Rafe and Vera gave each of the girls a puzzle and a piece of chocolate. They ran to their mother and handed her the chocolate before heading to their room to work on the puzzle.

Brenda put the candy into a dish on a high shelf before turning to the grandparents. "The girls really love candy, so I've rationed them one piece daily after a meal. I know it probably won't hurt them, but I use it for a reward for good behavior. Joe went out for groceries and will be back shortly. Besides, I wanted to talk to you about something. As you know we both work for Star Explorations who now have two space ships in operation and another in construction. We both want to attend the next Star Explorations training school with the goal of getting onto a crew of a space ship. Can you help us?"

Vera asked, "What about the girls?"

"While we attend school, Elizabeth will take care of them. She thinks the girls will be a good influence on her boys. After school we hope to alternate crew duties so at least one parent is available to take care of the children, and Elizabeth will help out as it becomes necessary."

Rafe said, "I'll need to talk to both of you and get an understanding of this sudden desire to get into space and how you plan on maintaining a stable family life with one of you gone for lengthy periods of time."

"Oh, I know it sounds crazy. Ever since we moved here we have been caught up in the general frenzy of getting into space. We both have skills that will be needed if we can attend the school."

Joseph arrived with bags of groceries and asked for help getting them into the house. After everything was settled, Joseph said, "I asked Brenda to broach the subject of us attending Space School. I guess I was afraid of what you would say."

Vera punched her son on the arm. "Joseph! I could care less if you two want to go to school, it's how it will affect the girls that's the problem."

Rafe nodded in agreement. "They need a stable environment to grow up in with two parents, like you and Elizabeth had. I don't think fostering them off on Elizabeth is going to work as she has her own kids to raise. Taking care of her two boys is really all she can handle at once. I want to talk to Vera and maybe we can come up with a solution."

Rafe and Vera went into the master bedroom and shut the door before teleporting back to Macon. Rafe looked into Vera's eyes before asking the question that was on both their minds. "Are you up to raising June and Rachael with occasional breaks when their parents are home on leave? We would be the stable influence in their lives without even the title of mom and dad."

Vera looked at Rafe, tears in her eyes. "Parents have always been given the short stick when it comes to their children. I don't think we have any choice if they really want to pursue this career."

After exchanging a worried expression they teleported back into the master bedroom in Wichita, where they joined Joseph and Brenda. Rafe gave both of them a stern look before speaking. "You're sure you want to go into space as a career?"

Joseph placed his arm around his wife and they both nodded in agreement. Vera stepped forward and glared at the two causing them to take a step back. "Rafe and I will give our approval, but only if we raise them in a stable environment. When one or both of you are available you may live with us in Macon until you no longer have Ship duties or the girls reach maturity. Talk it over until we are ready to leave for Macon."

Elizabeth and her family arrived with the usual ruckus two three-year old twin boy's make entering a room. This brought the girls from their room and the noise decibel increased substantially. The grandparents interacted with the children and almost like magic peace was restored. Vera gave the children tasks to do with promised rewards if accomplished within a set time period.

After the children left the living room, their parents all breathed a sigh of relief. Brenda looked at Vera with wonder. "How did you do that!"

Elizabeth smiled as she answered, "Practice, lots of practice. She had three sets of twins and by now she has it down to a science. Have you dropped the bomb on them?"

Joseph replied, "Yes, and they gave us one better. They said if we do this they will raise the girls and we are welcome to come visit when we are in town."

Elizabeth looked at the stricken faces of her brother and sister-in-law, and then at the serious faces of her parents. "Oh my. What are you going to do?"

Joseph looked at his wife, who suddenly started crying and ran out of the room with him following after giving everyone a shrug of his shoulders. Vera asked Elizabeth, "How are you getting along raising two three-year old boys?"

"It's a learning experience because none of my siblings were boy twins. They don't have to work very hard getting into trouble, but it's not malicious. They are just very curious about things and how they work."

"How about ESP? Have they come into their powers yet?"

"Not yet, but who can really say. They could be using a power we haven't recognized yet."

Pete and Jasper ran into the room closely followed by the girls. Jasper held up the puzzle box in triumph. "I solved it!"

Vera looked at him in surprise and held out her hand. "Let me see it."

The box floated to Vera's hand, which she then rotated looking at each side. "How did you solve the puzzle?"

Jasper's face turned red in embarrassment. "I peeked inside and saw how it was constructed."

"Jasper, that's cheating. Didn't your mother tell you it's bad form to cheat?"

"Yes, but I wanted to win the prize."

"My, my. I'm afraid you have won a different kind of prize than you were looking for. How long have you children been using your powers?"

The boys suddenly became very anxious as they looked at each other.

"Come on now. We already know about some of what you've been doing. Girls! Don't give me that innocent look. I know from your thoughts what you've been doing."

June gave Jasper a dirty look. "Now look at what you've done. We're all in trouble now."

Vera smiled at them. "No trouble, but we need to know what you can do so we can train you to safely use your powers. Alright, boys tell us what you can do."

The boys had telekinesis, the ability to mentally move objects, and weak telepathy powers. Jasper also could use his mind to look into objects, such as the puzzle piece. The girls also had weak telekinesis and telepathy powers.

Vera looked at the children thoughtfully. "You all are getting your powers early. Normally they don't appear until you are ten or twelve years of age, but I've noticed more are showing up shortly after they reach one. You probably will become very powerful as you get older, which means you need training and guidance in your abilities now."

Elizabeth said in shock. "I had no idea. They must have had these abilities for some time. Mother! I've been too busy watching the wrong things. I couldn't see the trees because of the forest."

"Elizabeth, you and Peter need to teleport the boys to Macon every day so they can attend ESP classes. I think they are going to enjoy them. I'll talk to Joseph and Brenda about the girls. Now you children! New ground rules until you start classes. Don't move hard objects or people through the air, as people may get hurt. Do you understand me?"

The children nodded. "I didn't hear you!"

"YES GRANDMOTHER!"

"That's better. Just remember what I said. I better not see any bruises on anyone. Right June?"

"Yes Grandmother."

"Okay, I bet I can find some ice cream if the girls helped me." Both sets of twins followed Vera into the kitchen. Joseph and Brenda found them all sitting at the kitchen table eating ice cream when they returned from their conference in the master bedroom.

Later, when the children had returned to playing games in the girls' room, Joseph said, "We have reached a decision. Neither of us had considered our mortality or the effect our absence would have on our children, or even how it would affect us. We no longer want to attend Space School, at least not until they are much older."

Relieved, Rafe and Vera smiled. "Good, we hoped you would make that decision; however, the girls have started getting their powers early and need to attend ESP school in Macon. Elizabeth's boys are further along and need to attend as well. Get with Elizabeth and teleport to Macon daily beginning Monday."

Joseph and Brenda together blurted, "What!"

Brenda looked at Vera. "When did this happen?"

Vera then related how they had discovered the children's abilities. "The children have gotten their powers early and need to be instructed in their proper use so they don't do harm to others or themselves."

Joseph shook his head in disgust. "Just think, we were ready to leave our kids with Elizabeth while we trained for the stars. Somebody up there has a wicked sense of humor."

Rafe hugged his shoulders. "You came to your senses and it didn't happen, so don't beat up on yourselves too much. Just concentrate on raising those beautiful girls."

After spending the rest of the day visiting with their children and grandchildren, Rafe and Vera teleported back to their apartment in Macon, pleased and relieved, but needing to reflect on all that had transpired.

CHAPTER 51

Another ten years passed with a big change in the structure of the SA Group. It had been 125 years since Rafe and Vera were infected with the age contagion and the membership now totaled over 1,000 plus 330 children, and were scattered in three countries besides the United States. Rafe and Vera thought the Group should be democratic rather than autocratic and asked the members to vote for a new leader if they so desired. Three members put their names in contention and a vote was held resulting in Rafe retaining the title of President and CEO for a period of five years, at which time another vote would be taken.

Rafe also gave other senior members titles according to their duties performed for the Group. The SA Group headquarters was moved to a new larger complex in Macon. The new headquarters and living quarters were three times as large as the old building. To outsiders the SA Group was a conglomerate investing in numerous business interests. The new complex resulted in the hiring of over a hundred personnel to staff the office buildings and provide security for the campus.

Adam made sure the complex was well protected by the latest in security devices and all nonmember employees were telepathically checked initially and every three months to make sure nothing had changed. The living quarters was an apparent glass tower, but was faced with transparent bullet resistant material rather than glass. It contained eighty large apartments with the latest in luxury appointments. The fifteen-story building rose from the center of the old business district, causing a revitalization of the entire area.

Rafe's apparent age was now in the mid-twenties and he still couldn't show himself as the public face of the SA Group. He hired a local public relations firm to publicize the Group's interest in community affairs. They named a fictional James Parsons as head of the Group and used a picture Adam painted of Rafe that vaguely resembled him if he was twenty years older. They touted him as an innovative businessman who was taking his business forward and Macon with him. The city had already grown with several new businesses following the SA Group and bringing new jobs with them.

The past ten years also resulted in further advances in the Earths' space program, both civilian and military. Star Explorations now had four space ships and Earth Space Fleet had two ships, one used mostly for training new crews. Star Explorations was considering sending a smaller ship to the Alpha Centauri binary system, 4.35 light years from Earth. Assuming the ship could obtain the speed of light, it would take 4.35 years to get there.

Star Explorations' engineers estimated it would take the ship ten months to achieve eighty percent of light speed and assuming that was the limit of its speed, it would take over six years to reach their destination. This was much too long for a human crew. However, if they sent the ship out guided by computers and teleported a small crew out every six months to check ship systems, it might be doable.

No one but senior Group personnel of Star Explorations would know of the teleportation of crews to and from the star ship. If this worked then they would have a crew on hand to explore both AC-A and B of the Alpha Centauri binary system before turning the ship home or to another destination, depending on the ship's fuel status.

Rafe and Vera Johnson had lived over two normal life spans, but the last 125 years were the most rewarding for them. They had no idea what the future held for them or the Group, but they hoped the membership would continue to grow until all humans were the 2.0 version and internal wars on Earth became a thing of the past. Humankind was destined to expand to the Stars and the 2.0 versions were the most likely to succeed. Maybe sometime in the future Rafe and Vera would be on one of those ships that would colonize a new world similar to Earth.

In the meantime, Rafe and Vera intended to do their best to continue to protect the United States and its interests from anyone who bore them ill well.

THE END

About the Author

Hugh A. Flowers retired after almost thirty years with the Federal Deposit Insurance Corporation as a bank examiner. He now spends his time reading and writing novels and short stories and traveling the world.

OTHER PUBLICATIONS BY FLOWERS

The Salvation Trilogy
Salvation
Angel's Triumph
In Perpetuity

Other
Emergence
Reclamation
Oklahoma Tomboy

www.ingramcontent.com/pod-product-compliance
Lightning Source LLC
Chambersburg PA
CBHW051422170626
46809CB00006B/2273